PUTTING THE PIECES IN PLACE

AND

LITERARY REMAINS

PUTTING THE PIECES IN PLACE

AND

LITERARY REMAINS

by

R.B. Russell

Tartarus Press

Putting the Pieces in Place and *Literary Remains*
by R.B. Russell

Putting the Pieces in Place was first published in a limited edition
of 400 copies in 2009 by Ex Occidente Press
Literary Remains was first published in 2010 by PS Publishing Ltd

This paperback edition published 2022 by Tartarus Press at
Coverley House, Carlton-in-Coverdale, Leyburn,
North Yorkshire, DL8 4AY

ISBN 9781718108615

The author would like to thank Rosalie Parker and Jim Rockhill
for their help in the preparation of this volume

CONTENTS

To the memory of
Fred and Grace Russell

PUTTING THE PIECES IN PLACE

Putting the Pieces in Place

The tape came off the first reel, threaded its way through the guides and heads, and flapped uselessly, rhythmically, as the full spool continued to turn. Nicolas Porter kept his eyes closed, not wanting to believe that the music of Emily Butler had come to an end. Finally, he looked with a smile at the young woman opposite and got up out of his armchair. He walked over to the vintage reel-to-reel machine and switched it off.

'This'll need rewinding,' he said.

'It will need a new reel,' Beatrice Grant replied. 'The original is cracked.'

'I have to admit that I am a little precious about such things. You know what obsessive collectors are like?'

Beatrice said that she didn't, that she had never felt the urge to collect anything, and Porter gave a short, self-deprecating lecture on how passionate collectors can be about the smallest of details. When he had finished he smiled again, rather guiltily, and said:

'But that did sound absolutely magical. It was everything I dreamed it would be. I suppose I should get a copy made; as a back-up?'

'That would be sensible, yes.'

'But no copy will ever sound as good as hearing it on that old analogue tape.'

'I suppose it's like your first editions,' she suggested. 'Reading a book on lovely paper, and in a nice binding, the words are still the same as in a cheap paperback, but the experience is different.'

'I don't know if it is quite the same analogy,' he replied, slowly, giving it consideration. 'The process of hearing is different. Analogue is warmer. The bass is thickened up giving it a fuller sound. It compresses the high end too, which is more natural to the ear. . . .'

'Alright,' she held up her hand to stop him. 'I believe you. I defer to you in all matters musical as well as literary.'

'But you can still tell me what you thought of the music?'

'It was quite beautiful, but classical music isn't my forte, you know? It's obviously very skilful and sounds romantic . . . The tone is wonderful.'

'Emily Butler was playing Mozart's Third, on a reproduction Stradivarius. We had to listen to this tape on an original RCA reel-to-reel player because I'm pretty sure that's what she recorded it on. I've a photo of her with this kind of machine in the background.'

'You really are an obsessive, aren't you?'

'You don't know the half of it, my dear,' he said, with an affected movement of his hand over his brow. 'But *you* are the heroine of the hour.'

'I couldn't have tracked down the tape without the information you gave me.'

'I have made my living, and my money, being a literary detective, you know. I have some idea of how these things are done . . .' He turned off the tape player's power at the wall, and then walked over to the bottle of wine which had been warming, open, by the fire. 'Now, would you like a glass? We agreed that we wouldn't drink anything until we had played the tape.'

'Yes, please. I think we have something to celebrate, don't we? Although my detective work isn't quite of the same order as yours . . .'

'What you've brought along tonight excels any of my finds.'

'Even your discovery of the *Medea*?' she was incredulous.

'For me, it is.'

Nicolas Porter knew that classical literature was all the richer for his famous discovery; he had not needed the eminent figures in the literary world to tell him that. The person that he had been the most pleased to impress, though, was his father, who had taught classics at Newcastle University. Porter was delighted to have risen in the old

2

man's estimation; his father had believed his son to be the philistine of the family because he had never been able to hold a pencil, brush or bow. His sisters were the artistic ones, he was always told, but then he unearthed the full text of Ovid's *Medea* and the achievements of his siblings had been eclipsed overnight.

'I don't know anything about literature,' Beatrice continued, 'especially the classics, but you managed to appear on the front pages of some serious newspapers.'

And he had earned himself enough money that he no longer needed to haunt provincial auction salerooms, trying to track down the relicts of authors in the hope of unearthing a cache of unpublished novels.

'I won't ask you how much you made out of . . . ?'

'Good!' he declared. 'Because I'm not sure I know myself; not exactly. I have no idea how much I spent getting it authenticated, but the debts kept growing. When I finally sold it at auction the newspapers reported the headline sum, but that is only half of the story. It was bought by an anonymous philanthropist on behalf of a museum, and they've still not settled the full amount. They have a deal with a publisher who has yet to contribute their payment in lieu of a royalty.'

'Will you tell me how you came by it?'

'There are legal reasons why I can't give you any names. It was incredibly convoluted because the collector who owned it had origin- ally acquired it from an institution thirty years ago. As far as *they* knew it was just some early Latin manuscript, and the collector who bought it from them didn't know any better for the first few years. When he came to read it he had his suspicions that it was copied from a far earlier Greek source, but he never got it authenticated. When I discov- ered, from the records of that institution, exactly who they had sold it to, I asked the owner if I could see it, but he refused. He wasn't one of those collectors who like to share their treasures, even to impress, or to make other collectors envious. Then, when he died, his widow passed it on to me, knowing that it had value, but not knowing what on earth it was.'

'And the problem is?'

'Not only is the widow who sold me the *Medea* threatening to take me to court, claiming I should have paid her more, but the original institution who sold it to her husband is threatening to do the same.'

'Will they get anywhere?'

'I don't know, and frankly, at this very moment I don't care.'

'But you're still happy that you've paid me ten thousand pounds for the tape of Emily Butler?'

'Of course! I haven't heard that music for forty years and it is still breathtaking.'

'You've heard it before?'

'Yes. There was a very sentimental reason for wanting that tape. And I've reached an age, and now the financial comfort, that allows me to indulge such sentimentality.'

He put down his wine and walked over to a case on a table next to a music stand. With great care and reverence he took out a violin.

'This is the very instrument that Emily Butler plays on that recording.'

'How on earth did you get that?' she asked, standing up to take a look, although he possessively kept hold of it.

'I have a contact in the world of violins who is the counterpart of me in the literary world. You see, although it isn't a Stradivarius, as was thought for many years, it is a very good, early copy, and has a lovely sound. Really good violins need provenance, and this one came up with an impeccable record of ownership. I know for a fact that it was hers.'

'You really are an obsessive. . . .'

'Did you know that this house was where she lived?'

Beatrice laughed at this: 'I am impressed, although, I suppose, there was a certain amount of luck involved.'

'In what way?'

'In the house becoming available?'

'For all collectors there's some luck, but if you are serious you have to persuade people to make things become available, and not just wait. But in the case of this house, it had been empty for years.'

'A desirable property like this?'

'Yes, but it has some serious drawbacks.

The whole of the front façade has subsided and should really be rebuilt. It would be cheaper to pull the place down and start again, but it's Listed and the planners wouldn't hear of it. And so it's been allowed to decay and has inevitably fallen into a worse and worse condition. And, of course, it has the reputation for being haunted.'

'Splendid! What kind of ghost? . . . Not your violin player?'

He looked slightly uncomfortable.

'It is!' she clapped her hands with delight. 'You are the most committed collector I've ever met. It's not good enough just to have Emily Butler's music, and the instrument she played it on, or even the house she lived in, but you must have her ghost as well!'

'So,' she asked, after a suitable pause, 'have you seen her?'

He looked up at the ceiling and admitted, reluctantly, that he had not.

'But it's not a visual ghost,' he explained. 'It's an audible one. It is said that music can sometimes be heard coming from this house.'

'Violin music?'

'I'm not sure. I've asked around, and although everybody knows the story, I can't find anyone who will admit to having heard anything themselves.'

'Are the stories recent?'

'I never heard them when I was living in the area in the early seventies. Emily drowned in a tragic boating accident in 1975, and the stories appear to date from after that. . . .'

'So, how long have you been living here?'

'Only a couple of months. I bought the place a year ago, but it's taken that long for the builders to make it habitable again.'

She sat back down in her chair and savoured the delicious tale.

5

'You do realise that your ghost isn't likely to play any music if you are constantly listening out for her?'

'I know, I know. And the odds are that if I not only heard, but also saw the ghost, I'd discover that it was her mother, not Emily! The thing is, I don't even believe in ghosts. I've never seen one, and don't really expect to.'

'But, you'd be happy to meet a ghost if she happened to be the right one?'

'Of course.'

He put the violin carefully back into its case and turned his attention to the bottle of wine. When he had refilled their glasses he sat down again, and she prompted him:

'So, you heard her play the violin in the . . .' she made the calculation, '. . . late sixties?'

'Yes. I suppose I was one of the very first to hear her. It was at a party, like in *Le Grand Meaulnes*. You know the book? I was about fourteen and had been out on a long walk on a hot august day. I'd gone miles, and was coming back down the Dale, thoroughly tired. And then I heard this unearthly, yearning music floating through the descending twilight of a warm summer evening. . . .

'It was odd, but I couldn't immediately identify it as a violin. I was a romantic lad . . .'

'Go on.'

'I've replayed the memory so often in my mind that I am afraid I cannot given a dispassionate, accurate account, although I'm certain the salient facts are correct. When I first heard the music I hadn't immediately understood where it was coming from, but further down the Dale I could see coloured lights. As I got closer I realised that there was a party, and when the music stopped and there was applause, I knew that I had come to the right place. I had to cross a few fields and then I was on the edge of a garden looking at all these people in summer clothes, all appearing somehow very refined and magical.

'I don't know how long I watched them, but eventually a young woman appeared in a white flowing dress, and she played the violin

6

again. It was beautiful, thrilling, moving . . . I was sure that nobody else at the party was appreciating her music like I was. I thought she was the most beautiful woman I'd ever seen in my life, and her music the most exquisite I'd heard. She would have been seventeen at the time . . .

'When she had finished I waited for hours in the hope that she might play once more, but she did not. Later, I asked around and found out who she was. And a few weeks after that I turned up on her doorstep, with some spurious excuse, but I was told that Emily Butler had just left for London. She had a place with an orchestra.'

'Did you ever meet her?'

'No. I followed her career, but she didn't get to play any of the major first violin or solo material until just before she died. She was never properly recorded; she was just about to go into the studio when the accident happened.'

'Are there many other collectors out there?'

'No, because they haven't known that there was anything to collect. . . . But I haven't asked you how easily you came by the recording?'

Beatrice had been patiently waiting for the opportunity to tell him her story;

'Well, you explained that her brother had disposed of the contents of the family home at an auction, and that's where the tape would have gone.'

Beatrice took her time, proud of her detective work: 'The auction records hadn't survived, but I was told about a man who ran a large junk shop in Penrith. At that time he used to make offers for unsold lots after the auction and a good proportion of the items nobody else wanted passed through his hands. The odds on the tape recording going to him were poor, but there was always the possibility of it. . . . Well, he remembered the tape very clearly. You see, he had a reel-to-reel player, and now had a tape to play on it. Only one tape, but he thought it was lovely and was happy to play it over and over again in his shop.

'And one day a customer came in and liked it so much that he bought it. Luckily the owner knew who the man was; someone called Bathgate. And though this Bathgate had moved to Venice I managed to track him down.'

'Astounding work,' Nicolas bowed his head. 'I hope that you didn't have to pay this man too much for the tape?'

'I assume that like the lady who sold you the *Medea*, Bathgate didn't know quite what it was he had. Anyway, he acted very oddly from the moment he saw me. When I told him what I wanted he rushed off and couldn't come back with the tape quickly enough. Strangely, though, after such an odd display, he seemed to want me to stay, but he was becoming rather creepy by then. Once I had what I wanted I left as quickly as I could.'

'The poor fellow,' Porter replied, shaking his head.

'How much I may or may not have paid for it is my own affair,' she said defensively.

'Don't worry, the money really is immaterial,' he assured her. 'To me that tape is worth so much more than anything else I have; more than her violin, or this house.' He paused and looked around him: 'You know, I call this the music room. This was where they'd have made the tape recording. There's a photo, a family group, taken in this room. I've recreated the details as faithfully as I can.'

'If the ghost feels at home she might deign to make an appearance?'

'You never know. Every night I wind up the clock and lock the doors. I have a little routine. And I pass this room on my way to the foot of the stairs and I invariably get a frisson as I pass the door. If I don't actually look in I feel that someone may be in here.'

'And if you *do* look properly?'

He laughed loudly: 'Then there's nothing at all. It took me some days to realise that the impression is caused by that mirror over there. My eyesight is not as it should be, and the figure I see out of the corner of my eye is my own reflection. You know, if I ever get up in the night I always pop down the stairs and listen, but I've never heard a sound.'

'I'm not sure whether to admire your dedication, or despair at it,' Beatrice told him, and he laughed again, and then decided that it must be time to eat.

℘

Nicolas Porter was not so much a collector who was obsessive; rather he was an obsessive who happened to be a collector. Neurotic about his appearance and the tidiness of his house, he was equally fastidious about his food. He had been busy cooking all afternoon, and ever since Beatrice had arrived he had continually checked his watch and disappeared off to the kitchen where he told her he was preparing his speciality dish. The smells that came through to where she waited were quite irresistible.

He suggested she browse in his library for a quarter of an hour, before he came back and sat her down in the dining room and was almost immediately gone again. When he returned he brought with him what he called salt crust baked duck. The meat was tasty, although nearly overwhelmed by the vanilla orange sauce which he had served with it. Porter admitted that the sauce was slightly too strong, but Beatrice was just as surprised by the fennel and citrus salad with which he seemed to be pleased. He had asked her to try the 'off-dry Vouvray' before pouring her a full glass, and though she knew little about such matters it did seem the perfect accompaniment.

Later, when he brought out the chocolate brioche dessert, they changed wines again, but this time he did not offer her a taster.

'I always drink Chateau D'Yquem with dessert,' he insisted. 'Or, at least, I have done since I sold the *Medea*!'

They finished with a large glass of Calvados which they drank at the table, Porter not being obviously inclined to move back into the music room.

'I haven't been entirely honest with you,' Porter admitted. 'I must apologise, but some of the lines of enquiry that you undertook I also followed up, a couple of years ago.'

9

'Why didn't you tell me?'

'I knew you'd approach Bathgate in the right frame of mind if you'd had to work for the information first. And also if you did not know everything that I did.'

'You knew that Bathgate had the tape?'

He nodded.

'So I didn't really need to tramp around auction houses and travel to Penrith? Looking up Bathgate wasn't hard, but presumably you could have arranged for an introduction to the man?'

'No, not quite. You see, I asked the same questions as you at the auction house, went to Penrith and on to Bathgate. I found him in Venice but he wasn't happy to see me.'

'None of this makes sense.'

'It will, it will.'

He looked into his glass for perhaps a minute and then told her the story.

෨

'Statistically speaking,' he explained, 'coincidences have to occur. If they didn't then something must be conspiring to order the world unnaturally. And if one looks into the statistics of this case it wasn't really that unlikely Oliver Bathgate would happen to walk into a large cluttered junk shop and hear the tape of Emily Butler playing her violin. You allow for the fact that the owner of the shop played it regularly; he appreciated the quality of the only piece of music he had in the shop. And Oliver Bathgate was an antiques dealer, and in his time would have visited junk shops all over Britain. Mind you, it would have been the last thing he would have expected to discover by chance.

'Bathgate bought it, and when I visited the shop a few years later the owner remembered Bathgate very well. His memory was especially clear because his customer had paid him a hundred pounds for the tape. And he had left a forwarding address, in case anything else turned up. Bathgate was so concerned that something else might surface from the sale of the Butler family's estate that when he moved to Venice he wrote to the owner of the shop with his new address.

'So there were no outrageous coincidences, and the trail was laid pretty easily for me to follow, just as it was for you afterwards. And as you have so recently done, I found my way to Venice to track down Bathgate, and like you, I knew nothing about the man . . . That is, until I got there.

'Had you been to Venice before?' Porter asked Beatrice. 'It is an astonishing city.'

'No,' she admitted. 'And as soon as I had the tape I was off to the mainland to catch a flight home!'

'I'm glad you came straight here.'

'I wanted to be paid the balance of my fee!'

'When *I* went to see Bathgate I was on the same mission as you, but I did not find him at home when I first arrived . . . I look back happily on my time in Venice. I rented an apartment and while I waited I visited the palaces associated with Byron and Corvo, Proust and Casanova. On the very first day I went to the Ponta Bergami and stared at the sad façade of the Palazzo Capello; the setting for Henry James's *The Aspern Papers*. The building was in a poor state of repair, as though untenanted since the time of Miss Bordereau and her niece. I often consider that my whole career has been based on the slender plot of that story.'

'How long did you have to wait for Bathgate?' Beatrice asked.

'A while. I went there with the intention of playing my "long game". It is a method I have used to advantage in many of my literary discoveries; a tactic that does have something underhand about it, I admit. All of my finds have been the result of almost infinite patience. Unearthing the *Medea* had been ten years work. . . .

'I arrived at Bathgate's address every morning by a narrow *calle* alongside a high-walled garden belonging to a neighbour. And after a week he was finally at home to respond to my knocking. He answered through the intercom and I said that I was from England. He was wary of letting me in and so I lied—I told Bathgate that I had known him many years before, and the lock of the door shot open with a hollow sound from inside.'

'And you found yourself,' said Beatrice, 'in that cavernous, dank, dark hall.'

'Yes, and Bathgate was standing at the head of that intimidating marble staircase, silhouetted against an unshuttered window.

' "Welcome to my Palace," Bathgate said, dramatically. "Although it is only a small one, and some experts insist on calling it a *Palazzo*. . ."

'A dapper man with grey hair and a goatee beard?' Beatrice checked.

'Yes. Did you go up to his apartments?'

'We conducted all of our business down in the hall,' she said.

'Then, you missed out on a treat. I was envious. Bathgate's *palazzo* was fantastic; he took me into the main room which was decorated with eclectic and fantastic artwork, and wooden and plaster angels, presumably looted from churches. And the view from his windows! The bright sun shone on the Grand Canal, and each building flanking it was an architectural wonder; even the most mundane of craft on the jaunty waters were transformed into things of splendour. Further up the waterway the crowds of tourists on the Academia Bridge seemed no longer gauche and annoying, but looked like celebrants in some mystery play.

' "My Palace has a picturesque history of ill-fortune," Bathgate told me, "although the majority of its previous owners have died comfortably in their beds at a very old age. I love its splendidly unbalanced façade. Unfortunately the coloured marble was cleaned and restored by its last owner . . ."

'Bathgate then apologised for not knowing exactly who I was, or why I was there. And so I told him the truth. I said that I had been born and brought up in the same Dale as Emily Butler. I told him that I had heard her play her violin when I was a teenager, and that I had been bewitched by it.

12

'I told him that we had met at that summer party, when she had played. I didn't say that I had spied on the gathering from the outside. I may have claimed that I had talked to Bathgate, but it was so long ago that it was natural the man had forgotten. I told him that I had found out, quite by chance, that Bathgate had a recording of Emily playing the violin. I claimed that I happened to be in Venice on holiday and had decided to look him up.

'There were problems with my explanation, of course, and I was prepared to continue lying to shore up my shaky story, but Bathgate was not interested in discussing them. He walked back to the window, to his view, and stood contemplating it for several minutes.

'Bathgate said to me: "I was paralysed when I first heard that tape. I was transported back fifteen years to that bright party where Emily had so impressed everyone by her playing. As I stood there in that rubbishy antique shop I was convinced that I was going mad; having an hallucination."

'Bathgate admitted, quite candidly, that at the time of the party he had been taking LSD, and twice he had later experienced frightening flashbacks. He said that hearing the recording was like one of those episodes—his heart raced, his mouth was dry and he nearly fell over. The man who owned the junk shop sat him down and brought him a glass of water. Eventually Bathgate asked about the music and the owner explained how he had acquired it. Bathgate was still trembling when he left the shop carrying the tape.

'But then he admitted that he had never been able to play it! He was living in London at the time. He bought a tape player and sat there on his own, with it all set up before him. He made certain he would not be interrupted, but he couldn't bring himself to turn it on. He sat up late into the night, always about to press "play", but never quite had the courage to do so. It was then that he resolved to move back to Venice.'

'But why couldn't he play it?' Butler asked.

'Bathgate wouldn't say anything at first. When he finally started to talk I assumed that he was changing the subject:

13

' "Venice is the most beautiful city in the world," he said. "People come here to forget, but it isn't a city that allows forgetfulness. It is inconceivably old and every day that passes is recorded in its stones, in its bricks and crumbling plaster. But, despite its apparent, eternal decomposition, it remains standing. . . . And those old warm bricks that shrug off the damp plaster to gaze narcissistically into these stinking jade green canals have always looked backwards. . . . And so the inhabitants of Venice must also dwell in the past. . . ."

' "I should not stay," he continued, "because the past can never be forgotten here. But in this city a personal tragedy may take comfort amidst the clamour of so many other painful histories. The insistence of my own story cannot be drowned out by those others, but it might find a kind of companionship."

'And then Bathgate laughed, slightly hysterically: " 'Drowned out'; that's an unfortunate choice of words," he said. "Unfortunate when Emily died by drowning."

'Then he turned and asked if I knew who he was.

' "Oliver Bathgate," I replied, rather lamely.

' "But do you know why I have the tape, and what it means to me? Do you know what Emily Butler meant to me, and what I meant to her?"

'I admitted that I didn't.

' "Do you have any idea of the circumstances surrounding her death?"

'I mumbled that I knew nothing aside from the fact that there had been a boating accident.

' "Yes, an accident. And it happened here, in Venice."

'Bathgate had walked towards me, threateningly, and stood with his face uncomfortably close to mine. I had to back away.

' "She fell over the side of my launch," he said. "While I was piloting it." A pause, then, "You didn't know that, did you?"

' "I'm sorry. No, I didn't."

' "And don't you think that it makes me feel just a little guilty?" he asked, with sarcasm in his voice.

' "Of course."

' "Of course!" he shouted, and the words echoed around the lofty room. "There hasn't been a day that's gone by without me knowing that I am the most miserable wretch on earth. I'd been drinking, you see. We were out on the lagoon and when she went over the side I didn't realise. I just kept going, way past the speed limit. And when I did notice, when I knew for certain what a terrible thing had happened, could I find her? I was too disorientated and befuddled to know where I'd been going. It was all I could do to get to the bright lights of St Mark's and call for help . . . And you want me to give you the only thing of Emily's that I have?"

'I said that I understood.

' "Of course you don't understand!"' Bathgate screamed at me.'

§

Porter looked at Beatrice, sitting opposite him:

'They had been in love, and he killed her. And now that he had the tape he couldn't bring himself to listen to it. He said that every note that she played on it would reproach him for what he had done to her.'

'The poor man.'

'Yes, but then he said that he sometimes thought that it would be better for everybody if he just threw away the tape! I cried out "Don't do that, for God's sake!" and he asked why not? He asked who the hell I was? He said that I wasn't even family. If I was, apparently, he'd have been happy to hand the tape over to me . . . And at that moment I knew that a dignified exit was required.'

'That's why you told me to say that I was a member of the family when I asked for the tape?' said Beatrice.

'Exactly.'

'But why didn't Bathgate at least ask who I was? Or how I was related? Why didn't he ask for proof?'

'Was he scared when he saw you?'

15

'Scared? Well, shaken, yes. He behaved very oddly.'

'There is a little more to explain,' Porter said. 'I knew that I would have to send somebody else to get the tape for me, and I had to make certain that the odds on that person succeeding were maximised.'

'And you allowed for something else? You expected him to be frightened of me?'

'I threw something else into the equation that I hoped would at least strengthen the claim that you were a relative of Emily's.'

'You asked me to do this because I look like her, don't I?'

He smiled: 'I asked you to track down the tape for me because I knew you were clever, and you've just proved it, again. That was important; without your intelligence it would have mattered little that there was a family resemblance.'

'Can I see a photograph of her?'

'Of course. I normally have a few around the house but I tidied them away when you phoned to say that you were coming. I didn't want to worry you.'

'Worry me? Now I understand. I look a lot like her, don't I? That was why Bathgate was so rattled when he saw me.'

'There is a striking resemblance.'

'Perhaps I should be worried? You have her music, her violin, her house, perhaps even her ghost. And then I come along, looking just like her, and I am in your debt by ten thousand pounds . . .'

'I promise that it is me, not you, who is in debt here. Without you I would have no tape. You must remember that I am an *obsessive* collector. Second best wouldn't be good enough . . .'

'And I would be second best?'

'You are delightful; pretty, intelligent, interesting . . . But you are *not* Emily Butler.'

He got up and walked to a bureau from which he brought out a framed photograph which he passed to Beatrice. Emily Butler had looked very much like her, she could see that.

'In the half-light of Bathgate's entrance hall you would have appeared to be her double,' Porter explained.

16

'Or her ghost?'

'I didn't know what he would do, but I knew that he would be shocked to see you. When I was looking for somebody to go there for me I was only hoping for what might pass for a family resemblance. It took me two years to find you, and I almost didn't ask because you looked too much like Emily.'

℅

Porter gave Beatrice Grant the master bedroom that night. She did wonder which of them was in Emily's old room, but she didn't ask; it wouldn't have been beyond Porter to discover which one it had been. She did not quite know what to think of the man, and with his generous payment for the tape she didn't feel that she had much right to criticise him. She was annoyed that he had not told her more before she went out to see Bathgate, but perhaps she would have behaved differently if she had known about her resemblance to Emily Butler. Grant was sure that she would not have acted the same in front of Bathgate if she had realised then what she now knew about his history. Grant consoled herself with the fact that no matter how much more of a right Bathgate had to that tape, it was not as though he ever listened to it. And did he really deserve any sympathy when he was responsible for her death? Porter's morality was suspect, but she did not feel concerned about being alone in the same house as him; she believed him when he said he was not interested in her. His obsession was with Emily Butler, and perhaps it was no more strange than the obsessions of many collectors. Porter simply had the money to indulge his passion to an extreme that others could not consider.

When she went to wash in the bathroom she could hear him down-stairs in the kitchen, clearing up after the meal, and she wondered whether she should have offered to help. However, she was so tired after her recent flights to and from Venice, and from the long drive up to Yorkshire, that all she wanted to do was sleep. When she was safely back in her room she undressed and got in between the cold sheets.

17

She was wondering about the psychology of Porter paying her so much money for what could have been a simple errand, when she must have fallen asleep. She couldn't judge the time at all but it was dark when she woke again, and she felt uncomfortable from all of the rich food she had eaten. She could hear music from downstairs, but was not surprised that Porter was presumably unable to stop listening to his new tape recording. Her first thought was that it was rather too loud and if she wanted to get back to sleep then she would have to go down and ask him to lower the volume.

Her mind was racing. She was too warm now, and unable relax because of all the food and wine she had drunk. She was beginning to be annoyed by her host, but a little later the music stopped. She waited to hear Porter come up the stairs. Had he fallen asleep down there? She seemed to be laying there for hours, listening out, despite her tiredness. She became even more irritated when she realised that she needed to have a pee, and she got up, hoping that she would not encounter her host on the landing.

The house was now completely quiet, and when she came out from the bathroom she stood there and let her eyes get used to the dark, deciding that it was a friendly, family house, and wishing that she might have somehow known Emily Butler herself. She wondered whether Porter was one of those collectors who would really share his treasures? She hoped that he might make her a copy of the music that he had been so thrilled to finally own.

Beatrice remembered what Porter had said about going downstairs and taking a look in the music room. She decided that she would do the same, and she would get herself a glass of milk from his kitchen while she was down there. She reasoned that she had to forget about her need for sleep if she was ever to succumb to it.

The moon was shining brightly through the landing window and picked out the stairs for her. The hall below was darker, but light was obviously coming in through the windows of the rooms at the front of the house.

As she walked past the music room, at the edge of her vision she saw something move. She looked back in and saw her reflection in the mirror and smiled at the illusion. Poor Nicolas Porter would never see Emily as those features stared back at Beatrice, even in the dimmest light.

She peered at her smiling reflection in the gloom, and was surprised to see that she was wearing something black, with a collar, buttoned high at the neck. She looked down at herself but confirmed that she was still wearing her white nightdress. In an instant she looked back up at her true reflection.

Beatrice's legs felt weak. She was not scared by what she thought she had seen, but she had no idea of what to make of it. She clutched the door frame and could not take her eyes off the mirror which was certainly now showing a true reflection. She was terrified a second later, however, when a quiet voice from within the dark room said, simply:

'Thank you.'

She backed away from the door, trembling from head to foot. A chair creaked from inside the room, as somebody unmistakably stood up. And then walking towards her from the shadows was a dark figure. She pressed herself against the wall she had backed into, and when the silhouetted form reached the door it switched on a light and was revealed to be Porter.

Her heart continued to crash in her chest, but she was able to breathe again, not having done so for several seconds.

'Thank you,' he repeated, smiling.

'What did you see?' she asked, trying to control her voice.

'A reflection in the mirror,' he replied simply.

'Whose?'

He shrugged. 'What I thought I saw for a moment, and what I actually did see, might not be the same thing. Who knows? What did you see?'

'I don't know. I don't know at all.'

19

'That's alright,' he said calmly, reassuring her that he would not ask again.

'Were you waiting for me to come down?' she questioned him.

'I hoped that you might do so earlier, when I was playing the music. When you didn't, I waited.'

'Did you know what would happen if I did?'

'No, not at all. But the way that I work, as a collector, is to put various elements together in such a way as may be advantageous. Then I observe the results. As I said earlier this evening, for all collectors there has to be an element of luck, but if you are serious you usually have to choreograph or arrange a situation, and persuade people to make things happen. It is not good enough just to wait, and hope.'

And with that he said goodnight, switched off the light, and walked towards the stairs, to finally retire for the evening.

There's Nothing That I Wouldn't Do

Most people seem to consider Nina Monkman to be a self-assured, confident young woman, but I have known her long enough to realise that this is not quite the truth. Her appearance of self-belief has often got her a long way, and it is something I have always admired and rather envied about her. I did meet her parents a few years ago and it was obvious that this is a family trait; they are also calm, confident people, and they have passed this on to their only daughter. None of them are arrogant; they are open and friendly, and I have always been a little jealous of their poise.

I first met Nina at school and we happened, by chance, to go up to the same University, where she studied architecture. After three years there it was just like her to decide to take her first year working in practice in Sweden, rather than remain in the city. She returned for two years to complete her M.A., but then spent her next year back in practice in Brazil. It would never have occurred to her that moving to a foreign country, where she did not know the language, would cause any difficulties, and she seems to have enjoyed both experiences.

Nina returned to England and spent a further year in the offices of a large architecture practice in London before taking her exams and qualifying, but I know that she found this last part of her education rather dull. I was therefore very surprised when she announced that she was going to study for a PhD. The only people I knew who had taken this course had been attached to the University where they had trained, but, inevitably, that was not Nina's intention. She had come across a Ukrainian architect whose recent work interested her and she had decided to go to a University in his country. Although the Berlin Wall had come down a few years previously the idea of anybody going

21

to live in Eastern Europe, albeit temporarily, was surprising. It was only a few weeks after making her decision that she left England again, now bound for Odessa.

We received letters and cards from Nina, but on her return at Christmas she expressed reservations about returning to the Ukraine the following term. It was unlike her to be so negative, and on our first reunion she refused to explain why she was so unwilling to go back. She was not her usual, buoyant self, but we felt it prudent not to ask too many questions at that point. Early in January, though, she stayed with me for a couple of days and was still evidently on edge and worried about something. With reluctance she agreed to explain.

That evening, as she sat in the armchair opposite me with a large glass of wine, she said that the problem was a young man called Taras.

'I'm sure I met him on the first day that I arrived in Odessa,' she said, 'He was not good-looking and I didn't really "notice" him until one day at the end of October when a whole group of us went on a picnic. It was unseasonably hot and we knew there may not be another fine day available to us that year. A merry procession of students took the train out to some dreary suburb and we walked up an interminable hill. I followed behind them with a heavy heart.'

'You weren't happy there, even then?'

Nina shook her head, took a deep breath, and told me what had happened:

෨

No, I was not happy, but when we got to the top of that hill we were suddenly in the countryside. They all ran, shouting, down this tree-lined road and for a moment I forgot my troubles and ran with them.

At the bottom of the valley a wide, shallow, clear river pushed through the fields and this was what we were all evidently making for. At the bridge everybody climbed the fence and ran down to the pebbly bank where, with few exceptions, the students stripped down to their underclothes. With squeals and shouts they ran to the water and threw

22

themselves in. I kicked off my shoes, tucked my dress in my pants, and rushed in after them. But the water was so cold that it hurt my legs. They ached so profoundly that I very nearly stumbled and fell, so I turned around and made my way out as quickly as I could. I walked awkwardly over the pebbles and up to a patch of grass in the sun. I sat down next to Taras, an English student.

'This is a lovely place?' he suggested, his accent sounding slightly American.

I agreed that it was, pleased to hear my own language spoken for the first time that day. I chaffed my legs to try and warm them.

'Every weekend,' he said, carefully selecting his words, 'We say, "let us go to the river". All summer we have said it, and never came. But finally we are here.'

'It's beautiful.'

'And the city is so ugly.'

I could not quite agree with him. The city is, in fact, very beautiful: at least in the centre. Fine eighteenth and nineteenth century buildings have survived the Soviet replanning, and many streets are delightfully lined with trees. A cosmopolitan port, it has never been of any military significance and so the old harbour has never been redeveloped. It retains a charm that surprised me when I first arrived two months before. The university buildings are likewise beautiful, and from inside them the views out down the wide streets and boulevards are elegant and impressive. My Hall of Residence is something entirely different, though; a mile from the city centre, it is a dark, oppressive essay in decaying concrete. It doesn't help that the Hall is so noisy; as a post-graduate of twenty-four I find that the eighteen-year-olds in the Hall already seem a whole generation younger than me.

One of my main grievances is that fewer people speak English there than I'd been led to believe. I was told that at the University, of all places, it would be the international language, but this isn't so in the architecture department. I do, finally, have a supervising tutor who speaks English. But English doesn't appear to be spoken at all outside of the University. I suppose I was fortunate to have a room in a corridor in the Hall of Residence with several English Language students, of whom Taras was one.

On that day we first talked he said:

'We will swim here,' he said, 'but we must not start eating and drinking until lunchtime.'

'Why's that?'

'If we start now we will finish the food and beer too soon. And then some will return, and the party is finished. . . .' He smiled and lay back on the grass, closing his eyes. 'Tell me again; who is the architect you are studying?'

'Alexander de Saussure,' I told him.

'I said that to my tutor, but he has never heard of him either.'

'He's very fashionable in England,' I told him, with a little obvious bitterness.

'Then the answer is that we are not fashionable here in the Ukraine?'

'I have a horrible feeling, that when I go back to England, he will no longer be in fashion there either.'

'Then,' he said, choosing his words, still with his eyes closed, and smiling as he found the right phrase, 'You will be a fashion victim!'

He laughed, and it hurt that he was right. It had been my fear from the moment that I descended the steps from the aeroplane and looked at the horrible nineteen-sixties airport building. I'd been seduced by some carefully selected photographs in a couple of architectural magazines, and had fallen for some excitable articles which suggested that de Saussure was soon going to be an architect with a great international reputation. He'd won a competition for an arts centre in The Hague and the drawings that had been published, alongside the explanation of his design philosophy, had convinced me that my career could be made by clutching on to this man's coat-tails. A year in the Ukraine studying his work and a few interviews with the great man himself appeared to me to be an easy way to obtain some more initials after my name, and hopefully a position in a good architecture practice. However, I admit that my enthusiasm may have clouded my judgment. It was only when I had arrived that I realised that his own practice had churned out a whole series of uninspired commercial buildings prior to his high-profile competition win. The philosophical underpinning to his work did not appear to relate to anything he had previously designed.

'Me and my friends,' Taras mused, 'are studying English so that we can leave the Ukraine and get good jobs in interesting countries. But you, you come to Odessa when you could remain in England! You are very strange.'

'It seemed like a good idea at the time,' I sighed, and as I did so he opened his eyes and his brow wrinkled into a frown.

'You are not happy here?' he asked.

'No, not completely.'

Taras sat up and took my hand, staring gravely into my face.

'What can we do to make you happy?'

'I don't know. Perhaps I should just pack my bags and go home?'

And then he kissed me. It was a nice kiss, a sensuous kiss. I did not think Taras good-looking, I was not attracted to him, but at that moment the contact and the warmth were so welcome that I responded. I closed my eyes, which I almost never do when I kiss.

Somebody wolf-whistled from the direction of the river and Taras pulled away, looking over to where most of the other students were still horsing around in the water. I lay down and a moment later he laid beside me, taking my hand in his.

'I would like to help you,' he said with a sincerity that made me feel uncomfortable, for I was rather equivocal about our sudden intimacy.

'I'm just in a bad mood,' I said.

'Okay,' he replied, but I was unable to interpret his meaning. He said nothing more and as we lay there I became concerned that I had offended him.

I moved onto my side and propped myself up on my elbow, sup-porting my head on my hand, and looking down at him. He was staring up at the underside of the trees. He was pale, dark-haired and rather skinny. I was worried about the difference in our ages; he seemed so young.

A bird flew over us and for a second he watched it. I looked into his eyes and they seemed very sad. I realised that telling him how miserable I was just after we had kissed had been tactless. To make amends I said:

'There are some good things about being here.'

'Like what?' he asked, expressionless.

'You,' I lied, or half-lied, for I suppose that I did like him. I was grateful for his company.

He considered for a few moments and then looked into my face, scrutinising me and, I assumed, doubting me. This annoyed me, so I added.

'I do like you very much.'

I wasn't going to go any further, and I certainly wasn't going to say that I found him attractive because that would have been very wrong. But my awkward words might have implied this, and he smiled and sat up.

'I like you as well,' he announced. 'And I want to make you happy. And you make me happy.'

I was pleased at his reaction. He looked about him and smiled broadly:

'It is a beautiful day, and a beautiful place. And I am in love with a beautiful woman from England.'

There was something about the way he announced this that pleased me. I was flattered, I suppose. All in all, the sounds of laughter and shouting from the river, and the sun's warmth as we sat on the grass, all meant that continuing to kiss Taras was an easy and a pleasant way to spend the rest of the afternoon.

I had no intention to deceive him, but that is exactly what I did. I acted out of motives that I am not at all proud of. I enjoyed that afternoon in the countryside, with the food and drink and the light-hearted company. I enjoyed the fact that Taras had said he loved me and thought me beautiful. Yes, he was a scrawny young thing and had features that I can only describe as bland, but I did not put much thought into what happened. I knew that in any other situation I would have declined his attentions, but I did not feel that I had a choice if I wanted to feel close to someone in that foreign country; and that was exactly what I wanted at that moment.

But following that afternoon I took to avoiding Taras. I was a little embarrassed, and I felt rather guilty. And then, one night a week later, he knocked at the door of my room while I was sitting inside at my desk working. I recognised his voice as he had said goodbye to a friend a few doors away and I had listened to his steps in the corridor as he had approached the door to my room.

I sat still, saying nothing, and he knocked again and quietly called my name. I knew he could not open the door from the outside and simply come in, and although my light was on he could not be sure that I was inside. I decided to pretend to be out.

'I know you're there?' he said hopefully, and I was worried that perhaps he had been outside and had seen my silhouette against the curtain.

'If you do not want to see me any more, I understand,' he said, slightly pathetically.

I did not like being so cruel, but decided that I should continue with the pretence; he couldn't know for certain that I was inside and it would hurt him less if I carried on the charade rather than answer the door and confirm his suspicions.

And then I heard no more. If he was still standing outside, listening, I could not tell, but I had not heard him walk away. Noiselessly I moved into a more comfortable position and continued to read the book from which I'd been taking notes. Five minutes passed, ten, and then I heard the door banging at the end of the corridor and footsteps came down and past my door, not stopping until they reached a position much further down the corridor where another door opened and closed. As they had passed by my room no words had been exchanged with Taras, if he was still there, and their pace had not changed as they walked by.

It seemed likely that he had gone, but I nevertheless got out of my chair very quietly and lay down on the bed to try and read a magazine. It must have been nearly a quarter of an hour later that I heard a group of two or three people walking down the corridor, and again they made no allowance for anybody standing outside of my door. I was feeling terribly guilty by this time and I decided that I would have to make it up to Taras. I resolved to go to his room, pretending that I had been elsewhere and had just that moment returned. I would invite him to the Hall bar for a drink.

I immediately felt much better for the idea, got up and put on my shoes. I let myself quietly out of my door, and there he was, standing against the wall opposite. He had been there all the time.

'Then you do not love me,' he said.

'Oh, Taras, I never said I *loved* you. I said that I *liked* you.'

'I will not trouble you any more.'

'Taras!' I said, moving a step forward and taking his arm as he turned to go. 'Come inside, for a minute, please.'

'There is nothing to say.'

'Please?'

He nodded, reluctantly, and walked into my room before me.

'Please sit down?' I asked him and he obediently sat on the chair. I perched on the edge of the bed and decided to lie:

'I do like you, very much, but I have somebody else back in England.'

'Do you love him?'

'I don't know,' I replied carefully, feeling that this was rather a good way of explaining my reluctance to get involved with Taras. I continued with the deception, telling myself that it was to spare his feelings: 'I'm having trouble deciding who I would rather be with; you or him. I couldn't let you in here before because I didn't think it fair.'

'Why?'

'Because if I let you in we might start kissing again.'

28

'I wouldn't mind.'

'No, nor would I. But it wouldn't have been fair on this other boy.'

'I don't care about him.'

I laughed at his honesty and he smiled back nervously.

'I like kissing you,' he said. 'But we don't have to go any further than that.'

'What do you mean?' I asked, genuinely not considering that there might have been any further to go.

'I wasn't planning to sleep with you.'

'Oh!'

I was taken aback by his abruptness. And then, I admit, a very stupid feeling came over me. My pride was hurt at the thought that this young man who had said that he loved me did not want to go to bed with me. It was a stupid reaction, I know.

He stood up and smiled down at me.

'How long do you need to decide between us?'

'I don't know.'

'I will wait for you.'

I took his hand because I suddenly thought that I was going to be alone again. My story was a fabrication; there was nobody else in England. If there had been then perhaps I could have endured my loneliness there in the Ukraine. Taras offered some comfort.

He ran his hand through my hair and said, 'You are confused.'

'I am,' I conceded, glad that this was the truth, even if I was wilfully misunderstanding him. I stood and faced him.

'I will try and help you decide,' he said and kissed me. And I decided to stop analysing the situation I found myself in.

A few evenings later, a Sunday, Taras took me to a party somewhere on the outskirts of the city. It was in a large but run-down house and although very few people there were students, they were all of his age. The music was heavy but tuneful in a meandering, aimless sort of way and everyone had to talk loudly to be heard above it.

It was very dark in all of the rooms, and crowded, and I became bored quite quickly because I could not easily join in with any of the conversations. Taras was considerate, though, and unselfishly acted as translator for me some of the time, but the talk was a little tedious. When people discovered that I was English they often wanted to ask me about well-known English celebrities because they were easy references. I had answered the same questions so many times before that it was with some relief that I found Taras was tiring of it all as well. He took me to a corner of a room at the back of the house that was even darker still and perhaps just a little bit quieter. Here we kissed, and in the gloom where we could not be seen I let him slip his hand up my shirt and massage my breast. I did try to push his hand away but without any conviction and I admit that I was enjoying myself as much as he was. However, I then tried putting my hand into his trousers and he pushed me away.

'No, not that!' he said, serious.

'I'm sorry,' I replied. I pushed back his floppy hair and kissed his ear. 'But you excite me. I would like to make love with you.'

'I know, but I don't want to, yet. I don't know you well enough.'

And now I felt a complete fool; cheap. I hadn't thought that he would still feel like that.

'I understand,' I said, annoyed, and we decided to leave, walking back to the Hall, hand in hand, but making little conversation. It was a lovely night, if a little chilly, but neither of us said what we really felt. When we were back in our corridor we kissed, pretending that everything was alright between us, and went to our separate rooms.

And I slept badly. My earplugs never quite muffled the sounds of the other students returning late, and noisily, to their rooms, and somebody in another corridor appeared to be having a party of their own. Everything combined to make me feel even more irritable and serious about leaving for home.

However, the following week I was too busy to worry about my problems. On the Monday my tutor suddenly announced that he was going to Kiev for two days and could take me along with him to see a couple of Alexander de Saussure's recent buildings. I just had time to return to the Hall to pack a few things, return to the School of Architecture, and leave with him in his very old Mercedes. I didn't have time to tell anyone that I was going, but Taras was the only person who might have been interested in my movements. I didn't leave him a note, and felt bad about this the whole time that I was away. The trip is a story in itself but I will make it brief.

Visiting Kiev went well enough and I was impressed both by the city and de Saussure's buildings. Unfortunately the car broke down on our return and we spent an unplanned couple of days in Uman. The car, we were constantly assured, would be repaired at any moment, but the hours, then the days dragged on. We stayed in a small hotel and my tutor insisted that he would pay for everything because I was only a poor student and the problems with the car were his fault because he had not maintained it properly.

On the first day there we went to a park and sitting on a bench he took hold of my hand and kissed it. I was horrified that he was about to proposition me and that he had engineered the whole situation. I was being rather self-centred, however, for what he wanted to confide was that he was homosexual and was considering leaving his wife and family for another tutor at the University. I don't know that I was able to give him any useful advice, but I listened to him dutifully and as compassionately as I could. It was a stressful couple of days.

Upon my return to Odessa I found a letter waiting for me in the Department saying that Alexander de Saussure would be pleased to meet me for an interview at his office that evening in the city centre. It was dated three days previously. I barely had time to grab my research notes and borrow a dictaphone, and I arrived a half-hour late and out of breath.

De Saussure's offices were in an elegant Victorian building of classical proportions and detailing, but the interior had been gutted to create a thoroughly modern set of working spaces. I was shown into a conference room, immediately dropped my notes, and despaired of making a good impression. However, to my surprise it went well. De Saussure was amused that I was so evidently flustered, and with good humour he showed me how to operate the dictaphone.

I felt untidy, ill-prepared and out of place, but for two hours he was happy to explain his design philosophy to me as it related to his recent work. Somehow I managed to ask intelligent questions and sounded as if I knew what I was talking about.

De Saussure struck me as handsome; a tall man with greying hair and large hands, he was a charismatic character and I liked him immensely. He made many references to other contemporary architects, to great architects and artists of the past, and provided me with much useful material for my PhD. He re-ignited my enthusiasm not only for his own work but for contemporary architecture in general. I had been unable to see any way forward with my thesis until that meeting, but suddenly I was enthused. De Saussure obviously sensed this and asked me if I would like to return the next day and attend a presentation.

When I returned to the Hall that evening I was worried that Taras might be standing outside of my door, but despite the fact that I had managed to leave the lights on in my room he was not there waiting. I reined-in my ego and worked late into the night, rising early the next morning to walk into the Department and transcribe the interview of the previous day directly onto a word processor. I hadn't finished at lunchtime when I had to stop to go back to the offices of Alexander de Saussure for the presentation.

Once again I was shown into the conference room where one of the architects explained that this was not to be a presentation to a client but to other professionals, engineers, etc, who would be working on the design if it all went ahead. The following week, he explained, the same kind of presentation was scheduled for the clients, and then it would all be repeated for the planners.

Alexander de Saussure was obviously comfortable before an audience and enjoyed presenting his new design for a development on a cliff-side some distance along the coast from Odessa. I could not understand much of what he said but the model he unveiled suggested that if it could be built then more awards would soon be forthcoming. From the north the building was understated and had very little visual impact, being partly underground with an earth roof. However, once a visitor was inside the building the main corridor would widen, brighten, and finally open out to offer a great atrium space with wide views out over the Black Sea. This southern façade, entirely of steel and tinted glass, was to be cantilevered out over the water and would be quite breathtaking.

I made notes and drew sketches, and became so absorbed that when de Saussure later addressed me I didn't immediately realise that I should look up.

'I have explained to my colleagues here that you are studying my work for your PhD,' he said, amused at my surprise. 'Would you like to give us your opinion of the project.'

'It'll have to be in English,' I replied, reluctantly.

'Of course. Most of us will understand.'

'Well,' I said, putting down my papers and pen as twenty sets of eyes were turned to me. I felt very uncertain of myself. 'I assume that the entrance is so modestly designed for environmental reasons, as well as for reasons of theatre. It has a minimal impact on the landscape and conceals what is to be discovered. I like the way that anyone using the building will progress through the earth, as it were, from the small-scale, relatively dark rooms, through to larger, lighter spaces, until the main route ends in the atrium with the curtain-wall of glass and the view out over the sea. To continue the route with the balcony, or half-bridge seems . . .'

He raised his eyebrows, encouraging me to continue, but I could not think of the right word. I decided upon 'inevitable' and he nodded, sagely.

'Ideally,' he said, 'at the end of the bridge the person who has been progressing through the building should be able to throw themselves off and become one with the air, with the elements.'

'And from the sea,' I added. 'Which is not an elevation that many people will witness, it is a startling and bold statement. There is something primitive, or primordial about the entrance, but the progression through to the unashamedly modern part is daring and marvellously handled.'

'Thank you,' de Saussure replied, evidently appreciating my comments. 'Unfortunately I now have to persuade these gentlemen that the earth roof at the entrance will be strong enough for the load, and watertight. And that the curtain wall and cantilevered portions of the building can be built with the delicacy I envision. Engineers, eh?'

I left the presentation very impressed and returned to the Department for a late night writing up my thoughts. I got back to the Hall of Residence some time after midnight and went immediately to my room and got into bed. Somebody was playing loud music close-by so I put in my earplugs and started to read. However, after my busy few days, I fell asleep immediately and awoke the next morning with my light still on and the magazine lying on my chest.

໑

It was a Friday and I got up early, determined to go back into the Department to write up my notes. My mind was full of questions that I wanted to ask de Saussure and I decided to put them into a letter, if only to get them into some coherent order. I jotted a couple of things down while I dressed, and then went to leave. I had been so wrapped up in my thoughts that Taras standing outside my door made me jump.

'So, you *are* in there,' he said simply. He looked tired, his eyes dark-shadowed. He was wearing a t-shirt and jeans that looked a little crumpled.

'Yes. You weren't waiting for me?'

'You were pretending that you were not in.'

'No,' I insisted, making the adjustment from being absorbed by architectural matters, to considering Taras, who I had not really thought about for almost a week. 'I use earplugs at night.'

'Is that so you can ignore my knocking?'

My heart sank. I asked him back into my room but he would not sit down. He looked about him, distracted and sad, waiting for an explanation. I apologised for not telling him what I had been doing, and related the hectic events of the last few days.

'Those are all good excuses,' he said simply. 'You have had a long time to think of them. But I know the real reason you are ignoring me.'

'What's that?'

'Because I wouldn't sleep with you.'

I grinned, which was thoughtless of me and he seemed to take it badly. I was horrified that over the last few days, while I had been pre-occupied, Taras might have worked himself into a state over our creaky relationship. How often had he come and knocked on my door, convinced that I was inside but hiding from him? Usually, I would have been elsewhere, but perhaps at other times I had actually been inside, but sound asleep with my earplugs in.

'Taras. I have been thoughtless . . . .' I started to say, but he leant over and put his finger to my lips.

'If this is all I need to do to have you, then I give myself to you,' he said, and started to take off his t-shirt.

'No, Taras,' I protested, but was unable to stop him removing it and letting it drop to the ground. He then started to unbuckle his belt and I decided that I had to take control of what was happening.

I grabbed his hands to stop him.

'You don't have to do this,' I said firmly. 'I respect you too much, and like you too much, and yes, I'd like to sleep with you, but not like this.'

'I don't mind,' he insisted. 'There's nothing that I wouldn't do for you.'

'Put your shirt back on,' I said, as levelly as I could.

He bent down and picked it up, holding it to his skinny chest.

'Do you love me?' he asked.

'Yes,' I replied, desperate for him to get dressed and out of my room. The whole scene annoyed me, and he annoyed me, although I knew that it was entirely my fault. 'Yes, I love you. But please get dressed.' It seemed the easiest thing to say.

He put his shirt back on, gloomily, deliberately.

'Why have you been hiding for the last few days?'

'I haven't,' I repeated, tired and frustrated. 'I've been working. Look, how about we go out tonight?'

He smiled at this and I told him to be ready at seven o'clock. I insisted, though, that at that moment I had to go back into the Department.

As I walked into the city centre and the School of Architecture my thoughts were at first of the mess that I had created with Taras. I was annoyed that I had told him I loved him, and that I had agreed to meet him later that day. Perhaps, by that evening, I might have been in a more receptive mood for his company, but my thesis was rather more important to me at that moment and by the time I arrived at the Department it was once again uppermost in my thoughts. I share a small room there with another, harder-working postgraduate student, but that morning he was not in. With the place to myself I spread out my papers on both his desk and mine and started to see how my thesis might take shape. At any other time I would have wasted half of the morning walking down to the office to see if there was any mail for me, going to the coffee machine, and even wandering into the studios to see what the other students were up to, but that day I set immediately to work. I could see how the PhD could be divided up into a number of distinct sections, each having a separate building as a case study, and I put my notes in piles with photographs, drawings and copies of magazine articles. Just doing this brought ideas to mind, associations and themes that I would want to explore. I made notes of these before they slipped from my mind, and wrote down references to the work of other architects that I would need to follow up. It was exciting to realise just how much of my thesis could be written with

36

the aid of my interview with de Saussure, but slightly worrying that I would need to do so much extra research to back up what he had told me.

Once it all seemed to make sense I rationalised my piles of papers and turned on the word processor to start transcribing the rest of the interview from the Dictaphone. While I was waiting for it to boot up my supervising tutor put his head around the door and coughed, startling me.

'I'm sorry,' he apologised.

'I didn't hear you coming.'

'I have just had a telephone call from Alexander de Saussure,' he informed me. 'He asked whether it would be right for him to offer you a position in his company?'

'A job? Doing what?'

'He called it "International Public Relations".'

'Goodness! Really?'

'Yes. He telephoned to discuss whether it was . . .' he struggled for the word, '. . . ethical, to offer you the position. He doesn't want it to conflict with your studies.'

'It won't, will it?'

'It might. But as long as you put plenty of hours into your PhD, you could be in a better position for research if you are working for him.'

'I don't know what to say.'

He shrugged. 'You will have to talk to him,' was all that he would say before he left.

I waited for the news to sink in, but as it would not I walked down the corridor to my tutor's office and asked if I could telephone de Saussure. He agreed, got me an outside line and held on until the call was through to the architect himself. Then he left.

At some time in the middle of the following night I awoke and remembered Taras. In the pit of my stomach it gave me an unpleasant, hollow feeling. I wondered what on earth I was doing? I had thought that I was in control of everything but suddenly I doubted myself. Quietly snoring beside me was Alexander de Saussure.

In his office the architect had offered me a very good position with an enviable salary and insisted that although I would have to regularly visit the Ukraine I could work from London. I refused to accept such a proposition immediately, and although he said that this was entirely reasonable he started to joke that he was upset that I couldn't accept there and then. In the same spirit I told him that I was a difficult woman to persuade, and that he would have to try harder. We flirted rather, and to show that I wasn't ungrateful I agreed that he could buy me dinner. It was a silly game, but I didn't want him to think that I would simply accept any offer that he cared to make. What was more, I told him that if he was taking me out it would have to be to an expensive restaurant.

We got on very well while I teased him over what I did or did not think of his offer, and he insisted that if I was to keep him waiting for an answer then there would have to be small forfeits in return. For example, he insisted that I chose the wine, and insisted that I chose well, so I simply decided upon a very expensive bottle. When he tried to top up my glass and I demurred, he reminded me that the wine had been my choice and that it was not cheap. When we had finished eating he said that he thought he could persuade me to accept the offer that very night, but we would have to have liqueurs with our coffee so that he could have the time to talk me around.

Next to the restaurant was a hotel with a dark, comfortable bar, and we went there afterwards to continue our conversation. I knew the implications of this and I was happy for the evening to come to its inevitable conclusion.

But at four in the morning, in the hotel room which was too warm and stuffy, though luxuriously appointed, I did not feel so certain of myself. I had no real qualms about who I was sharing a bed with, but I was concerned as to how Taras would feel that I had stood him up. Thoughts of him in that oppressive Hall of Residence went around and around in my thoughts. I lay under a very thin sheet feeling hot and uncomfortable. It took a great mental effort to relax and think of other things before I was able to sleep again.

I returned to the Hall of Residence at some time in the middle of the morning and was pleased that Taras was not hanging around. Somebody, Taras I assumed, had left what looked like a large, sealed jiffy bag outside of my door so I picked it up and let myself in. Although I had showered at the hotel I was still in my clothes from the day before and I was about to change them when I casually examined the contents of the parcel that had been left for me.

The bag looked new but it was stained an unpleasant brown at the bottom. I tore it open and tried to tip the contents out onto my desk but they seemed to be stuck. Looking in I could see something dark and felt instinctively that shaking it vigorously was preferable to putting my hand inside. What fell on the desk with a thump appeared to be a large lump of old meat, bloody, gristly and fatty and starting to dry up. I dropped the bag and backed away, appalled that somebody could have left such a thing for me. I couldn't believe that Taras had done it.

It took me several moments to compose myself. I found an old plastic bag and with a ruler I pushed the thing lying on my desk into the bag. I felt nauseous at the pressure I had to use to move the weight of the lump of old meat, and at the extra effort required because it had slightly adhered to the desk. When it fell into the plastic bag the sudden weight of it made me feel shaky and I dropped it and jumped back, unable to stop the stupid reaction. Gingerly, and without looking into the plastic bag, I then put the stained jiffy bag inside as well.

I washed my hands in the sink and then wiped down my desk and threw the soiled tissues into the bag, which I then tied up. I detested the thought that by carrying the bag up the corridor I was somehow associated with whatever it was that I couldn't identify. When I dropped it into the large dustbin outside I felt so much happier, although I returned to my room with some hesitation, worried that there might be something else to confront.

The damp patch on my desk had dried by the time that I had changed my clothes, and although I wasn't sure that I was in the mood for work, I decided to go back to the Architecture Department. I certainly didn't want to stay around in the Hall, and I was desperate to tell somebody who might appreciate the news about my job offer of the previous day. I was still shaken and angry, but as I walked out of the grounds I was already thinking about what had happened between myself and Alexander de Saussure, and wishing that I had some close girlfriend to whom I could confide.

As I reached the gate into the street Taras appeared before me. He walked directly out in front of me and I stopped, my heart thumping.

'Did you find it?' he asked quietly. He looked terribly ill.

'So it was you,' I said, appalled, but unable to think of anything other than his terrible appearance. He was unnaturally pale, his skin almost translucent, and this was emphasised by his stubble and his dark shadowed eyes. He was wearing an old, stained coat, which he had pulled exaggeratedly tight about him with dirty hands.

'What the hell was it?' I asked, but as I did so I suddenly thought that I knew.

'It was for you,' he said, his words pained and awkward.

ò

Nina Monkman stopped her narrative and stared down into her glass of wine as if to find something there to replace what she could see in her memory.

'You are going to think me mad . . .'

'Are you suggesting . . . ?' I started to ask and she nodded vigorously.

'A prank,' she said determinedly. 'It was a trick, a horribly cruel trick. He had every reason to be angry with me, but why so nasty? Why so macabre? He pulled open his coat and his shirt and his trousers were completely sodden with what appeared to be blood.'

'What did you do?'

'I did what any other self-respecting woman would do, of course. I had hysterics and ran.'

'Where?'

'Away, from him. I don't quite know where I went, probably only two or three streets away, and then I calmed down a little, and went back to Alexander. He must have wondered what kind of madwoman he had been with the previous night, but he listened to what I said and we went to the police, and then they listened patiently to what I had to say.'

'And what did you say?'

'Only what I told you . . . I told them what happened. I said that it could only have been a sick trick but they asked me what I thought Taras had meant to suggest. I couldn't say it, though.'

'And what did the police find?'

'That Taras is missing. In the dustbin they found the bag, with his blood on it, but nothing inside. There were still traces of blood on my desk, but in his room it was everywhere.'

'What do they think happened?'

'They don't know and they won't say. But they asked me so many questions, and they didn't want me coming back to England for Christmas. They want to ask me more questions when I return next week.'

'Are you going back?'

'I think I have to. I have to know for sure that it was all a horrible joke.'

In Hiding

For the first time since his arrival in Arkos the Right Honourable David Barrett, M.P. was up early, washed and dressed and standing on the quay. Behind him the town seemed angular, dusty and harsh, but the sun was bright and glittered off the sea. In the distance the island of Elga looked green, fresh and inviting.

There were a number of fishermen about at that hour, stretching out their nets to dry and talking with good humour amongst themselves. They didn't seem to mind him staring at them, trying to fathom their actions. At least Barrett had now seen them with their boats: it had appeared unlikely that their craft were intended to be purely picturesque.

It was cool enough to stand in the sun and enjoy its warmth without discomfort, and the Englishman felt it on his face as he closed his eyes. When he opened them again it was to see a boat approaching from the island.

A man in a red shirt sat in the back of the small craft by the outboard motor, the sound of which reached Barrett a few moments later and increased in volume as he came into the harbour. Barrett assumed that this must be Simon. There was nowhere obvious for him to tie up, though, so the pilot of the boat pointed to a small wooden jetty a short distance away and turned in that direction.

Barrett walked over to meet him, stepping over the paraphernalia of the fishermen, watching as the man cut the engine just before the jetty and let the boat continue under its own momentum. He was not intending to stop, however, and as the boat came alongside Barrett, he motioned for the English M.P. to jump aboard while it was close enough. It rocked and lurched as the man stepped in, and immediately the pilot pulled at the engine and it started up again. Barrett marvelled that anyone could appear to be so at ease on the water, moving about the boat gracefully, turning it and giving the engine full throttle once he had it aimed back in the direction of the open sea. His passenger sat towards the front and once he had composed himself he enjoyed the slight breeze and the sprays of water that came over the side from time to time.

'I assume that you're taking me to see Taylor?' he shouted over the noise of the engine.

The young man smiled, apparently in agreement, and Barrett told himself to relax. Even if this man wasn't Simon and didn't speak a word of English what did it matter? He had become so tired of his predicament that he no longer cared what risks he took. What could be worse than the calamities that had so recently befallen him?

The boat left the harbour, passing a couple of birds which Barrett assumed were gulls; they seemed unconcerned at both the boat and the small wake that made them bob up and down. Barrett could see further up the mainland as Arkos shrank behind them, and noticed that Taylor's island was still quite sheltered, despite being a half mile out at sea. Along the coastline to the north there appeared to be army buildings of some kind, but they may well have been older fortifications. They were too far away for him to be able to see whether they were still in use. To the south the coastline looked a little gentler, though still rocky. The tourist beaches were at least a couple of dozen miles further away with their stretches of inviting sand.

The island of Elga grew closer, and through the dark green of the trees Barrett could make out two houses. They were both built of the dull yellow local stone and one looked run-down and perhaps burnt-out? Then the sun reflected off something brightly and was immediately gone again.

The boat soon started to skirt the island and they made for what Barrett now saw to be a very small harbour with one other similar boat in it. The engine was cut, as before, and they coasted in and alongside a low concrete arm in which were set rusty iron steps. The young man deftly took the rope and climbed up, pulling it through an iron ring. The boat stopped with a jerk and was then secured against the wall. The sea here was clear, unlike the harbour at Arkos, and Barrett could see the sand a few feet below him. Fish darted past and apparently out into the wide water of the Mediterranean.

He stood uncertainly and climbed up after the pilot, who turned and offered him a hand.

'Welcome to Elga,' said the young man with an unmistakeable northern English accent.

'Thank you.'

Just ahead of them was one of the houses.

'You're expected up there,' Simon suggested, but Barrett took his time to look out to sea, wondering if he could make out a coast on the far horizon. It was strange to be on an inland sea; having been brought up on the south coast of England he had always assumed that such stretches of water went on forever, getting colder and wilder. But this was enclosed, safe-seeming.

Barrett turned back to the house; it was magnificently situated. A series of stone terraces led up from the harbour. Trees pressed all around this side of the island, but Barrett could see that they thinned further around, allowing views to the north. It seemed so much cooler there than in the town. There was a breeze blowing, and the stone balustrade, when he touched it as he ascended the last few steps up to the house, was still cold. There was vegetation everywhere, with brightly coloured flowers. And there were lizards, motionless, willing the sun to burn with more heat. Next to him, in the grass, a cicada shrilled, and high above in the blue vault a bird called.

Taylor appeared, standing on the top step in front of the house.

'Welcome to my domain,' he said with a broad smile on his great, square face.

Only two days previously Barrett had booked himself into a Spartan hotel in the small, dusty Greek port that the guidebook had insisted had little to commend it to the casual tourist. He had arrived in darkness, and it was without great hopes that he had drawn back the curtains on his first morning. He had no idea of what to expect and, frankly, it could have been worse. There was a small bay with boats in the harbour, but the buildings were too modern to be attractive, and perhaps the boats were too functional to really be pleasing to the eye. He had been woken early by the sound of the cars and scooters under his window, the noise of which echoed around the semi-circular port long after they had passed out of it.

At that moment he tried not to think of why he had ended up in Arkos, but, unbidden, recent memories of his wife's face, the Prime Minister's anger, and the newspaper reporter's obvious enjoyment of his plight rose up before him. He had been able to face up to the scandal for only so long. When his Party had publicly chastised him he still had the support of his wife, but when she decided that she should distance herself from him, then it had all become too much to bear. Friends slipped away, becoming mysteriously unavailable, and his family suddenly found it impractical to see him. For almost a week, when he thought that he had the support of those around him, he had been able to ignore the fact that he really had made a career-ending mistake.

On his first morning in Arkos he borrowed the guidebook from the hotel lobby and read about the local archaeology. He thought that perhaps he should try to see it, but he found life much more relaxing if he simply sat in the little café in the middle of the harbour and watched the world pass by before him.

The café was dark but bustling and he had formed the notion that he would sit there and write. Despite all that went on around him, he was trying to explain on paper the set of circumstances that had allowed him to appear to pocket the old lady's half a million pounds. It was a technical argument, and one that he felt he should be able to defend. On the first afternoon, though, he had started to lose interest, and he ended up playing draughts with an old fisherman who came in to drink retsina. The language barrier meant that they could not talk and that suited Barrett.

It was at the end of his second day in the café, when he had all but abandoned writing, as the sun was setting splendidly over the sea, that a man was suddenly at his shoulder.

'Hello there. Barrett, isn't it?'

He looked up and saw a very tall man; he was large in that way that denoted aristocratic blood. Barrett was only a Socialist for the sake of his political career, but he had never liked this kind of person with a booming voice, air of confidence and expansive gestures. He was over-sized, he assumed, because generations of his family had been well-fed at the expense of ordinary people.

'Yes,' he agreed, reluctantly. 'I'm David Barrett.' He had already decided that if challenged he might as well reveal his identity.

'I'm Taylor, Ferdinand Taylor. You remember? We met at Hugh Golightly's party, after the Derby, oh, twelve years ago?'

Barrett stood up reluctantly and had his hand engulfed in Taylor's. It was squeezed mercilessly.

'Twelve years, is it?' asked Barrett, who was not sure if he recognised the man.

'I'm afraid so. I've been here for ten years, you know. Rarely see a pale English face. So why are you in Arkos?'

'Don't ask!'

'Oh, like that, is it?'

Barrett nodded and offered the man the chair opposite.

'How is old Golightly?' the man asked.

'Oh, you know, still stinking rich.'

'Still able to lose a fortune on the horses each year without ever touching his capital, eh?'

'I'm surprised you remember me?'

'Oh, I had years working as a journalist. Trained myself to remember faces and facts, gossip and indiscretion.'

He looked pleased with himself, but was concerned at his companion's hang-dog expression.

'What's up, old man?'

'I just can't believe my bad luck, that's all.'

'I'll try not to take that personally.'

'Well, I've come all the way here to the middle of nowhere to escape the British press, and who do I bump into? Only a bloody journalist!'

'I've retired, dear fellow, I've retired.'

'But do you chaps ever hang up your notebook? Isn't it worth a few thousand quid for you to phone your old paper and cry, "hold the front page! David Barrett's in hiding in Greece"?'

'No, not anymore. I left England under a cloud myself. But what have you done, old fellow, what have you done? If your whereabouts is worth that much money...?'

'You really haven't heard?'

'No. There're no British papers to be had here. So, have you been caught shagging your secretary?'

'No. It's financial . . . .'

'No need to justify yourself to me. I'm well out of that game.'

'I'm not sure that I believe you.'

'I'll come clean. Ten years ago a certain newspaper editor was discovered to have had a gay affair, despite the anti-homosexual rants in his newspaper . . . ?'

'It sounds vaguely familiar.'

'Well, I was the one who sold the story to his rival newspaper.'

'I hope you were well paid?'

'Handsomely. But then, I had to be. Because *I* was his lover.'

'Really?'

'Yes. And they had to pay enough to make it worthwhile that I was a part of the story. And they did. And I have taken an early retirement . . . here.'

'In Arkos?'

'No, not quite. I have a small island just out there,' he waved his hand in the general direction of the sea. 'It's called Elga.'

'But why here? Because it's remote?'

'Well, an old school chum owned it and was talking of selling-up. When I looked into it I was impressed that I could afford a whole island. Arkos itself was dismissed in the particulars as a "small and friendly port where hotels overlook the boats and the nets of the fishermen".' He waved out of the café window in confirmation.

'So, do you want to know the details of my disgrace?' asked Barrett, feeling that perhaps, after all, he would like to justify himself to somebody who might listen without having been prejudiced by the rabid newspapers.

'Tomorrow. Tell me tomorrow. You come over very early and I'll show you around my island. And we'll swim, and have lunch, and then maybe, only maybe, we'll drink enough retsina for me to be bothered with your story,' he smiled again. 'But if I can drag you away from whatever you're writing, you must tell me what you've been up to while you've been here. Where are you staying? The hotel at the end?'

'Yes, I didn't think there was much choice?'

'No. Simon's family stayed there sometimes when they used to visit. When did you arrive?'

'Only two days ago. I read about the archaeology. I've been meaning to look for the ruins; there was once meant to have been an Oracle at Arkos.'

'Most of the remains have long gone. The port's been developed over the centuries. There're some old building on the hillside above us. There're a few bits and pieces on Elga, but nothing of significance.'

There was an awkward pause. Barrett knew that he should be asking Taylor about himself but he could not quite bring himself to.

'So, have you burnt all of your bridges, then?' Taylor asked, at length.

'I didn't think you wanted to know the details until tomorrow?'

'I don't. I was just wondering whether you were planning on going back at some time and trying to salvage your life. You never know; people do bounce back, if they've got the strength, and arrogance. Or are you intending to spend the rest of your life in this hole?'

'I suppose I intend to go back some time. Perhaps when all this blows over, and I'm no longer in the news.'

'Wife and children?'

'Wife. No children.'

'Well. Perhaps we'll talk properly tomorrow?'

Taylor stood up and took Barrett's hand once more:

'Tomorrow. I'll send the boat for you, at about nine.'

And with that he turned and left.

Barrett was dumbfounded. He finished his drink, picked up his papers and walked back to the hotel, its presence announced by an illuminated sign on the dusty roadside. It was a small establishment, although it echoed disconcertingly like a grand palace.

His room was small and sparsely furnished but it had a balcony. The hotel stood at one end of the harbour, facing the buildings on the other side of the bay, but he could still peer out to sea and to the island he guessed was Elga; it was a dark shape against the light evening sky. Barrett stared at it for a long time from the balcony while the frequency of the cars lessened on the road underneath his vantage point, and after a while only the occasional scooters and motorbikes buzzed loudly below him. He was waiting for lights to shine on Elga, but they didn't appear.

℘

The island seemed to be very lush compared to the mainland, although the little terraces that stepped back down from the house to the edge of the sea were overgrown with pale, dry grass. They were probably old, abandoned fields. Barrett could see one of the old wartime buildings through the trees near to them and tried to remember which army might have built it. The air was alive with the sounds of insects.

He followed Taylor around the side of the house and he could see that it was bigger than it had at first appeared, being ranged around an open courtyard, overlooking the terraces and out to sea. Several of the windows were shuttered, but there was one large glazed opening in the middle of the range of buildings.

'There are good stone slabs under this,' Taylor kicked at the grass that covered the yard; it was thick, sharp stuff, interwoven with

49

straying creepers and brambles. 'The fountain's never worked,' he said as Barrett was trying to understand the arrangement of stone and rusted metal in front of them.

On the far side there was a barn and a couple of cart-sized entrances, and Barrett expected to see a few chickens. No part of the building was particularly interesting from any architectural point of view, but with its clay tiles and small windows it made a pleasing composition. He noticed that Simon was no longer with them.

Taylor led him inside, where it was dark and cooler still. Once his eyes had become accustomed to the gloom he could see that it was very tastefully converted. The stone flags in the kitchen were highly polished, and the big bare table in the centre looked newly scrubbed. It was well and expensively appointed, and from a large stainless steel refrigerator Taylor produced two large bottles of beer and opened them. He sat at the table and placed one of the glasses in the place opposite him, inviting Barrett to sit there.

'You look well,' Taylor said, pouring his beer. The words were considered, measured.

'I feel better,' replied Barrett, doing the same. 'I hoped I'd left all my troubles miles behind me, in England, but in Arkos it didn't really feel like that. But here, now, on your island, it's different.'

'I understand. It's special here. It seems like so long ago that I escaped from my own past. But go on, tell me, what occurred back in "Blighty" that drove you here. You might as well unburden yourself, man!'

'The short version of events,' Barrett explained, 'is that about twenty years ago, starting out as a solicitor, I had the dubious honour of acting as Executor for an awkward old lady. Her financial affairs were so incredibly convoluted and slipshod that just about all of her estate would've disappeared into legal fees if I hadn't taken a few short cuts. One of the main liberties that I took was with regard to some assets that should have been transferred to a very questionable evangelist church. They appeared to have several ministers and no congregation, and two of the ministers were convicted criminals. It didn't trouble my conscience that I was able to acquire the assets myself for a very advantageous sum. It was completely wrong legally, but morally? Well, I didn't think they should get the money.'

'But it's come back to haunt you?'

'Yes. They church had known for some years what I'd done, but were waiting for the moment to use the information to their advantage. I was about to be promoted to the Cabinet and they tried blackmailing me. I refused to go along with their demands so they told the newspapers about my activities twenty years earlier.'

'And the newspapers have torn you to pieces?'

'They wouldn't have been so interested in me if I hadn't recently been arguing for more controls on the Press.'

'Do you consider yourself unlucky?'

'Yes! Exactly. What I did was wrong, but it still doesn't trouble my conscience. It is simply bad luck that it came out. I just wish, right now, that I had the resources to buy myself an island. This looks like paradise to me.'

Taylor sipped his beer, staring out the window, and Barrett took the opportunity to do the same.

'It's not quite paradise,' the host said, slowly. 'It should've been.'

'I've told you my woes . . .' Barrett invited him.

'I didn't invite you here so that I could tell you mine, though.'

'It only seems fair.'

'I suppose it always helps to hear of somebody else's misfortunes. It wouldn't hurt to have some one else to sympathise . . . not that I expect that to ease the pain.'

'But if it is painful, you don't have to.'

'It was once unbearable, but the years pass. . . . I wake up every day here in "paradise", but immediately I remember what happened and it's all spoilt for me.'

He sipped his beer once more.

'You see, I met Simon in Arkos one day, about seven or eight years ago, much as I met you. He was on holiday, and I wanted company, and I invited him over here to Elga. And he never left.'

'He seems like a nice chap,' Barrett said, by way of filling the gap, but was surprised to see Taylor's expression.

'So, you saw him?'

'Of course, when he brought me over.'

'He brought you here in the boat?'

'As you arranged, yes. As I said, he seems nice.'

He looked aghast:

'But Simon died, just over three years ago. There was a fire, and it was my fault.'

'So who was the young man in the boat?'

'There was no young man.'

'But who piloted the boat? I didn't do it myself?'

Taylor looked at the surface of the table and simply shook his head.

'So you've seen him too,' he mumbled quietly.

'He's not a ghost.'

'No? Are you sure of that? Are you very sure?'

'I'm certain. But, look, what is this? I mean, you told me you would send him across to pick me up from Arkos.'

'Did I?'

'Yes, hang it all! If this is some attempt at a practical joke…'

'No, I assure you,' he said, looking back up and searching for something in Barrett's face. The gaze made the man uncomfortable; his host was in earnest.

Barrett suggested:

'Let me go and fetch him in? The man out there who collected me is very real; flesh and blood.'

'If you like,' replied Taylor calmly, as though convinced that Barrett would be unable to do so.

He got up from the table and, leaving his beer behind him, he walked out into the bright light of the Greek morning. Simon was not in sight, and might take some finding, Barrett realised, but it was not a large island, and the first thing he would do was go back down to the boats to make sure that there were still two tied up. Before he could get there, though, the young man in the red shirt appeared over to his left with a wheelbarrow full of logs. As he appeared to be coming in Barrett's direction he simply stopped and waited for him.

'Hello again,' the visitor said when the man drew close. 'This might sound odd, but can I ask you a couple of questions?'

'About Ferdinand? I thought so. I hung around because I knew that something might happen.'

'You do realise that he thinks you don't exist?'

'I know. He thinks I'm a ghost,' said the young man with a grin. 'Perhaps I'd better explain.'

He sat on the cool stone balustrade to the steps and said, in a business-like fashion:

'A few years ago there was a fire. It started off as a bonfire. It got out of control. When Ferdinand bought this place there were two houses and both were fully furnished. He emptied the contents of the main house into the second and then moved his own stuff in to the first. And then when I moved here I brought a lot of my own possessions, and we stored the surplus we didn't need in the second house. Then we had a hare-brained scheme to rent out the second house and so had an enormous bonfire to dispose of all the rubbish we'd accumulated. We'd been drinking because it was so hot, and we'd thrown more and more rubbish on the fire. But it was too close to the house, and eventually the whole building went up as well. He got the idea in his head that I was trapped in the burning house when all I'd done was go down to the shore to try and fill up some buckets with water.'

'He thought you'd died?' asked Barrett.

'Yes, poor old Ferdinand. Wouldn't be budged from the idea, even when I turned up safe and well.'

'That must have been awful for him.'

'Yes, for the both of us. He had a breakdown. I don't know if you've ever tried reasoning with someone who is in such a state? It was as though he didn't recognise me. Well, he had to be hospitalised. And he was in and out for five or six years while they tried to find the right balance of drugs. But to ease his psychosis the drugs they gave him made him physically ill. We tried so many combinations, and each had to be left for months to settle down to see if they'd have the desired long term effect.'

'That must have been dreadful.'

'It wasn't good. But his family came over and stayed and were very supportive. And then about two years ago, when he was very ill again, we decided to remove all of his medication. Within weeks he was fit and well, almost entirely restored to his old self. The doctors were surprised, but it worked. The only problem was that he still had the idea that I'd died in the fire, and that it was his fault. We decided, me and the family, that in all other respects he was so much better. And as it had been so long since the fire his grief seemed almost bearable to him. So we simply left everything like that.'

'And he thinks that he sees your ghost?'

'His family look after his financial affairs and I'm paid to stay here and look after him. I cook for us, clean, look after the place. And he simply thinks that he's haunted.'

'You're a pretty substantial ghost!'

'I should say so!'

'But what should I do? Go back to him and act like everything's normal?'

'Everything *is* normal, apart from his one strange belief. Yes, go back, talk about England and old friends.'

'But that's wrong, surely.'

'In what way?'

'Morally. I mean, the man may be deluded, but you're colluding with that delusion, reinforcing it.'

'What should I do? Go back to experimenting with different doses of drugs? Let them fry his brains with ECT again?'

'They don't do that in this modern age. Go back to Britain rather than stay in this ratty old country . . . Go private . . . See some specialists . . .'

Simon was obviously annoyed and was choosing the words for his reply with care.

'Thank you for your advice, but with all due respect, you don't know what you're talking about. The medical care in this country is just as good as in the UK. And we did go private, although it offered nothing that all the alternatives didn't, except a larger bill. And yes, for your information, even in this enlightened age they do still resort to electrocuting patients because, barbaric as it seems, it can have positive effects.'

'I'm sorry, I was only trying to help,' Barrett defended himself.

'No. Real "help" means being here when he is going through sheer physical and mental hell and can't even feed himself. "Help" is spending the whole day trying to get a very big, uncooperative and belligerent man into a bath because he stinks so badly but doesn't notice. And then when he's in the bath you don't only have to wash him but you have to hold him up so that he doesn't simply slip under the water and drown. Because he's so confused and unable to do anything for himself . . .'

'Okay, okay,' Barrett backed away. 'Point taken.'

'The state he's in at the moment is as close to normal as you could imagine. And it's a blessing.'

'I'll go back and pretend I didn't see you.'

'You do that,' Simon said, almost with a threat in his voice.

Feeling rather aggrieved Barrett walked back to the house. Taylor was in the kitchen and appeared to be preparing food, although it was still quite early.

'We shall have a picnic,' he declared. 'I'll show you around my island first, by which time we'll have worked up an appetite.

'I'd like that. You can point out the archaeology.'

'There's very little left,' he explained as they started around the shoreline, travelling clockwise. 'The army were here in the Second World War and destroyed most of it. They built the little harbour, and there are a few old pill-boxes, and other horrible things in concrete.'

Neither of them said anything as they passed around the second house, lacking its roof and the inside blackened and empty. The holes for its windows were like sightless eyes and seemed to watch them, reproachfully, as they passed by.

'Is there anything you miss about England,' Barrett asked Taylor.

'I suppose so, but they're not realistic things.'

'What do you mean?'

'If I lived there I'd still want to be in a house in the middle of nowhere, without a telephone or television. Just like here.'

'Are you completely cut off from the world outside?'

'I've got a radio, and sometimes I listen to the World Service, but that isn't a realistic picture of what's going on, is it? I think back to my childhood with fondness, and if I returned I'd expect unreasonably endless sunny days in the house I grew up in. But they weren't endlessly sunny, were they?'

'No. It still rains quite a lot.'

'I suppose so,' he agreed. 'But after a few years here I even started to imagine that everyone wears bowler hats and drives Triumph Heralds. I think of men drinking warm ale in coaching inns, and women in flowery dresses in gardens full of night-scented stock. . . .'

'Do you miss the people?'

'Not really. There are good people and bad people wherever you go. Mostly good people. There are as many interesting and as many dull people here in Greece as there are in England.'

'But you think of England nostalgically?'

'When I'm in a good mood, I suppose so. When I'm well, and happy, I remember the great times, and the stupidity and fun of my old job. But when I'm down I remember the bad times, and the depths to which I descended just to get a story to fill up a few column inches.'

Taylor stopped walking. They were at the northernmost point of the island and he was staring out to sea, his eyes searching the horizon for something. In two places Barrett had noticed small areas of sandy beach, but the rest was rocks. They continued their walk, and when they had almost circumnavigated the entire island they cooled their feet in a large stony pool. Taylor insisted that they eat their food looking out to sea rather than back to the mainland, so on a large flat rock he spread out the cloth in which he had wrapped the bread, feta, tomatoes and ham. In a string bag they had carried two bottles of wine and two glasses, but one had broken. Taylor was saying that he couldn't be bothered to go back to the house for another when, in the distance, Barrett saw Simon. His red shirt was unmistakable, and now that he had started to saw up logs they could also hear him.

Taylor noticed that something had caught Barrett's attention and turned as well, and so Barrett looked down at the food and broke off a piece of bread. He scraped some feta on to it and looked at it carefully, not wanting to know whether Taylor was looking at Simon.

'So, you can see him as well?'

'Yes,' Barrett admitted.

'Good,' he said, with a certain finality. 'I told them I didn't want any more of their pills. I told them I was perfectly sane.'

'I don't think that discussing it will help.'

'You are probably right.'

And with that agreement Taylor then went on to regale Barrett with a succession of entertaining stories, many of them quite unbeliev-able, dating back to his days as a journalist. He was quite unashamed that he had worked in the 'tawdry' end of the business, and claimed that all of his best stories were the result of 'pillow-talk'.

'Not that I had the pleasure of the pillow myself,' he said. 'We paid young men and women, depending on the tastes of the target, to wheedle their way into the affections of useful people and it was amazing what stories they would tell.'

'Wasn't it immoral?'

'But we were usually exposing the immorality of the people we targeted. Let's call it "amoral"?'

After they had finished the second bottle of wine Barrett realised how sleepy he was, with the alcohol and the heat. Taylor talked on, becoming more and more indiscreet, and his listener wished that he had a notebook to take down the stories because some of them were priceless. He desperately hoped that he would remember one about the early career of the current Prime Minister; it might just help if he ever wanted to go back into politics.

Sleep, however, overcame the unfortunate M.P., and Taylor's stories merged with dreams which were inspired by his recent problems back in London and when he awoke he could not disentangle the two in his fuddled mind. He was lying on his back and his bones ached abominably from the rocks he had unwisely chosen for a bed. The skin on his face felt tight and smarting from the sun and he realised he must be burnt. He couldn't work out how long he had been asleep, but Taylor was no longer there. Barrett had not imagined their picnic, though, for the remains of the bread were on the ground beside him, and there was a little wine on his shirtfront.

He stood with great discomfort and looked back at the island. It couldn't be more than ten acres altogether, and though he couldn't see his host, he could make out Simon in his bright shirt walking from the house towards the little harbour. He decided to go after him, believing that now would be a good time to leave, if the young man thought he could do so without appearing rude.

Barrett walked with care over the rough ground and while some distance away Simon turned and saw him coming. He crossed his arms and waited, and when they were close enough he was the first to speak.

'I'm afraid you've rather caught the sun.'

'I guessed I had. Taylor left me to sleep. Is my face that red?'

'Very. You're going to peel badly. Ferdinand's having a siesta indoors, which is the best place to recover from a liquid lunch,' he beamed. 'Oh yes, you will peel...'

'It's a shame someone didn't wake me. But I was wondering, would it be a good time to leave?'

'If you want to. It doesn't bother me. I'd only end up having to cook for you tonight as well.'

'How does Taylor explain the fact that his ghost cooks for him?'

'I'm not sure if he questions it or not,' Simon replied, walking back towards the boats. Barrett followed him.

'His mind does use a kind of logic of its own, to understand the world, but it's not one that makes sense to anybody else. He lives in an alternative, parallel universe, and we have to respect that.'

'But why? There are some objective absolutes; some rights and wrongs we can all agree upon.'

'Are there? Are you a Christian? Do you believe in God?'

'Yes, but what's that got to do with it?'

'Well, why is believing in ghosts any more unreasonable than believing that there is a God?'

'Because a belief in God is more of a working hypothesis than a real proposition.'

'So you don't believe in God as anything other than a concept? That's fine. But plenty of people believe in God as a very real being. And they think that Christ really was conceived by a virgin, and performed real miracles, and died and yet came back to life. You respect the views of people who claim this as real and true?'

'Of course.'

'Well, all that strikes me as a lot more bizarre than Ferdinand's beliefs, even though I can prove to myself that he's mistaken.'

At which point they had reached the boat and Simon untied the rope and jumped in, helping Barrett to follow him. Without another word the young man started up the engine and with the sound roaring off the concrete wall he turned the boat and gunned it for the mainland.

Barrett refused to consider the argument that he could not really refute. His head was throbbing abominably and he felt unequal to an intellectual dispute of any kind. He enjoyed the cool air on his face, although the movement of the boat as it sped over the light waves made him feel nauseous. He didn't look back at the island, but resolved that once in his hotel he would have to make a decision as to what to do next. Perhaps a phone call to an old friend would let him know whether the fuss had died down at home. He had a horrible fear that his disappearance might actually have made things worse.

In Arkos Simon stopped the engine before the jetty, as before, and allowed the boat to continue up to it under its own momentum. He didn't allow Barrett more than a second or so to clamber out of the boat, which he somehow managed without falling back into the water. He turned to Simon to thank him for the ride, but the engine was being fired up again and the young man was taking himself back off and out to sea.

Barrett now felt truly alone for the first time since he had left England. He had been offered a kind of friendship but had refused it. He walked towards his hotel feeling physically and emotionally very tired. When, he asked himself, might his luck start to turn? At the edge of the road he waited for a lorry to pass and a porter from the hotel came up beside him and they crossed together.

'You have caught the sun rather badly?' he said with a tone of voice that was balanced artfully between concern and amusement.

'Yes, I fell asleep outside, in the open.'

'And you went to the island?'

'Yes, to visit a fellow countryman.'

They were both walking towards the hotel. Barrett did not want the company, he needed the sanctuary of his room as soon as possible.

'You are both from England?'

'Yes. We all are, all three of us.'

'All three? But there is only one Englishman on the island.'

'The owner, yes, and the man who took me over there in the boat.'

'I meant the man in the boat. He lives there alone but he is a bit strange. He talks to ghosts.'

'No, you're getting it muddled up. The man who lives on the island thinks that the man in the boat is the ghost.'

'No, sir. The man in the boat, I saw him. He lives there alone, although he comes here and says he is looking after many people on the island. The boys go over there sometimes and watch him talking to people only he can see.'

They stopped at the door of the hotel and the porter opened it so that Barrett could go in first.

60

'I think the boys throw stones at him and break his windows some-times, but he scares them and they don't go there often. Certainly not at night.'

Barrett went up to his room and washed and changed, but did not go down for dinner that evening. He sat on his balcony and stared at the island out on the horizon. After the sun had set and darkness crept in from the east, no lights appeared on the island.

Eleanor

David Planer and I walked into the hotel bar through opposite doors and met in the middle of the room before anyone else could accost him. I was able to offer my old friend a drink, which he accepted, almost with alacrity. I commented on his apparent desperation.

'I am a silly old fool,' he said, patting his breast pocket. 'I have just had a shock. Old men like me should know better. You see, we don't grow any wiser as we get older; there must be a moment in our later middle-age when we start to un-learn everything.'

I was not able to immediately reply because I had managed to catch the barman's eye as we had walked over. I put in an order for a pint of best bitter for him, and a vodka and orange for myself, which annoyed a convention delegate in front of me. He turned round and started to complain that he had been waiting to be served long before we had walked up. However, when he saw that I was with David Planer he smiled and insisted on shaking his hand:

'It's a great privilege to meet you,' he insisted

'If only it was,' David replied, sorrowfully. He was possibly the oldest person at the convention, and looked rather out of place in his jacket and tie. However, I knew that this was as informal as he could bear to dress. 'Would you please forgive me?' he asked the younger man, and then turned to me: 'Sarah, could we go through to that little lounge at the back where it'll be quieter?'

I agreed and he immediately turned and started to walk away. Once I had paid for and picked up our drinks I followed him, but he had not been able to walk far; he was having to acknowledge other convention-goers who had recognised him as the creator of 'Eleanor'. It was probably a quarter of an hour later that we managed to find a couple of chairs together where we were able to speak with a little privacy.

'I've never felt comfortable at any literary events, let alone a science fiction convention,' he said. 'The first time I went to anything like this I was so excited to see some of my literary heroes that I wasn't able to talk to any of them.'

'But now *you* are one of those heroes.'

'Hardly. It was twenty years ago that *Eleanor* was published. My one and only novel.'

'Why would you want, or need, to write another? It must have sold hundreds of thousands of copies worldwide?'

He shrugged: 'But that's not necessarily been my doing, has it?'

'Whose would it have been, then?' I asked, and took a sip of my drink.

'Why, Eleanor's herself.'

'Do you think of her as a real person?'

He laughed, and then shook his head, silent.

I prompted him: 'When she was first conceived, when you thought her up, was she already fully formed and real?'

He considered:

'Yes, in a way, I think she was. It's just that at the start I didn't know her very well. I had to find out about her, and over time I thought that I had . . . When the book was published, and people asked me about it, it was as though she had gone from my life, and I was simply remembering an old friendship.'

'You inscribed my first edition for me at the launch,' I remembered.

'I hate to think how much you'd have to pay for it if you bought it today!'

'The first edition had quite a large print run, though, didn't it?'

'Something like two thousand copies. For a small press it was quite a lot of books, although nearly half of them were pulped after the first two years. The publishers were happy; even selling just a thousand or so made them a profit, and I got a reasonable royalty. We all thought that was the end of Eleanor in our lives.'

'Was it a wrench for you when she left?'

'No. At the time I was glad we'd parted. You see, the novel had been going around in my head for years, and I'd written and re-written permutations on the same theme and the same character so many times . . . When the book came out and I was asked about it I actually had problems remembering which of the various plots was the current one! But Eleanor herself was a constant.'

'She came back into your life, though?'

'Yes. And that was why I was calling myself a silly old man.'

'I'm sorry, I don't understand? I meant the Americans. What did you mean?'

He shook his head again.

'As I was coming down here, from my room, I shared a lift with Eleanor.'

'What, your character?'

'Yes. She was standing there, in the lift.'

'And did she recognise you?' I asked playfully.

He laughed again, but this time I saw tears in his eyes, and he had to turn away and wipe them.

'You see, I told you I was a silly old fool.'

Once he had calmed himself David took a sip of his beer.

'You saw someone dressed up like Eleanor?' I asked. At length he was composed enough to answer:

'Yes, I suppose that's all it was. But for a moment it made me question everything. It made me wonder whether she was real or fiction . . . whether I had merely described a living person, or maybe I hadn't written about her at all. Maybe senility really is catching up with me?'

'You've still got *all* your marbles.'

'Don't be so sure of that. I forget my keys, my spectacles . . .'

'Oh, I do that all the time!'

'But this Christmas I had a long talk with my granddaughter, Rachel, thinking her to be my daughter, Tanya. The poor girl was rather upset that her grandfather was starting to lose the plot. Don't worry, it's nothing horrible like Alzheimer's, but my doctor says, at my age, the onset of senility is no surprise.'

'I'm sorry.'

He shrugged. 'When you get older it doesn't seem *quite* so terrible as it might have been when you were younger. I mean, it still makes me bloody angry. It's getting confused that upsets me most.'

'And seeing someone dressed as Eleanor . . . ?'

'Exactly. I wanted to talk to her, you know. But she's not my Eleanor any more. As you say; "the Americans". She went away from me when we sold the rights to the book to that television company in the States. I never did see the pilot; perhaps, if I had, I would have vetoed the project.'

'Didn't you even see the script before they made the series?'

'Yes, I did, but it was so different from my book that I actually felt guilty that they were paying me for it. I wouldn't have known it was based on my Eleanor if they hadn't told me.'

'A few years ago I met the writer,' I said. 'He admitted that he'd read your book a dozen times and become obsessed by her. He fantasised about her living around the corner from him, and what the consequences would have been. That was why she was uprooted and placed in suburbia, kicking against the preconceptions of white, middle America.'

'His Eleanor wasn't dangerous, like my Eleanor was.'

'No. But it was quite radical at the time that she was even slightly alternative; a pierced nose and a tattoo, unable to cook and her house a mess . . . But she could still teach the perfect all-American little women around her the values of friendship, love, decency . . . It was heart-warming stuff.'

'I never saw it, and I didn't want to.'

'Did you see it when it was re-made though?'

'No. I was just happy to get paid twice!'

'The actress that the second company hired was much better. *Eleanor* became a hit over there primarily because of the actress, and clever marketing. They got it programmed prime-time on the biggest channels.'

'Do you know,' he chuckled, 'we even banked a percentage of their merchandising? It included a whole line in women's fashion!' He smiled properly for the first time that evening. 'No, I never met the American chap, but last year I finally met the Japanese artist who turned her into a comic book character.'

'Did he apologise for ripping you off?'

'Yes, he was polite and very contrite. He claimed he didn't know at the time that he was in breach of copyright.'

I snorted in an unladylike fashion: 'But his graphic novels explicitly named your book as the inspiration for the series . . .'

And then I noticed that David's attention was elsewhere. In the doorway to the lounge was a woman with electric blue hair. She was obviously looking for someone. David half-rose out of his seat and seemed to be a little shaky on his legs. I got up to steady the old fellow and he looked knowingly into my eyes, and then immediately back at the woman. She was now walking into the main bar and out of sight.

'That was Eleanor,' he said quietly. 'Perhaps she was looking for me?'

'Perhaps. But then again, at these kinds of conventions there are always one or two women dressed up like her.'

He looked at me steadily but excitedly, his eyes fixed on mine:

'No, Sarah. That was *my* Eleanor.'

'The one you met in the lift earlier?'

'Yes, but also the Eleanor of my book.'

'Shall I go and find her? I'll ask her to come over here and say hello?'

He looked nervous now, and agitated. I helped him to sit back down and he looked up at me:

'Would you do that?'

I went back into the bar but she was not there. Perhaps she had not found who she was looking for and was now searching elsewhere in the hotel? It could be that she had found whoever she sought and that they had left together. I went to the Welcome Desk in the lobby and explained to a couple of people from the convention committee that David Planer wanted to meet the young lady dressed like the heroine of his famous novel but they could not identify whom I meant. I described her as tall, with blue hair, dressed in the Goth style, but still they denied all knowledge of her.

On my way back to David I put my head around the door of the main conference room but it was empty. I looked into the bar once more, but she was not be seen there either.

'A part of the trouble,' I explained to David an hour later in his room, 'is that she doesn't look quite like the Eleanor from the television series, from the graphic novels, or the computer games.'

'No, well, she wouldn't,' he assented. 'That's because she is the real Eleanor from my original book. And only I know what she looks like!'

The convention organisers had told him that as Guest of Honour, David could have whatever he liked from the mini-bar without concerning himself with the bill. We were therefore availing ourselves of the miniature bottles of spirits. He had decided that the so-called best bitter in the bar was unworthy of the name.

'Did you know that the Japanese fellow, I can't pronounce his name,' David continued, 'had his own model for Eleanor? I thought that comic artists would just make it up, out of their heads. But he drew a real person. Not that he told her! She was a woman he loved from afar, and he called her his muse!'

'So he had a habit of working without permission?' I asked.

'That's a little unfair,' he chided me. 'Once his comics really took off, and were published by a large corporation, they did the right thing and I received all my royalties.'

He had calmed down by now. When I had reported back on my failure to find the woman he wanted to meet, he decided that he would like to return to his room. In my absence a very large, bearded Norwegian had been trying to explain something to David about the Velvet Underground and he looked relieved to be saved by me. As we left the bar he had been rather unsteady on his feet, and I was a little worried about him. Now, sitting in his room swirling the drink around in his glass, he was relaxed and contemplative.

'But,' he said, 'I could see little relationship between the character I had created, and the gun-toting heroine of his comics.'

'You have to call them "graphic novels", especially at a convention like this. But I agree; as far as Japanese readers are concerned Eleanor is a weird-looking western woman rushing around beating the shit out of bad guys.'

'And her sex life . . .'

'As a sub-plot it is bizarre.'

'At least that doesn't get into the computer games!'

'Have you ever played them?'

He looked at me over the top of his spectacles with an expression that suggested that I did not know him as well as I thought.

'They're very good,' I explained. 'But they're based very much on the Japanese version of Eleanor.'

'The strangest thing of all is to compare the American incarnation of Eleanor, all wholesome and good, with the Japanese one.'

'But they do have a lot in common, apart from being skinny, with dyed hair, piercings and tattoos. All of them are outwardly strong characters but inside they're a mass of uncertainties and contradictions. I rather liked that description one academic gave of her as a "flawed *femme fatale*".'

'My poor old Eleanor has been attacked by as many people as have defended her.'

'The problem is, although she's a realistic, crazy, mixed-up woman, she's also rather sexy. No matter how multi-dimensional you want to argue she is . . .'

'Well, from her appearances in my book, through television and on to comics and now computer games, her character has been well explored...'

'Yes, but in all of those media she still *looks* like an escapist male fantasy. . .'

'Her fans include a substantial number of women; they say she's a strong, realistic role model.'

'Post-feminist?'

'Exactly. But I suppose that at the end of it all, I'm jealous.'

'In what way?'

'Well, if I'm to be quite honest, she was originally my own escapist fantasy.'

'There's no sex in the book.'

'Does there have to be sex?'

'No, I suppose not.'

'You see, she was *my* Eleanor, and now she belongs to everybody.'

That evening I took David down to the main convention room and stood by him on the small platform. I introduced him to the audience simply as the man who had created 'Eleanor', and recommended to them that if they were true fans of his heroine then they really should read his original novel.

David then insisted on remaining standing, and even more than he would with me, he played up to the image of the elderly conservative who did not understand modern technology. He explained what books were, to those who had not read one before, and their advantages over other media with which, he admitted, he was not well-acquainted. He acknowledged the television as something he had seen in the houses of friends, and pretended not to understand anything about computer games or the internet.

He then talked about the *femme fatale* in literature, starting with Salome, and moving through to the heroine of Lawrence Durrell's *Alexandria Quartet*. This was as modern as he was willing to allow his literary references, but then he started talking of film and became more expansive. I knew that he had always loved the cinema and he obviously enjoyed talking about the alluring and seductive women of the silver screen who had so fatally used their charms to ensnare their lovers. Myrna Loy obviously had an important place in his heart, as did Theda Bara and the wonderfully named Musidora. He loved *film noir* and cited examples of *femmes fatalse* played by Barbara Stanwyck and Rita Hayworth, and then moved on to the sixties and explained that along with Jules and Jim he too had fallen in love with Jeanne Moreau in François Truffaut's classic film. With a little embarrassment (at being almost up to date), he admitted to having been impressed by Sharon Stone in *Basic Instinct*.

He explained, though, that *femmes fatales* were not always the villains they seemed, and that the best are very often anti-heroines. Here he introduced the character of 'Eleanor'. He explained that he had set out to honestly describe a woman who had a strong sense of right and wrong, but, unlike most heroines, was really rather flawed. Because her many faults and weaknesses threatened to overcome her, she could only be viewed as an anti-heroine. He publicly apologised to her for endowing her with so many failings, but concluded by saying that there were enough of them to take the fancy of other creative minds, and hence she had flourished in the hands of other artists. They had explored sides of her personality that he had not even dreamed of.

I think that everyone went away from his talk charmed and amused, and hopefully some of them read David's novel as a consequence. At the end he agreed to answer a number of questions from the floor, but when he had finished, and I had to leave, he was still happily chatting to a number of fans who had further questions for him.

I went to the Welcome Desk, to find out what time our table was booked for dinner and, as I waited, the woman whom David had previously called 'his' Eleanor walked past. I excused myself from the Desk and hurried over to her without thinking of what I would say:

'Excuse me,' I introduced myself. 'I was looking for you.'

'Really? Why?'

'You came into the lounge this lunchtime, where I was sitting with David Planer.'

'Oh?'

'Yes, and he commented that you are the double for his original "Eleanor".'

'I'm sorry, but that doesn't mean anything to me.'

'You know . . . Planer wrote the novel, *Eleanor*, that became the American tv series, and the Japanese graphic novels, and the games.'

'You'd have to ask my husband. He's the science fiction fan. I'm just the long-suffering wife.'

'Well, the character is pretty well-known,' I replied, lamely. '*Eleanor* wasn't a science fiction book, but the science fiction crowd have rather taken her over.'

She said nothing, obviously waiting for me to explain myself further.

'Planer is one of the guests of honour here this weekend, because the character he created is . . . ah . . .'

'So well-known?' she prompted.

'Exactly. And, well, the point is . . . other people have portrayed her, and depicted her, and none have ever been quite as Planer, the original author, ever imagined her.'

'But *I* am as he imagined her?'

'Yes! And, well, this sounds a bit odd, but would you mind saying hello to him?'

'Of course not. I'm just going to find my husband, and then we'll meet you in the bar?'

I agreed and watched her walk away. I thought to myself that she didn't seem David's 'type', but then realised that this was unfair of me. I had first met him when I was in my late teens and he was fifty-five, and he had always seemed to be a frail old man to me. There was no reason at all why he should not be attracted to a tall, strong woman in fishnets and leather-boots, with a shock of dyed blue hair.

I went to rescue Planer from his inquisitors and explained that he would be able to meet the woman he had seen in the lift. He asked 'Does she know she's my Eleanor?' and I was able to say that I had explained the situation. He made hurried excuses to those who still had questions for him, and he took my arm and went eagerly into the bar.

We found Eleanor easily; it was quieter than before because a presentation had just started elsewhere. She was sitting with her husband near the door.

'I am delighted to see you again, my dear,' Planer greeted her. The husband looked wary; he was a tall man with very long black hair, and his hands were tattooed in a gothic script that I couldn't actually read. His body language suggested that he was very protective of his wife, but David charmed the both of them. For a half hour he talked as if the woman really were his Eleanor, and he explained, for the benefit of the husband, her various adventures and incarnations.

While he talked I had the time to decide that David Planer's Eleanor was good-looking in an oddly individual way. Her features were slightly too large, but her freckles and her cheekbones were all that any of the artists that had depicted her could have asked for. Her figure was also real, unlike the graphic novel interpretation; she had very long legs, but I noted, with some satisfaction, that they were quite chunky, and although the make-up made her look younger, she had to already be in her early forties, and was therefore slightly older than I was. As with the Eleanor from David's book she had several piercings in her ears and one in her nose, along with a tattoo on her forearm. I have never thought piercings or tattoos to be particularly attractive and I was surprised that David, conservative as he was, did not condemn them on a woman.

'Would you like to know my real name?' she asked, towards the last.

'Oh no, please don't say anything!' he insisted in what may have been mock horror. 'You *are* my Eleanor.'

She agreed that she was, and that small incident summed up the meeting. She and her husband were both indulgent and considerate, and when they left they gave David their address in Montreal. They insisted that he should visit them, and he promised to try.

With old-fashioned courtesy he stood up as they did so, and as they left the bar he watched them go, beaming beatifically.

At length he said: 'Thank you, Sarah.'

'What for.'
'For finding her for me.'

The following day was the last of the convention and I was surprised
not to see David at breakfast. I asked the hotel's front desk to check up
on him and they assured me that he was fine but did not want to be
disturbed. I didn't see him until after lunch when he came through to
the bar to say goodbye. He looked tired and was walking slowly with
all of his seventy years apparently on his shoulders. I told him so; I was
worried, but he smiled indulgently and explained that the previous
night had been the best of his life. He implied that something had happened after we had said goodnight, after dinner, but wouldn't say any
more. He insisted, however, on us agreeing upon a date to meet one
evening in a town where we would often rendezvous. Almost immediately his taxi arrived to take him to the station and back off to Lincolnshire.

ԑ౧

Although we talked briefly on the telephone once or twice, David and
I were not in touch for another three weeks. When we met up for dinner it was where we usually arranged to meet. It was a small town with
a choice of excellent public houses, and was conveniently mid-distance
from where we both lived. We arrived separately, but at the same time,
and walked from the car park together over the small bridge. I asked
him if he was going to tell me what had occurred on that last night of
the convention, but he said that I would need a drink in my hand first.

We had our usual choice of the three pubs that served food, and in
winter we usually decided upon whichever could offer us a table near
an open fire. This involved looking through the windows of each of
them, and sometimes going in, only to leave again if the favoured spot
was already taken. I was a little frustrated that he would not immediately tell me what had happened, but we decided on the Blue Bell
without too much fuss. I sat at a table near the fire while he bought the

drinks and came over with the menu. He then made it clear that he would not tell me his news until after we had made our decisions about food.

When all was settled and ordered, he leaned forward over the table:

'That evening, after you had formally introduced us, I saw Eleanor again.'

'Ah, so that was what happened. I did wonder. . .'

'I went up to my room after dinner, and she was waiting for me. We talked for hours.'

'What about?'

'About her, mainly. Oh it was lovely! And I don't think that she left until five o'clock in the morning. Fancy, an old fool like me entertaining a beautiful woman in my room until the early hours!'

'Lothario!'

'Well, there's more,' he said, confidentially. 'When she left I gave her my address. And just a couple of days afterwards she came to my place, for lunch.'

'With her husband?'

'No, she came alone. You know that there are so many different Eleanors: the American Eleanor, and the Japanese one, and now the Canadian one . . . And you will want to know which one came to visit.'

'Well, presumably, we're talking about the Canadian Eleanor?'

'No, we are talking about my original Eleanor.'

'Not the woman from the convention? But she was the woman you gave your address to, surely?'

'My Eleanor and the Canadian one are so similar as to be almost indistinguishable. Even I can get confused between the two. I told you that senility is creeping in.'

'What happened?'

'We had some business to discuss.'

'What kind of business?'

'Well, it was to do with sorting out her life. You see, I left her slightly high and dry at the end of my book.'

I did not have a comfortable feeling about this.

74

'We talked about all the things you'd expect,' he continued. 'The things you'd have predicted her to talk about; love, money, sex. We sat talking and talking and talking. She was next to me on my settee, and held my hand, and poured out her heart. She explained things that I didn't know from her past. And she told me what had happened after I left her at the end of the book. How she laughed at her American "cousin", as she called her. And she admitted that she was afraid of her Japanese counterpart. And you know what really touched me, and made me happy?'

'No, what was that?' I asked warily.

'She said that, in many ways, she wished that she hadn't ever been taken from my book, and pawed at and ogled and looked up to, and despised by all those people who didn't even know her. But, I admitted to her that she had more than paid my bills for the last twenty years. It only seemed fair to be able to share it.'

With a horrible clarity I knew what must have happened:

'You mean, you gave her some money?'

'It's her money really.'

'Oh David! What have you done! She's only a woman who happens to look like your Eleanor. How much did you give her?'

'That's between me and her.'

'She's swindled you! You silly old man.'

'That's very uncharitable of you,' he said, not at all annoyed by my outburst. 'Eleanor and I discussed this at the hotel that night, so I was prepared. When she came to see me I had already been to the building society and it was all arranged. I gave her a cheque for four hundred and fifty thousand pounds.'

'Oh David! Is it too late to stop the cheque?'

'Sarah, you are forgetting something?'

'What's that?'

'Eleanor is not real. I'm not that senile yet. Remember, I made her up, twenty years ago. She's only a character from a book.'

'But *you* seem to be the one who's forgotten that! You're the one who gave her your life savings!'

'But what can a fictional character do with my cheque?'

'The woman who visited you isn't fictional, though. She's real enough, and able to cash that cheque.'

He smiled at me and shook his head:

'No, Sarah. I tell you, it *was* my Eleanor who visited me. I knew what you would say when I told you, so I went to the Building Society this morning and confirmed what I already knew. She hasn't cashed my cheque. The money is still in my account.'

෨

David told me that Eleanor visited him twice more during the following year. The first time she had arrived on an August morning with a picnic hamper and they had gone driving around Lincolnshire churches together. This would have been extremely thoughtful of her as it was one of his favourite pastimes, but it would hardly have been the way that any of the incarnations of Eleanor would have preferred to spend her day. Later, at Christmas, she had been with him for two days, staying overnight in his little cottage. She had never asked for any more money, apparently, and he told me that she had in fact bought him gifts. One was a rather bright red tie that he was very unsure of, but had worn to please her. Another was a very tasteful gold tie-pin, and as he had never owned a tie-pin before he rather treasured it.

She visited him again just before he died last year. He was seventy-two and went quietly in his sleep. There were a few obituaries, and two newspapers chose to print pictures of the television series Eleanor rather than the author. Radio Four read *Eleanor* as their Book at Bed-time, which they insisted was a repeat, but which I had never heard before. I think that there was only one sour note: an article in the *Guardian* complaining that Eleanor remained a very bad role model for women.

There was an impressive crowd at the crematorium and I helped his daughter, Tanya, with the arrangements. There were few family members, but many friends. All of these were outnumbered, however, by the admirers of his work, and by his work I mean the character he had created. The Japanese artist who had interpreted Eleanor in graphic novels flew over from where he was now living in America, but the writer of the television series who had first popularised her was not able to attend. Two different women had asked if it would be unseemly to attend dressed in their 'Eleanor' costumes and David's daughter had begged them to dress as outrageously as possible.

I was asked to read a passage from the book of Job at the service, which I agreed to do, a little nervously. As I looked out over the mourners those two women in their bright costumes stood out from the black that everyone else was wearing. I started to read the text that I had been given and as I reached the part about an 'iron pen' I looked up and saw for the first time the electric blue hair of David's Canadian Eleanor. I smiled at her, she grinned back, and I lost my place. Everyone was very understanding when I said that such a large crowd was a little off-putting, but how it would have pleased David. I returned to the beginning of the passage and managed to read it without making any further mistakes.

After the service I stood with Tanya, her husband and their daughter Rachel as everyone filed slowly out past the flowers. The two women in their extravagant costumes were complimented by the family, and Tanya was very moved by the few words of obviously heartfelt tribute that the Japanese artist paid to her father. I could see the Canadian Eleanor coming towards us in the line, her dyed hair standing out from the shades of mourning. People seemed to move so slowly and it had been then that I calculated that at least two thirds of them were really only attending because Eleanor meant something to them. And yet the woman that David imagined really was Eleanor was passing among them unnoticed.

When the woman came up to the family she said how sorry she was that David had passed away, and then recognised me as his friend from the convention.

'Hello,' I said. 'You live in Montreal, don't you?'

'That's right. My husband told me that Mr Planer had died and I felt compelled to come over. It's my first trip outside of Canada since that convention. It'll sound silly, foolish even, but the old man had an affect on me.'

'And you've really not been back to England since then?'

'No,' she replied. 'I often thought of it, to see Mr Planer, but he might not have welcomed me.'

'He would have loved you to visit,' I assured her. 'He was rather taken with you.'

And then she was gone. I saw her in the distance later, but not to talk to again. At the time I wondered whether David would have left her anything in his Will, but he had not. I was co-executor of his estate and I know that all the money went to his daughter and granddaughter. While finalising his financial affairs I took the opportunity to look through his bank and building society statements, but no large sums of money had been taken from his account before he had died.

A few days after the funeral, once the Will had been read, a very small party of us went back to his Lincolnshire cottage. It was strange to let ourselves in his front door without knocking, and to walk around his rooms, so fussily but tidily furnished. His two old cats had been re-homed, and a thin layer of dust had already accumulated on the polished surfaces.

Rachel was looking over a shelf of books in his study when she took down his own copy of *Eleanor*. She said that she had never read it, and asked her mother if she might have the book. Tanya took it and looked through it before handing it back to her, saying that her grandfather would have loved her to have it. I can still see her in my mind, sitting in the sun-lit small-paned window, reading those first few pages.

Rachel asked if I wanted to have anything of his to remember him by, but I could not immediately think what it should be. We went from room to room while she wondered what to keep, what to sell, and what to give away. Up in his bedroom she opened a wardrobe and despaired of what to do with so many old-fashioned clothes. It was on the back of the door that I saw his ties, and it was impossible not to notice a bright red one amongst them. Rachel thought this rather funny, saying that she couldn't imagine him ever wearing it, but I was able to tell her that he had done so, at least once, to please the person who had given it to him. I looked around the room for the little gold tie-pin and there it was on his rather prim dressing-table. Rachel was happy for me to take that as well as the tie, saying that he had been wearing it the day before he had died. David would call me a silly fool, but I keep them both on my bedroom window sill with my signed first edition of his book.

Dispossessed

Everything went right for Jayne just as it appeared to be going wrong. Or, at least, that's what she assumed. To begin with she lost her home and her job. For ten years she had looked after the house of an old lady in Chelsea and it was an enviable position. Jayne had just come out of college and a family friend recommended her to the elderly woman when the previous housekeeper left to get married. Jayne didn't think there could have been an easier job available, and for a decade all she had to do was make sure that the house was cared for. Her employer was looked after by nurses from an agency, and there was already a cook and a cleaner engaged. The old lady's dog, a large, rough-haired Scottish deerhound, ancient and lumbering, was looked after by the cook. For everything else, and there was very little else, Jayne had been at liberty to hire gardeners or handymen as and when they were required, and she simply spent a great deal of her time reading, watching the television, or entertaining friends in the large living room into which the old lady never came because she was bed-ridden.

Jayne did not take many liberties, but because the old lady was also deaf, her employer did not notice when Jayne's friends occasionally did. The wages were good, especially as Jayne was provided with board and lodging, and, in that way that one can be when young, it never occurred to her that anything had to change. But then the old lady died.

The family descended upon the house immediately and to Jayne the old woman seemed to be buried with indecent haste. When the Will was read immediately afterwards the house was divided up amongst a dozen different family members and they decided to put the building up for sale. Jayne was out of a job and had lost her home.

At the same time her relationship with Paul fell apart spectacularly. She was distraught that she only had a week to find somewhere else to live and her boyfriend, in front of all of their friends, made a callous joke at her expense. Jayne wasn't in the mood and she took it badly. He compounded her humiliation with another joke and then she said a few things about him which were quite unpardonable. There must have been a dozen of their friends present and their jaws dropped simultaneously. Jayne left the party immediately, and when she got back to the house she sat by the phone and waited to see who would call her. But nobody did.

She was too angry to do anything useful for days. The house was emptied around her; first by relatives taking the nicer items, and then by auctioneers who stripped the place down to the floorboards. Jayne swore at the family members and was ignored, and she even threatened the men from the auction house, who told her that they would phone the police if she didn't get out of their way. It all seemed to happen around her at great speed and she was powerless to do anything.

Jayne then made a mistake that very nearly got her into even deeper trouble. A van turned up outside the house and she let some tradesmen inside. She didn't care who they were or why they were there and she simply left them to their business, which was to steal a number of expensive light-fittings and other easily removed architectural features. Jayne hadn't realised what had happened until much later that evening when the estate agent arrived to look over the house and draft the particulars. The police were called, and the next day various family members had a meeting from which she was excluded, although they were obviously gathered to talk about the way in which she had let the thieves inside. One couple were convinced that Jayne had colluded with the men who, as far as they were concerned, had walked off with a part of their inheritance. There was talk of trying to press charges against her, although nothing came of this. However, the goodwill cheque that she had previously been promised failed to materialise.

On the last day she was in her bedroom, putting her few meagre possessions into black plastic bin bags, with no idea of where she was to go. A tap came at the door and a tall thin man introduced himself as Mr Rogers. She had seen him about the house, with other members of the family, and had perhaps talked to him before? But she had not realised that he was aware of the position that she found herself in. Later, looking back, she supposed that she was still in shock, and she wished that her old friends might have made allowances for this at the time and perhaps offered to help.

Mr Rogers stood in the doorway and ascertained that Jayne now had no accommodation. He explained that he felt sorry for her and was annoyed by his own family for throwing her out on the street so callously. He was understanding, and after expressing what appeared to be genuine sympathy, he explained that he owned a large block of flats in south London and she was welcome to stay there, rent free, until she found something more suitable. She was not sure that she even thanked him, but she took the small manila envelope, which contained a couple of keys, and stuffed it into her handbag. He didn't say how long she would be able to stay there, but he said that the building was rather in need of modernisation and her neighbours would be mostly students. With a solicitous smile he suggested that he could arrange for someone to take her bags there, and so Jayne shrugged and simply left the dead lady's house carrying her handbag. As far as she was concerned the family were simply trying to get rid of her, and she complied. She was tired of fighting the inevitable.

Jayne walked out into the summer sunshine of the affluent Chelsea street in which she knew she no longer belonged. The old lady's ancient dog was the only creature to watch her go. She walked out and just kept walking, with no idea of where she was going or why.

It was then, at her very lowest ebb, that she met Andrew Hurst. He was sitting by himself outside a flower-bedecked pub and he asked her if she could tell him the time. She did so and he swore colourfully, surprising her. She didn't know why she had bothered to ask him what was wrong. After all, he could not have been in any worse position than that in which she found herself. He explained, apologetically, that it was a long and stupid story and that she wouldn't want to hear it, but Jayne was in an argumentative mood. She insisted he tell her and he proceeded to relate how he had been taken in by a confidence trickster. A man who had claimed to be an old school friend had come up to him in the street and had somehow borrowed a hundred pounds from him. The deal had been that they would meet later, at that pub, when the man would return the money. Andrew admitted that he had known as soon as his so-called friend had walked away that he would never see him again, and he was angry with himself.

'It's just about impossible for me to sympathise,' Jayne said flatly. 'You see, I'm in a position that makes yours look trivial.'

'Tell me?'

'And it's an even longer story.'

'In that case I'll buy you a drink and then you can tell me.'

And that is what happened. It seemed so natural to confide her troubles in a complete stranger, but he had asked for her story and so she told him, in exhaustive detail. She felt that by inflicting it upon him she would be somehow getting a small degree of revenge on somebody, but the result was something that neither of them could have expected. They went on to a restaurant and Jayne spent almost the whole night complaining. She ended up in his flat near the British Museum, and in his bed, and they were together for almost a year.

&

For weeks on end Jayne would forget that she had the keys to a flat in Balham that probably contained her possessions. Moving in with Andrew happened so quickly and so naturally that her previous life seemed to be something from the distant past, to be looked back at from across a great gulf of time. Andrew was very well-off; he had a position with a bank that sent him to various European cities and allowed him expenses that paid for her to travel with him. He bought her new clothes and jewellery, and had proposed marriage within a few days. These material things she accepted without complaint, but marriage seemed to be an altogether different proposition and she put him off time and again. Eventually he stopped asking.

Andrew told his mother that Jayne seemed to him to be something of a blank canvas. Five years younger than him, and considerably less worldly, he had introduced her to his twin passions of opera and rugby and in no time at all she had come to share his interests. Andrew's mother thought it an odd comment to make, but she soon saw his point, for her own interest in gardening was quickly communicated to Jayne and the young woman seemed happy to spend the weekends with her, helping in the garden at their house in Surrey.

Jayne's own family was small and distant, and Andrew's large and boisterous set of relations came as something of a revelation to her. They were immediately accepting of Jayne, and even took her part when Andrew bemoaned her lack of interest in marriage. She enjoyed their company, and life was good.

Andrew's announcement, a year later, that he was seeing another woman came like a physical blow to Jayne. He returned from work one evening, poured her a glass of wine and explained, awkwardly, that he thought that he might have found somebody else. She was unable to speak, unable to think; she looked around at his expensive apartment, full of his expensive things, and knew in an instant that she was no longer a part of it. She got up to leave, while he talked about helping to get her a flat of her own, paying her an allowance for a few months, and she decided that there was nothing around her that she could call really her own. He asked her to stay, to talk and sort things out, but she found her handbag and her coat and simply left the building.

It had happened again.

It was a short walk to the main road where she would find a taxi, although she had no idea of where she would ask it to take her. Looking in her bag to see what money she had to pay a fare she saw in the bottom of it the crumpled manila envelope that she had been given all those months ago. The address was on the envelope, and she decided that she would go there.

The block of flats in Balham was not particularly salubrious. A four-storey red brick structure, it looked like it dated from the time of the underground stations, and was not in good repair. The door was covered with graffiti and had obviously been reinforced against vandals. The windows either side of it had been bricked up and the intercom had been smashed. She had two keys and the larger one effected entry.

In the dark hall a light came on automatically and revealed a staircase in front of her and short corridors stretching away to the left and right. The other key had a plastic cover over the top which bore the number 12, and a small sign on the stairs showed that it would be on the floor above.

The door to her room, when she found it, was of featureless varnished wood, and once unlocked would not allow her inside until she had put all of her weight against it. Once admitted she ventured tentatively into a very small room, containing a bed, a small table and a wardrobe. The grey evening light came in warily through a frayed yellow curtain and Jayne's first thought was that it was a room for somebody to kill themselves in. It was in every way the opposite of what she had just left behind, or had been forced to leave behind, and the differences filled her with despondency.

The minute kitchenette and the bathroom with its small shower might have made her laugh if she had been able to draw on any inner resources, but all she could do was sit at the table with her head in her hands, unable to think about what she might do next. The rest of the world seemed a great distance away from that small, drab room, and she tried in vain to remember the name of the man who had given her the key to it. What had he done with the bin bags of her few possessions that he had promised to send along?

Eventually, unwillingly, she laid down on the bed, very still. There were other tenants in the building and she heard them coming and going during the evening and late into the night, making more or less noise. She listened to the sounds of the building, amazed that just as it seemed to be quiet at last, another door would crash shut somewhere above or below, or she would hear footsteps, or a distant cough. Somebody had a dog, somewhere, and from time to time it would bark, monotonously, for minutes on end.

It is always disconcerting to wake up in a strange room. Jayne found it doubly hard to work out where she was because she could not remember quite where she had expected to awake. The large, modern, airy bedroom she had shared with Andrew was already something from the past, and was certainly a place now denied to her. Remembering the circumstances in which she had been given the keys to the cramped flat brought back memories of the room in the old lady's house. But she didn't seem to be able to recall where she had ever lived before that time.

Hunger sent Jayne out to buy breakfast in a small café, and then she walked around the district to get her bearings, spending time in an arcade of stalls selling antiques, but buying nothing. As she looked at the jewellery and ornaments, silver and brass, glassware and pottery, they all looked like so many items that had once belonged to people who were now dead.

The miserable mood stayed with her as she returned to the flat. She had not brought any provisions back with her to prepare her next meal, or even a cup of tea, and she was standing in the middle of the main room, indecisive, wondering what to do, when there came a knock at the door.

She remained still and said nothing. She continued in silence after the next knock, but then a key was fitted into the lock and the door started to open.

'Hello? Who is it?' she demanded, frightened, backing away.

'Oh, you're here? It's Terrence Rogers,' stuttered her visitor. He put his head around the door nervously. 'Only, I've knocked from time to time, and never found you in before.' He opened the door and stood half in and half out of the room. 'I was worried, because you never seemed to be here. I didn't know whether to let the flat to somebody else. If you don't want it, that is?'

Jayne said nothing; he took this for acquiescence and somehow insinuated himself inside the room, with the door half closed behind him. They faced each other over the small piece of thin carpet, both in their coats.

'You look well,' he suggested awkwardly, to which she gave a short, noiseless laugh. 'Are things not okay?' he enquired solicitously.

'No, not really,' she admitted.

'Can I help at all?'

'Being able to come here helps, I suppose,' she said, wondering how it could possibly be that she was grateful for such an unpleasant place to live. In every respect the flat was dingy and depressing and all that she wanted to do at that moment was leave. If this man (she had forgotten his name again) had not been standing between her and the door she might have rushed out immediately, and perhaps returned, ignominiously, to Andrew.

'You're very welcome to stay here as long as you like,' he smiled, revealing a set of small teeth that were yellow and a little too far apart from each other. 'I just didn't know if you were using the flat.'

'I wasn't, but I might be. I mean, well, I've nowhere to stay again.'

'I'm sorry to hear that. Do you have a job at the moment?'

'No, I didn't need one. I was with someone . . .' she started to explain, and then decided that she would rather not tell him anything. 'But I'll have to get one.'

'Well, don't concern yourself about the rent until you've got some money coming in. And then we'll sort something out. You know? We'll come to an arrangement. And I can always offer you something better than this.'

'Oh, don't worry,' she shivered involuntarily. 'I'm sure I can find something else on my own.'

'I do have other properties, nicer properties, that you could stay in.'

'I'm not sure what work I'll be doing. I mean, I don't know what I'll be able to afford, or where would be convenient.'

'Don't worry,' he tried to sound reassuring. 'As I said, we can come to some arrangement.'

And then Jayne seemed to be watching the claustrophobic scene being played out, somehow, from outside of herself, as if she was watching it through a camera placed high up where the wall met the ceiling. What happened didn't seem to be happening to her directly.

The man took a tentative step towards her with his hand out, and when she didn't react he took another step and put the hand on her forearm. Jayne was unable to move, for she did not seem to be the same woman as she was watching down in the room. She looked on, and listened as he reassured her of his friendship, and his desire to help her. Because she did not move he seemed to gain in courage and took her other arm. He gave her a kiss on the cheek before letting her go with a smile that suggested he had made a conquest. He was relaxed now, and brought out a packet of cigarettes from his coat pocket. He asked if she minded him smoking and Jayne shook her head.

'I have a nice flat coming free at the end of the month,' he considered. 'Near Victoria, very central, but it's up high and you can hardly hear the sound of the traffic.'

Again she said nothing, being rather more interested in the displaced view of herself and the room, and wondering if this was what was meant to be an 'out of the body' experience. Surely it was only meant to happen to people at the point of death? She felt curiously indifferent to everything, even the thought of dying, but then she did not feel that she was going to die.

The man had his cigarette in one hand and a lighter in the other, but he did not put the two together. He was too busy talking about the flat she could stay in, and then he took another step forward.

'I really like you,' he said, quite grave all of a sudden. 'And I'd like to make sure that you're okay, and looked after.'

An alarm was sounding somewhere in the distance, as though the woman below was trying to communicate somehow with the woman above.

'Is there anyone looking out for you at the moment?' he asked. 'Anyone who cares for you?'

Jayne was wondering if the woman below would answer, and when she didn't he put his cigarette and lighter back into his pockets. He took a further step forward and kissed her softly, tentatively on the mouth. Suddenly his hands were inside her coat and she could feel them over her, around her, and with a shriek she pushed him away.

Jayne had returned to herself. She hadn't seemed to feel anything at the time, but now she could remember how his stubbly face had pressed itself against hers, and the way that one hand had clutched at her waist while the other pressed at her breast.

He was apologising, mumbling now after all of his eloquence.

'Please leave,' she said simply, wiping her lips clean of his spittle, and pulling her coat closed. She felt as though her clothes were all rucked-up, rearranged and uncomfortable.

'Don't be like that,' he said, apologetically, looking at the ground. 'I like you a lot. I thought you might like me. I mean, I've helped you, and there's more that I can do.'

'I don't need your help,' she said quietly, fearful for the first time, feeling exposed and vulnerable.

'But you do,' he said slowly, looking at her now with more confidence. 'You've had my flat for free for nearly a year. And you're welcome to keep using it. You do rather owe me . . .' he started to say, and then became defensive again. 'I don't mean in any monetary way. There's no proper obligation, nothing written down. What I've done for you I've done out of friendship, and I supposed you might like to be friendly in return, that's all.'

Jayne was now firmly back in her own body, although the emotion she felt was something quite alien to her. There was an anger inside her that she was not repressing, but channelling. With deliberation she asked.

'How do you want me to repay you?'

'Friendliness, just friendliness,' he said, half pleading, almost grovelling.

'In what way would you like me to be friendly?'

'However seems right to you, and natural.'

She considered, and nodded, letting her coat fall back open.

The man smiled and walked forward very cautiously. With a careful, slow movement, as though he did not wish to startle her, he put his hand forward and onto her waist.

'Is that alright?' he asked.

Jayne said nothing, but tensed at his touch. He moved around to her side and put his face into her hair. She heard him breathe in appreciatively, and then she felt the hand move down and it was going inside her skirt.

'No,' she said, and reached down and stopped him. He started to resist her attempt to take his hand out and she forced the nail of her thumb into his wrist.

He shouted out, but she did not release her grasp. He tried pulling away, and suddenly she was able to direct all of the pent-up fury and aggression through her whole body, down her arm, and into her thumb. She felt her nail break the skin and still she pushed while he shrieked and shrieked. Still she pushed, not seeing anything around her but concentrating her energy into forcing her thumb into the wound while the man thrashed and flailed around her. She felt her nail break and still she pressed until he managed to hit her, somehow, and she fell over onto the floor.

She lay looking up at him; there was blood all over the man. He was hugging his arm to his chest and looking up at the ceiling, not wanting to see what she had done to him. 'Why did you do that? Why did you do that?' he was repeating wildly, taking his breath in deep, sucking lungfulls.

Jayne sat up cautiously, scared of the man who himself seemed very frightened. Her chin hurt where he had hit her, but her neck was more painful; his punch had knocked her head back with a jerk.

He was obviously in a worse position than she was. His white shirt was black with blood, and it had run down and was staining his trousers.

'I thought you liked me?' he said, now sounding hoarse, still looking fixedly at the ceiling.

She was worried that he would turn on her, so she stood up carefully, slowly, ready to run to the door. She was thinking of how quickly she could get there and open it when a voice from outside called:

'You alright in there? I thought I heard screams?'

The man now stared at her, fearful, and she called back:

'Alright now, yes. We had a fight, there was an accident. But we're okay.'

'Are you sure?' the voice asked warily. 'I was worried.'

Jayne went cautiously to the door and opened it far enough to look out at a young man, with an even younger woman standing a couple of paces behind him.

'Thanks for checking,' she said, with a composure she did not feel. 'I was being very stupid, but we're both okay.'

'Good,' replied the young man, nervous and unsure, but obviously relieved that he could back away and leave. Jayne saw him go to the stairs, and then, keeping the door open in case she needed to escape, she looked back into the room. The man still stood there, stiffly, holding his injured wrist up to his chest, and the blood was now starting to puddle around his feet. She shut the door cautiously but kept her hand on the lock.

'I think I've cut one of your arteries,' she said slowly.

'Shit,' he said through his teeth. 'It hurts so much I want to cry. Do I need an ambulance?'

'Probably.'

'I'm sorry; I think I can feel something running down my legs.'

'It's blood.'

He laughed; he was trying to keep down the hysteria: 'Is that good? I thought I might have pissed myself.'

'That might have been better.'

'I have to keep pressure on it, don't I?'

She shrugged.

'What shall I do?'

When she didn't answer he looked down, apprehensively, to where he held his hand, and then, fearfully, took his wrist from his chest. It adhered slightly to the sodden shirtfront, and he stared down at the wound she couldn't see. His eyes rolled upwards as his head fell to one side and then he collapsed in a noisy and ungainly heap on the floor. His bleeding wrist was flung out, wound uppermost, and Jayne watched while the blood pulsed outwards.

She had still not closed the door, and drawing her coat around her she left the room, the building the street and the unconscious man whose name she could still not remember.

Jayne took a taxi back to Andrew's flat; she had no idea of where else to go. She still had a key and let herself inside cautiously, but he was out at work and she had the place to herself. Her coat had hidden her bloodstained shirt and skirt, and she immediately stripped off in the bathroom, threw these in a bath of cold water, and took a shower. Details of what had happened came back to her, but she made a conscious effort to try and repress them.

When she turned off the shower she listened, but the police were not yet knocking at the door. She dried herself quickly and in the bedroom found that Andrew had not taken her clothes from the drawers and so she was able to get dressed. Back in the bathroom she tried to get the blood out of her clothes. It came out of the lining of her coat surprising easily, but her blouse was stained and so was her skirt; in desperation she doused them in cleaning fluid.

Looking in the mirror she could see that she had a bruise on her chin which was now hurting more than her neck, and she could say that the man had hit her first. She had been trying not to think about what had happened, but she decided that if asked she would say that he had tried to assault her; she could argue that she had grabbed his wrist in self defence and what had then happened was the result of him refusing to take his hand out of her skirt. She repeated this to herself time and time again, rehearsed her explanation, making herself believe that her version of events was true. There were questions that might be asked, though, such as did she let him get too close when she could have sent him away? Had she really needed to keep driving her nail deeper and deeper into his flesh? She tried not to dwell on them, though they kept coming to the surface of her mind. She had the most trouble not questioning why, even now, she had not called an ambulance for him?

The cleaning fluid had removed the stains from her blouse and this now simply needed rinsing several times to get rid of the smell, but her skirt was ruined and she threw it in the bin outside. When all was straight in the bathroom she had to wash her hair again so that she would be able to dry it and get it straight, and then she applied her make-up.

By the time Andrew returned from work she was almost calm. However, when she saw him she lost all of her self-possession. The scene that followed was emotional and confusing, because at first he assumed her mood was entirely due to his revelation about the other woman. Time and time again he assured her that he had made a mistake and he wanted her, Jayne, after all, but she did not seem to listen or understand. He was entirely in the wrong, he insisted, and he pleaded with her to forgive him and to come back. Finally he began to understand that there was more to her distraught state than his own actions.

Eventually she was able to recount her story; the story that she had rehearsed so many times over the previous few hours. Andrew's reaction was that she should simply call the police and report the assault, at which point she had to admit that she had left the man, probably bleeding to death. How, she demanded of Andrew, as if it was his fault, was she to explain the fact that she had not called an ambulance.

He poured them both a drink and took time to consider what they should do next. Jayne was relieved that he should want to take over the decision-making, but then took some convincing when he decided that he should go back and check on the man. He calmly explained that her reaction to the assault was quite normal in the circumstances, although it would certainly complicate matters. He suggested that they return to the flat and review the situation when they had ascertained how the man was. Perhaps, he suggested, whatever they discovered, all they had to do was remove her possessions from the flat, and nobody need ever connect her with what had happened there. It was with the greatest reluctance that she got into his car later that afternoon and returned with him to Balham.

They were able to park outside the door. The building did not look any different to her, but he pointed out that there was a large sign, only partly vandalised, advising no entry. The downstairs windows were all boarded up and she admitted that she had not noticed any of this before. After his insistence that they go back to the flat he now seemed reluctant to go inside and even insisted that the key would not work. She now took it from him and, pushing at it violently, opened the door.

Inside she pointed up the stairs, and as they started to ascend they heard footsteps in the corridor downstairs.

'Hoy!' called out a voice and Jayne's heart, already low in her chest, sank, and she could not stop herself from leaning against the wall, then sliding down it to the floor. They waited until a man came in sight, and she was surprised that rather than wearing a police uniform he was wearing a fluorescent jacket and a hard hat.

'You're not supposed to be in here,' he insisted. 'How did you get in?'

Andrew held out the key.

'Is she alright?' the man asked, nodding towards Jayne sitting on the floor.

'She's fine, just a little tired,' Andrew said. 'We just wanted to visit one of the flats.'

'They're all empty. There's nobody here. The place is due for demolition next month.'

'We'll only be a couple of minutes.'

'I can't let you do that, sir.'

'It's not dangerous, is it?'

'No, sir, not exactly, yet. But next week they'll be coming in to strip out what can be salvaged; then it will be.'

'In that case,' Andrew explained coolly, 'Won't you look the other way for a few minutes while we visit the flat of an old friend, for old times' sake?'

'Well, if you make sure you're gone in five minutes . . . and you understand that we didn't see each other . . .' he conceded. 'But only five minutes, mind.'

'We won't be any longer,' Andrew agreed. 'And we didn't see anybody.'

As the man walked away Andrew helped Jayne to stand.

'He didn't say the place was being demolished,' she said weakly.

'Who? The man who attacked you?'

'Yes, him.'

'Well, maybe you were too upset to realise what was going on?'

'Perhaps,' she agreed, and led him reluctantly to the door to the flat, just off to the left at the top of the stairs. Andrew tried the key, but the lock refused to move. Jayne leant back against the wall of the corridor and waited while he fought to get the door open. When he had succeeded she refused to go in with him. She watched him walk inside and try the light switch, which did not work. Through the partly opened door she heard him move across the room and open the curtains and then there was silence, a brooding silence that seemed to echo up and down the corridors just as surely as any shout would have done.

Then she heard movement again, but could not decide what he was doing inside. Eventually he reappeared at the door, frowning:

'He's not in here.'

'Is that good or bad?' she asked and, taking a deep breath, walked forward.

'But there is something,' he started to say, hoping to stop her going inside.

He was too late. Once in the doorway she could see the black shape on the floor by the wardrobe and her heart lurched so violently that she thought she would be sick if her throat had not suddenly constricted, and then she saw that the large form lying there was not the man. There appeared to be a large, dead dog lying on top of a small pile of black plastic bin bags. Something hammered in her temples and she felt dizzy. She could not be sure, but it looked like her former employer's dog.

Andrew went over and knelt down by the dead animal.

'Is this your stuff?' he asked, pulling out some books and cassette tapes from the bag nearest to him.

She nodded.

'Well, then let's take them and get out of here.'

He tried to pull the bags out from underneath the body of the dog but they ripped and the contents spilled out. Gathering together a number of items he tried to add them to the one bag that he had managed to retrieve.

'Shit,' he said, looking at his hands. 'All this stuff's covered in blood.'

'Leave it,' she said quietly.

'But these are yours things.'

She backed out of the room.

'Leave it all.'

'No, wait a minute,' he was calling to her as she turned and started to run to the stair. 'I think this animal might still be alive.'

'Leave it!' she screamed. 'Leave it!'

LITERARY REMAINS

Literary Remains

When I look back on my life in Eastbourne in the late 1980s I find it amazing that I could have ever had enough time and energy to accomplish what I did. I had returned from University but decided, after three years of freedom, that I could not possibly move back in with my parents. My father thought me foolish, paying rent on the squalid little flat that I took in the centre of town when my bedroom was still available in the comfortable, large family home in The Meads. My little sister was still living there, and visits showed me that staying with them would have been just as suffocating as it had been before I left. There were times in my flat when it was cold, and the lack of space irked me, but, compared to living in my parents' super-heated house just a mile away, it was everything that a single twenty-one year old woman could want.

To pay the bills I took a part-time position in a large, modern bookshop; part of a national chain. It was just a few hundred yards from my flat, and I enjoyed working there. I was good at my job, being one of the few members of staff interested in literature, and I could have got on and perhaps made a career for myself with the company, but I refused to go full-time, and that annoyed my boss. I had completed my music degree, largely at my parents' expense, and had horrified them both by joining a local rock band. I played rhythm guitar, and we spent many nights each week travelling around the south-east of England in an old Bedford van. We played gigs wherever we could get them. It was fun, and surprisingly lucrative; when you cover other people's well-known songs at weddings and other private parties you get paid handsomely, but there was never any possibility of moving into the big-time. We could each of us earn a couple of hundred pounds a week when we were busy, and invariably drink as much as we liked at all of the free bars.

I also had my own band, writing material with a couple of old school-friends who had never moved away, but we rarely played to more than a dozen people in the local pubs. I think that my mother had once had hopes of me playing the violin or cello (my instruments at university) with the London Philharmonic Orchestra, and she would refer to my music degree with great sadness. I did put my abilities to another use, however, giving guitar lessons to a couple of friends of the family. Somehow I managed to get by pretty well financially.

I also had a boyfriend at the time. His name was Pete and he was the lead singer in a rock band in Brighton. I seemed to spend far too much time trailing around after him, and splitting up, and getting back together. He was unable to resist any of the groupies that followed him around, and I was too prone to forgive his weakness for them. When I wasn't playing gigs myself I was following his band, and I never seemed to spend an evening at home. Despite this busy schedule I somehow managed to get a great deal of reading done at that time. I was obsessed with Joseph Conrad, and had several shelves of his books, and books about him, and I even considered going back to University to try and take an English degree. I was aided in my quest for his books not by the bright, modern shop in which I worked, but by Tilly's bookshop at the end of Grove Road.

Tilly's has been in its present location for years and is a superb resource for book-lovers who have the patience, as I had then, to wade through piles and piles of assorted, and ill-sorted, second-hand books. Unlike Mr Brooks' bookshop on Station Road in Brighton, which was even more of a mess, the owner of Tilly's had no idea of what could be found in his stock, or where. When the shelves had become full, in some dim past time, more books had been piled in roughly the right place on the floor in front of them. These piles became deeper and higher until such time as it was almost impossible to navigate between them. Only the dedicated bibliophile could ever find what they wanted, and I was dedicated. I don't think that I ever paid much more than a couple of pounds for a book, but after a year or so I had managed to unearth most of Conrad's major works from the area roughly corresponding to where they ought to be found on the shelves. My acquisitions included a number of first editions (the less expensive ones), and a chance meeting with a first editions expert in the shop where I worked got me interested in the idea of collecting books for reasons other than simple reading pleasure.

Inevitably I visited Julian Tovey's bookshop, near my family home in the Meads. With the passion for collecting growing within me it soon became a place of pilgrimage. Certain of Conrad's books only seemed to be available as first editions at that time, and those that I hadn't already acquired were rather expensive. It is a slippery slope, and collectors will have done far worse things than me to aid their collecting, but I have to admit that I became something of a book tart, prostituting myself, in a manner of speaking, to assuage my collecting habit. I rather led Julian Tovey into thinking that I fancied him, and he started to do favours for me. He must have been in his forties then, and seemed so much older, but he was good-looking, in a dusty, bibliophilic sort of way. His home-life was not happy, as he explained to me, many times, in detail. He was obviously flattered by the attentions of a much younger woman, and back then I had a great figure and long, naturally blond hair. I started to work in his shop, on a casual basis, in return for books, and he also gave them to me as presents. I persuaded him to give me outrageous discounts, and often I was bought dinner. It was in return not only for spending a few hours minding his shop when he was away, but also for letting him think that I might have gone to bed with him if we didn't both have partners; I claimed that my relationship with my cheating boyfriend was more serious than it was.

It was one Saturday afternoon in Julian Tovey's shop that I first met Ernest Robertson. When he walked in off the street Robertson was simply an old man who had come in to browse. It was immediately obvious that he didn't really want to buy anything, but he looked over the small stock, and then, rather pointedly, asked if Mr Julian Tovey was available. When I told the old man that the proprietor was at a bookfair he said that he would come back another time, and was disinclined to leave any message with me. He seemed absolutely ancient; his back was bent and his teeth were quite obviously not his own. He had very uneven white stubble that suggested that he probably couldn't see well enough to shave properly, and he exuded a peculiar old man's odour. I didn't think that I had been particularly friendly to the old chap, but apparently he had returned and told Julian that he had been rather taken with his 'young assistant'. According to my boss he had sold him a number of very collectable books of ghost stories, and promised more, all because I was such a fine adornment to the shop! I remember thinking that all of this was a little creepy, but sure enough he had sold Julian several rare books by M.R. James, H.R. Wakefield and Arthur Machen. The only downside, Julian pointed out, was that they were all devalued by Robertson scrawling his own name on the fly-leaf of every book in biro pen. Of course, to an expert in the field that would now *add* value to the books, but back then nobody was interested in Ernest Robertson. He only became revered by collectors just after he had died.

I didn't think to take any interest in the books, but a few months later I entered Tilly's bookshop just as the same old man was leaving, and he lifted his hat to me with a gesture that couldn't have been in fashion for at least fifty years. Mr Tilly was looking through a collection of paperbacks that Robertson had just sold him, and he passed me a copy of 'The Heart of Darkness', saying that Robertson had written over it so much that it was worthless. Well, it had no value to me either; I had a first edition of *Youth* by then, in which the story had first been published, but I decided to read what the old man had written on the book. I leant against Mr Tilly's counter and tried to decipher the handwriting.

I had not paid much attention to any Conrad criticism, but I rather liked what the old man had to say about the story. He was commenting on it from a psychological point of view, suggesting that the narrator and Kurtz were both different aspects of the author himself, and, in explaining this, Conrad himself came off rather badly.

Tilly told me that I could have the book, making it obvious that it was nothing to thank him for. He pointed out that the man didn't seem to realise that his note-making would not appeal to most people who might try and read them after him. Robertson had sold Tilly a number of horror anthologies, and these were by far the most defaced.

Out of interest I paid for a copy of the book that appeared to be the most heavily written-in. Mr Tilly thought this rather perverse, which it was, especially as collections of ghost stories were not to my taste. I read the individual tales over the following couple of weeks; I wasn't a slow reader, but I was still consuming Conrad, as well as working and travelling most evenings with my own bands, or following that of my erstwhile boyfriend.

ഇ

Half of the stories in the anthology I had bought were enjoyable, but half of them were too dull or creaky to impress me. A couple were excellent, I thought. I read each without attempting to decipher Mr Robertson's notes until afterwards, coming to my own conclusions before reading his, and we broadly agreed. He, though, had an admirably clear insight into why certain stories were successful, and others less so. I remember that the very first tale in the book was called 'Thurnley Abbey' (I forget the name of the author) and I didn't think a great deal of it. Mr Robertson described it as 'melodramatic tosh', and went on to explain how the gothic horror story had evolved since the days of Mrs Radcliffe, and suggested which other writers had handled similar themes with much more style. The book also contained 'The Wendigo' by Blackwood, which he described as 'almost perfect', although I found it over-long. He wrote that the story described a fear of nature, but also a reverence for it, and listed numerous words and phrases used by the author that subtly pre-figured the denouement of the story. It struck me that Mr Robertson obviously had a first rate mind, and I should really revise my opinion of the old man.

I returned to Tilly's and bought many of the other ghost story and horror paperbacks sold to him by Robertson. I was attracted by the criticism, but in the process became hooked on the stories themselves. I didn't think to mention this interest to my sometimes employer, Julian Tovey, for perhaps several months, when he told me that old Mr Robertson was himself the author of ghost stories. He told me this rather dismissively, as though it was as low a classification of literature as science fiction (his *bête noire*). However, by this time I was unashamedly a fan.

According to the database we used at work, Robertson had written four collections of short stories, a novel, and had edited two anthologies of classic ghost stories. All of his books were out of print, but on a foray into Brighton I found three of his own collections in the cellar of the Trafalgar Bookshop, and both of his edited collections in the paperback exchange in The Lanes. The novel eluded me for a while, but I got that through a booksearch service. With a sense of timing that couldn't possibly have been worse, it was while I was reading these new acquisitions that I heard that Ernest Robertson had died.

I read all three of the collections in the week before his funeral and was overwhelmed by them. His ability to suggest the psychologically chilling, without ever resorting to anything graphic, was masterful. And I had just about finished his novel, *Cadogan Square*, about an old tramp in a London square who is victimised by the *nouveau* residents who want to lock him out of the little communal garden because he lowers the tone of the place. The tramp is never once referred to as Pan, but it is implied that the modern world has reduced him to a derelict clinging to this one little piece of nature in the artificial city. How could the author of such a subtle and moving tale have been known to me, living so close, and yet I never once realised who he was?

The Guardian printed nearly a full-page obituary of Robertson. I found out later that he had once been a staff writer on that newspaper, and later a reviewer for them, which was why his death, and career, were given such prominence. Other newspapers did not mention his passing at all. Then, somewhat unbelievably, he was cited by a well-known actress as being one of her favourite authors, and suddenly Robertson had a posthumous profile that he could never have expected. There was an article on collecting his books in a trade magazine, and in both the new bookshop where I worked, and in Julian Tovey's, we had several people enquiring after his work. Within six months his books had been reprinted by an enterprising small press, and one collector offered me fifty pounds apiece for the annotated anthologies I had bought from Tilly at fifty pence each.

I have to admit that I resented the turn of events. Even my boyfriend's band wrote a song which they claimed was inspired by one of Robertson's stories. I was rather miserable about the whole situation, asking those who talked about him whether or not they had attended his funeral, as I had, and pointing out that there were only six of us at the crematorium. It rankled that my personal literary discovery had been taken over by so many others, but there were still many other things in my hectic life to distract me. I broke up with my boyfriend, very messily and painfully, without leaving myself with much dignity, and my father had a car accident that was causing a great deal of upset because the fault was his and he was being prosecuted for careless driving.

I stopped going around to Julian Tovey's shop at about this time. I was simply unable to give him more than the occasional hour every now and again, minding the place when he went to auctions or fairs.

It had also started to get a little awkward between us, especially when he knew that I was single again. It was at least a year later that he turned up unannounced at my flat one day, a thing he had never done before. He stood nervously on the doorstep, and asked me if I could help him out for a few hours. I was going to decline but he explained that he was going to clear the books from Ernest Robertson's flat.

'I somehow expected to find more books,' said Julian. 'He'd been selling me the gems from his collection for a few months before he died . . .'

'Yes, and all the rubbish he was selling to Tilly's.'

'But a bookish chap like that . . . And by all accounts a recluse . . . I've bought libraries from collectors like him before, and their rooms have been piled from floor to ceiling with books . . . with books even kept in kitchen cupboards, and once, believe it or not, in the cooker.'

It was a summer morning, and already furiously hot. We had let ourselves into the dark, dusty, but immaculate flat with a key provided by the solicitor. It was very musty and peculiar-smelling, but tastefully furnished and four of the five main rooms had just one or two book-cases in them.

'The old chap's Will has been in dispute,' Julian Tovey explained, as he went down on his haunches to inspect a bookcase in the living room. 'Would you open the curtains for me, please? I can't see what there is in here.'

I put down the neatly nested cardboard boxes I was carrying and pulled open the long, heavy, red curtains.

'Yes,' Julian went on, scanning the spines. 'He owned this whole building, and it's worth a lot of money; you know, enough to make it worthwhile for two different groups of distant relatives to argue over. But it looks like their solicitors will see the majority of it by the time they've stopped squabbling. And Robertson had a few sitting tenants in the other flats, which apparently complicates matters.'

He stood up and walked to the other bookcase:

'Luckily they've agreed to sell the contents of the flat and put the proceeds into a fund. And happily they accepted my quote for the books some time ago.' He pulled a small number of thin hardbacks from out of the bookcase and was riffling through them. 'Normally I'd just put all these in boxes and sort them out back at the shop, but I've got no room in there at the moment, what with the builders . . . So my plan is to separate the books here; those I want for stock from those I want to sell at auction. And of those for auction, some can go up to

London, and the rest, any rubbish that remains, I'll just put in the local, general auction. I expect Tilly's will buy them.'

I left Julian and walked through to the dining room where, again, I opened the long curtains to the big windows. I admired an elegant grandfather clock that had a spider living in the top left corner of the dial, and wondered why Julian wanted me to help when there were so few books? There were no more in this room than in the last, but there were a reasonable number in the study; this time there were two very large bookcases on either side of the door. In the first one I saw the small row of books he had written himself, and taking a couple down smiled to see that he had written his own name in the front of them with the date of publication. I would have liked to have them myself, but by then even Julian knew their value, and he probably had some well-heeled collector lined-up to buy them for a few hundred pounds each.

There was only one bookcase in the old man's bedroom. There was no room for any more because it also contained a wardrobe, a cup-board, a chest of drawers and a dressing table, along with a big brass bed. The guest bedroom, in contrast was more Spartan. There appeared to be no books in there at all, so that was the extent of the collection. I had inspected the whole place before returning to Julian, who had removed his jacket and already had volumes piled up around him on the floor.

'Can I open the windows?' I asked, feeling uncomfortably warm now that the summer sun was shining in through them.

'By all means,' he replied, taking a book off one pile and putting it on another. 'Apart from the heat, it smells too much of the previous occupant.'

The windows, though, were locked. I asked:

'Do you have keys for them?'

'No, just for the front door of the building, and for this flat itself.'

'Can I poke around and look in drawers and cupboards for them? They'll only be small keys I expect.'

'You might as well. And if you see any books, take them out. The deal is that I've paid for his library, so *any* books are now legally and morally mine.'

The first cupboard was well-stocked with bottles of spirits, but the second contained files of what looked like utilities bills and bank statements. However, there were a couple of proof-copies of his novel and I passed these over to Julian. Despite the growing heat in the room I had just about forgotten that I was looking for keys to the window-locks, and taking off my jacket and putting it over the back of a chair I set to looking through a bureau with my mind more on books. Here I made a discovery that was to keep us busy for quite some time. Two big box files appeared to contain the typescripts of his published stories, each neatly paper-clipped and annotated. The bureau also held a few piles of other miscellaneous manuscript papers, some very old photograph albums that didn't appear to be his own family's, and a heavy pile of fragile 78-records.

I eventually left Julian poring over the manuscripts and went into the study. Here, in a series of cupboards, I found piles of paperbacks, and though they had little value in themselves, they all contained their owner's signature and would thus be of interest to collectors. They had been hidden away, out of view, I decided, because their tatty, gaudy spines would have upset the look of the room.

'When I came to value the collection,' Julian admitted, standing in the doorway after I had called him through, 'I didn't think to look in the cupboards. If they're all signed then they're worth at least twenty pounds each, if I don't flood the market with them . . . and as long as interest in Robertson continues. Well, it looks like I got myself a bit of a bargain, and we'll need more boxes. And I'm going to have even more of a space problem at the shop. And is it me, or is it getting hotter in here? I don't suppose you've found those keys to the window locks yet?'

I hadn't, and had all but given up looking for them. I spent the next quarter of an hour filling several boxes with the paperbacks, sealing them with tape and writing 'Robertson: paperbacks, misc, signed', on them. When I walked back through to the living room to get more boxes Julian was in his shirtsleeves and was looking at the manuscript material I had found:

'Do manuscripts constitute a part of his library?' he asked me carefully.

'I imagine that would be open to some debate,' I said, raising my eyebrows at him.

I took two more empty boxes and went back to the dining room. I put the books in carefully, pleased that they fitted neatly and without too many voids. When I had finished I realised that Julian was behind me.

'There is always the chance,' he said, slowly, 'that if I don't take those manuscripts then somebody from the family, who doesn't know what they are doing, will just throw them away?'

'It's possible,' I admitted, standing up and looking over my shoulder at him. 'But,' I turned back to the boxes, 'it's got to be your conscience that decides . . . And if you sell them, you might need to prove that they are one hundred percent yours to sell . . .'

'I know,' he replied, closer to me now. 'It's got to be my decision.'

And then he was directly behind me, his hands very gently on both of my arms.

I froze. In all the time we had known each other, and I had flirted with him, there had never once been any physical contact between us. I could see how it frustrated him, but I had told myself time and again that I did not want a relationship. But, as I stood there, unmoving, I considered that Pete was no longer an issue, and perhaps I did rather like Julian . . . But I had taken time to consider my response and he moved away.

'I, I'll, um, go and get some more boxes,' he said nervously, backing off. 'I wasn't expecting to find these other books. And, I'll, ah, have to consider the ethics of taking those manuscripts, while I'm gone. I'll bring us back something to eat and drink. Are you okay here on your own for a while?'

Without turning, I said that I was, and he promised to be back within a half-hour. I decided that I did not want to think about what had just happened. I hadn't previously felt thirsty, but his mention of something to drink sent me to the kitchen where I found a glass and, having run the tap for a while to make sure that it was fresh, I gulped down a glass of water. There was something slightly unpleasant about drinking from the thick old glass, but I decided it was just the thought of it having previously been used by a slightly smelly old man.

I looked, without much curiosity, through the kitchen cupboards, and eventually went back to the dining room where it now felt even hotter than before. I undid the cuffs of my shirt and rolled up my sleeves. I was glad that I was wearing a skirt rather than trousers, but my tights now felt uncomfortable against my legs and I was glad that Julian had gone out so that I could remove my shoes and take them off then and there. I took them into the sitting room, stuffed them into the pocket of my jacket and felt a little better.

Still trying, consciously, not to think of what had just happened between the two of us, I wandered about the flat. I was considering going out for some fresh air myself, but on walking out into the hall-way I distracted myself with the thought that there was a nice marquetry cupboard in the bedroom, and that it might, too, contain more books. Being smaller than the two main reception rooms it seemed another few degrees hotter in there, and because the window was not as large as any of the others it seemed more close and oppressive. I knelt down by the bed and opened the doors of the cupboard to find, predictably enough, more books. I pulled some out; Dennis Wheatley at first, then a whole pile of Eleanor Brent-Dyer's 'Chalet School' books, which struck me as somewhat odd. A number of Olympia Press books then came to hand, and I put them up on the bed, knowing that Julian would be able to sell those at something of a premium. A couple of 'Emmanuelle' books then revealed themselves, followed by other seventies paperback erotica. For the first time it seemed a little odd, sitting in the bedroom of a dead man that I had not really known, looking through his books. And here was his soft porn collection.

I am not a prude, but I had never really come across much pornography before. I had led a pretty sheltered life really, and I had only read, and been excited by, odd excerpts from my mother's Jackie Collins novels. It was something about the suggestive titles of Mr Robertson's collection that made them more erotic than if I had simply come across a pile of old Playboy magazines. I opened up a paperback called *Chains of Silk*, but couldn't immediately find anything of interest, and then another titled *They Called it Sin*. It was an American paperback, but with a British price overprinting the original which had been in cents. The cover showed a rather prim young lady who, nevertheless, was revealing more of her legs than she had necessarily intended. I started to read the first page, as she expressed her shame about some incident that she promised to reveal shortly, when suddenly I sensed Julian was standing behind me once again.

I whirled round in surprise and lost my balance. Putting my hand out to stop myself from falling, my weight went on one of the paperbacks which immediately slid out from under me. I fell, hit my head, not hard, on the cupboard, but recovered myself from a very undignified position in an instant. But Julian Tovey was not there.

I stood up, brushed down my skirt, and was annoyed that I had sprained my wrist. I felt a fool and strode out to the hall where I decided that Julian must have retreated in order to spare my blushes (although I thought it rather rude of him not to make sure that I was alright), but he was not there. When I checked, he wasn't in the living room, or the kitchen, and I even looked into the bathroom, despite knowing instinctively that there was nobody else in the flat, and probably there never had been. It was only when I returned to the bedroom and sat on the bed that a feeling of uncertainty crept over me. I was sure that I had seen somebody behind me, and if it was not Julian, then who or what could it have been? Of course, I had read enough ghost stories by this time that I immediately thought of Mr Robertson, but even in my slightly frightened state that didn't seem an idea worthy of any attention. I knelt back down by the cupboard, resuming the position in which I had previously been reading, and immediately had the same feeling of somebody standing behind me. This time, though, I was not so scared, and despite my heart suddenly lurching in my chest I had the presence of mind to realise that there were some clothes hanging on the back of the door which must have caused the illusion. When I investigated I found a long silk dressing-gown hanging over the top of two jackets which had given it some bulk.

I would have finally left the flat for the cooler, cleaner air outside, except that I now felt very tired. Despite the fact that it seemed to be the main source of the musty, old man's smell, I lay down on the bed. I didn't want to move for a while and my wrist was hurting. Not long afterwards I faintly heard someone in the building down below, but they must have either been leaving, or perhaps entered another flat, because no other sounds came through to the bedroom. Anticipating Julian's return I was ready to get up off the bed, but once I realised that it was not him I allowed myself to relax.

I know that I must have fallen asleep, because I started dreaming about my ex-boyfriend, Pete. I assumed that I had only just started to doze, because when I awoke I was a little confused as to where I was. For a moment I thought that I was actually on Pete's bed in his house in Brighton. Then I remembered that I was alone in Mr Robertson's flat.

Oddly, it was dark. It appeared that the curtains had been drawn again. I sat up, trying to regain my composure, and was surprised to feel a trickle of sweat run down from between my breasts over my stomach. I suppose that this in itself was nothing odd, for it was oppressively hot in the room, but at some point I seemed to have taken off my shirt and I was only wearing my bra on my top half. I got off the bed and pulled down my skirt, which appeared to have ridden up, and was about to leave the room when I heard somebody walking across the hallway, presumably (if my bearings were correct), between the kitchen and living room.

My first feeling was anger. I must have slept for longer than I had thought and Julian had returned and must have come into the bed-room to pull the curtains across the window. But what else had happened? At the very least he must have seen me half-dressed, but had *he* removed my shirt? I couldn't understand it, because it did not appear to be in the room.

I was too annoyed to care about modesty. He must have seen me like this already, so I decided that I would simply confront him. I walked determinedly down the hall and into the living room where, inexplicably, once again the curtains had been closed. As I entered I thought I saw something move behind the curtains themselves, and without thinking that it could be anyone other than Julian I strode across the room and pulled them back.

There was nobody there. The bright sunlight was blinding, and down on the street a couple of young men looked up at me, probably attracted by the movement of the curtains. It took a second before I remembered that I was only wearing my bra and skirt. I jumped back from the window, now really angry with Julian.

I turned back to the undoubtedly empty room and heard the sound of movement once again. This time I judged it to have come from the dining room.

'Julian, you bastard!' I called out, almost running across the room and into the hallway from where, again, I certainly heard the sound of something heavy move. I strode into the room and found nobody there. Only now did I think that perhaps the sounds were actually coming from the flat above.

The thought calmed me. I opened the curtains in the dining room, carefully this time so as not to expose myself to anyone outside, and leaned on one of the bookcases. I told myself that I was in a stupid state. The sounds upstairs were probably from whomever had let themselves into the building earlier. Despite the heat of the flat, and the reassurance that I had given myself, I shivered. Looking down I saw that I was bathed in sweat, and I saw that there was a mucky smear on my arm from where I had leant on the dusty furniture. I needed to find my shirt, or, failing that, my jacket from the sitting room. I'd then go and have a wash in the bathroom.

I was now quite calm, walking from room to room. My shirt was still missing, but my jacket was where I had left it, and going into the bathroom I really felt quite at ease. It was only as I was shutting the door that I realised that the curtains had been drawn again when I had collected my jacket from the living room.

I re-opened the bathroom door gingerly and looked out. It was un-doubtedly dark back in the sitting room, but perhaps I really had closed them when I realised that the two young men could see me from the street. It was possible that I had misremembered, but from further down the hall there should have been more light coming through from the dining room door. I knew for a fact that I had opened those curtains.

There was nothing to be heard, inside or outside the flat. I do not know what made me walk into the hall and press myself up against the wall. Something compelled me to inch along it towards the door of the dining room. Nothing, however, could make me look around the doorframe. Moments passed, perhaps minutes, I do not know, but I soon felt that there was definitely somebody, or something in there. How they had moved between rooms without me seeing them I did not know, but perhaps there were interconnecting doors I hadn't noticed? I was grasping at impossibilities, and my mind reeled. Only now that I was so close to it did I feel the need to move away. I tried to tell myself that there had been nothing in the room earlier, and that my fear had actually conjured whatever it was out of the ether, but that did not help me. I sensed the presence of a man in there, a big man. Involuntarily, as I breathed in, I gulped and made a sound like a sob. Perhaps he was just around the door jamb, his body up against the other side of the wall to where my own was pressed. I held my breath, expecting to hear his breathing, but I had the notion that whoever was in there was mirroring my own actions on the other side of the wall.

I tried to picture him, and with some sense that I could not name I knew that he was bigger than me. Perhaps much bigger. I hardly dared breathe, and I cursed the hammering of my heart. I realised that my chest was pressed hard against the wall; I was scared that the noise of my heart would use the partition as a sounding-board, magnifying it so that he could hear it!

I moved slowly and only ever so slightly away from the wall and I heard a corresponding movement inside, and it could not possibly have been something as small as a man that moved!

I turned and ran across to the main bedroom in blind panic fear, slamming the door behind me. Without thinking, and with a strength I did not realise that I possessed, I lifted the chest of drawers by one corner, high enough to allow it to pivot on one of its back feet, and swung the whole thing around and across the door.

I took two steps away as I heard another movement outside in the hall; it was a sound that seemed to be from something that took up the entire space behind the door.

A third step back and I fell onto the bed, and I believe that the surprise made me scream. It was a stupid, stupid sound; unreal as it rang in my own ears. I wanted to be safe inside the room with the barred door, but that was not safe enough. I swept the floor clear of books in front of the cupboard and climbed inside that, pulling the doors shut behind me so that I was now in complete darkness. My knees were up against my chest and I was sitting uncomfortably on books but I had no thought for that. A whole pile of paperbacks had fallen against me and their shiny covers felt cold against my wet skin. I listened, and listened, knowing that as yet nothing had tried getting in through the bedroom door. As before, when I had been standing outside the dining room (and I was appalled that I could have been standing there at all, out in the open, so exposed, so close to whatever it was), I could not discern moments from minutes. Perhaps I could not differentiate minutes from hours, because I seemed to be in there, in the dark, for so long. I could hardly breathe. Perhaps I was running out of oxygen, because my head began to swim.

And then I heard another noise. It was not the chest of drawers moving as it would have had to do if the was door opened. It was that horrific, indefinable something that I had heard before in the dining room. Whatever it was had somehow found its way into the bedroom without moving the obstruction I had put in the way. Perhaps it was the realisation that I had nowhere else to hide that made me finally lose consciousness.

I felt as though I awoke almost immediately, but I kept absolutely still. I had no idea of where I was, or if anyone was there with me. It was dark, and perhaps I could not move, even if I had wanted to. I had been unconscious, I knew, because until that moment my body had been relaxed. My heart was starting to race once again and I fought to regulate my breathing, hoping that if anyone was there they would think me still asleep. I opened my eyes only a fraction and could see nothing at all. I sensed something, material perhaps, pressed up against my face, and a horrid smell was almost suffocating. With infinite care I moved a little and felt that I might be tied up, but no, the position of my limbs was wrong. I tried to shift my weight and could not turn, but my left arm was free and moved over something soft, like sheets. I was able to pull whatever it was from off my head and I saw that I was in the bedroom, but now on the bed, and tangled in the bedclothes. I felt certain that I was alone, and with great difficulty turned the other way and pulled my other arm clear. I then used both arms to slide myself out of the knotted sheath of bedclothes. The curtains were open and I could see that the chest of drawers was back again in its right place, and the door was slightly ajar.

I felt no fear now. Whatever had been in the flat with me before seemed to no longer be there. When I looked around the room again I saw that my shirt was on the floor in the far corner.

In pulling myself clear of the sheets my skirt had come down to my knees and I pulled it back up. With the greatest care not to make any noise I went over, picked up and smoothed down my crumpled shirt, which I then put on. When dressed, I walked gingerly out into the hall and noticed that all the rooms seemed to be light. The curtains were obviously now open, but I didn't go into any of the rooms to look around. I quietly walked down to the door and let myself out of the flat.

I knew that my make-up and hair would be a mess, and my shirt had lost two of its buttons, but I needed to leave immediately. I went down the main stairs, my legs stiff as though I had walked for miles, and I appreciated the clear, clean air. Once out in the street it was better still, though the bright sunlight made my eyes ache and bleached the colour from everything around me. I needed to walk back home at a sensible, reasonable pace, without giving in to a need to run. I felt that panic was still within me, deep down and I had to continue to control it.

As I crossed the road by the theatre Julian pulled up in his car, returning, so he told me, from a frustrating scavenge for cardboard boxes. He pointed out that I looked unwell, and he was quite content for me to go home and leave him to the work that remained to be done at Mr Robertson's flat. He had decided, he informed me, that the manuscript material that I had found was rightfully his. When he drove off it was all that I could do to continue and not collapse on the pavement that seemed almost to be moving underneath me.

Of course, Ernest Robertson's posthumous reputation looks unassailable to us today, especially with the reprinting of his work by large commercial publishers, and with the critical acclaim given to the previously unseen stories that Julian Tovey has edited. I didn't re-read any of Robertson's books again until recently, when I worked my way though all of the stories consecutively, over just a few days. I felt compelled to write this account, I suppose, under his influence.

Forcing myself to remember what happened twenty five years ago has been a revealing exercise for me. I am a very different person now to that girl in her early twenties, and I wonder how I would react today to such events? Probably, nothing like that could happen to me now? However, my main concern is that the story I have told has been filtered through the consciousness of someone who is now too old and perhaps too knowing? But I do not believe that I understand more than I did then, and it may be that I see less?

117

An Artist's Model

Justin had been humiliated many times in front of his fellow students. On a regular basis they were all made to put their work up on the studio wall for a Criticism, when their tutors would patiently explain exactly how and why their art failed. But their work was not exhibited solely for the appraisal of the professional staff; all of the first year students were expected to comment, and even others from the second and third years were encouraged to come along for the show. If the tutors could be harsh and appeared to have favourites, then the other students were often downright cruel; it often felt as though as much effort was expended by them in the destructive criticism of their peers than on the creation of their own original work.

However, there were those who sailed calmly through this process. As ships on a bright and sunlit sea they never seemed to experience any hazards; they were not asked awkward questions, and their weaknesses appeared to pass unnoticed. Others, however, like him, always faced bad weather, and knew that storms were approaching long before their leaky vessels had ever set out upon the water.

Justin usually argued with his critics. He told himself that it was his way of surviving the attacks on his work, but his belligerence made him enemies. The tutors were convinced that he rarely learnt anything from their comments, and that he never followed their shrewd advice. Perhaps they were right? Perhaps he argued because he knew that he did not have the talent of his peers?

His embarrassment and disgrace this time, though, was not meant to be a public one. The only tutor who appeared to have any time at all for him, Archer, a man who enjoyed championing the underdog and was viewed with suspicion by his own colleagues, had come up to Justin after lectures one morning and taken him aside.

'I know that you've still got a couple of assignments before the academic year ends, but I should tell you that your future here is in doubt,' he informed Justin. 'Your first year hasn't gone well. Already there are those among the teaching staff who don't think you should come back for a second year in the autumn.'

'Do you mean I should "loosen up", as Barrett suggested, or should I be more "disciplined", as Locke recommended,' he asked facetiously.

Archer was an affable man and Justin knew that he was being unfair.

'I mean, you need to put in more hours in the studio,' Archer said patiently, stroking his neatly-trimmed beard. 'You need to be seen to be more dedicated.'

'I already put in twice as many hours as anybody else.'

'Perhaps you do, but not in the studio. You spend too much time working at home. The studio environment will help your art to develop, and might just save you.'

'I'm not sure that it will. There's always somebody around to tell you that you're on the wrong track. At least back in my digs I can concentrate.'

'I'm not going to argue with you. You need to be *seen* to be putting in long hours,' he said, and after a pause: 'And you need to get on with the tutors.'

'Well, that works both ways.'

'I agree,' Archer bowed his head, and then looked up with a smile: 'But I think I have a solution.'

'Which is?'

'I'm moving out of the first year studio. I'll be going into Mr Hemmingway's old room; I'm sorry to say that due to his illness he won't be coming back. I've always worked with the students in the communal studio, but I recommend that you take over the space that I'll be vacating.'

'But that's right next to Mr Locke's office! You know how much he despises me?'

'Exactly. And that's why you have to be there when he arrives in the morning. And you must still be there, working, when he leaves at night.'

'Am I allowed to say no?'

'Of course you are. But unless changes are made I can guarantee that you'll be asked to leave at the end of term.'

The conversation had taken place outside of the main lecture theatre, and although they were to one side of the corridor somebody had obviously noticed the short, older tutor in earnest discussion with the tall, gangly student. Their conversation was overheard, so by the time that Justin returned to the studio it was common knowledge that he was about to be thrown out, and in the meantime he had to be under the close supervision of Locke. Justin was ready for a fight, but even those students who were normally aloof from failures like him seemed to be sympathetic. When it was time for Justin to move his equipment from one end of the studio to the other there were a number of friends ready to lend a hand. He had arranged his easel, paint-boxes and desk, and recreated the still life that he was working on, when Mr Locke appeared, and made a sound that approximated to 'harrumph', before going into his own room.

The art school was a long, thin Victorian building on four floors, and each of these was essentially a large open space lit by tall north-facing windows. At each end an office had been created for the tutors to use as private studios with partitions which were partly solid and partly glazed. It was up against one of these that Justin was now expected to work, and he had placed his easel in such a position that he could not be watched by Locke from his desk or his easel. The light was noticeably different from where Justin had previously been working and the composition of his still-life had to be re-organised. So far he had only sketched-in the outlines of the skull, the suitcase and the bottle of wine, but it was annoying to have to start again. Judith, however, seemed happy to help him; her easel was now nearest to his, and together they came up with quite a pleasing arrangement in which the different sizes of objects did not seem to be in quite such an awkward relationship to one another as before. Justin then took another sheet of cartridge paper and taped it to the board on his easel. With a new stick of charcoal he began to painstakingly draw the outlines of each item. He started to delineate them very softly, and made a few changes before going over the lines with a little more pressure.

'That's pathetic,' announced Locke from behind him. 'Make those lines darker, lad.'

'They will be, when I'm sure of them.'

'I can see what your problem is. It's lack of confidence. Don't be such a coward!'

'Thank you for your advice…'

'I've been watching you for the last few minutes,' he announced, his voice suggesting tiredness and exasperation. 'You know exactly where the line should be strong, and where it should be weak. You use the charcoal in such a pathetic fashion. Don't go over the same line time and time again to thicken it up; have the confidence to use more pressure when and where it is needed.'

Locke was a massive man. He was well over six and a half feet tall and seemed almost as wide. He was not overweight, nobody would have the nerve to call him that, but he was broad. His hands were what always surprised people the most; he had great thick fingers, and it seemed impossible that an artist could ever have such unwieldy-looking digits.

With a dismissive sniff he walked away, and for once, rather than continue to argue, Justin simply turned back to his drawing. He had a yet heavier heart; if this was to be the result of working in such close proximity to Locke then he would walk out long before they asked him to go.

Justin worked through lunch and Locke returned to his office late.

'Are you still outlining those objects? Put some bloody effort in, lad,' he bellowed, and Justin decided that he would show the old bastard. He worked in the uncertain way that he always did, but he was still there when many of his fellows had wandered off to the bar that evening, or had left to go home. Locke didn't leave until seven, and Justin had the satisfaction of watching him depart before him. With the studio empty of everyone except Chalmers at the far end, Justin walked over to the south wall and looked out of the window by the sofa where the more gifted students seemed to congregate. Justin watched the tutor's bulky, but now foreshortened figure appear out of the main doors below and then disappear along Infirmary Road. It was the student's cue to leave for the evening.

The next morning Justin was in early, meaning to arrive before Locke, and was annoyed that the tutor himself did not get in until nearly mid-day. By this time Justin had discarded his first drawing, started another, and after some more discussion with Judith he had made a pretty good fist of the picture.

'Now, have the confidence to give those forms proper shadows!' Locke bellowed as he passed Justin's easel and strode into his own office. The student took a deep breath and sat down to compose himself. He deepened the shadows, somewhat hesitantly, and continued to make ineffectual changes to the study for the next half hour. When Faulkner walked over, he had come to borrow some tape from Judith, he considered the picture and suggested that there was scope for even more shadow and therefore more depth. Justin did as he recommended and soon Judith glanced over at his work and agreed that it did look more impressive. However, the objects themselves appeared weaker as a consequence, so he went over them with the charcoal, not with confidence so much as annoyance; he turned greys to black, then shaded grey those areas that had previously been white. He added more gradations of tone, even though he could not honestly see them in the objects before him, and two other students who happened to have business in Locke's office said, as they passed, that the sketch looked good. Finally he could see that it was working, and gaining a little in confidence he made yet bolder marks on the paper, and it was not too late in the afternoon when he allowed himself the luxury of sitting back on his stool and putting his hands behind his head.

'Admiring your work?' Locke asked from behind him.

'No,' he lied, defensively.

'Good. Now, you've done enough on that picture. Knowing when to stop is as important as anything else you can learn here. What I want to see over the next two days are at least two more, different studies of the same objects.'

'But what's the point? I've put in all this work in preparation for the painting. Why should I waste it?'

'It'll not be wasted, you ignoramus. You'll learn something new each time you start another study. And I want at least two more.'

Justin's second study was undertaken while he was in the blackest of moods, and he refused to speak to anyone. He later admitted to himself that he had wanted the second drawing to be second-rate so that the first would become the basis of his final painting. He did, however, apply the lessons he had learnt from the previous picture, and though it *was* inferior, the result was not as bad as he had expected. In fact, he rather liked certain aspects of it, and when he came to rearrange the objects for his third attempt he was able to make a few refinements to the structure of the picture. He left himself more room for the shadows, and by denting the suitcase (in what Judith termed an act of vandalism), he gave so much more scope for texture, to a whole massive plane that had previously dominated the composition but which had been lacking in any real interest.

He began his third picture with some nervousness, but this was caused by his desire to create something at least as good as the first. It took him a full day to complete, and he was still adding a few last refinements when Locke left his office that evening and simply commented:

'That's better.'

Justin stopped work and let the words sink in. They were as much encouragement as he had ever received from Locke and, given the rarity with which this tutor ever bestowed praise upon him, it was quite a positive step forward. It had been a hard-won comment, he considered, and he was not sure that he could keep up this level of effort. He decided, though, that he too should finish for the day. Out of a recently developed habit he walked over to the window and watched the tutor leave.

Tiredness suddenly swept over him. It was eight in the evening and it was the simplest of calculations to work out that he had been in the studio for twelve hours. He had not eaten since breakfast, but the thought of going out to find food suddenly seemed beyond him. He slumped down on the overstuffed sofa. Without much thought he looked around the studio before him. It was always a mess there, but the bizarre collection of objects they had all brought in for their still-life compositions gave the place the look of a bric-a-brac shop. Eddison's large, stuffed parakeet was probably the most outrageous thing there, he decided.

Before he could think about getting up and leaving, he fell asleep, dreaming about the brightly coloured bird.

According to the clock on the wall to his right it was just past midnight when he awoke. A few of the studio lights were still burning (nobody would come and turn them off; it was common for the students to work very irregular hours), and from the floor above he thought that he could hear a radio playing. He rubbed his eyes and stood up shakily before going to collect his coat and satchel. He noticed as he walked over that there were lights on in Locke's office and his first thought was that somebody was in there without permission. He did not consider that Locke might have returned.

He walked warily over to the door but glimpsed the tutor himself inside, and he appeared to be quietly talking to someone. Well, that saved Justin the trouble of confronting anybody who shouldn't have been there. He wondered what Locke would think if he saw Justin still working! But he could not carry that off; when he had returned the tutor was more likely to have seen Justin sleeping over on the sofa. He decided it would be best to unobtrusively leave.

He switched off the lamp by his desk and bent down to pick up his old satchel. As he did so he saw a movement at the edge of his vision and turned to see a woman's face. It was only there momentarily, and he wondered if it was some optical illusion. He realised what had happened when she reappeared a second later, only to turn her head away. Through a glazed panel of the tutor's office he had seen her reflection against the window to the night sky outside. The light inside had made a mirror of the window, and at that angle he had seen her reflection.

Almost immediately he saw her again. He moved closer to the glazed panel and watched Locke and the woman walking around the office, talking. It looked as if the tutor was considering where he should get her to pose so that he could draw or paint her. Justin could hear their voices indistinctly, for they were still talking quietly, almost conspiratorially, but he felt no unease about spying on them. He watched as Locke decided where she should be placed, and then found a chair for her and arranged her pose. She was wearing a black dress of some silk stuff which had a high neck and bare arms. She was slim but had a full figure, and he was appalled to see Locke manhandle her; he forced a cushion between the chair and the small of her back, thus pushing out her chest. He hated the way the man's big hands took her arms and moved them apart, pushing back her shoulders. Locke knelt down in front of her and with one hand under her foot he unceremoniously lifted up her left leg and put it over her right. He retreated out of Justin's view, and then came back and placed a lamp to her left, going back and forth to get the light correct from where he would be standing at his easel. The quiet talk continued between them, and the man must have started drawing. Justin could not quite see him from where he stood outside the office, but he thought that if he went around to the door he would be able to look over the man's shoulder and see him at work.

Justin, however, quietly moved his stool over to where he had been standing watching. Carefully, so as not to make any sound, he took his pad and a thick Hb pencil out of his satchel. He sat down, and for a while he simply stared at the model. Then he drew a few tentative lines; he sketched the oval of her face and framed it with her short, dark hair. A light line showed where her eyebrows would be, and then he drew in the eyes and nose. The mouth came easily, but her jaw-line proved troublesome. He went back to the eyes, the dark shadowed eyes, and then to her cheekbones which suddenly brought the drawing alive. The jaw-line, when he came back to it, appeared quite naturally. They had been quiet inside for a few minutes, but there was a muted conversation again. When Justin looked up from his pad she had moved and then Locke was at her side, changing her pose.

This time Justin had only drawn the outline of her head and shoulders, suggesting the shape of her hair with a few uncertain strokes, when once again Locke walked over and made her stand up. He suddenly turned to the corner of the office and appeared to look straight at Justin. He froze.

And then Locke turned and walked back towards his easel; he was evidently unable to see Justin through the glazed panel; it was dark where the student was sitting, but Locke's office was ablaze with light. It had given Justin a fright, but he made sure that he did not risk attracting any attention by moving.

Locke again reconsidered the pose he wanted the woman to be sitting in. He once more walked forward, and he almost pushed her into the corner close to where Justin was watching. He made her sit on the edge of the desk, and while he was preoccupied Justin's nerve deserted him and he drew back. Leaving his satchel, but taking his coat he slowly and quietly moved away. As he padded off across the studio to the door to the stairs he looked back and could see Locke through the door of his office, now at his easel again, and working furiously

The following morning Justin woke late, exhausted after three long days in the art school, but especially from his last, late night there. In his room in the house that he rented with two friends he lay on his bed looking up at the bright ceiling, knowing that it had to be mid-morning, but purposely not looking at the alarm clock on the floor by his bed.

He had slept soundly, although he did not feel that he had bene-fited from this. Because he had fallen asleep almost immediately he had returned home he had spent little time thinking over the events in Locke's office. It was only now, with the light of the summer morning through his curtains slowly clearing his head that he wondered why it was that Locke was drawing the woman in his office so late at night? A number of possibilities played out in his imagination, including a scenario in which she was his mistress. She certainly was not one of the usual art school models, and the possibility of there being some mundane, prosaic explanation of what had happened seemed unlikely. They had been working too late at night for that to be a possibility.

Eventually Justin got up and found himself some breakfast. He washed, pulled on his clothes, and walked back into town. Other students were leaving the art school for lunch when he arrived, but their greetings were cheery enough and nobody seemed surprised at his lateness. Justin often arrived late, having worked at home in the mornings, and it had only been in the last couple of days that he had been the first to arrive in the studio. Up on the first floor he walked to his own easel, but peered into Locke's office to see that there was nobody inside. In the communal studio, however, it was busy. Those who had finished their work in preparation for the afternoon Criticism may have been going off for lunch, but those who were left behind were busily finishing pictures and rehearsing their arguments in defence of the artwork they would soon have to exhibit.

Justin took his three studies from out of the plan chest that he now shared with Judith. Looking them over he was rather pleased with his efforts, and decided that last-minute titivation would add nothing positive to them. It was only then that he opened his drawing pad, left on the desk from the previous evening. He flicked through the various drawings until he found the sketch that he had made of the woman.

Life drawing was one of his weakest disciplines, but he was pleased with the results. Late at night, tired, without much thought and certainly no premeditation, he had produced a lovely drawing. He did not have much time to admire his work, however, as Jennings and Fredricks appeared from behind Judith's easel and insisted on seeing the studies for the still-life Justin would be pinning up on the wall that afternoon. They were looking for work that they could pre-judge, and dismissed his as being too good, 'for once'. Fredricks was annoyed because two of the tutors' favourites had come up with some outstanding sketches. Another, however, had obviously not put in any work at all, and his single study was decidedly poor, apparently. They were confident that although the student deserved to be lambasted by tutors and fellow-students alike, he would talk his way out of any suggestions that he had not worked as hard as everybody else.

'You know what they're like,' Jennings moaned. 'They'll search for the positives in it, and congratulate him on not needing to put in all the work that us lesser mortals have to.'

The three of them sauntered between easels and offered support to everyone, genuinely in many cases, hypocritically in others. The time for the Criticism was heralded by the scraping of furniture on the wooden floor as a space was cleared in front of the long blank wall reserved for the exercise. Chairs and stools were brought over as some of the more eager students took their places at the front. Justin went to his easel for his pictures and turned back to the room as Locke appeared, apparently for the first time that day.

'I hope you have at least *three* preparatory drawings for us,' he warned as he went into his office, shrugging off his coat.

There was never any arrangement as to the order in which the students showed their work. With the old belligerence rising up within him Justin walked out in front of everybody and declared, with uncharacteristic forcefulness, that unless anybody else wanted to go first, he would put up his work and get the ordeal over and done with. Then, with his back to them, he pinned up his pictures. He could hear them commenting, but it all sounded relatively non-committal for once. When he turned to face them Locke was sitting down next to Archer and two other tutors were joining the crowd.

'Explain yourself then,' Locke insisted.

'Well,' he said, trying to control his nerves, 'this was my first attempt, and I was pretty pleased with the result.' He decided that he would disarm his critics by honesty. 'Normally I would've decided to rest on my laurels, but it was suggested that I try and improve upon it. I thought the composition good, the massing of shapes interesting, and the light made it quite clear in what relation the various parts stood alongside the others.'

He moved over to the second picture. 'This attempt,' he admitted, 'wasn't so good, but I did manage to tighten a few things up that I had rather ignored in the previous attempt. The third picture, it seems to me, improves enough upon the first to have been a worthwhile exercise. I do realise that I've rather neglected the background, but my plan is to do a little extra work this weekend, in preparation for starting on the final picture next week.'

'Well . . . ' Locke considered, as though he was about to make an immediate comment, but then he stopped and turned his head to one side, squinting at the first picture. He stood up slowly and walked over to the second drawing, which he only looked at briefly. He then moved on to the third one.

'Well . . .' he repeated. 'I'm glad that you've finally seen fit to listen to your tutors.' He looked directly at Justin. 'Frankly, your second composition is an abject failure. But the third is more than adequate. Work on that background over the weekend, and on Monday we will let you all know in what medium you are expected to complete your final picture.'

Locke returned to his seat and Justin took his cue to remove his drawings.

'Well?' bellowed Locke. 'Who's next?'

ॐ

After the Criticism Justin joined the others in the bar where it was generally felt that he had done well. When a number of them had drifted off he decided to return to the studio to retrieve his belongings before going home. The Night Porter had just come on shift and greeted him in a friendly enough fashion. He told him that if he was staying in the studio then he would be on his own that evening. Justin thanked him and climbed the narrow stairs, not thinking of anything particularly. He was not surprised to see lights still burning on his floor, although there was no reason for the students to be in the building; no new work would be set for them until Monday. Justin walked in and saw that the most brightly illuminated space was Mr Locke's room.

Justin made his way up to it with some caution, and past the door. He desperately hoped that he hadn't been seen by the occupants; Locke and his model. The man appeared to be just starting out on a painting and had posed her in the corner where Justin had seen her the previous evening, just before he had left. The student did not turn on his own lights. He found his satchel and took out his pad and pencil. He placed his stool where it had been the night before and turned to look into the office.

She was sitting right by the window, in profile. She did not seem to have seen him. Her eyes did not once look in his direction. He was convinced that she was unaware of his presence. In the borrowed light he sketched her profile—the shape of her face from brow to throat in one long sinuous line. He was bewitched, and realised that he was also inspired. The curve of her eyebrow worked perfectly at a stroke. He caught the shape of her lips exactly. And her eyes, large and heavy-lidded, filled him with joy as he reproduced them perfectly on the paper. He admired his handiwork and decided that it could not be improved upon. He turned over to another blank sheet and looked up.

She was now looking directly at him. She smiled for a second and he froze. Now that his eyes were accustomed to the dim light he knew that she must be able to see him. In the smallest of movements her eyes flicked down to his pad and back up to him. She smiled, slightly. It was a sign for him to continue, and he did so, hesitantly, knowing that his embarrassment, his rudeness in fact, would be far more profound if he were to stop now.

Justin drew a large oval and divided it in to two, just as he always did when drawing portraits. He drew in the line of her hair, which was up around her ears now, and sketched in the eyebrows, nose, eyes and mouth. Her cheekbones were wonderful, he considered, and he smiled to himself. Then he blushed. Could she see him blush in that light?

He considered her face once more and was amazed at its perfect symmetry. No face is ever that perfect, he thought, but hers made him take an unnecessary deep breath and he forgot what he was doing for a moment. He had to compose himself. But the drawing would not now work for him.

He heard Locke talking to his model and she replied, smiling slightly, but whether she smiled at Locke or him he did not know. He looked around his space and decided that he could not move his easel for fear of making a noise. He leant over and took up a board that Judith used and saw that she had already taped a blank piece of paper to it. Well, he could replace that for her he decided, and taking a piece of charcoal he turned back to the woman.

She was still in the same position. As soon as he looked up to start drawing again she smiled ever so slightly, and ever so fleetingly.

Justin worked fast. He would normally take his time, but he had no idea how long Locke would allow her to hold the pose. The charcoal in his fingers travelled over the paper at a rate that seemed almost impossible to him, although he had seen others work that fast. He made mistakes, but he smudged them away and drew over them with bolder, thicker marks. Twice he drew her eyes, only to decide that they were wrong, and the surface of the paper was dangerously damaged by the time that he had removed the errors and drawn over them in an intense black. Her cheekbones were too accentuated, he decided, but they would have to remain. He was adding the shadows under her neck when she suddenly turned away and was gone. There were voices, and he expected her to return at any moment, but the minutes passed and she did not. Finally he heard the door open, and unable to breathe for fear that she would have revealed him to Locke, he waited to hear the door close once more, and voices and footsteps receded down the studio towards the stairs. When he was certain they were gone he put down the board and allowed himself to relax.

When he was calm he carefully removed the drawing from Judith's board and put it away in his drawer. He replaced her paper, put back the board, and then considered going home. It was not quite twelve, and he looked out into the dark night in the hope of seeing the tutor and the model walking away along Infirmary Road. But they had long since disappeared.

Although Justin would normally have spent the whole of the Saturday morning in bed, especially after another late night, he awoke early and was desperate to return to the studio to take a look at his drawings of the night before. By the time he got there, however, Jennings was standing at Judith's easel discussing with her the Criticism of the day before. They were the only two other students in the building and they were in precisely the position to see the charcoal drawing if he tried to take it out to look at it. He was able to take a surreptitious look at it, however, and was pleased with it. He took his pad with him down to the library, though, and was able to look at those sketches without fear of discovery.

As he stared at them an unaccustomed confidence crept over him. He could draw, and pretty well too, when he was inspired. And who-ever Locke's model was, she inspired him. It was certainly very strange that she modelled for him so late at night, and there was obviously something clandestine about their relationship, but this had been to Justin's benefit. If she had come into the studio at any other time he certainly wouldn't have been able to draw her. And she had conspired with him too. Although they had not spoken there was now a relation-ship established between them. A very odd and tenuous relationship! He shook his head and closed the pad. The librarian had seen him and gave him an amused glance over the top of his glasses:

'We're closing at lunchtime today,' he warned Justin, who decided that he might as well attempt a little research while he was there. He had promised that he would put some thought into the background of his painting; it would not do to make it too neutral because that would risk the wrath of Locke, who expected to see some development. On the other hand, it would not have to draw the eye away from the objects in the foreground. He found a few obscure examples of still life pictures in a book of American modern art and made some photocopies.

Back in the studio he was invited by Jennings to go to the pub for lunch, and he agreed. They met some other students and he stayed with the merry party until mid-afternoon, when he killed time going into town and doing a little shopping. He had decided that he would be staying late in the studio again, but this time he was disappointed. He was the only one there at six that evening and he stayed until one o'clock, but Locke and the woman did not turn up. While he was there he lounged on the sofa, out of sight of Locke's office, and using Judith's board once more he worked on ideas for the background to his picture. Making himself stay there in the studio, waiting, he tried out a number of possibilities, and by the time he left he was again feeling positive about his work.

Justin stayed away from the studio during the day on Sunday, but returned that evening and once again saw nobody at all. He heard a rowdy bunch of students walking past, obviously thrown out of the King's Head around the corner, and they appeared to be threatening to come inside, but the Porter would never have let them enter the building in their state. Justin walked back home that night feeling more dejected than he had since Archer told him that he was to move his new position in the studio. On the long walk home it was as though all of the triumphs of the previous few days had never happened. Forgetting his excitement at drawing Locke's model, all he could dwell on now was the fact that he would have to start work again on the still-life the next day, and under the eye of Locke.

Monday dawned bright and warm, as though summer was really getting into her stride, and despite his dark mood, Justin felt the infectious anticipation in the studio when he arrived. The presentation for the next project would be made at eleven, and apparently neither Locke nor Archer would be there to make it. Throughout the year they had both been adept at adding extra, unnecessary requirements to the work of their students, and everyone hoped that they would simply be asked to produce the painting they had been preparing for in some reasonable medium. It was a badly kept secret that they would be working in oils, but the official announcement had yet to be made.

Turbot arrived; a third year tutor they did not normally see in their own studio. He was all smiles, and asked for quiet.

'Now, you've being preparing for a still-life. You will be given two weeks to complete it in oils.'

There were a few whispers from among the students.

'Those of you with surnames beginning A-G are to go down to the workshop and pick up the materials for your pictures between now and three o'clock. The rest of you can go along after three. Unlike last term your canvases will not have been prepared for you. The stretchers have been made up, but you'll need to put the canvases over them yourselves. You can bring the staple guns up here, but make sure they are returned. There'll be a pot of rabbit-glue size in the studio, but you'll have to buy the primer yourself.'

The students were starting to discuss this among themselves, but Turbot quietened them down.

'You will need to pay for the materials when you pick them up from the workshop. And one last thing. You've been presenting your preliminary designs on the paper we supplied for you. The canvases we expect at the end of the fortnight are twice as large . . .'

The noise level from the students rose with a certain amount of indignation at this.

'You must be very careful getting them up from the workshop,' Turbot had to raise his voice. 'We don't care if you damage your stretchers, but do be careful with the paintwork in the stairwell!'

The students were not pleased. Although they had been prepared for oils, they had not been warned about the scale they would have to work at. There were complaints about the amount of paint they would have to buy. Of course, they would all simply scale up their earlier studies, but Justin suddenly pictured the vast expanse of canvas he would have to cover.

The studio was busy that afternoon and evening with all the students vying for space and helping each other to fix their canvases over the stretchers. They were all sizing their pictures before they left, intending to come back the next day to prime them.

Archer had appeared later in the afternoon and he made his way over to Justin and asked him what he thought of the assignment.

'To be honest,' he admitted, 'I'm a little worried about the size of the canvas.'

Archer smiled conspiratorially:

'Why not add some marble dust to give it texture? Put it on with a damp cloth when the size has properly dried. There's some just inside my office door, if you want to help yourself.'

'That's great; thank you,' but Justin did not feel any more confident.

'Try using larger brushes to block in your picture,' the tutor suggested. 'And perhaps add some body to the paint, beef it up so it will go further; I use wax, you could try that; then, later, for the finer work, you can work into it with smaller brushes, as you're more comfortable with those, and revert to purer paint and glazes.'

There were other students for Justin to talk to, but they slowly faded away, in ones and twos, until only he was left in the studio. He was hoping to be able to apply the primer that evening, but knew that he had to let the size dry properly first. He hung about the studio listlessly, trying to read a novel someone had left on their desk, and thinking about Locke and his model.

135

At about ten that evening it was dark. He judged it to be the right time to paint on the primer. When he had finished, his brush was washed and his space tidied up, and with nobody around, he decided to take out his charcoal drawing from where it had been in the plan chest. All day as he had worked with others around him he had been aware that it was there. A part of him had hoped that somebody might have discovered it; he wanted it to be admired, knowing that it was rather well-executed. But even if his work was not properly appreciated, he decided, any critic would have been taken with the beauty of his model. The picture, however, had remained undiscovered, and he knew that for the moment it was best that way. How could he explain to anyone what had happened in the studio late at night? And even if he was believed, and not thought badly of, that very evening there would be at least a dozen other students waiting there with him to see if the tutor and model would return.

He put the drawing on the easel and stood back from it. As he did so he bumped into someone standing behind him.

'Adequate, lad,' said Locke.

Justin turned in horror and then backed away.

'Barely adequate. Where's the passion?'

'I'm sorry, I can explain . . . '

'No you can't.'

Locke strode across to Justin, whose easel barred any escape he might have wished to make. Locke grabbed him by the scruff of his shirt and started to drag him away, over towards his office. Justin now saw that the woman was there too, waiting by the door. Locke let go of Justin and waved her inside. Then he pushed Justin in after her.

'This is passion,' pronounced Locke, going to his own easel and taking off the sheet that covered it. There was a full length drawing of his model, sitting in the chair just as she had when Justin had drawn her himself. From Locke's position, though, she was in profile; she was looking through the glass; she was looking to where Justin had been sitting drawing her.

'Look at this, and learn what passion is!'

From a portfolio he produced a large piece of tan card with the model standing depicted in gouache. She was facing the artist this time, and it was well done, certainly. It was executed with simple, bold lines and large blocks of confident shading.

'Can you see how much better this is than your own feeble effort?'

Justin was unable to think straight. His thoughts were in conflict. Should he admit the superiority of his tutor's work and hope to get out of the situation by grovelling? Or should he say that he thought his own work to be as good as Locke's, as he really believed?

'They're . . . they're . . .'

'They're what? Spit it out.'

'They're, well, different.'

'What?'

'You can't compare them. They're different.'

Justin was prepared to accept verbal abuse, to be humiliated by the man's words. He had been surprised when Locke had manhandled him into his office, but he did not expect physical violence. Locke took a step forward and punched him firmly on the nose.

Justin did not have time to pull away, because he had not known what was about to happen. He did not know whether he cried out or merely kept silent, but the blinding pain exploding in the centre of his face made him unaware of what happened in the following few seconds. He simply found himself sitting on the floor with his nose hurting like hell and blood gushing from it down his face and over his shirt. He opened his mouth, not necessarily to speak, but blood rushed into it and so he shut it again. He felt unutterably foolish and then he noticed that the man and woman were fighting. She was calling him a brute, a beast, and slapping him hard about the face. Justin felt he should get up and intervene, for compared to Locke she looked small, thin and fragile, but the tutor was not reacting to her assault. She punched him ineffectually in the chest and he moved back, and then she stopped. He laughed at her.

In reply, and with a look of determination, she punched him hard between the legs.

This made him double up and shout, breathlessly, 'Bitch!'

Locke stayed in that position for some moments, then, very stiffly and painfully, he stood upright again. With a pained calmness he reached for something on a cupboard that was just out of Justin's line of vision. Then he strode forward and determinedly pushed his hand out towards the woman's throat.

From where he was still sitting on the floor Justin had not seen quite what had happened. She had disappeared from his view behind the desk and was making strange noises that frightened him. He was compelled to get up, his hand still trying to stop the blood from running out of his nose, although whenever he touched it his nose hurt abominably. There were still those strange sobbing sounds he couldn't identify, sounds magnified by the silence of everything else in the whole vast building. He groped his way shakily around the other side of the desk from his unmoving tutor, distracted by the pain he was in.

She was lying there, on the floor, her head at his feet. He became faint and saw her as though she were upside down. It took a moment before he understood what had happened; her hands were at her throat, but unable to grasp the hilt of the paperknife that had been driven into it. The knife had made a wound through which she was now desperately trying to breathe. The woman's eyes looked up into his and then suddenly she gasped in a huge, horrible attempt to get oxygen into her lungs. Her body went into spasm once, and then she was still.

Justin looked over at his tutor, who was still staring at the woman he had killed.

He had killed her, Justin repeated to himself, he had killed her. And then Locke looked at Justin, who now tried backing away from the desk, towards the door. The tutor shook his head, and moved quickly to block the student's exit. There was an impasse as neither now moved.

Justin cast about the room, looking for any heavy object with which he might defend himself; he even thought of throwing himself out of the window to escape.

Locke stepped forward and his fist connected with the side of Justin's head. There was a flash of light, and then, instead of pain, darkness, and nothing.

Justin opened his eyes and his mind reeled. He was unable to understand anything that he saw. He was sitting in a chair, at a slight distance from a long table behind which were seated Archer, Turbot, and another man he did not recognise. He looked down and he was wearing a suit.

'Are you alright?' Turbot asked.

'I feel a little dizzy,' he replied, noncommittally, putting his hand up to his nose and finding everything to be quite normal. There was not even any discomfort. In fact, physically he felt quite well. He looked again at the other people in the room, who stared back at him expectantly. He turned around in his chair but there was nobody else with them. They were in a small lecture room he had not been in before, on one of the upper floors.

'I'll put it to you another way,' Turbot was saying, in quite a relaxed, friendly tone, 'how do movements in contemporary art inform the rather traditional way that you choose to paint?'

'I'm sorry, I'm a bit confused,' was his reply. He stood up, almost involuntarily, but had to grab at the back of the chair to stop himself from falling over. His legs were very weak.

'Would a drink of water help?' asked Archer, concerned.

'Perhaps we should end it now?' the other man suggested. 'We have been quizzing the poor chap for nearly twenty minutes, and there are other students to interview.'

'Agreed,' said Archer. 'We will let you know the result in due course. Don't lose any sleep over it, though. You've done well.'

The three men stood up and Turbot extended a hand from behind the table. 'Well done, Justin. As Mr Archer says, don't worry about the classification. You've done yourself proud over the last three years.'

Justin took a breath and walked across the carpet to accept the handshake.

Archer added. 'I thought at one point in the first year that you were going to fail dismally. And then there was that terrible, terrible business with poor Mr Locke and Miriam. I do think that both of you coped with the tragedy very well. You got yourself together and the improvement has been very marked.'

'And I'm proud of you,' the third nodded sagely. Justin did not know who he was. 'I've seen how hard you've worked this year, and you'll have your reward.'

When Justin had shaken the third proffered hand he left the room, bewildered. Outside in the dark hallway two other students looked up at him nervously; Eddison and Jennings. From the studio at the far end there came the sounds of excited whispering. Justin, however, remained outside of the lecture room door. He was overwhelmed by the knowledge that time had somehow suddenly passed, but he did not know what had happened between what had occurred in Locke's office and finding himself in what appeared to be a *viva voce*.

'You alright?' whispered Eddison, and at that moment the door opened and Jennings was called in.

'You look a bit shaky?' Eddison continued once the door was shut again. 'Did they give you the third degree in there?'

'No . . . I don't know,' he replied, and started to walk away.

'That was a joke!' Eddison pointed out in a harsh whisper.

Justin looked back over his shoulder and wished the other student good luck.

As he neared the light from the studio door he could make out Judith coming towards him from the brightness ahead, and as they approached each other she held out her arms. He stopped a foot before her, but she came right up to him and gave him a very affectionate, intimate kiss.

She sensed his uncertainty and pulled away.

'Did it go badly?'

'I don't know,' he replied honestly. She seemed to expect more, so he said: 'I suppose I'll have to wait and see.'

He didn't recognise all of the students, and the surroundings of the third year studio seemed very strange. He evaded their questions and walked over to the window that gave a view up Infirmary Road. He found himself alone with Judith who hugged him, worried, but he did not feel able to respond.

'It's her, isn't it?' she asked, letting him go.

'Who?'

Judith seemed confused by his obvious ignorance.

'She's downstairs waiting for you.'

He frowned.

'Miriam?' she said, refusing to believe that he did not understand her. 'Your model?'

And then she pointed to a three quarter length oil painting of the woman that Justin believed that he had only recently seen murdered by Locke.

'Miriam?' he asked

'I don't know what's up with you,' Judith said, suddenly angry with him. 'But I think you've got to make a decision between her and me. I know that neither of you are ever going to explain what happened the night that Locke was killed; I've known that since we've been going out together. But you've spent so much time with her, painting your masterpiece. If that doesn't get you a 2:1 then nothing will . . .'

'A 2:1?'

'Depending on your *viva*. But that's not what I want to talk about. If she was just your model then you won't need to see her again. You can go down and tell her to go away and leave you alone. But if she's more than that to you . . . well, then go to her, but we're finished.'

He walked up to the portrait that he could see was well executed. Could he really have painted it? It was not badly done, and it was in oil, which was not his favourite medium. Perhaps it was a little stiff and slightly lifeless, but the personality of the model lifted it. The line of her cheekbones, the curve of her eyebrow. . . . Was she really waiting for him downstairs?

And Judith had referred to Locke being killed?

He turned around but Judith was walking away. He was alone and confused, but downstairs, waiting for him, was a woman called Miriam whom he hoped would be able to tell him what had happened.

Llanfihangel

It was perhaps an hour into the evening that I first really noticed Sally's friend, James. He was a large, fleshy, almost bald man who tried to hide his weight by wearing a white linen suit that was perhaps two sizes too big for him. He hadn't said a great deal over the dinner table, at least, nothing that I remembered as very interesting, but now I couldn't stop looking at him and suspecting that I had seen him somewhere before. My interest had been aroused, I know, by the fact that I had caught him, several times, looking in my direction and then lowering his eyes to his food, or suddenly switching his attention to one of the many other guests he had not previously been speaking to.

He was now in an armchair opposite me as I drank a second cup of coffee and he was enjoying one of our host's large liqueurs. With the conversation fragmenting between the different guests around the room I said:

'We weren't properly introduced before. I'm . . .'

'Stop!' he insisted. Then, slowly, 'I know you already. You're Christopher Turner.'

'Yes.'

He smiled, and shook his head slowly:

'You really don't recognise me, do you?'

'I decided there was something familiar about you before we sat down to dinner.' I don't know why I immediately lied, but something about his manner put me on the defensive.

'But you don't know where you've seen me before?'

'No, it's been annoying me all evening,' I continued what was, after all, only a partial untruth.

'James? There was nobody at your school by that name?'

143

'Of course,' I said, hesitantly, trying to remember anyone from thirty years ago by that name. 'There was a James Wilson? . . .' I said, getting ready to list as many of the Jameses that I could remember from the distant past.

'Could I perhaps be James Wilson?' he asked, a slightly sardonic pleasure evident in his cold smile.

'No, I saw him just a couple of years ago.'

'So who else was there?'

'James Tobin?'

He raised his eyebrows, and I was annoyed. I felt intimidated; only an old school-friend could bring back all the lack of self-confidence that had afflicted me as a boy.

'You're James Tobin?'

'Imagine me rather slimmer, and with more hair...'

James Tobin had always been rather large, but I wasn't going to be rude. I remembered him as rather more sharp-featured, but many years had passed, after all. He also looked older than I thought he should have done.

'Well I never,' I said, feigning an instant remembrance. 'It all comes back to me now. You went off to university, to study advertising?'

'Yes. But I have to admit I've forgotten what you did?'

'Polytechnic. In Brighton. Electronic engineering.'

'Did I know that?' he asked genially. 'I'm sure I did. And you were with that pretty girl at the time?'

'Julie? No, we split up before the end of the sixth year. She decided that Neil Priest was likelier to succeed in life and hitched up with him. They're married, living not far from where I live now. I keep in touch, but...'

'Do you remember Sara?'

'Sara who?'

'You went out with her as well, didn't you?'

'No, not with a Sara. My only other girlfriend was Cara Penrose.'

'Ah, I was getting around to mentioning Cara. Have you seen her in the last few years?'

'No, not since school, actually. I've no idea what happened to her.'

'I met her recently.'

'Really, how is she?'

'She's not been too well. She's had a bad time of it, poor thing.'

'That's rather sad. I've always had a soft spot for her. I didn't treat her too well. You know, I left her for Julie, which was a mistake.'

'Well, I met her in Wales. Like you, she didn't recognise me at first. (Perhaps I've changed more than I think?) You know, you're the only two from school I've met subsequently, and you were once a couple.'

'That's a coincidence.'

'Well, you know what they say about coincidences? Statistically speaking, they have to happen from time to time. You have to start getting worried when they don't happen…'

'I suppose so. But, what's happened to Cara?'

'She's been ill. She had been married to some chap, I don't recall the name. He met her after school and she didn't want to dwell on him. He knocked her about a bit.'

'That's awful.'

'Yes, and they were together, married, for some years. Anyhow, he died, apparently, a few years back, and for all his faults, which were many, he left her with a rather magnificent house in Wales; border country, near Hereford. It was in Hereford that I met her. She is really rather attractive, you know.'

'She was rather plain when I knew her.'

'She's blossomed. Handsome might be the word now. And this chap's money and background obviously brought out an elegance in her. You know, she dresses well, and obviously looks after herself. She's got a good figure, but that might be the illness…'

'What's wrong with her?'

'She didn't say exactly, and I didn't like to pry, but I assume it's cancer. She's been having treatment, and apparently it's working. She insisted that she isn't going to die, or anything like that. But it's been costly. She went private, because that's what she'd always done with her husband, and one day she discovered that he hadn't left her with as much money as she'd thought. It turns out that she's actually in debt, thanks to some very incautious investments he made just before his death.'

'And she hadn't realised this when they'd wound up his estate?'

'No, it's a complete cock-up, apparently. She's furious with the solicitors, and she'll try and sue them, once she's well again.'

'She'll have to sell the house, I assume?'

'That was my immediate reaction as well. She told me that she'd put it on the market for the best part of a million pounds. And then a prospective buyer had had a survey done and it's got subsidence. She hadn't noticed the cracks, apparently. She got quotes for remedial work, but it's so bad the recommendation is to tear the place down and rebuild it. The house is actually a liability.'

'Poor Cara!'

'The stupid thing is that the house isn't about to fall down. It'll stand without being any danger to it's occupants for another fifty, perhaps a hundred years. But the engineer's reports make it unsaleable. She's effectively penniless . . . And she can't work because of her illness . . . And she can't even get social security because they argue that she's got the asset of the house, which, at the moment, they refuse to believe she can't sell.'

'So what's she doing? Is anyone helping?'

'She hasn't a family to help, and there's nothing left of her husband's family. She's no friends to talk of—*he* wouldn't let her have friends.'

'Is nobody helping?'

'Well,' James Tobin coughed, embarrassed. 'I have given her some money.'

'That's very good of you.'

'It's a little awkward. I have some savings, not much, and I haven't been able to tell my wife.'

'Oh, she doesn't know you've helped Cara?'

'No, well, I gave Cara two thousand pounds. It's a big chunk out of our savings, and how do I explain to my wife that I gave it to an old school friend, who I didn't even know well at the time? In fact, she needs twice the amount again, soon, or she'll end up in court, or worse. My wife would ask where I met her, and I'd say on a business trip, and then she'd ask if she's good-looking, and I'd have to lie and say no. And she'd think that I was getting something in return...'

There was a pause, and then I asked the obvious question:

'And are you?'

'She's been very grateful. And I know that she's desperate, and I realise that from the outside it looks like I'm taking advantage . . .'

I sat back in my chair. At some point in his story I had moved forward in the seat, but now I wanted to put some distance between this obscene man and myself. I had noted that he looked old and fleshy, and now I noticed the red veins on his nose that suggested too much alcohol, and the curdled look to the whites of his bleary eyes. He was obviously rather vain, wearing flashy cufflinks, but looking for flaws I saw the dirt under his fingernails, and a stain from the evening's food on his rather ludicrous cravat.

And, of course, all this was against the picture that had been drawn of poor Cara, attractive and helpless, and preyed on by this bloated and unpleasant man. I'd never liked him at school, in fact I suddenly remembered various instances at school when I had been rather revolted by him. It also seemed creepy that a person I didn't know well, many years ago, still remembered my old girlfriends as pretty. He had mentioned a Sara, and must, I now decided, have meant Sara Howard. We'd only been good friends, but he was probably envious of that friendship as well.

'Would you give me Cara's address?' I asked, businesslike, taking a pen from my pocket and wondering what he could write it on.

'I'm afraid not, old friend,' he said.

'Why not? I'd like to write and offer to help.'

'Well, although she's desperate, she's very embarrassed about her present position. I actually suggested that she might have some old friends who could help out. I wasn't necessarily thinking of old school friends, but she insisted no. It's pride, I assume. She said that the few people who'd remember her wouldn't remember her fondly.'

'Well, that's rubbish,' I said, feeling my way carefully and cautiously. This monster of a man, her so-called 'friend', held the secret of her whereabouts, and had to be played carefully. I was at a loss to know how to get the information out of him.

'I have a friend,' I started to make up the story as I went along, 'who is a lawyer, who could help her. He's very good, and as a favour to me he could at the very least deal with the social security people in a single phone call. And then he could certainly help her realise the value of her property...' I was noticing the flaws in this story as I went along, but decided that confidence might just get me through. 'What's her married name, and address? A phone number would be useful.'

'I'm sorry,' he shook his head heavily. 'She has a firm of solicitors on the case already. It wouldn't be possible to bring someone else in just like that.'

'Look here. I want to help. I can't bear the thought that she's in such distress.'

'Who's in distress?' asked Sally, our hostess, who had abruptly turned her attention away from the small party looking at a pile of records on the coffee table.

'An old school friend of ours,' I said.

'Oh, James was asking about you earlier because he said that he thought he was at school with you! What a splendid surprise.'

'It turns out that a mutual friend is in a terrible state at the moment,' I explained. 'James has very kindly been helping her out, and I want to do my bit too.'

'Of course you must!'

'All I have to do is persuade James to let me know her address.'

'It wouldn't be quite right,' he explained patiently, 'to give out such personal details when I've been particularly asked not to.'

'Rubbish!' Sally exclaimed. 'If she needs help, you've got to both help. After all, you are all old friends.'

'Exactly,' I agreed.

'Well,' he said, reluctantly. 'Now isn't the time, or place, really. It's late, and I ought to be going soon. Perhaps we should meet tomorrow? I'm only in London until the weekend. I could sound her out about your offer by phone in the morning. And at lunch decide where to go from there?'

And that was the end of the party. James Tobin left with the promise to let me pay for the meal the next day, and Sally was inordinately proud of her achievement in reuniting old friends who would be able to be such a help to each other. I asked her how she had met James.

'A delightful coincidence. We met on the train coming up from Devon, and we got into conversation. It seems that he was a good friend of my late brother when he was in the army!'

&

After a good night's sleep, and with a full morning before I met with James for lunch, I should have had time to question quite what had happened that previous evening. To a dispassionate outside observer, one who was not desperate to chivalrously help out an old girlfriend, and rescue her from a rather repugnant dragon, it seems obvious that I should have been more cautious. Coincidences were natural, as he had explained, but that he should also have known Sally's late brother was extending the lengths to which coincidence could comfortably be pushed.

But he played his part so well. At the café the next day he appeared in a hurry, and apologised that he could only stay for a short time and would only have a starter with me, and no wine. It was me who suggested the writing of the cheque for four thousand pounds, and he who was very unwilling to take it. He told me that he had talked with Cara on the telephone that morning and she was very uncertain about accepting help from me. He explained that he would pass on a cheque from me made out to her maiden name, with a note of my address, and then it was up to her whether she bank it and get into contact. He played the part of grudging go-between very well, and I came away from our brief meeting believing that I had managed to get around his attempts to block direct contact with Cara. For the rest of the day I was rather pleased with myself, and that evening I dug out of the attic my old photograph albums. It was then that I realised what had probably happened.

I had no formal class or year photographs, but I had several of a school play, and quite a few taken on the very last day of school. There was Cara, in two photographs, and I admit that I went rather misty-eyed over them. And then, in another photograph, there was James Tobin in the background. It was unmistakably James Tobin, and how I had accepted the man at the party and in the restaurant as him was beyond me. Yes, James was quite a large boy, and his sharp features would undoubtedly have become blurred if he had gained further weight, but the profile of his nose was unmistakable, and it was not the nose of the man who had recently claimed his identity. The more I thought about it, the more the impostor also seemed too short.

I couldn't sleep that night. I kept replaying our conversation over in my head and realising that he had offered very little information, and had expected me to guess his name, and to suggest who my girlfriends had been. And yet I didn't want it to be so. I wanted his story to be true so that I could play the gallant friend to Cara, and, less selflessly, not have been the dupe of a con-man's trick. Ungallantly I was unable to believe how much better it would be if it was just a trick because then it would mean that he had never met Cara, and that she was probably happily married, living in Surbiton with three children.

I did not really need to lose any sleep, because as soon as the bank opened in the morning I could arrange to have the cheque stopped—it would be that easy—and indeed that's exactly what I did. My account was untouched, and I never heard from 'James Tobin' again. It was a curious sensation; like narrowly avoiding a car accident.

Of course, I alerted Sally, who told me that she had very much doubted that 'James' had ever been in the army with her brother ('he was obviously not a military man'), but she couldn't see that he had gained anything from her apart from a free meal and entertainment.

LLANFIHANGEL

The incident appeared to be effectively ended. I didn't tell Sally, or anyone else about the cheque I had written and then had to go to the bank to stop. I was not defrauded, and if I was to be honest, I felt a complete fool for ever having been taken in. I considered going to the police, but made the excuse that there was no way that I could do anything but give a vague description of a fat man in a white linen suit. It was a pathetic excuse, of course, because the real motive was my embarrassment. I should have considered the possibility that I might be able to stop others from being defrauded by him, but I preferred to try and forget the whole thing. And I did, for about a month.

The handwritten envelope appeared on my doormat with the other mail and I didn't even stop to look at the handwriting or the postmark. I started reading without looking at the 'Nr Hereford' address at the top of the page, and was baffled by the first couple of lines and had to look at and decipher the signature before it all came back to me, and my heart started pounding horribly. It read:

> Llanfihangel House
> C—H—
> Nr Hereford

Dear Christopher

I think that I understand why you did what you did. I know you offered help for all the right reasons, and then withdrew that help with equally as valid motives. I immediately tried to bank your very generous cheque for £4,000, and would have replied with great thanks, but other pressures kept me from writing. And then I was informed that the cheque would not be honoured.

Dear James has been so kind, and so generous, and if I come through this unscathed it will be him that I have to thank. He tells me that you remember me fondly, and that is more than I can hope for.

> With love,
> Cara.

151

Guilt overwhelmed me. How could I have doubted the man calling himself James Tobin. Hadn't Sally said that he had never tried to defraud her? Perhaps he was just as stupid and socially inept as he had been at school and I had misread the whole situation. There was a phone number on the letter and I called it, unhesitating, to try and put things right with Cara. The line was dead, though, and I wondered if it had been cut off. Pathetically I noticed that the letter had been sent with a second class stamp. How could I have been so fanciful and dramatic as to believe that I would have been the target for a confidence trickster? I wanted to rectify my appalling mistake there and then, but I couldn't just leave everything and drive up to Hereford.

Perhaps a little explanation of my own situation is required at this point. I am married to Judith, and have two children, Trish and Tom. I manage an electrical goods shop in the west of London, and I desperately want to find another job without such demanding employers. At the time of the dinner party at Sally's my family were on holiday in Norfolk without me (I had already used up by annual holiday entitlement by taking time off when my mother had died earlier that year). Judith and the children were back home when I received the letter from Cara, and I have to admit that I hid it from my wife. I hadn't told Judith about meeting 'James Tobin' because I was embarrassed, and I decided not to tell her about the letter because it seemed to put me in an even worse light. I hadn't wanted to tell her that I had been taken in by a con-man, and now I didn't want to admit that I had believed an old friend was a con-man and that I had acted so badly towards a different old friend.

I should have explained it all to Judith as soon as she returned from Norfolk. Not doing so made it harder to tell her now. With the arrival of the letter I should have insisted in taking the day off work and driven straight up to Hereford to put things right. But I was a coward. There are no other ways of explaining myself. That day I sat in my little office at the back of the shop and wrote several letters to Cara, apologising, explaining, and either enclosing or not enclosing a replacement cheque. I had got myself into a stupid state. With hind-sight the best thing would have been to have written and explained everything, and said that I still wanted to help. As I drafted and re-drafted letters a sentence crept in which said 'I think that it would be best if we met so that I can give you a replacement cheque in person.' I kept reusing the same line, word for word, and then I suddenly saw how creepy it might look and excised it. On some level I wasn't admitting to myself, wasn't I doing just what James had done? And by doubling the amount of the gift was I just trying to look more impres-sive than him?

My thought processes were getting more and more convoluted, and the next thought that lodged itself in my mind was that we would really have to meet because her letter may just be a further flourish of the confidence trickster. Simply sending her a cheque in the post, an accomplice could bank it tomorrow and after the minimum number of days had passed they could simply withdraw it all.

But doubting Cara's existence made me feel inordinately guilty again. Believing in her made me feel as though I was being tricked. I didn't feel that I could tell anyone, and I continued to prevaricate and sent no reply as the days passed and I slowly got on with my life. I always intended to tackle the problem, but I always put it off.

I hate to admit that it was six months later that I finally went up to visit Llanfihangel House. My shop is a part of a chain and our Bir-mingham store had been experiencing problems which had led to the dismissal of the manager and under-manager. I was sent up there for two weeks to straighten things out while decisions were made on new appointments and possible in-shop promotions. I started up the motorway as planned but almost immediately took off on a very long detour. In Hereford itself I telephoned the shop to say that my car had broken down and that I'd be unable to make it in that day. For good measure I phoned Judith and complained of the same thing. She was sympathetic, picturing me hanging around some midlands garage while I waited for the fictional fault to be mended.

From the letter Llanfihangel House was in a hamlet called C—H—, some ten miles inside the Welsh border. The place was marked on my map, but the black dot seemed to represent an area of very scattered houses without any centre, and I didn't find the house without first getting lost in a maze of high-banked lanes and odd-looking hills. It was a huge Victorian pile on a rise, surprisingly hard up against the narrow road. I parked in the weedy drive and walked around to the front door which was boarded up and with a 'Condemned' notice stuck to it, and a further sign saying that the site was patrolled by a security firm from Welshpool (though this seemed very unlikely). By climbing through a very overgrown flowerbed I could see through the front room window that it was empty. It was so still and quiet, but that was probably the impression any townie would have received in that part of the countryside.

At a loss to find any local walking around the lanes who could tell me the story of the house and its owner I even tried at the doors of a couple of houses that could hardly have been called neighbouring, but nobody answered except some vicious-looking dogs at one farm. I drove to the nearest pub, perhaps two miles from the house, and though they provided me with a decent lunch, neither the landlord nor the patrons could give me any information whatsoever.

I returned to the empty house and parked once more in the driveway. Looking at the outside walls from inside the car I realised that I was examining them for the cracks that, Usher-like, threatened to topple it. It was an impressive brick-built Victorian affair, out-of-keeping with the local architecture. The driveway ended in garages that would once have been a stable-block, and these were joined to the house by a long wing that must have been kitchens and store rooms. When I finally got out of the car the place seemed even more unnaturally quiet than it had before.

I don't know what I expected to achieve by returning to the house, but I found myself aimlessly walking around its choked gardens, looking up at its big empty windows and various, changing rooflines. It was missing a few slates, and the woodwork was in sore need of new paint, but it did not appear to be in bad repair. Without realising what I was doing I was peering in through an old conservatory which housed only a few broken remains of cane furniture. The door had another 'Condemned' notice on it, with the smaller print explaining that it was private property, that trespassing was forbidden, and that the owners had no liability if anyone was injured by it. I tried the handle and the door opened.

In London, of course, they would have had to completely board-up the windows to deter vandals, and not just downstairs. I'd seen some houses where they'd even bricked them up to stop people from getting inside and lighting fires, or turning it into a squat. I suppose it was well out of the way here. And Llanfihangel House didn't have anything inside worth stealing, or vandalising. There were no period fittings or furnishings. It was bleak and lacking in any character. My footsteps on the bare, wide boards echoed off the pictureless walls, and a smell of damp was almost suffocating. It was bright without any curtains at the large windows, and simply dusty. I passed from room to room downstairs not seeing anything of any note whatsoever, and stood in the hall wondering whether there was any point in climbing the stairs to the next floor. What was I there for?

It was dark with the front door boarded up, but the sun was coming in through the etched glass fanlight above, and slanted brightly across the wall forming a strange, stretched shape. Without the light at this angle I wouldn't have seen the wrinkle in the wallpaper that travelled from the floor to ceiling. I followed it with my hand, and then with my fingernail I scored the paper along the edge and it tore. It wasn't a crack that I could see into, but a ridge where something had shifted fundamentally in the wall. It was then that I realised what I might find out there.

In the depression by the front door that was meant to take the mat there was a debris of ignored post. It looked like impersonal stuff, mainly, but on the top of it I could see a printed invitation to the opening of a local gallery, addressed to a Cara Penrose.

If only I had simply telephoned directory enquiries the whole thing would have been clear. How many Cara Penroses could there have been living in the Hereford area, just inside the Welsh border?

The only thing that was certain was that James was right: Cara had lived here in a house suffering from subsidence. I looked through the rest of the post and saw that those letters at the bottom of the pile had not been moved since the 21st November. That seemed odd. And then I noticed, poking out from the envelopes and leaflets a familiar piece of stationery. It was my letter to Cara. It was the letter I had given to James Tobin containing my note and the cheque. He had scrawled 'By Hand' in the top left hand corner, so he had delivered it, but it was not opened.

Now, up until this moment I had walked through the empty house without a thought to any atmosphere it might have had. I was sitting on my haunches by the front door with my back to the dark hall when I suddenly had the idea that someone was behind me. It was absurd, of course. Nobody could have walked around in the house without their footsteps making a din on the bare boards, and I had been in that position by the door, motionless, for perhaps a half-minute. An unpleasant tingling at my spine and a feeling of cold rushed over me and for several seconds I wasn't able to move. I was listening. In fact, all my senses were straining for the least suggestion that I was not alone in the house; that there was something there. I didn't move, but far from being paralysed, I was forcing myself to be still, so that if there was anyone behind me in the empty house, I might not cause anything to happen until I was ready to move! Finally my muscles screamed at me to change my position and with a dread fear such as I've never before experienced, I turned my head and looked back in horror at the completely empty hallway. There was nothing at all there, but I could not shake off the feeling that threatened to overwhelm me.

I stood up gingerly. And without looking anywhere other than straight ahead I walked out of that dark space, and through the lighter rooms into the conservatory and made my way outside. At no time did I look back, and even when I was in the car and had reversed out of the drive, I did not once look in the mirror as I drove away from Llan-fihangel House.

I was too disconcerted to notice that I was low on fuel, and it was only when the light started flashing on the dashboard that I realised I must find a petrol station. Being stranded out in that tangle of lanes did not appeal to me. I wasn't quite certain of where I would find the main road and had a horror of discovering myself back at Llanfihangel House; perhaps doomed to keep coming across the same lane and landmarks, with the great Victorian house inevitably appearing at the rise in the road.

It did not happen. Almost immediately I found the road I wanted, a sign showing Hereford as seven miles distant, and a petrol-station. It was an old-fashioned, slightly intimidating 'attended' service, and I was asked by a dour old man in overalls if I was there on holiday. I said, no, and added that I had been trying to look up an old friend and he insisted on knowing who. I decided to tell him, and he replied that the lady who'd lived there was dead.

'Killed herself,' he said without any consideration for any feelings that I may have had. My stomach lurched.

'About a year ago,' he said.

'Surely not that long ago?'

'Oh, it must be. Hanged herself from the banisters in the hallway. Postman saw her though the front door one morning. Her husband had died a couple of years earlier and left her with huge debts, so the local paper said.'

'It must have been some time in the spring,' I insisted. Arguing over when it had happened was a good way of deflecting the conflicting feelings of guilt and confusion.

'No, it was definitely before Christmas, because at Christmas the house didn't have its lights out around the windows, like it used to do, even when she was there on her own.'

'You're wrong,' I insisted. 'She wrote to me only this year.' I had her letter burning a hole in my inside jacket pocket.

157

'If you say so,' he said, as annoyed with me as I was with him.

But I also had my unopened letter to her in my pocket.

I still had not told anyone the details of this story, though there was not a day when aspects of it did not surface in my mind, when questions did not appear before me, or waves of guilt pass through me. Twelve months on from the dinner party at which I first met the man calling himself James Tobin we received another invitation, and this time Judith was able to come too. At the last minute a fear that 'he' might have been invited as well made me suggest that we should not go. However, baby-sitters were on their way, taxis were booked to take us there and collect us afterwards, and Judith had not seen some people from that circle of friends for two years and was eager to go. I had no choice but to agree.

As we sat down to dinner early that evening I was relieved to see all the seats taken and that there was no balding, fat man present in his white linen suit. I was rather enjoying the evening, having had a couple of cocktails before starting on the wine, and with the added comfort of knowing that a taxi would be taking us home. I relaxed and put everything from my thoughts but the trivial chatter of the dinner party. It was as I was being served with the sweet that Sally asked me, from the head of the table, what had happened to my friend in distress from a year ago. Completely unprepared, I simply gawped at her, unable to think of what to say. My unnatural inability to reply meant that in a matter of a couple of seconds the whole table had their heads turned to me. Even those who had not heard what Sally had asked were expecting me to say something.

Finally I excused myself:

'It's, well, a little distressing. Do you mind awfully if I tell you later?'

It was Sally's turn to be embarrassed, and she apologised for saying the wrong thing, and everyone tactfully started or resumed talking among themselves. Only Judith continued to stare at me. Naturally enough she was rather perplexed, and I mouthed the word 'later' across the table to where she sat.

The moment we moved out of the dining room, before even Judith had the chance to come over to me, Sally was by my side and apologising profusely.

I told her that it was nothing. Over the last course of the meal I had had time to think of what to say to Judith, and decided to keep it simple:

'I met an old school friend here last year,' I explained to her, as Sally continued to stand with us just outside the living room. Everyone else had gone through and were being offered drinks by the host. 'He told me of another friend who was in financial difficulties, and though I offered to help, he wasn't very willing. I don't quite know what happened. It was a bit of a muddle. I had no contact address for him, or her.'

I looked at Sally: 'James Tobin, that's what he said his name was, wasn't it?'

'Oh, you silly!' she exclaimed. 'All you had to do was ask me. You know, a month or so ago he brought me some of my late brother's things, the sweet man.' She was directing this at Judith now: 'By coincidence Christopher's school friend was in the army with my brother, you know. Though if you saw him you wouldn't believe he could ever have fitted into a uniform.'

'So you've got his address?' I asked.

She frowned. 'Actually, no. He just turned up one day with a box under his arm, as he had said he would. I was going to write to thank him, but didn't know where to write. What did you say his name was, Tobin?'

'So, not only do you not know his address, but you don't know his surname?' I pressed her, receiving frowns from both women.

'I gave them lunch…'

'Them?'

'Him and his wife, a quiet woman…'

'His wife?'

'Yes. She was very quiet, a little odd, called Cara, I think . . . Any more questions?'

No, I didn't want to ask any more. I didn't want to hear anything else. I just didn't want to think about any of it. The last time that I had been to Sally's for dinner I hadn't availed myself of her husband's liqueurs, but this time, knowing that a taxi would take me home, I got really rather drunk.

Una Furtiva Lagrima

Samuel Miller discovered the photograph tucked away in the back of his father's wallet. The hospital had given it to him along with the other items the old man had been carrying when he had been admitted. Samuel felt awkward looking at it as he sat in the hospital grounds, as though his father was at his shoulder.

The photograph was of a woman that Samuel did not recognise. It had become creased and dog-eared over time, the paper soft and slightly yellowed, but the image had remained colourful and sharp. The son had always felt that at some past time there had been another woman in his father's life. But he could not now ask him who she had been.

He stared at the woman who stood tall and confident in what would have been a fashionable dress; her hair in a style that was starting to come back into vogue. She was striking, without being obviously good-looking, and he understood why his father might have admired her. Samuel was now the age that his father would have been when the photograph was taken.

It was perhaps a whole year afterwards that Samuel started to read the papers his father had written regarding this woman and was able to give her a name, Clare Macdonald. He had described their relationship, and the scandal that surrounded her due to the murder of three small children. At no time while alive had his father ever mentioned that he had once been caught up in events that had made the national press.

It was a full two years later that Samuel finally took the papers with him to see Clare Macdonald in North Yorkshire. As he drove there, the car slowly covering the miles, he tried to picture the woman as she would look now. Like his mother, she would be in her very late fifties, and he wondered if time would have treated her as unfairly. Since his father had died Samuel's mother seemed to have aged terribly; her loss had taken her strength from her and she seemed smaller and slower. It was as though something inside had been broken beyond repair.

Clare Macdonald, Samuel supposed, would also be some crabbed old lady with wispy grey hair and shapeless cardigans, but he was wrong. The woman who eventually answered the door of the stone built house on the hillside overlooking the small town was tall and still quite handsome, despite the inevitable lines. In the photograph she had had long blonde hair, which was now dark and not quite shoulder-length. It trailed unkempt about her face. She was older, yes, but she had not yet become an old lady.

However, she had appeared so unwilling to answer the door after he had rung the bell that he had nearly left without seeing her at all. At first, through the closed door, she had asked him what he wanted.

'Are you Clare Macdonald?' he asked.

'My name's Lykiard,' she insisted, after a pause.

'But you were Macdonald before?'

'May I ask who wants to know?'

'My name's Samuel Miller.'

There was a further silence. He knew that she had heard him, but he could not understand why she was taking so long to reply. It was already twilight and the temperature was dropping; returning to his warm car suddenly seemed like a good idea. The longer she hesitated the more his self-possession began to desert him.

Eventually he heard bolts drawn back and the door was opened a fraction, obviously on a chain.

'You said, Samuel *Miller*?' she asked, suspicious.

'Yes, that's right.'

Through the gap she appraised him warily, but with obvious delight.

'I can see it now,' she said slowly, unhooking the chain and opening the door properly. 'Bloody hell. Ambrose's son?'

162

'Yes.'

She ushered him inside and shut the door quickly. She then locked it again, which disconcerted Samuel. Having done so she seemed to relax, and she looked at him again in the dark hallway.

'And how is that no-good father of yours?' she asked.

'He died about three years ago.'

'Oh,' she replied, deflated, lowering her eyes. 'I'm sorry to hear that,' she continued, distracted. 'Three years?'

She did not move, and after a time he coughed and she appeared to suddenly remember he was there.

'Won't you go inside?' she asked, gesturing for him to walk into the brightly-lit front room. Samuel turned to face her as she closed the door to the hall and then sat down.

'Dead?' she asked, flatly.

Samuel remained standing, wondering if he too should sit down.

With an effort she composed herself: 'So,' she said, looking into the fire in the grate rather than at the young man who had brought her the news. 'Three years ago . . .'

'Yes.'

'It has taken you all this time to come and tell me?'

'I didn't know that you existed,' he replied, and then added, 'at first.'

'Oh.'

There was a further silence and he looked around. It was a nice room, cosy without being cluttered. There were just a few pieces of antique furniture and a number of framed watercolours on the walls.

'Did your father not mention me?' she asked.

Still she would not look at him.

'Well, he never said anything about you when he was alive; at least, not to me. But he wrote about his time with you, in London, and then meeting you later, up here in Yorkshire. He left some papers behind, as a kind of record.'

'And what did he write about me?'

'Quite a lot, but it's rather complicated.'

'What did he seem to think of me?'

'It's obvious that he loved you.'

'Perhaps he thought he did.' She now looked up at Samuel: 'Did he write why he never came back up here to me?'

'He didn't write that down,' Samuel replied. 'But I do know the reason he didn't come.'

'You do? Well, I've been waiting for ten years or more to find out.'

As he looked down at her upturned face he could see that her eyes were shining.

'Please take off your coat and sit down,' she said. 'I'll offer you a drink in a moment, but I think that first you should tell me what happened.'

'Of course. Well, he tracked you down after many years, and was delighted to have found you. Your meeting meant a lot to him. But he said he had to go back to London, to sort things out. And you told him to come back to you within a week, didn't you? To return within a week or not at all?'

'He wrote that?'

'Yes.'

She nodded in agreement.

'Well, the day he came back to London from seeing you here he had an accident. He was run over by a car and was unconscious for several days. He was desperate to return to you, but he wasn't even able to walk with crutches for months. He had to keep seeing specialists. And there were complications...'

She stood up purposefully and looked as though she was about to leave the room. Instead she glared at Samuel, accusing:

'He could have written!'

'He wasn't even able to feed himself for the first few weeks.'

'He could've phoned. Or dictated a letter!'

'He probably didn't want anyone else to know his secret.'

'That's pathetic,' she considered, looking away again. 'He told me he would leave your mother for me. Why didn't he just tell her about our plans? Why was it a secret? And why the hell didn't he come back to me later, when he was better. I only told him to come back within a week because I was afraid he wouldn't return at all. I'd have forgiven him for being late; a week late, a month late even. Bloody hell, even a year! Why did he never come back to me?'

She was trembling, and Samuel could see she was setting her face not to cry. She tried not to give in to what she was feeling, but big tears ran down her cheeks. Her shoulders shook and she sat down once more, hiding her face in her hands.

With some reluctance, afraid of being drawn further into something that he now regretted having started, Samuel crouched down beside her and put his arm around her shoulders. Now she seemed quite small and insubstantial. She struck him as quite bony, and there seemed to be such a gulf between them.

'What the hell did I do to your father,' she asked through her hands, not looking up, 'that he couldn't come back to me?'

'I don't know what happened.' He wanted to console her. 'My father was a romantic. He took you at your word.'

'Was I so frightening that he was scared of returning after my silly deadline?'

'I don't know.'

'He simply went back to your mother?'

'Yes, but he had no choice. Somebody had to look after him while he convalesced. If it's any help, they never really got on after the accident.'

'No, that's no help at all! It makes me feel worse that I did that to him. When he didn't come back to me I assumed it was because he was happier with her. But please excuse me. I must pull myself together.'

Samuel gratefully removed his arm and she sat up, forced a smile and wiped away the tears with the sleeves of her dress.

'Look at you; a young man having to put up with a stupid old woman and her decade-old disappointments in love. All this time I've been wondering whether your father would one day have the courage to come back. But for the last three years he wasn't going to because he was dead.' She looked at Samuel: 'How did it happen?'

'A heart attack.'

She nodded but said nothing, so Samuel continued:

'I didn't see a great deal of him after I left home. He must have come up here to see you just as I was going to University. I didn't realise he was about to leave my mother for another woman.'

'What am I thinking?' she said, standing up once more. 'Can I offer you a drink?'

'Well, I've got something here for you,' he said, reaching into the deep pocket of his coat. 'I know from my father's papers that you like it.'

'Mari Mayans! Thank you.' She seemed incredulous as she read the label of the bottle. 'I haven't seen a bottle of absinthe since, well . . . But do you mind if I open a bottle of wine instead? I don't think absinthe is quite the right thing to drink right now.'

'How about drinking it *with* red wine? He said you used to do that.'

'Ughh, how could I have done it? And sometimes I used to mix it with brandy, like Toulouse-Lautrec.'

'He said.'

'Really? These papers; they must be rather detailed? Oh, well, no matter. It *is* good to see you, even if you do bring such bad news,' she said awkwardly. 'Your father meant a lot to me, despite what I thought he'd done to me. And it means a lot to me that you're here, to explain . . . You will stay the night at least? I don't get many visitors, and we can talk about your father.'

'I wasn't intending to stay, but it's become later than I expected . . . I drove up from Southampton.'

'Goodness! That's far too far to drive back tonight. So that's settled. The bed in the spare room is all made up.'

She already had a bottle of wine open on the mantelpiece and a second glass appeared to be at hand. She poured the wine deftly and as she handed Samuel his she started to propose a toast:

'To . . . well . . .' and they touched glasses. 'Well, to anything. Your stupid father, perhaps? Sorry, I shouldn't call him that.'

'It seems right.'

'No, I was the stupid one, telling him to come back in a week, or not at all . . . not realising he'd take me at my word.'

'What about your husband?' Samuel asked, then realised how awkward he sounded.

'Thomas? We separated a few years ago, after your father let me down. He still lives down in the town.'

She offered Samuel a cigarette, which he declined, and took another gulp of wine. She seemed more confident.

'My father said that you'd given up smoking?' he said.

'In this famous record of his, I suppose?'

'Yes.'

'He must have gone into a lot of detail?'

'He did.'

'That's rather unfair of him. I mean, you've now got the advantage of knowing about me, but I know nothing of you. Did you bring his papers with you?'

'They're in the car . . .' he replied.

'Do you think he'd have wanted me to read them?'

'I don't know. Perhaps not. I mean, I don't know who he wrote them for.'

'Never mind. You haven't taken your coat off yet. Perhaps you can tell me what else he wrote?'

He laid his coat on the floor behind the armchair, considering how to describe the large pile of miscellaneous papers his mother had inherited but had never thought to read; the papers he had almost thrown away but which had caught his attention the moment he started to look through them.

'The first part's handwritten, and is about him meeting you in London. It's about what happened there, with the children, and the court case. It's about you becoming a couple.'

'A short-lived and very unconvincing couple.'

'When he was . . . twenty-five?'

167

'That sounds about right,' she drew in a deep breath. 'It seems like such a long time ago. You'll understand why I try not to think about what happened. I didn't go to prison; I was never even charged with anything, but I was vilified in the press.'

'He says that. And he says that he believed you were entirely innocent. That's why he gave you an alibi.'

Samuel was about to go on but was aware of a sudden and apparent drop in temperature in the room. The coolness emanated from the woman in front of him. She was looking at him aghast.

'What did he say about the alibi?'

'Just that he didn't believe that you could have ever had a part in what happened to those children.'

'Did he write that he was with me that night? Or did he lie in his statement just to help me?'

'He doesn't go into any detail.'

'Why not?'

'I don't know.'

'I think I need to read these papers of his!'

'I don't understand. Either he was with you or he wasn't?'

'Exactly. And I've never known. You see, I had a drink problem and have never remembered anything about that night. I was too drunk. My employers didn't seem to care that their unqualified *au pair* was an alcoholic. They went out and left me with three children to look after. I put them to bed, got drunk, and woke up in your father's bed the next morning, three streets away.'

'The night that it happened?'

'Yes, the night they were killed. At around two in the morning all three of them were murdered in their beds, but your father said I had gone around to his place at about midnight. I've never known if that was true. I was so drunk I could've been anywhere. I can't account for what happened.'

'And the killer was never discovered?'

'No. The parents came back from the party to find their children murdered and their *au pair* missing. I know I could never have had a hand in their murder, but I should have been there for them. I should've been there to defend them.'

'My father doesn't seem to have held you responsible.'

'Everyone else did. I was their main suspect until your father made his statement. And as the police couldn't find the killer then the newspapers attacked the drunken young woman who had failed to protect the victims.'

'But if you'd stayed there that night you might've been murdered too?'

'Possibly, and there've been times when I wished that had happened.'

'I know it was a long time ago, but there must have been forensic evidence? Surely they must've had some idea of who the killer was?'

'All they ever knew was that the murderer entered by the unlocked front door, wearing gloves, and smothered each of the children while they slept. They used a pillow that was never found. The parents blamed me, and I've always understood that. I've lived with this guilt all these years.'

'Guilt for a crime you never committed?'

'Guilt for a murder that I should've prevented. And your father saved me from life imprisonment.'

'Even without his alibi they wouldn't have found you guilty.'

'You don't know what it was like; the police, the newspapers, the family, all needed to catch the killer and it was as if it didn't matter who that was. It would've been so convenient to pin it on me...'

'My father wrote that the statement he gave threw suspicion on him as well.'

'Yes. It was even suggested that we were in it together.'

'For what reason?'

'Who knows? What reason did the real killer have for murdering three innocent children?'

'I'm pretty sure my father's account of all that was written before he tracked you down. He wrote that he was rather obsessed by the memory of you.'

'He admitted that when he came up to see me, yes. He said that he'd always loved me, and me running out on him after the investigation . . . well.'

'Why did you leave him?'

'It wasn't your father I left, but London. I had no choice. I was helped to move here with a new identity, to start again, and it almost worked. I met Thomas Lykiard, we married and I took his name. When your father turned up on my doorstep, just as you did tonight, I was so glad to see him. I wanted him. He had saved me all those years before. And I thought he was the one person who could tell me what I'd really done that night. But we both skirted around it all . . . You don't want to know the details, what with you being his son, but we had a fantastic week, and we didn't discuss that night. And then he said he had to go back to London. I pleaded with him to stay, but he said he had to get back. It was probably because you were going to University, and there was something about his business. He was going to tell your mother he was leaving her . . .

'And I decided that he didn't return to me because that would have meant telling the truth about the night the children were killed. I decided that if he really couldn't bring himself to do so then it meant that I didn't leave the house when he said I did.'

'It wasn't his fault he didn't come back.'

'No, not immediately. But then for years he left me believing that I was probably there when the children died.'

'I'm sure that wasn't the case.'

'How could you possibly know?'

'I couldn't, I'm sorry. I just meant to say. . . .'

'I know. I'm sorry too. I shouldn't have a go at you. Whether I was there or not, I wasn't in any state to defend them anyway.'

'It must've been horrible. But nobody could *still* blame you, not after all these years?'

'Oh, I know that they do.'

'Who?'

170

'Ignore me,' she shook her head. 'The problem is that thinking about it fills me full of self-pity and self-loathing.'

Sensing the awkward silence that was to follow she asked him how he had found her.

'There was an address in the papers my father left behind. And he mentioned your married name.'

'So why has it taken you so long to come up and find me? To tell me?'

The wine made him feel slightly giddy. He realised that he had not eaten since lunchtime. He put down his glass while Clare waited patiently.

'My father was always rather distant. When I read his papers I wasn't sympathetic. I was angry that he'd considered leaving my mother. But, then again, I didn't understand why he stayed with her if he had really loved you, as he claimed. I didn't care about you. . . . though I suppose I wanted to meet you out of curiosity. I wasn't particularly interested in his broken promise to you. But as time went on I felt I had a duty to try and find you. I never got on with him that well, but he didn't deserve to be thought of badly by you. Although you told him you expected him not to return, you must've thought he'd made a conscious decision not to come back. I wanted to explain to you that it had been out of his control.

'When I went to see him in hospital. On my first visit he didn't wake up, and I remember him as looking very old. . . . He was unconscious for a few days, and when he woke up he was very confused and shaky. That was scary. I remember helping him with a glass of water and he seemed very strange to me. He'd fractured his skull and there was inflammation . . .'

'I had no idea. All that time I was up here cursing him for not returning.'

'I know that he wanted to come to you. He was frustrated that they wouldn't allow him to be discharged. I seem to remember that when he was finally able to talk he did mention leaving my mother, but she said it was due to the concussion, and all the pills they gave him.'

'He could have come back to me,' Clare shook her head, looking down at her hands.

'I don't think he believed you would allow him to do so.'

She put out the cigarette and poured more wine into both of their glasses. Then she lay back in her chair, looking at the ceiling.

'I don't know what to think,' she considered. 'And then you turn up out of the blue.'

'I'm sorry. I should've phoned first.'

'Yes, you could've given me some warning, and given me time to prepare myself.'

'I thought that if I told you on the phone I wouldn't have been able to explain properly . . . you wouldn't have understood.'

She sat forward:

'I'm glad you came, really. There're too many things I've never understood. I don't suppose anybody's life is so well plotted as to make sense at the end: there never is a neat final scene in which the clever detective explains who did it. In lieu of explanation, let's try alcohol? Stay here and I'll get another bottle.'

She stood up, but did not immediately leave the room. She looked down at him once more.

'You think that your father was distant towards you because of me,' she suggested.

'I didn't say that.'

'No, but I sensed it.'

'My father's mind was always elsewhere. He only engaged with the external world, our world, on a superficial level.'

'You judge him harshly.'

'I've every right to. He was a dull man.'

'To you, perhaps, but what was going on inside his head?'

'Who cares? It's how you externalise yourself that's important. How you show love, or friendship, or creativity.'

'But we all live inside our own heads. We're all prisoners of our own minds. We all see the world differently, individually. What you see here, right now, is not necessarily what I see.'

'Okay, so we interpret things in our own way, but we all see the same things on the surface.'

'Do we?'

And she turned and left the room.

Samuel blamed the wine for his inability to understand her. She came back with another bottle that she passed to him to open. While he did so she went to an old record player by the window and turned it on.

'Enrico Caruso,' she said. '*Una furtiva lagrima* by Donizetti. Your father and I both loved this recording. . .'

'And it was on your turntable, waiting . . . ?'

'We've always been waiting.'

'Who are "we"?'

'Everyone concerned with what happened that night. Look, I've been waiting all this time for your father to come and tell me, categorically, that I had already left the house when the murders took place; that I was simply negligent, a bad *au pair*. The parents wanted to hear him say I'd turned up after the event and that he'd lied. The newspapers didn't care what he said as long as they could blame someone.'

'But you did finally escape it all?'

'I tried, but they followed me.'

'The newspapers?'

'Them as well, but after a while most of them gave up. . . .'

'Not all of them?'

'No. Those involved in the case that wanted to, well, they managed to track me down.'

'Like my father did?'

'Unlike him, some never left me.'

'I don't understand.'

She shook her head.

'It took some courage for you to come up here and see me,' she said. 'A woman you don't know, who was involved in an horrific murder.'

'My father said you were blameless. . . .'

'Let me finish. I don't know if I am blameless. I know I never killed anyone. But there's a good possibility that I was there when it happened. And if that's so, why don't I remember anything about it? It's driven me mad, literally.'

'How do you mean?'

'I had to see a succession of psychiatrists.'

'Nowadays they'd call it post-traumatic stress.'

'They've called it that, and they've called it "survivor guilt", and goodness knows how many other things. But it has apparently made me psychotic.'

'Which means?'

'I'm not a psychopath,' she said. 'Psychosis means losing touch with what is commonly accepted as reality. In my case I see things that other people deny the existence of.'

'But knowing that they're not real must be a step on the path to recovery?'

'No. You see, I've taken anti-psychotic drugs, and tried various therapies, but nothing has ever helped. They've only made me feel ill. So, several years ago I told the doctors that I'd stopped seeing things and they left me alone.'

'So, you're not on any medication now?'

'No.'

'But you seem quite well?'

'Apart from what I see, yes, I am.'

Nervous, he asked, 'So, what do you see?'

'The children.'

'Oh.'

'I sometimes think I should have had the courage to move into a town, a city even. Everyone around here recognised me from the newspapers anyway. I could've moved into a terraced street, with neighbours either side of me, and opposite. Then maybe I wouldn't have seen the children outside my window when it's dark.'

'What do they do?'

'They are waiting.'

She was looking towards the heavily curtained window.

'What are they waiting for?' he asked.

'For me to tell them what happened. At night, when I look out of the window, it's as though nothing else is out there; I just see them.'

'And they're always there when you look out?'

She nodded.

'Would it help if I looked out now, and was able to reassure you that they aren't there?'

'No. Don't get me wrong, if you said you didn't see them I'd believe that you couldn't. But that wouldn't mean that if I looked out as well that I wouldn't be able to see them.'

'But you know it's the psychosis.'

'No, I'm only told that it's the psychosis.'

'I'll look anyway,' he said, getting out of his chair.

'No, wait.'

'Why?'

'What if you see them as well?'

'Well, then that'll mean you're not psychotic; that they're really there.'

'But that would be worse.'

Samuel's hand had been raised to pull the curtain aside, but now he let it drop. There was not a sound from outside. There were no cars passing in the road, but then the house was fairly isolated. Perhaps the heavy curtains insulated the window, which could well have been double-glazed, but it seemed wrong that there was no noise at all from outside.

He turned around and looked at Clare Macdonald who was replenishing his glass with wine.

'I understand if you want to leave,' she said quietly.

'No,' he replied, at length, realising that he didn't want to. Not that he was afraid of what, or who, he might meet out there.

'If they are waiting for you to tell them what happened...'

'I thought that one day I might be able to.'

175

'But if they can't ever be told?'

'I don't know. As I said, you're welcome to leave.'

'No,' he repeated, quietly. 'I think I'll take you up on the offer of a room for the night.'

'Good. The curtains up there are already drawn.'

'Thank you,' he said, quietly, sitting back down and taking up his glass. 'I'll leave in the morning,' he decided, and they both looked into the fire and said nothing.

Another Country

Up until the moment I approached the door everything had been effortless. My connections from Amsterdam to Bialystok had been on time, and there, at the airport, had been my old friend David to greet me. He eased me through the process of hiring a car and had sent me on my way with a detailed set of directions that finished on the very road that Adam Krasicki gave as his address. I had to go just over the border, it was quicker than flying direct to the country I wanted, and the Customs procedures between the two countries were surprisingly uncomplicated and informal. The roads were all good, and at the end of my journey there was even a parking space outside of the very building I sought. It was a busy thoroughfare, with fast-moving traffic, but I turned the car in to the side of the road without having to make any awkward manoeuvres. When I switched off the engine it was with some satisfaction.

The day was bright and clear. When I got out of the car I decided that, despite the fumes and noise of the traffic, it was a fine city. The buildings lining the street were late nineteenth-century and mellowed, with sooty ornamentation. There were trees at regular intervals along a wide pavement, and there were small areas in front of each building so that they stood back from the road. I had always had the idea of Eastern European cities being dour and grey, featureless and windswept, but this seemed very civilised indeed.

The building displayed its number clearly and Krasicki's name was on a plate by the door, with a number suggesting a flat on the third floor. There was no bell to ring, so I let myself in and I walked up the stairs with a light heart, not a little proud of myself.

In one hand I carried a bottle of Scotch Whisky, a drink I knew Krasicki to appreciate, and under my arm a parcel containing copies of the paperback printing of his novel, *Terminus*. We had published the first edition a year earlier, to great critical acclaim, if not huge sales, but this reprint had better distribution and was already pre-ordered in substantial numbers by the major retailers.

Outside the door to his flat I put the parcel on the ground and knocked. It was only now that things started to go wrong.

The door partly opened, but before I could see what had happened I could tell by the hollow sound of my knocking, as it echoed inside, that the flat was empty. I pushed the door further and looked in, not having the courage at first to cross the threshold. There was no furniture in the hallway or in the room that I could see leading off from it. I noticed indentations in the linoleum that showed where furniture had once stood, and there were light patches on the walls where pictures had obviously been hanging. A bare flex came down from the ceiling, and even the light switch had been removed.

'Hello?' I called, a little stupidly, but by way of easing my conscience as I stepped inside.

I have always disliked empty buildings. I don't expect to come across ghosts, or any other potentially malevolent presences; I simply find a succession of empty rooms dispiriting and depressing. Even the cleanest-looking room appears dirty and grimy when the furniture is removed: cobwebs will have been hidden by cupboards, stains concealed by rugs, cracks lost behind the folds of curtains. Krasicki's accomodation was not in bad repair; there was a carpet in what I took to have been the bedroom and it didn't look too worn; the paper was not peeling from the walls, but there was a pall of neglect that enveloped the place.

There was nothing at all, apart from the small plate by the door outside, to suggest that Adam Krasicki had ever lived there. Well, that explained why he had not been answering letters. I was annoyed with myself; there was always a risk that he would not be at home when I tried to visit, but my worst fear was simply that my arrival would have been inconvenient for him.

As I left the flat, wondering how on earth I might find a forwarding address, and assuming that I was going to have to retrace my journey all the way back home, I bumped into a woman on the landing outside. She looked somewhat angry, and addressed me in a language I knew nothing of. I said I spoke English, but she did not understand.

Surprised at my own cleverness I put up my hand to stop her flow of words, and put down the parcel which I then unwrapped. The books were upside down and Adam Krasicki's picture on the back cover appeared first. I showed this to her, and repeated his name slowly, but she looked just as unimpressed, and there was no hint of recognition. She made it clear that I was to leave, and I did so, hastily, but despairing that I had travelled so far, to a foreign country even, and that my quest was to have been in vain.

The woman was shouting down the stair-well at me as I descended, but I stopped in the hall, considering what to do. Suddenly she was quiet and a few moments later a door slammed. That was all. I had been rather shaken by what had happened.

I went back to the car and sat in the driver's seat, wondering what to do. My mobile phone put me immediately in contact with my office, and I was assured that I had the correct address, which I already knew. I informed them that I would be returning sooner than expected.

I put the phone back into my jacket pocket and was about to look at the map when I saw what appeared to be a policeman on the other side of the road. Without great hope of success, I grabbed one of the books and got back out of the car. A gap in the traffic did not open up immediately, and by the time that I was across both lanes and on the other side of the road he was walking away from me. I ran up to him and said:

'Excuse me.'

He turned and said something I could not understand. I asked if he knew English and he smiled helpfully but continued in his own language. I showed him the picture of Krasicki on the book, and then took out of my pocket the address I had written down.

'He's not there,' I said, knowing that the words would communicate nothing, but hoping that my accompanying actions might.

He nodded sagely, took the book, and considered what I might mean. He then nodded again and I worked out that he wanted me to follow him.

It appears to be no problem for a policeman to cross a busy road. He simply steps out into the traffic with his hand up to stop the cars and they obey. I followed him to the building I had already visited. I would have liked to tell him that I had been there already, but I decided that it would be fruitless. We went in and I climbed up to the third floor again. He looked surprised that the door was open and the flat was empty.

He walked in, calling out before him, much as I had done earlier, and again the woman appeared. This time I could see that she was certainly from the flat opposite.

I was completely unable to follow the direction of their conversation, but she appeared to be annoyed with him, and he was not happy with her attitude. Both tried to talk to me at one point but I was forced to simply shrug and look apologetic. She then went back to her own flat and me and the policeman appeared to be waiting for her to return. When she did so she was holding a map and I guessed that Krasicki may have left a forwarding address after all.

The map was not detailed. I told them to wait for me this time, hoping they would understand that I would return. I ran back down the stairs and out to the car in the street which I had left unlocked, although nothing had come to any harm. I picked up my own, new map from off the passenger seat and locked the car. When I got back upstairs they were dutifully waiting for me.

The policeman found the street that I presumably required, which appeared to be on the outskirts of the city, and he laboriously traced with his finger the route that I would have to take. While he did so the woman returned to her flat once more, but came back after a time with a pen and wrote a series of numbers and letters on the back of my hand. I assumed that this would relate to the address.

I am not well-travelled, and I had been lulled into a false sense of security by the ease with which I had found my initial destination. The second address proved more problematic and it was dark by the time that I arrived at the right road. The place I had ended up at, though, did not appear to have conventional houses lining the street, but barrack-like buildings arranged irregularly along it. There was no obvious military presence, but neither did it look residential. A single track led off from the road and appeared to head towards further barracks, but I was relying on my car headlamps and they did not seem to penetrate very far into the blackness. I parked, and was seriously considering returning to the centre of the city, to find a hotel, when I saw a man in the distance and I decided to ask him for help.

Once again language proved to be a barrier, but I showed him the numbers and letters written on my hand and his face brightened to a smile. He was probably only thirty, very tall and with slightly protruding eyes. He beckoned me to follow him, but I first retrieved my parcels from the car. He waited patiently until I had locked it, and then surprised me somewhat by insisting on taking me by my one free hand. He led me over to a path that passed by the nearest building, and it was then that I began to have grave misgivings. We followed unlit paths between these old barrack buildings, most of which, though by no means all, had some lights on behind net curtains. I soon became completely disorientated. Even driving out to this god-forsaken spot I had not worried because I had my car, a good map, and the roads were well signposted. If this man's intentions were not good then I was in trouble because, at the very least, I had no way of finding my way back to the car. Eventually, though, he stopped before a building that looked like all of the others we had passed. He bowed gravely and deeply, and said something, and I noticed with profound relief that what was written on a small sign by the door corresponded with what was written on my hand. I thanked my guide, bowed as he had done, and when I looked up he was gone.

I took a deep breath and walked up to the door. I knocked, but there was no answer. I knocked again, and waited, but still nobody came. I stood there in growing despair, and looked at the address on the door again, which was illuminated by a thin, rosy light. When I put my hand by it I saw that it did not have the final letter that my address did; a letter 'C' was missing.

Despite my fears my mind was relatively calm and I decided that perhaps these building might have a number of dwellings inside them. I tried the door and it opened.

There was a lobby inside, and a corridor running down the spine of the building. My reasoning had been sound. There was a very dim light, but a large switch inside the door threw the place into harsh illumination. Before me were doors lettered 'A' and 'B', and the next one I came to was 'C'.

℘

Adam Krasicki sat forward in his armchair and stubbed out the remains of his roll-up cigarette.

'I'm here because my mother needs me,' he said. 'It's not out of choice.'

He looked considerably older than in the photograph on the paperbacks that were piled up on the table next to him. He had allowed me to put them there when I had arrived, along with the bottle of spirits, but he had not touched either.

'So you went to my flat and found it empty? You did well to find me here, but it wasn't a good idea. You should have just gone back home. You could have posted the books.'

'They were an excuse. We were worried about you. We hadn't heard from you for so long . . .'

'And you want my next novel, perhaps?'

182

'That isn't the only reason; the welfare of our authors is important to us.'

'I liked that old place,' he said, meditatively. 'It was a bit of a dump, but I did like it. For several years I sat in there, writing, and at the time my old possessions always seemed to mock my lack of success . . .'

'What have you done with them?'

'What I was able to fit in my bedroom are here with me,' he pointed to a door off the main room. 'There is not enough room here even for my mother's stuff.'

The living room certainly was very full. There was little floor space because of the furniture, and on the furniture were boxes and piles of shapeless material, themselves covered by ornaments and other more utilitarian items. The walls were covered in pictures; mainly glossy landscapes.

'There are only two bedrooms, hers and mine. She's bedridden, and her equipment takes up much room.'

They were meant to be talking quietly because she was apparently asleep.

'But at least that other place was my own. Now I live here, with all the . . . rubbish . . . that she has collected in a lifetime.'

'It must be awkward.'

'Awkward? Yes, very. She's very demanding, the old cow.' .

There was a pause.

'My place was a dump,' he continued, 'but at least it was mine. My furniture was old and battered, the books on my rickety shelves were cheap paperbacks. I lived in a dull, dull world, and then, one day, as if my magic, stacked on the floor in front of me were ten beautiful new copies of a novel that apparently I had written. That *I* had written! I was the king of the world!'

'You've every right to be proud of that book.'

'I should've been just as proud if they'd been cheap print-on-demand paperbacks from some fly-by-night small press. But no, these were substantial hardback volumes, with bright embossed dustjackets, published by a real mainstream publisher. And on each one was written praise from one of my great literary heroes, proclaiming me, *me*, as the most exciting writer of my generation!'

'It must have felt good?'

'For a minute, perhaps, or for an hour. I don't know. Maybe I believed in it all for a whole day? But it wasn't real. None of it was.'

'You weren't dreaming. I can vouch for that. And now it's been reprinted in paperback.'

'You should have seen those first few copies that I received,' he said, meditatively. 'The books lit up the room, glowing with a supernatural brilliance against the grey world that I normally inhabited. I told myself that if I were to suddenly have a heart attack at that very moment then I should die happy. In fact, what could have been better for my reputation than an untimely death on the eve of the publication of my great work? Everyone would have had to imagine the even greater novels I would have gone on to write.'

'It received excellent reviews.'

'Exactly. All was as I'd dreamed it might be. And I was going to be flown to London; there were launch parties organised . . .'

'But it didn't seem real to you? Well, I suppose it was all a little unexpected.'

'You don't understand. This novel was not really any different from my previous attempts and they had always been rejected. So, why this one? How was it any different?'

'Well, surely that's a good thing? All the time and effort you put into those won't have been wasted. You could let us have a look at them as well?'

'No, I can't, because I did discover the difference between those earlier efforts and my sudden, unexpected triumph.'

'And that was?'

'Simply that I didn't write the book that everyone is raving about.'

'Rubbish! I work alongside your editor and I saw some of your correspondence.'

'Ah yes, Joanne Reed. So you work with her, do you? And do you know how Joanne Reed changed my book?'

'How?'

'Subtly . . . but enough to make it somebody else's work . . . her work, not mine. I entered into a contract with the devil herself.'

There was a horrible groaning noise from his mother's bedroom.

'Let me check on the old cow, and then I will come back and explain'

'I had sent the manuscript to Weber's believing that the time and effort was completely wasted, but I had a large enough ego to think that maybe, just maybe, they'd consider it publishable. I was resigned to waiting a couple of months before the standard letter arrived telling me that they had no interest. I can't really afford to send off the same manuscript simultaneously to several publishers, especially in foreign countries. The very evening that Miss Reed appeared I was preparing another copy for posting to what I thought was a more realistic hope. It was to a company in Minnesota who seem to publish any kind of crap as long as they can put some lurid artwork on the cover. Well, I was writing the covering letter when the bell rang and I answered it to a smart-looking young woman who asked for me by name. She was Joanne Reed, from Weber's, and that she was making a detour en route to a convention. She was there to say that she wanted her company to accept my manuscript.

'Well, I would've invited her inside, but my flat didn't seem at all the place to entertain an elegant publisher who had flown all the way from London. So I took her to the smart wine bar in the adjacent street. I hoped it would impress her, and I knew that none of my boorish friends would be there at that hour to interrupt.

'We shared a bottle of sparkling white wine and I sat there while she made me feel like the great author I'd always wanted to be. She loved my characters and my descriptions, and said that they had already decided that they would offer it to their American partners after it had been published in Britain. I splashed out on another bottle of wine.

'She did have a few suggestions to make, however. She was an editor, after all, and pointed out that any changes would be made in consultation with me, and nothing would be altered without my agreement. She explained that great editors are only appreciated by their authors; nobody else ever knows they exist. I rather liked this, because I had already realised that there were a few infelicities that needed addressing, and if somebody else was happy to tidy those up for me, then all well and good. English is not my first language . . .'

'Your English is exceptional, let me tell you.'

'Thank you. People have always been very complimentary. But I know that my written English is not always correct. But that was no problem; I would receive the credit for the work of a professional. I asked for an example of what she wanted working on.

'She did not mention problems with my English after all. She explained that one of my failings was pacing. There were occasions, she said, when the novel would benefit from me taking more time to describe certain events; usually to tease the reader and create suspense. She would point out to me, she said, where a paragraph, even a few pages could be inserted. If I agreed I would simply have to add a little padding, perhaps with direction from her. I agreed to this quite readily, and asked if there was anything else.

'She did not want to go into specifics there and then, but she suggested that there could quite easily be a little more development of my main character. She liked the whole concept of the anti-hero I had created, but wondered if he couldn't actually appear to be sympathetic at the beginning of the book. A few tweaks here and there would make the indignities that he suffers appear to be the fault of his enemies. It would cause the reader to question all of their assumptions if the one person in the book they naturally identify with was to turn out to be morally repugnant.

'I liked the idea, but I was horrified that I'd have to take the book back and start re-writing it. Her first comments had led me to believe that proofs would be in the post shortly, and after a few typesetting errors had been corrected publication would naturally follow in a few weeks. When I looked worried she assured me that in most instances one or two changes of emphasis in a sentence was all that was required. She said that she could easily effect these; in fact, she was happy to do this for me and send the changes to me for my approval.

'Other than this, she said that there was the routine editorial work. There was no shame in having your grammar and punctuation tidied up. And I have the habit, apparently, of repeating the same words and phrases just a little too often. All it needed was a thesaurus, she explained.

'Well, what was I to say? I agreed to everything. I saw her go off to her hotel in a taxi and I went back to my flat. I was impressed that she wrote to me the next day from her office in London. I was flattered. I know flights are cheap at the moment, but you're the second person from your office who has bothered to fly all the way out here just to see me.'

'We have great hopes for your next novel, and your career,' I pointed out.

'But before publication things did not go as I expected.'

'In what way?'

'Miss Reed asked me to write a little more. It was mainly descriptive pieces she wanted; a paragraph here and there offering the thoughts of my characters. Sometimes she wanted me to explain how my character had moved from one location to another. I thought many of these a waste of time, but I did as she asked.'

'She is one of our best editors. And you can't fault the finished book.'

'Then she wrote and asked for excisions.'

'Were there many?'

'No, not many, but they were important. The main one explained the whole philosophical idea behind the book. And so I refused.'

'Maybe she felt that the central philosophy came through without explanation?'

187

'That's exactly what she said. And she told me that unless I changed it the book would not be published.'

'Oh.'

'Exactly, "Oh",' he repeated annoyed. 'But what could I do? Would I risk publication by such an important company as Webers, just for the sake of a few paragraphs? I agreed, with very bad grace, and told her not to delete another single word.'

'And how did she take that?'

'Ha! She said that all she wanted to do was to make it perfect. She asked me to add a couple of sentences which made it clear that my main character, rather than simply observing the horror at the heart of the book, was himself one of the monsters that so disgusted him!'

'Oh.'

'You keep saying "Oh"!' Krasicki had slowly worked himself up into a rage. 'You say it like you understand!'

'I apologise.'

'You don't understand at all, do you?'

'I must admit that I don't. You see, the whole book is a wonderful exploration of the idea of the monster in modern culture.'

'That's what all the damned critics say! But that's not what I intended. It is NOT meant to happen that the character of the book turns into the horror that he observes around him!'

'No, he doesn't realise it . . . That's why it's so clever, so subtle, so . . .'

'But my book was not clever, or subtle, or anything else. Miss Reed did that to it.'

I stopped myself from saying 'Oh' again. There was very little that I could say. I understood exactly what had happened. Joanne Reed had seen that there could be something great in a book where it did not yet exist. It had not taken much work to include it, but it had been at the expense of the author's original, second-rate intention for it. No wonder the man felt humiliated. I shrugged:

'I don't know what to say.'

'There is nothing that you can say.'

'All you can do, I suppose, is accept the glory, and move on to your next book.'

'There is no next book. I have realised what a poor author I am. I have not written a word since then.'

'But that's nonsense. Even if the central idea of the book has been changed from your original intention, it contains insightful ideas and images, scenes and characters . . .'

'No, it doesn't! I happen to have put together ideas from books I've read and films I've seen, but I am so poor at writing that you would find it hard to recognise the source material!'

'I refuse to believe that. For a start, you write so beautifully!'

'Do I? Well, I went back to my original manuscript and compared it to the published book. There is not a sentence that has not been altered, sometimes quite noticeably, often less so. Your Miss Reed has re-written my book.'

There was a noise from his mother's bedroom again. Krasicki shouted something at her as he stood up, and then he swept the books from the table beside him as he left the room. The bottle wobbled but regained its balance.

I composed myself, hoping that he would be calmer when he returned, but I could hear him actually shouting at his mother, and she was making odd, shrill noises herself. I wanted to stand up, and decided that when he returned it would be best if I looked concerned, but relaxed.

When Krasicki came back he came over and stood before me. He glared at me, too close, and I said, carefully:

'I'm so sorry that you feel this way. But at worst your book is a collaboration.'

'Ha! That is one way of looking at it, I suppose. I concede that the great lump of clay that she used to sculpt my book was supplied by me.'

'But apart from you and her, nobody else knows this. Well, I do now, but I won't say anything.'

'Don't they know? Doesn't the whole literary world know?'

'Honestly, I don't think that they do.'

'But that's not good enough. That woman has destroyed me.'

'Well, what do you want to do about it?'

'What do *I* want to do about it? Shouldn't you be asking what *you* are going to do about it?'

'Me? I'm afraid that I'm just a publicity officer in the firm. I have little influence.'

'But you are a representative of the publisher.'

'Not really.'

'Oh yes you are. And I will have my revenge. I've had to come back and live in this stinking hell-hole to care for that thing back there that my mother has become. I've no friends, no dignity.'

I did not know how to take his comments. I was in no doubt of his anger, but what form would his revenge take? I was tired and had hoped to meet an author who would be pleased to receive copies of his new book. I had gone well out of my way to find him, and expected some gratitude, but Krasicki was far from grateful.

At length he smiled and said: 'Get up.'

I did so, cautiously.

'Now, in there,' he pointed to his mother's bedroom.

'No, I'd rather not,' I told him, not believing what was happening. I should have left then and there, but I stupidly watched as he looked in a box under the table. He stood up and there was a hammer in his hand.

'In there,' he snarled now, and only then did I realise what trouble I was in. He lifted the hammer, threateningly, and I did as I was told. I went into the darkened room and heard the door shut behind me.

'Now,' he said from behind the door. 'It is your turn to stay here and look after her. If I stay here I will end up like her.'

I could make out nothing at all in the room, apart from some very heavy breathing in the corner. I heard Krasicki moving around in the living room and then, unmistakably the front door opened and closed.

When I was sure that he was no longer inside I opened the bedroom door a little and looked out. The place appeared to be empty.

Behind me, in the borrowed light from the front room, I could see the massive form of something in the bed. There was the framework of a large, complicated piece of machinery around it.

I shut the door behind me and crossed the apartment quietly, letting myself out of their front door having first checked that there was nobody waiting outside in the hallway. I then opened the main door and looked out into the empty night. At any moment I expected Krasicki to loom up out of the darkness, hammer in hand.

I shut the door behind me and hurried down the path, having no idea of where I was going. I just had to leave. The pathway forked before me and the route I chose came to an abrupt end. I ran over some rough ground, and then I was passing alongside another of the barrack buildings. There were stars visible, so I decided to keep heading towards the brightest one that was low in the sky, but I must have miscalculated because as I jogged past yet another of the buildings I had a premonition that it was one that I had seen before. Of course, they all looked alike, but I checked the numbers and letters with those on my hand and it was the Krasicki's.

Twice this was repeated, and finally, exhausted, I regained my courage and re-entered the building. With the greatest care I opened the door to their rooms; Krasicki himself did not appear to be inside, but his mother was calling.

I waited until morning and tried to leave again by daylight, but it was impossible. I had tried my mobile phone a number of times but there was no signal. I attempted to talk to the neighbours, but they could not understand me. Those who were willing to let me in to their rooms did not have telephones. Now in daylight I tried walking away from the Krasicki's building in one direction, with the sun before me, but I always managed to become disorientated and end up where I had started. At midday, as the same barrack appeared before me yet again I returned to Krasicki's rooms.

His mother was crying, pleading, and I went in to her. Really, she is a trying old woman. At first her appearance scared me, repulsed me, made me physically sick, but I've become used to her now. I've been here for what seems like weeks and she always appears to want something. We have a kind of system so that I can understand when she is hungry, thirsty, needs moving in her bed, or when the sheets need changing. I hate her, but I cannot discover any means of getting away. I don't know what's wrong with her but I have a suspicion that Krasicki will have to return here one day and then I will be able to make my escape.

Loup-garou

I first saw the film, *Loup-garou*, in 1989, in a little arts cinema in the centre of Birmingham. I had driven there for a job interview and, as usual, I had allowed far more time for the journey than was required. I had reasoned that it should take me two hours to travel there, to park, and to find the offices of the firm of accountants where I desperately wanted a position. The interview was at two thirty, so I intended to leave home at midday. I had worked it all out the night before, but then became concerned that the traffic might be against me, and I decided to allow another half-hour for the journey. That morning I checked my map, but no car parks were marked on it and so I added yet another half hour to the time I would allow myself. Leaving at eleven o'clock seemed prudent, but I was ready by half-ten and, rather than sit around the house worrying, I decided to set out.

I know my nervousness about travelling is a failing, but I've always lived and worked in this small provincial town and it is not a day-to-day problem. On this occasion it was made very obvious to me just how irrational my fear of being late for appointments really was; the traffic was light and the roads clear and I was in the centre of Birmingham by a quarter to twelve. I found a car park with ease and was immediately passed a ticket by a motorist who was already leaving, despite paying to stay the whole day. I parked, and as I walked out on to the street I could see the very offices that I wanted directly opposite. I had two and a half hours to kill.

For no reason other than to pass the time I looked into the foyer of the cinema which was immediately adjacent to the car park. Pegged up on a board was the information that a film called *Loup-garou* was about to start, and that it would be finished by two o'clock. It seemed the perfect solution to my problem.

I doubt if there were more than five or six people in the cinema. It was small and modern and the seat into which I settled myself was not too uncomfortable. I was in time to watch the opening credits slowly unfold. The sun was rising over a pretty, flat countryside, and the names of the actors, all French, slowly faded in and out as the light came up over fields and trees. It was beautifully shot, and a simple, haunting piano piece repeated quietly as the small cast were introduced, and finally the writer and director, Alain Legrand. I noted the name carefully from the information in the foyer when I left the cinema two hours later.

The film was incredibly slow, but each scene was so surprisingly framed, and the colours so achingly vivid that it was almost too lovely to watch. The sunlight, a numinous amber, slanted horizontally across the landscape as we were introduced to the hero, a boy who was walking from his home in the village to a house only a half-mile distant. The camera was with him every step of the way. There was a quiet voice-over, in French, that was unhurried enough for me to understand it. The boy was kicking a stone and noting that he had a theory that four was a perfect number, as exemplified by a square. Therefore, if he kicked this stone, or tapped the rail of a fence, he had to do it three more times to make it perfect. If, by some unfortunate mischance, he should repeat the action so that it was done, say, five times, then he would have to make it up to sixteen – four times four. The penalty for getting that wrong was huge; the action would need to be repeated again and again to make it up to two hundred and fifty-six, or sixteen times sixteen.

It was a rambling dialogue, and a silly little notion such as any young lad might have, but I was immediately struck that it had been an affectation that I myself had had as a teenager. Predisposed toward our hero on the strength of this, I was rather looking forward, as he was, to seeing his sweetheart, if the director would ever allow him to arrive at her house. When he eventually knocked at the door, predictably we had to wait for the mother to answer it, and for him to be shown into the comfortable, dark kitchen. He had to wait, of course, for the girl who, he was told, was brushing her hair upstairs and would not be long. He talked to the mother, stroked a cat and looked out of the window. Finally the object of his affections descended the stairs.

At this point I sat forward in my seat. The young girl looked exactly as my wife, Yvonne, had looked at that age. She was pretty, with startlingly blue eyes, and long blond hair. I was delighted by the coincidence.

They took their time, of course, in going outside to where the sun was now higher in the sky. I felt a frisson as they sat close together on the bench outside the door, and, unseen by the mother, he tenderly kissed the nape of her neck as she bent down to look into a box of buttons. I marvelled at the film-maker's art. As the boy's lips brushed the girl's skin she slid her hand through the buttons in a way that was incredibly sensual. Then she picked out a heavy green one, shaped like an apple, and asked him if he knew that it had once belonged to the costume of a famous clown?

Up until this point I had enjoyed the coincidences I had found in the film, but this was stretching them too far. My mother had also had a very similar button in a sewing box, which was also said to have once belonged to a well-known clown. I did not know what to make of its appearance in the film.

The hero and heroine then decided to take a walk through the fields, talking of love and their future. And then, in the woods, there was the most delicately handled love-making scene, shown to us through carefully concealing trees. When he eventually walked home we had another voice-over where he declared his love for the girl whom he inevitably calls Yvonne.

After a few more meetings between the two of them, the only scenes involving several other actors are played out on a day of celebration; their last at school. Here another character is introduced, an older boy who clearly has an interest in the heroine. I immediately cast around for the equivalent character in my youth. There had been jealousies in my relationship with Yvonne when we were still at school, but I had finally married my childhood sweetheart. Completely lost to the apparent reality of the film I hated this potential suitor with a passion. Suddenly it is revealed, in a scene where Yvonne tentatively kisses this second boy, that we had been watching the earlier love-making scene at a distance through our hero's eyes!

The film then changed in style. In an instant the long, beautifully framed scenes from a single static position were replaced by abrupt, short images from what appeared to be a hand-held camera, and which were presumably meant to be from our hero's viewpoint. It conveyed the black rage within him. He was retracing the journey to Yvonne's house from the start of the film, but this time at a run. He was looking all about him in desperation. When he arrived at the farmhouse he hammered at the door, and when the mother answered it she told him that the girl had gone out. He rushes off across the fields and into the woods, and as the hurried camera-work shows his journey the view-point subtly moves down from the eye-level of a young man to that of an animal running, finally, over the floor of the woods. For only a few moments we see the lovemaking couple once again. The hero rushes upon them and there are terrible screams and the wild movement of the camera makes it impossible to see what is happening. The screen goes black, and just as the audience is getting restless and wonders whether the film has finished, or if the reel has not been replaced by the projectionist, the picture slowly comes up to show an incredibly languid sunset, and the hero, looking dirty and ragged, crying uncontrollably, walks slowly back to the village.

We are back to the earlier, slow direction. He slips unnoticed into a dark garage, and in the dim light we see him loop a length of rope around the rafters. The music has started by this time, a variation on the opening theme, and in front of one long apparently unedited shot we watch him climb a chair, tie the rope around his neck, and kick the chair from under him. By now it is so dark that we can't make out the details of his horrible death, and the music has taken the place of the sounds in the garage, but the imagination makes up for what is not shown.

I was emotionally drained by the film. I emerged into a Birmingham afternoon light, deeply affected by the closing scene and not thinking particularly of the earlier coincidences. The rage that had been in the hero as he rushed to find the lovers seemed to grow in my own breast and it was a while before the shock passed. Eventually I remembered and was able to reflect upon the uncanny similarities between the hero's circumstances and my own. I could not work out what was real, what was my imagination and what had been the film-maker's art. I was standing on the pavement outside the cinema, angry at the injustice of the film. To this day I do not know how I managed to compose myself for an interview thirty minutes later, and how I made the short-list.

When I arrived home that evening and related the events of my day, the film assumed more importance than the interview. Yvonne listened to my description patiently, amused, and said that she too would like to see it. I had written on a flier taken from the cinema *Loup-garou* and the director's name, 'Alain Legrand'. She pointed out that *loup-garou* meant werewolf, which I had not registered at the time. 'You've been watching horror movies then,' she asked, and I had to agree that it was horrific.

Having unburdened myself to my wife, and, I am embarrassed to admit this, having cried while re-telling the story, I felt remarkably better, and with a little distance was able to be amused by the coincidences of the film. Perhaps I had made too much of them. As I lay in bed that night I told myself that if there was anything supernatural about the apparent coincidences, anything at all, then it was there to show me how lucky I was to have made my childhood sweetheart my wife. I looked at her as she slept beside me, at her tangled blond hair and fine skin, the shape of her nose and at her soft, parted lips. For the first time that day I thought of the hero as an actor rather than as myself, and I slept soundly.

I did not get the job when I was called back for the second interview, and in retrospect I am glad that I didn't. At the time I was disappointed, but my life carried on comfortably and provincially, and city
life has never since appealed to me. On my return to Birmingham for
the ill-fated second interview I looked in at the cinema but the film
they were showing was apparently a Norwegian 'comedy of manners'.
It didn't appeal, and I did not have the time to watch it.

Almost immediately *Loup-garou* became something of a joke
amongst our friends. I had explained what had happened one evening
to another couple at a dinner party, and my wife saw a tear in my eye
as I explained the plot, and a great deal of fun was had at my expense.
I played up to it, and berated my wife for leaving me for another in her
filmic existence, and letting me, presumably, attack her and her lover
and then commit suicide. My wife was quite fascinated by the idea of
the film, and between ourselves we resolved that we would try and see
it. Obscure French art films don't often appear on the provincial film
circuit, though, and it was some years before I saw any reference to it
anywhere.

For a while I bought a few books about werewolves, fiction and
non-fiction, but it struck me that the power of the film didn't derive
from the legends, but the way in which the film had been put together,
and my fascination for the subject quickly waned. My interest in
foreign cinema grew, though, along with my video collection, and soon
I was quite knowledgeable on the subject of art-house European
cinema. In my researches I found a reference to *Loup-garou* in the
biography of the director, Alain Legrand, which claimed that the film
had never been distributed because it had fallen foul of the censors
(because it appeared to condone under-age sex). A few years later it
appeared on the internet in a French language film database which
claimed that not only had it never been distributed, but had never even
been edited. These claims were repeated, word for word, on other
databases, and although a large reference book on European cinema
later corrected these errors, those entries remain unrevised on the
internet. The reference book added that those critics that had seen

Loup-garou reported that it contained some of the most beautiful, as well as some of the most amateurish camera-work they had seen. The only other reference that I discovered in the intervening years was on a 'werewolf' website, where it was described as 'disappointing', and 'hardly to be described as a werewolf film at all'. Nowhere could I find any reference to it being made available in any form. Without any hope of success I programmed the details into internet search-engines with no result, and left it as a permanent 'want' on an auction site, which I refreshed every year without success.

And then only a couple of weeks ago I had an email notification that the film was being offered for auction. A private seller had a dvd to sell that he admitted was an unauthorised copy from an unreleased studio video. I didn't hesitate to put £50 on as my maximum bid, and despite there being no other apparent competition, with a day to go I raised it to £100. I watched the end of the auction on a Sunday evening, waiting for the flurry of last-minute bidding, but none came. I won the dvd for the minimum bid of £5.

It arrived in the post two days later, sent by a Frenchman living in London. There was no accompanying receipt and the dvd was blank, with no artwork. Yvonne and I had decided to make an occasion of watching it, and planned to wait until the children were in bed. We had opened a bottle of wine in readiness, but a nagging headache that Yvonne had earlier complained of became worse, threatening to develop into a migraine, and she decided to go to bed.

I watched the film anyway. I knew that I'd be happy to see it again in a few days time when Yvonne was feeling better, but after all this time I could not wait.

In the quiet house I sat down before the television, and pressed 'play' on the remote control. The credits came up as they had done in the little cinema over fifteen years before. The picture jumped a couple of times at the beginning but settled down after that and the quality was good. The sound was clear, and the music was just as haunting as I remembered it. A part of me was worried that it wouldn't be quite as I remembered it, but it still looked beautifully shot, and I waited to see the young boy walking out towards the farmhouse. He duly appeared, and explained in the voice-over about his obsession with the number four. A shiver ran through me.

When the camera panned slowly around Yvonne's family kitchen I noticed a number of things that I hadn't seen on my initial viewing; the first being that their dresser was similar to one that my wife's family had once owned. The mother, too, looked a lot like her own mother. I drew in a breath as the young Yvonne started to come down the stairs, but suddenly found myself completely bewildered.

The girl that appeared was certainly not the girl that I remembered. This actress had dark hair, and was slightly plump as opposed to the skinny little thing from before.

As though wilfully ignoring my confusion the actress assumed the role as though it had always been hers.

Outside the door they sat on the bench as I remembered, and the whole scene with the buttons was repeated exactly as I had retold the story to others over the years. As far as I could tell, the walk across the fields and into the woods was the same, scene for scene, and the love-making was carefully, and enigmatically, handled as before. I could understand now that there might be some who would protest that the actor and actress were under-age, but almost everything was inferred by the viewer; suggested but not shown by the director.

Disillusioned at my apparent inability to remember the film correctly I watched the scenes with the alternative suitor without quite the same passion as before. I had retold the story of the film on so many occasions and nobody had ever said that I had changed any details, therefore I must have reported it wrongly from the very beginning—immediately after I had seen it!

I was too annoyed with myself to enjoy the rest of the film, and suddenly it seemed to drag interminably. I made myself watch it, wondering if I'd even bother showing it to Yvonne, when the final scenes eventually appeared. The attack on the love-making couple was as sudden and almost as unexpected as before. But again I had got the details wrong. It was not the hero but the other boy who made his way back to the village, and into the darkened garage. He climbed the chair and fixed the rope. Barely perceptible in the dark, and with the sound masked by the music, he hanged himself.

The credits came up and I turned it off. I put the dvd back in its blank case and decided to go and get myself ready for bed. I locked up the house and turned off all but the landing light, where I stopped to look in at Yvonne, who was sleeping.

I sensed that something wasn't quite right, though, and walked into the room.

There, in our bed, was a dark-haired woman. I stood quite still, not wanting on any account to wake her. I found myself trembling, though, and backed out of the door, not knowing what to do. There, at the top of the stairs was our wedding photo, and I had problems standing as I saw myself, in a picture from twenty years ago, beside a pretty, plump, dark-haired woman.

I must have fallen asleep on the sofa that night, and the next morning was the usual whirlwind of getting the children's breakfast and taking them to school before I myself carried on to work. I murmured something to the darkened bedroom before I had left the house, trying not to think who was lying under the blankets.

I am not sure how I got through the day. All that I could think of was that my wife had changed. This was a ludicrous proposition, especially as the wedding photograph showed that it was my error. I certainly didn't feel mad, but through the whole day I examined every possibility, and the only one that made any sense was that I had made an error of vast proportions. This did not convince me, of course, and it was with the greatest trepidation that I made my way home that evening. I parked in the garage and stood in the gloom, not wanting to go indoors. Despite the turmoil that my mind was in, I realised that I was not thinking about the dark-haired woman in my house, but of my confusion between the heroines of the film I had seen. It was when I found myself thinking about the last scene that I decided to go indoors.

My daughter greeted me in the hall as though nothing was at all amiss. Indeed, she announced brightly that 'Mummy is feeling better and is up, out of bed.'

I walked through to the kitchen where the dark-haired woman was preparing dinner. My other daughter walked out with a cheery 'hallo' as I walked in, and the woman saw me with a smile. She walked over to me and took my hands in hers.

'You watched that film last night, didn't you?' she asked.

I agreed that I had.

'I understand,' she said. 'We were meant to watch it together, but after all these years you couldn't wait to see if it was the same as you'd remembered it. I hope you don't mind, but when I got out of bed this afternoon I wasn't up to anything other than sitting in front of the television. I decided that I might as well watch the film as well. And you were right; it's astounding, but you didn't remember the end properly, did you?'

I shook my head.

'But you were right about Yvonne . . . she *is* just like me.'

And she hugged me, and although I could not see her face I knew that she was crying. I should have felt love for her, but all that I could think of was the dark garage, and the rage that was growing within me . . .

Blue Glow

David Riley knew that he spent rather too much time watching the world go by as he worked at his desk in the window of his shabby flat. He looked down on a busy city street and in a couple of months he had come to recognise the familiar faces of those who lived and worked there. By their routine he could tell how the hours in the day were progressing. It was all mundane stuff; people in shops and offices coming and going, deliveries being made, and residents leaving and returning to their homes, like his, above the slightly tawdry businesses that lined the pavements.

When David first moved in he had been distraught, but soon began to feel a certain contentedness. Everything had been greatly simplified by his divorce, the failure of his business and his subsequent bankruptcy. It had been a painful, purgative process, but he believed that he had come out of the other side of it all somehow refreshed and ready to start his life again. It was liberating to have lost his debts and the personal and business complications that had surrounded his previous existence. And it was similarly cathartic to find himself without any real possessions. He had no commitments or obligations to anyone and, most important of all for his peace of mind, he had also left behind him the creative drought that had been so damaging to his old business. He might now be working freelance for somebody else, but his new job was genuinely interesting and he was good at it.

But no matter how absorbing his work he could only stare at the computer screen for so long before he had to look away and rub his eyes. He had just turned fifty and acknowledged that he had to take regular breaks. Working from home certainly helped. There was nobody to notice if his mind wandered and he spent rather too long aimlessly staring out of the window and it was one day as he was doing this that he saw the man whom he later believed was called Tedor Pienkowski.

This man on the pavement opposite was in his thirties, wearing sunglasses, and he was casually but expensively dressed. David didn't know why he had caught his attention. Perhaps he had seen him before? The man walked with a certain confidence; almost a swagger. He had his hands in the pockets of light-coloured trousers and David could see that his shirt was hanging out at the front. He was obviously happy, carefree, being light on his feet and almost dancing along the pavement. His head was down, under a hat, but David almost fancied that he could tell the man was singing to himself. He wore a fleece under what looked like a very expensive jacket, and the collar of the fleece was turned up in a way that David's ex-wife would have frowned upon. It was this man's ease that caused him to stand out from the other passers-by.

As the man continued to walk along on the opposite side of the road from David's vantage point he delved into his trouser pocket and pulled out a key-ring which he twirled around his finger several times. Then he turned suddenly through ninety degrees and with his back to his audience fitted one of the keys into the lock of a door that David had not previously noticed. The next moment the man was inside and out of sight. David assumed that it was the entrance to a flat like his own; a flat above either the bookmakers or the jewellers.

David peered at the windows above both of these businesses which were directly opposite and a minute later he saw the man's face. He was looking down along the street, as though expecting to see some-one.

David looked too, and in only a few moments the person who must have been expected appeared. David saw her before the man did because she was approaching on the other side of the street, from the direction of the park, and the angle was in David's favour. She was young and thin, wearing a tight pair of jeans and a white padded jacket trimmed with fur. David guessed that she was on her way to the man's door because her walk was similar to his: confident, expectant. Sure enough she produced her own key and followed where he had previously gone.

David Riley decided that theirs was an assignation and returned to his computer, amused, satisfied that he had guessed what they were up to. It was just another of the many unimportant dramas that he glimpsed from his window.

David didn't see either of them again for another week or two and then it was not from the window of his flat but in the general store at the western end of the road. He had gone in to buy a bottle of wine and was talking with the owner when the man entered. He didn't take off his sunglasses, although it was dark inside the shop, and he selected a bottle of wine with care. When he had made his decision, because David and the owner were still talking, he put a twenty pound note down on the pile of newspapers on the counter between them.

'Great minds think alike,' he said, noticing that David was also clutching a bottle. The man's attention, though, was caught by the young woman walking past the window. He insisted that he was in a hurry and didn't want any change. David thought this recklessly generous until he noticed that there would not have been much change from the twenty-pound note anyway. He paid for his own rather cheaper bottle and left in time to see the man walking by the side of the woman down towards their doorway. For a moment David couldn't understand their body language; there was a calculated distance between them. Then he realised that they were presumably trying to be discreet about their relationship.

At the door the man took out his keys and unlocked it while she looked around them, almost as if she were checking that they were not being followed. If that was her intention then she did not notice that David was walking directly towards them, noting their every movement. He decided that she was very pretty, although the dark make-up around her eyes was not necessarily very flattering.

While she was looking about her the man had opened the door and, as she had not noticed, he placed a kiss on her cheek and rushed inside. Playfully she protested and stamped in after him. Once again they were gone.

And as before David Riley forgot all about them, and it might have been three or four weeks before he saw the couple again, together for the last time. He was returning home from a meeting at the offices of his new employers and the two of them were standing outside of their door. As he recognised who they were she turned away from the man and walked decisively off towards the park. He was staring after her and even with his back to David he could see by the man's posture that he was upset. David continued to walk towards him, warily now, and was about to cross to his own side of the road when she disappeared around the far corner. The man turned and they recognised each other. David didn't know if the man knew him to be a neighbour, but he shook his head slowly, sorrowfully, and went back inside his door.

That night David noticed that there was a dull blue light in the windows of the flat over the road. He had not noticed it before and was fascinated. He stood at his own window, his lights off, and watched. Twice David saw the man looking out; he appeared to be bare-chested, with a glass in his hand, and he stared down the street as if hoping that the woman would return. It was from this date that David began to look out for him regularly, and he saw him leave about noon the following day.

Usually the curtains were drawn in the flat opposite, although the blue light crept around the edges of the curtains at night. However, he didn't see the man himself for perhaps another week, when he appeared in the street carrying a plastic bag emblazoned with the name of an expensive local wine merchant. It may have been that David had missed the man's comings and goings and this annoyed him. He knew that for some reason he wanted to make his acquaintance, although he did not understand how he might do so, or why.

206

Quite who the man might be nagged at David, and the following week he decided to make some enquiries. He wondered if he might get information from the staff working in the bookmakers below the flat, and to that end he looked in the newspaper and, turning to the racing pages, found a horse upon which to put a bet. He didn't want to spend anything other than the minimum amount so he chose a horse with long odds and went over the road. In fifty years it was his first time inside a betting shop and it seemed rather dark and seedy. The old man behind the counter peered at him threateningly and asked if he could help. David stammered out the name of the horse and the race, and received a very suspicious stare in return, presumably because it was such an unlikely runner. He then failed to find anything other than a large note in his wallet and felt so intimidated that he didn't consider that he could ask for change.

'To win?' asked the man, incredulous.

'Each way,' said David, attempting to make the bet easier to justify. He felt foolish, but nevertheless he had the courage to ask if the old man knew the name of the people in the accommodation above.

'I should do. It's my flat,' the bookmaker said shortly, still suspicious. 'He's got some foreign name. But he's not renewing his lease. It's a pity; he's renovated it, and decorated it nice. He put in a whole new kitchen and bathroom. I could do with another tenant as good as him.'

'It'll be for rent then?' David asked.

'Yes. Do you want to go up and see it?'

David said that he did. He explained that he only lived over the road, but made the excuse that he was looking for something better in the same area.

'I'll get you a key and you can go and take a look. He won't mind. He's never there.'

The old man disappeared into the back of the shop and eventually reappeared with the key. 'Make sure the door's locked properly when you've finished.'

David was pleased to be out of the bookmakers and his pulse raced as he stood outside the front door to the flat. He knocked first to make certain that nobody was at home, but when he unlocked it he felt as though he were trespassing, even though he had the landlord's permission. David didn't know what to expect inside, but it was surprisingly airy and modern. It was very simply and very tastefully furnished, but the bedroom appeared to be in the large front room where most people would have had their living room. It was dominated by a large bed covered by a heavy dark blue bedspread. What he would have expected to be the bedroom contained just an exercise bike and nothing else. The place didn't tell him much, but if the price was right he was indeed tempted to take it. His own flat, while serving its purpose of accommodating a single later-middle-aged man, was cramped and in poor repair. His kitchen was particularly old-fashioned and he rather coveted this one with its expensive-looking units and modern appliances. Over the years he had always told himself that his surroundings didn't particularly matter to him, but the contrast between the two flats made him envious. The only thing in favour of his present position was that it was furnished, and he supposed that he would have to buy new furniture if he were to move.

He looked up and noticed that there was a curious light fitting in the centre of the ceiling. He flicked the switch by the door and three blue bulbs winked on. He was pleased to understand the strange illumination he had seen from his own flat opposite.

As David was considering the impracticality of the lights he heard keys in the lock down below. He automatically backed further into the living room, feeling like an intruder. He heard the door open and close, and somebody started to climb the stairs. Although he told himself that he was there with the permission of the landlord, David wasn't looking forward to explaining his presence.

'Hello,' he said, awkwardly, as the tenant of the flat reached the top of his stairs.

'Who the hell are you?' the man asked, stopping, surprised and suspicious. 'What are you doing here?'

'The landlord told me I could come up and look around. He said you were moving out?' David held out the key for him to see.

'The old bastard could've waited 'til I was gone.'

'I'm sorry, he said it would be alright?'

The man looked around him.

'I suppose it is,' he said, a little mournfully, calmer. 'There's nothing for me here any longer. I don't even know why I've come back today.'

'You've somewhere else to move to?'

'What?' he asked, appearing to have already forgotten that David was there. He was rubbing his eyes under his sunglasses, which he still retained although he was indoors.

'Have you another flat to go to?'

He laughed. 'We don't know each other, do we?'

'No,' David replied, defensively.

'Good. Then I can tell you that I do have somewhere to go to, yes. I have a family. This was somewhere for myself, somewhere private.'

'Ah, I understand.'

He looked searchingly into David's face: 'Good.'

'But it didn't work out?'

'You could put it that way, she . . . well . . . You don't want to hear it.'

'It's okay. I think I saw you a couple of times. I just live over the road. My place is in poor repair, and I'm looking for something better.'

'We were trying to be discreet.'

'Don't worry, I don't know anyone to tell.'

The man shook his head, considered, and then said:

'It isn't possible to communicate to somebody else just how terribly you can be in love, is it? Intellectually somebody might say that they understand. Perhaps they can try and relate it to their own experience? But that unique feeling of exultation when you're in love can't ever, ever, be appreciated by anyone else. Perhaps it can't even be appreciated by the person you're in love with . . . ? And when it goes wrong, when you are still as furiously in love, but you find yourself thwarted; it is as though you are falling, forever from a tall building . . .'

'I'm recently divorced,' David said, wanting to suggest that the man didn't have a monopoly on bad experiences.

'I'm sorry. Did you love her?'

The question took David aback. It seemed like such a stupid one, to which he ought to have retorted 'Yes, of course,' but he acknowledged that it would have been more honest to say that he had simply been fond of his ex-wife.

'Not passionately,' he admitted.

'That's the difference between us, then. I'd say that my love for Alice is, was, a vast, magnificent love that rips through my whole being.'

He walked across the main room to the window and peered out, distracted.

'I'd better leave,' David said quietly, and the man nodded, without looking at him.

David Riley was very tempted to take the flat, but told the landlord that he would think about it. The more he thought about moving over the road the more certain he became that it was a good idea. He hoped that some of its elegance, and that of its former tenant, might rub off on him. It was when he had returned to his own dilapidated accommodation after that first awkward viewing that he could see how substandard his own place was in comparison. And he knew that the seediness of it had transferred itself to him personally. Since he had been there, living alone, working from home, he could spend several days without seeing anybody and he had started to neglect himself and his appearance. He was getting overweight, and was no longer shaving every day. The way that he looked could be rectified immediately, he decided, and the following day he made sure that he shaved, showered and put on smarter clothes.

He was confident that he presented an altogether better appearance when he went out. It was an omen, he hoped, discovering in the newspaper that the horse upon which he had placed his bet had miraculously come in third. He felt some confidence as he went in to the bookmakers this time, and while the old man begrudged him his winnings he seemed genuinely interested that David might have had some inside knowledge. Buoyed up by his good fortune, David agreed to the old man's terms for the flat and put most of his winnings down as a deposit on the rooms above. With what remained of the money he went and had a haircut.

He and the landlord agreed on a date of the 30th July for moving in, a Monday, and David calculated that he had just less than three weeks to make all of the arrangements. He was given a key so that he could go in at any time and measure up, but this felt a little strange as the present tenant presumably still had his belongings in there. Over the next few weeks David didn't see the man in the street, though, and at night there was no longer any blue light around the curtains which were permanently drawn.

The three weeks before he could move into the flat passed slowly, partly because David became more and more critical of the rooms he was about to leave. He was constantly tempted to go over the road to look inside his new flat again, but could never summon up the courage in case the old tenant was still there after all. Finally the thirtieth of July arrived and he had his few possessions boxed and ready move. At nine in the morning an old friend, Julie, arrived to help him, as she had insisted.

They each took a box across the road to the flat and let themselves in from the street and climbed the stairs. Julie went ahead, chatting all the time, but stopped just inside the door to the front room.

'What's wrong?' David asked, and she stood to one side so that he could see. The curtains were closed but some light came in, mixed with the blue light from the ceiling, and revealed that lying on the bed in the large, elegant room, was a naked man. He was on his front, gently snoring, and David did not immediately identify him as the previous tenant.

Julie and David started to withdraw quietly, but the man awoke, peered over and saw them. He looked confused, and realising his nakedness he dragged the sheets over himself.

'What the hell?' he asked. He groped for his glasses almost blindly, located them on the bedside table and put them on. Turning, he recognised David. 'It's you?'

'Yes,' David replied, trying not to look too surprised by the situation in which he found himself. 'I'm meant to be moving in today.'

'No,' the man insisted, slightly groggily. 'It's only the 30th today.'

'That's the date I was given by the landlord.'

'But the stupid idiot told me I'd got 'til the end of the month.'

'Ah,' said Julie, obviously amused by the scene she was witnessing. 'There are 31 days in July.'

'Do you think the landlord knows this?' David asked. Julie was the only one who felt comfortable enough to laugh.

'We haven't been introduced,' the man said to Julie. 'My name is Tedor Pienkowski. I am pleased to meet you. I would get up and shake your hand . . .'

She turned red and giggled.

'Give me a moment to get dressed,' he asked. 'And we'll decide what we are doing.'

David and Julie agreed, and moved into the kitchen.

'I suppose I might as well leave today,' the man called after them, as if it was of little concern to him.

'Well, I don't have to move in until tomorrow,' David countered. 'Although the overlap would've been useful, I could leave it until then.'

The man did not reply and a second later was overcome with a fit of coughing.

Neither Julie nor David put down the boxes they were holding. They listened as he continued to cough intermittently, and in between they could hear him moving around.

'Are you okay?' David asked. 'If you don't mind me saying, you seem unwell.'

'Since Alice left me,' he eventually called back, but did not continue the sentence.

'We can return later,' David repeated. 'You'll need some time to remove your things. Have you got people to help you move?'

'No, no people,' he admitted, appearing in the doorway, dressed. 'I've only got a few bits and pieces here anyway. A bed, a wardrobe, these chairs and a table. Obviously I'm not going to take them back home . . . Do you want them?'

'Well, not really. I've got a new bed being delivered tomorrow.'

'Cancel it. Save yourself the money. Have everything here for nothing. I'd only have to pay to get rid of it.'

'Well, if it helps . . . ?'

'It will,' he assured David.

Julie put her box on the table and while David still held his she looked around the kitchen admiringly.

'I'll leave my key with you,' he said, offering it to David, who now had to put his own box down before accepting it. 'Please, return it to the landlord for me? I won't be back.'

'Are you sure you want to leave everything?' David asked.

'Quite sure,' he said. 'I hope you are happy here. There were times when I certainly was.'

'That's very generous of you,' David started to thank him, but this was dismissed by an impatient gesture of the hand.

'Goodbye,' the man said, then turned and went down the stairs.

'Goodbye,' David called and listened as the door was opened at the bottom of the stairs and then shut.

'Blimey,' he said, incredulous.

'Don't complain,' Julie insisted, and pushed past him, back into the front room. He followed her and watched as she ran her hand over the end of the bed: a substantial and expensive-looking example in steel and brass. David watched her looking at the few tasteful pictures on the walls, and nodded towards the discreet hi-fi system in the corner of the room.

He walked over and looked into the drawers of the nearest bedside cabinet and found them to be empty.

'This is really odd,' he said. He assumed that he had also taken over what looked like expensive linen on the bed. The dark blue bedspread was heavy with a faint paisley pattern and he ran his hand over it appreciatively. Pulling it back he could see a dent in the mattress and wondered if that was quite as good quality as the sheets, which he would have to wash and use himself—his own were probably too small for the bed.

'He's left all of his clothes in here,' Julie pointed out as she looked through the wardrobe. 'And some shoes.'

David was having to take his time and consider the implications of what had happened. He watched Julie pad excitedly back to the kitchen.

'Did you notice that he couldn't see without his sunglasses on,' she asked.

'They must be prescription glasses: tinted.'

'There's a fancy coffee-maker in here,' she called through. 'And a juicer, and a microwave. He's left everything. You've done rather well,' she assured him. 'Oh, and there's a couple of bottles of champagne in the fridge. Perhaps we should open one to celebrate your good fortune?'

When they had finished exploring, Julie with excitement, and David with some wariness, not quite believing what had happened, they moved his boxes in from over the road. Later that morning his new bed arrived and he turned away the disgruntled delivery-men. For lunch she had brought sandwiches and they shared a bottle of the champagne before he took his time arranging his few possessions. She amused herself by discovering those left behind by the former tenant.

'Tedor Pienkowski,' she announced. 'It's written on a business card here on the windowsill. Sounds Polish?'

'It could be. Did you think he had an accent?'

'I don't know, but he had money. All these things he's left behind are good quality and barely-used.'

'It was a love-nest,' David explained, taking his turn to look into the wardrobe at the expensive clothes that made his own look rather tawdry. He eased on a very smart, comfortable jacket.

'I can't help but think he'll see sense at some point and come back.'

Julie admired the jacket, straightening the lapels and saying that it suited him. She brushed it down and noticed that there was something in the pocket. She fished out what appeared to be a piece of torn blue silk, and inside it was a gold ring.

'You've got to get this back to him,' she said. 'This looks personal.'

'I suppose that the landlord might have a forwarding address,' he agreed.

But the landlord had no address for Tedor Pienkowski. He simply had a business card like the one left in the flat with a name and mobile phone number on it, but there was no other information and the number was inoperative. David tried directory enquiries, to no avail, and the following day asked at the City Hall, but they could not locate anyone with the name Pienkowski living in the city. Widening his search he obtained the phone numbers of several Pienkowskis in the country, but none admitted to knowing anybody with the first name Tedor.

David had unpacked some of his boxes, but he liked the uncluttered feel of the flat that the man had left behind him. The new tenant set up his computer and most of his possessions in the small back bedroom and allowed the large bed to remain dominating the front room. When Julie visited some weeks later she told him that he had kept the place unchanged out of guilt, or fear, that Tedor Pienkowski might return. He disagreed, but had to admit that he was in some ways modelling himself on an idealised version of the former tenant. A part of him was uncomfortable doing so, but he felt better for using the man's exercise bike to get into shape, wearing his expensive shirts, trousers and jackets, and he gained in confidence as a result. It had been very strange to wear somebody else's clothes at first, but he soon thought of them as his own. When he next went in to the office he even had the self-belief

215

to mention a project that he had been working on privately and somehow managed to persuade them to take it up. A half-hour meeting stretched over the whole afternoon and he came away with an offer of a full-time, permanent position, a very good salary, and his own room in their offices.

Julie admitted that he was a changed man, more assured, and she was obviously taking an interest in him. He was not inclined to reciprocate, but her feelings towards him further added to his confidence. He had long thought that she was the plainest woman he had ever met, but he wondered if with such a blank canvas for a face, something might be done for her with the careful application of a little more make-up?

It was a month later, when he returned home from work, that David met Alice. For perhaps the first time since he had moved into his flat, David had not thought of Tedor Pienkowski at all that day. He had spent the morning worrying about a meeting that he was having with his bosses, but that afternoon his ideas had been well-received and he knew that they would be acted upon. He had walked home looking at himself in the shop windows and not even glimpsing a slight reflection of Pienkowski in the image that he now presented. Remembering the other bottle of champagne in his fridge he decided that he would open it on his return and perhaps ask Julie around to share it with him. The only reason he could think of for not doing so was the fear that she would see it as an encouragement to her obvious feelings for him.

As he let himself into the flat and bounded up the stairs he was considering how to re-start his social life outside of the new friends he had made at the office, where he seemed to be well-liked. The idea of the champagne was in the back of his mind as he wondered whether he wanted to meet up with his old friends at all, or start completely afresh. He threw the keys on the kitchen table, took down one of the champagne flutes he had inherited from Pienkowski and removed the bottle from the fridge. Starting to open the foil around the top, still lost in thought, he turned and nearly dropped the bottle when he saw that somebody was standing in the kitchen doorway.

'I had to come back,' she said disconsolately, her head down as she stared intently at her sandals. She was wearing a shirt patterned all over with rosebuds, and a pair of jeans.

David didn't know what to say. It took him a second to recognise her. She looked up slowly and started when she saw that he was not Pienkowski.

'Who are you?' she asked, her hand on her heart, backing away.

'I live here.'

'But where's Tedor?'

'He moved out about a month ago.'

'But all of his stuff is still here.'

'He left it all behind when he went.'

'Where did he go?'

'I don't know. He didn't leave a forwarding address.'

'You're even wearing his suit,' she noticed, incredulous, her retreat halted.

'As I said, he left all his things.'

David put down the bottle and she stood glaring at him, which he found disconcerting. She had no right to be there, in what was now his home, and yet he felt that he was the intruder.

'You still have a key?' he asked.

'Yes, he gave it to me. I assumed he was still here.'

'I'm sorry,' David said. 'But there's something he might *not* have meant to leave. It might be yours.'

She frowned.

'I'll get it,' he insisted, and she backed further away onto the top stair as he walked towards and then nervously around her into the front room. On the bedside table there was the piece of blue silk in which the ring was still wrapped. She had not followed him in so he walked back and handed it to her.

'Is it yours?'

She looked down at the piece of silk without opening it and her face crumbled. She almost groped her way past him to the bed before falling on to it, weeping uncontrollably.

It was not a situation to which David had any idea of how to react. He did not know this woman, and she was, after all, in his flat. He decided to take off his jacket and hung it up in the wardrobe. Then he took off his shoes and put them out in the hall. When he returned to the woman she was still sobbing.

'Can I get you anything?' he asked.

She sat up, unwillingly, and wiped her eyes on the sleeves of her shirt. Eventually she replied:

'You were opening a bottle?'

He agreed and went back to the kitchen, grateful to have something to do. He wasn't sure if the champagne was expensive or cheap, but he had been about to open it anyway. The cork came out quietly and he filled two flutes, which he then took back into the front room.

'I assume you're Alice?' he asked, handing over the glass.

'Yes, Tedor told you about me?'

'He said that you were in love, but you broke up?'

'Yes. I wasn't meant to come back. I promised him. And now you have no address for him?'

'No. I'm sorry.'

'He was an extraordinary man,' she said, quietly. 'It wasn't like any other love.'

'He said that.'

'I really do believe that he loved me with a passion, and an intensity, that no man has ever had for a woman before.'

The suggestion that their love was somehow better than anybody else's annoyed David.

'Why did you break up then?' he asked.

'Because it was too intense.'

'Oh, I see,' he replied, changing his tone to one of sarcasm, although she did not seem to notice it.

'No, you don't,' she said simply. 'When I first met Tedor he acted so oddly,' she explained. 'He seemed to like me, to seek me out, but then he would shun me. At first he said that we couldn't have a relationship because I was married. I said I'd leave my husband for him, but he insisted I shouldn't. This went on for a while and nothing happened between us. Can you imagine what it is for two people to be so attracted to each other, and to not even touch?'

David shrugged, knowing she wasn't looking at him and wasn't really interested in his opinions.

'And then one night we gave in. We could never remember who succumbed first, or whether we both did at the same instant.'

After a pause she sipped her champagne and looked up at him. 'I am sorry. Is this embarrassing you?'

'No,' he said, and then added, maliciously, 'It doesn't really interest me.'

She could not fail to understand his tone this time. She put her wine on the bedside table and stood up.

'No, and why should it interest you?' she asked. 'You've just taken over the outside, surface appearance of Tedor. You could never understand the man that he was.'

She was waiting for a reply, and she gave David time to consider it. He took a moment to imagine how the former tenant would have acted. After all, he was no longer the rather bitter failure who had once been the old David Riley, but was the rather more confident successor. This woman was in distress, in his flat, and he should be acting more sympathetically. He remembered something of what Tedor Pienkowski had said to him and repeated it by way of explanation:

'No, I don't understand the man he was. He was obviously in love with you and it just isn't possible for another person to understand the love that somebody else feels. They might say they understand, relating it to their own experience, but being in love is unique, and sometimes terrible.'

He spoke slowly and calmly and at the end she was nodding. He decided to embellish the truth a little.

'Tedor and I discussed love. We discussed the exultation you feel when in love, and we discussed the awfulness of it when it all goes wrong. He said that the feeling in your stomach is as though you're falling, forever from a tall building . . .'

She looked puzzled: 'But you said you were not interested?'

'I apologise. That wasn't the word I should've used. I should have said that I could never understand, or appreciate, what happened between the two of you, because it was so intensely personal. Just as you couldn't hope to understand the love that I have felt at times in my life. You talked about external appearances, and yes, perhaps that's all we ever understand of anyone, no matter how close we get to them.'

'That's what Tedor used to say,' she agreed. 'He insisted that we were closer than any two people had ever been, and yet we could not fully understand how the other felt.'

She sat back down on the bed and reached for her glass. David sat beside her and she didn't seem to mind.

'I'm married, with two children,' she said. 'I've always thought of affairs as seedy, distasteful things that people have when they're bored with their husbands or wives and don't have the courage to do anything about it. But I do love my husband, and I would do anything not to upset my children. But my love for Tedor . . . It sounds like I'm making excuses, justifying myself, but it isn't . . . wasn't . . . like that. What we had was beautiful, special . . .'

'And you offered to leave your husband for him?' David asked, as sympathetically as he could.

'Yes. I was willing to explore the idea. But really, ideally, I wanted everything. I was unrealistic, I knew it then and know it now. I want my family and I want him. I want them both at the same time.'

'But if you had to choose?'

'Then I would choose Tedor. I should have chosen him while he was here. Now it's too late and I don't have a choice.'

'But when you told him you would leave your husband, he said no?'

She took another sip of her drink and then nodded.

'Why was that?' he asked, quietly.

She sniffed: 'I don't know.'

'He said something to me about his family.'

'He had a family, but I don't think he had a wife, children . . .'

'But you're not sure?'

'He said that he didn't, and I believed him.'

'So why didn't he want you to leave your husband?' David asked as patiently as he could.

'Because he said he was no good for me.'

'Not worthy?'

This time she took a sip of her drink and then shook her head.

'No,' she said. 'I mean yes, you're right. Not worthy. . . .'

David got off the bed and walked out to get the bottle from the fridge. He was interested to learn more of Pienkowski, although a little ashamed at himself.

With her glass refilled Alice turned and drew her legs up under herself on the bed. With her free hand she smoothed down the bedspread.

'Tedor said that if I tried coming back to him he'd be gone.'

She looked around the room.

'Actually, I love the fact that you've changed nothing in here. It's almost like he's still here. You've even kept the blue lights.'

'Yes. I ought to change them. They're not bright enough, but they create a nice atmosphere.'

'It was because of his eyes. He couldn't stand certain higher wavelengths of light. But you're right. The blue gives the room a kind of calm. And he chose things for the room that went well in that light.'

'It was very generous of him to leave it all.'

'He was always very generous. This shirt I'm wearing is one that he bought for me when we were first together. Even these jeans, these shoes. . . . They were all very expensive, and I had problems explaining these gifts to my husband. I always told him they were cheaper than they were, or that I'd bought them in charity shops.'

'And how did you explain the ring?'

'I never showed him. And then I gave it back to Tedor when we parted.'

'But it is rightfully yours. You'd better take it.'

'No, as I say, I gave it back to him. If he passed everything on to you then it is yours.'

'I would like you to have it,' he said, believing that it was the right thing to do.

'No. It was very expensive. I could accept it from him as an expression of his love, but not from you.'

And then David felt angry. Did she think he was trying to give her the ring as an expression of his own love? He didn't know what to think, but she was obviously comparing him with Pienkowski and finding him wanting, deciding that he was the lesser man.

'I'm afraid I have to leave,' he suddenly said. 'Finish the champagne and let yourself out.'

She started to cry and he went into the hall and put his shoes back on. Returning to the front room he took the jacket out of the wardrobe and tried not to notice that rather than prepare to leave, she had in fact, got into the bed and was crying into his pillow.

David left the flat and walked for perhaps two miles, all the way into the city centre and out to the river. For a while he watched the sluggish black water flow between the warehouses and then he went for a drink in a dreary public house that was almost empty. With reluctance he walked back to his flat, taking his time in the hope that Alice would be gone. It was dark when he returned and he could see that the lights were on in the flat above the bookmakers. When he climbed the stairs he was annoyed to find that she was now in his bed, apparently asleep. Not only had she left the lights on but music was quietly playing. Her empty glass was on the bedside table alongside the ring on top of the piece of blue silk.

David went into the kitchen and poured himself some more champagne. Alice had returned the bottle to the fridge and had fixed on the top an elaborate stopper that he had previously seen in the drawer but

222

had not known how to use. He finished the champagne before starting on a cheap bottle of red that Julie had given him as a flat-warming present.

After a half-hour of drinking, with ill-humour, he went and turned off the lights in the front room, along with the music, and took a pillow from beside Alice. He then pulled the cushions off the chair and made himself an uncomfortable bed in the back room. When he returned to the front room he removed the blue bedspread, not caring if he woke her up. He knew that in the morning he would ache from sleeping on cushions on the floor, but assumed, correctly, that the alcohol he had drunk would help him get through the night.

The following morning David did not experience too much of a hangover, but ached terribly, as he had predicted. When he went into the front room Alice had left and he was glad. His routine had been upset and he was up an hour before he would normally have been getting ready for the office. He didn't think that he would be able to go back to sleep, however, so went about shaving, having a shower and breakfast, and decided that he might as well go into work early. His personal office there was still something of a novelty after so long working from home.

When he was ready and came to open his front door he was startled to see Tedor Pienkowski standing there, about to stuff an envelope through the letter box.

'Hello,' said David, amused to see that, if anything, Pienkowski was even more surprised by their meeting than he was. 'What's this?'

The man looked worried and asked if he could come inside for a moment. David had the distinct impression that the man did not want to be seen out in the street with him. He was still wearing his trademark sunglasses.

'I have some things for you,' said Pienkowski, having to edge around the door in the confined space before pushing it closed behind him. 'But, can I ask, first, did you sleep with Alice last night?'

'No!' David surprised himself at the volume of his denial. They were standing in the very cramped area between the door and the bottom stair so David moved back up onto the first step to put more distance between the two of them. The extra elevation, however, was disconcerting.

'Why do you ask?'

Pienkowski tried to dismiss the subject with a wave of his left hand while he proffered an envelope with his right.

'You should contact Alice,' David insisted. 'You've hurt her badly.'

'I know, I know. But things have happened. And I need to tell you that my name isn't Pienkowski.'

'No?'

'No. I used a false name to protect myself, and Alice. Now I have to go back to my old name and my old life. So I don't need my Pienkowski identity, and I thought that you might like it.'

'Why would I want your old identity?'

He shrugged:

'I have a car registered in that name, and a bank account. I don't want them and don't need them. The details are in this envelope and you should take them, and use them.'

David accepted the envelope out of curiosity and the man made the awkward manoeuvre to re-open the door in the confined space and squeeze around it to leave.

'But hang on,' David said. 'Can I ask a couple of questions?'

'I have to go,' the man insisted, and was back in the street and walking quickly away.

David followed him out, locking the door behind him. He took his usual route to the office, resolving not to look into the dubious envelope until he was at his desk. He settled himself in his new room with a coffee and closed the door. When he tipped the contents of the envelope out before him he found a set of car keys and a note to the effect that they were for a green E-type Jaguar that was parked in a garage near the flat. There was also a log book, MOT certificate and the insurance paperwork. In another envelope were details of a bank account in the name of Pienkowski, including the PIN number and a card for withdrawing cash.

During the day David considered the implications of what the man appeared to be offering him. He certainly did not want to take over the fictional identity of Tedor Pienkowski, but he could quite clearly see that all he had to do was go to an ATM machine and draw out whatever money was in the account. And as he didn't drive he could sell the car, bank the cheque in Pienkowki's name, and likewise remove the funds from the account once they had cleared. What he had not been able to work out, though, was why the man who had masqueraded as Pienkowski had not done this himself? Did he not need the money?

If these questions occupied his thoughts all day, then there was another which also nagged at him. The man had asked whether David had slept with Alice the previous night, but he hadn't appeared particularly jealous. The obvious implication was that the man knew she had been at the flat. Had he been watching them? Perhaps he had only been following her?

That evening David did not go home directly, but went out of his way to pass by the bank and check on the balance of the account that was in the name of Pienkowski. He had not tried to guess what the sum might be and was astounded to find that it was just over seven thousand pounds. He then went to the lock-up garage and discovered that he did, indeed, have the keys and ownership papers for a vintage E-type Jaguar that appeared to be beautifully maintained.

Rather than go straight home he visited Julie and explained what had happened. Once again she was more enthusiastic than he was about his good fortune.

'But is it all legal?' he asked.

'I don't see that it's *illegal*. The money and car were his and he's every right to give them to you, if he wants to.'

'But why should he do that?'

'I don't know. He must have a good reason.'

225

When David said that he was going home Julie seemed reluctant to let him leave, and somehow they ended up compromising on her walking back to his flat with him. She insisted that he buy a bottle of wine on the way and she put her arm through his in a proprietorial manner that made him feel uncomfortable. Once again he looked at his reflection in the shop windows and was not sure that they looked right as a couple. Their steps were in time, though, and she nestled disconcertingly well against him as they walked. There seemed something inevitable about what was going to happen and he felt a dread of which he was ashamed. He reluctantly opened the door to the flat and watched as she seemed excited and eager to get inside. Her spirit, though, was dampened immediately she walked into the front room and found Alice lying on the bed.

'What are you doing here?' Julie demanded.

'It's nice to see you,' David said, relieved. 'Would you like to join us in a drink?'

Alice smiled at him as though Julie was not there, and accepted.

'Tedor has given me his car,' David told her.

'Why's that?'

'I've no idea. Nothing he does makes sense to me.'

Julie gave her opinion:

'I don't think David should worry about questioning it. Never look a gift horse in the mouth.'

They both turned to her, and she stared back at them.

'What did I say?' she asked, annoyed.

'Nothing,' said David, and Alice agreed.

'No, come on,' Julie insisted, and Alice looked down and bit her lip, stifling a laugh.

'What's so funny?' Julie demanded, and then turned to David. 'What's she laughing at?'

'I don't know, really I don't.'

'Come on, what does she find so funny?'

David looked at Alice and then back at Julie. It was cruel and he couldn't help but say it: 'You, presumably.'

'I'm not stupid,' she explained. 'I can see when I'm not wanted.' To which neither David nor Alice replied.

'I'll go then?' she offered. Her anger turned to tears when he politely offered to pay the taxi fare for her to go home.

David and Alice watched together at the window as Julie walked off up the road, having just stumped down the stairs and slammed the front door after her. He looked over to his old flat where the curtains were drawn closed, in time to see them moving, as though somebody had been looking out of them right up until that very moment. He had the idea that whoever it was had also been watching Julie walk away. David thought of how he had sat at that window, not so long ago, watching people coming and going.

They drank the wine while standing looking down into the street and, although David tried to listen to what Alice was saying, he found himself giving all of his attention to the curtained windows of the flat opposite, wondering who its new occupant might be. He occasionally thought that he noticed a slight movement, but he certainly could not make out who might be there. As it became darker, however, he began to notice that around the edges of the curtains there was a slight blue glow. To anybody walking down the road and looking up it might have been assumed that there was a television on behind the curtains of a darkened flat, but the light didn't flicker or move. He knew that Alice had seen it too, and when she said she had to leave he begged her to stay. She insisted that she had to get back to her family and he watched her go from his vantage point by the window, expecting her to cross the road. However, she walked off up the road, and though he watched for a long time she did not return.

David went to bed late that night. The light still crept around the edge of the curtains opposite, but tiredness finally overcame him. The next morning he looked out and could see nothing, although he watched the windows and the door to the flat until the last possible moment before leaving for work. That evening he returned early and set up a vigil once again, but still he saw nobody. Again, in the evening when it was dark, he could see blue edging the curtains.

There was only one conclusion to draw and he decided that he had a right to know what was going on. He left his own flat and walked across the road. Without taking any time to think of what he night say he rapped on the door and waited, but nobody answered. It was a pattern that was repeated for the next two nights, and then, as he sat at the window in the early evening towards the end of the week he saw Julie approaching. He wasn't sure if he would admit to being in; he knew that he had treated her badly, but he missed female company. He had not seen Alice and did not know if he would see her again.

Julie walked along the pavement opposite, but rather than cross the road she knocked on the door to his old flat. It was opened almost immediately by the man who had called himself Pienkowski. Julie disappeared inside upon an instant.

David was furious. He left his own flat once more and strode across the road. He again rapped on the door before standing back a pace and crossing his arms defiantly. He was ready for an argument, though he did not know on what basis it would be conducted. When nobody answered he rapped again, and still there was no response. Were they up above him at the window, looking down, perhaps laughing? He had the courage to look up, but the angle was wrong and he would have had to step out into the street to see if anybody was really there. Suddenly feeling foolish he did not want to be seen and so he slunk back down the road and walked around until it was dark. He bought himself a bottle of wine in the general store before returning home, not daring to look back across the road.

David did not see Julie leave the flat that night. He sat back in his room with his curtains open and the lights off so that he could observe without being observed, but the drawn curtains opposite seemed to mock him. Again, the following morning, Friday, he saw nobody before he went to work, and that evening there was still no movement, and certainly no visitors. The following day, Saturday, he watched listlessly and was surprised when there was a knocking at his door. He had not seen anybody arrive, and was happy to discover that his visitor was Alice.

'I thought I'd better knock,' she said, 'rather than let myself in with my own keys.'

He let her pass, and she climbed the stair. He detected that her manner was somehow strange.

'I'm rather relying on you to have some wine,' she said.

'I do have a bottle, though it's still a little early.'

Alice walked through to the kitchen, took off her coat and leant against the table.

'I've left my husband,' she said, biting her bottom lip and trying not to cry.

'For Tedor?'

'No. I haven't seen him. I don't want to know where he is, or what he's done.'

David frowned, but said nothing. He opened the bottle and got out two glasses.

'I know where he . . .' he started to say.

'I don't want to know,' she insisted.

'Okay,' he agreed, and passed her a glass.

She drank half of it in one gulp and looked at him.

'So what are you going to do?' he asked.

'I was wondering if I could stay here?'

David nodded, and she smiled.

'I've always liked it here,' she said. 'I've decided that you're not like Tedor.'

He did not know what to think. She was young and good-looking, but, like the money and the car he had accepted from Tedor, he was suspicious of her. His apparent good-fortune was not something he trusted at all.

He motioned towards the front room and she followed him. When he was back at the window he could still see no movement at the flat

229

opposite, and he looked both up and down the road in case any of the pedestrians happened to be the man or Julie.

'Is that my ring?' Alice asked, standing just behind him. On the windowsill was the piece of blue silk.

'Yes. And I still think you should take it,' he said, not turning around.

'I will accept it from you,' she said.

When he tried to turn he brushed against her. She was standing closer than he had realised and she had unbuttoned her shirt. She took his hand and placed it on her breast.

With an attractive young woman pressing herself against him David was unable to think of anything other than a natural desire. She kissed him once, and then covering herself up leant past him and started to pull the curtains closed. He noticed as it became darker inside that she must have already turned on the blue ceiling lights. She was closing the second curtain when he noticed that outside Julie was letting herself out of the flat on the opposite side of the road. He had nearly missed her!

He apologised to Alice and insisted he would return, but ran out of the room, down the stairs and then out onto the street. Julie was about to turn the corner at the top of the road and he had to run to catch up with her.

'Julie, stop!'

She wouldn't halt so he grabbed her arm and turned her around.

'What were you doing over the road?' he insisted.

'Where?'

'In my old flat, with him.'

'None of your business,' she said, dismissive.

'But what's he doing over there?'

She shrugged David off and started to walk away, quickly: 'That's personal.'

'But why did he want to change places with me?' David asked, catching up and walking alongside her, matching her brisk pace. When she stopped he was taken by surprise and had to stop too and turn to face her.

'You really don't understand, do you?'

'No.'

She paused and looked up, obviously trying to decide on what to say. At last she met his eyes and asked:

'Do you still have his blue lightbulbs in your living room?'

'Yes,' he replied, defensively. 'I haven't got around to changing them yet.'

Julie smiled at him and with a very slight shake of the head said with pity in her voice:

'If you don't know now, then you never will.'

And then she turned and walked away, slowly now, knowing that he would not follow her.

A Revelation

I spent nearly forty years working for the District Council in their Housing Department, and now that I've retired I look back and wonder whether I wasted my life there? It was a good, secure job, but do I have anything to show for all that time? It wasn't as though I particularly enjoyed my job, or had colleagues that I considered good friends.

I recently saw my successor, Leadley, and though he passed on news of a few people I remembered, he admitted that nothing much had changed since I left.

'I bet you've a great fund of anecdotes about our old tenants,' he suggested.

'When I first started in the Department I found all the tenants fascinating,' I admitted. 'I remember on my first day in the job visiting the house of a man who had removed his living-room ceiling and painted his floor joists to look like beams. He'd plastered the underside of the floorboards, but as his family walked around upstairs great chunks of plaster fell down into the room below.'

'Well, we still have some pretty strange tenants today.'

'I'm sure you do. Collins always used to say how endlessly fascinating they were; all of those bizarre relationships, hobbies and pets you'd come across. But, somehow, for me they quickly merged into a grey monotony of humanity.'

'Oh,' he said, as surprised as I was at my miserable tone.

I decided to play up to the idea of the grumpy old man and with a smile added:

'For me the job was only ever enlivened by the occasional appearance of an outside lavatory that the council should've long ago condemned.'

He chose to interpret my comments as a joke and took the opportunity to laugh and leave, but I was being honest. In all those years there was only one tenant who had really stayed in my mind, and that was an occupant of 49 Coast Road.

I first visited the address when we were undertaking a survey of all the council's housing stock, to see what state it was in and where our maintenance priorities lay. Many of the houses have been sold off, of course, but the survey dragged on over the summer and into the autumn and in the end even I was hauled out of the office to try and get it finished before the winter set in. The survey wasn't popular amongst the staff and it wasn't going down too well with the tenants, either; most of them saw it as the council snooping on them.

It was a thankless job; various members of staff took it in turns to go out, and usually looked around as few houses as they could get away with. Once I had started to help out I understood why. I remember walking up the front path to Number 49 with the wind pulling at the papers on my clipboard, and icy rain dashing against the back of my neck. I'd been sitting in my car, parked outside with the heater on for some time, and it made it feel even colder outside.

If the doorbell worked I couldn't hear it, but a figure at last appeared behind the frosted glass and it was opened on a security chain. My notes told me that the tenant was a Mrs Johanssen.

The woman was dressed from head to foot in grey. I can still remember her. She stared at me, uncomprehending, as though visitors were not just infrequent, but completely unknown.

'Good morning,' I declared with the forced cheerfulness I had adopted for visits. 'I'm from the council. You will have had a letter a few weeks ago to tell you that we're surveying all the council houses. Would it be convenient if I came in now?'

It was my usual opening, and most people would let me inside. The complaints didn't usually begin until I was through the door.

'Yes, you can come in,' the woman said.

Her voice was lifeless, for all that there was a slight foreign lilt to it. She was tall and lean in a dress that was tightly cut around a fine figure for a woman who might be fifty. She was slightly stooped, though, with a sort of down-trodden look. But she might have been good-looking for all that; you know, in a way that was handsome rather than pretty. Perhaps, if she hadn't such a blank expression?

I was inside, the door was shut behind me, and I followed her down the narrow hallway. Her kitchen was clean and cold and clinical. There was a smell of bleach, and no clutter anywhere; even the calendar on the wall was unillustrated. It was certainly different to my kitchen at the time. I'd just moved out of my parents', better late than never as my colleagues often joked, and into my own flat. I had yet to perfect any housekeeping skills; this appeared to me to be the other extreme.

'What do you need to see,' she asked, again with no emotion.

'It's a very basic survey,' I apologised. 'We're not checking anything structural. We just need to know what services you have and whether they are up to date.'

'Would you like a cup of tea?' she asked.

Whether or not to accept tea from a tenant was a question we often discussed in the office. Our reply would not necessarily have anything to do with how thirsty we were, but how friendly the tenant was and how hygienic the house appeared to be. If it was offered immediately you wouldn't always have had time to inspect the kitchen, so you might not know if it was a good idea. Drinking a cup of tea also obliged you to stay longer, so whether you accepted or not depended on the house and the tenant. 'No thank you,' I replied, as politely as I could. 'The first thing in here that I need to know is how recent your kitchen units are.'

'They are in good order,' she replied.

It certainly looked as if she was right. I opened one, wide enough so as not to appear to be prying, and it seemed in good repair.

'And your sink,' I said, ticking the 'good' box against 'Units' on my form. 'It's one of the old Belfast sinks with a wooden drainer. We're trying to replace them with stainless steel...'

I was talking to myself really, ticking the appropriate boxes.

'I like my sink. There is no need to change it.' Her diction was quite precise and slightly unnerving.

'If you say that then you'll never get it modernised. I'm afraid that it's usually those who complain loudest who get the most out of the council. It shouldn't be like that, of course . . . Now, do you have modern pipes, or do you still have the old lead ones?' I asked. 'May I look under the sink?'

'If you need to,' she agreed, folding her arms.

Underneath there were the usual items: cleaning fluids, floor cloths etc. The pipes were lead, as I'd expected. From a quick glance around it was usually possible to fill in the forms with a fair degree of accuracy without checking all the details. I suspected some of my colleagues never got out of their cars at all but judged a property by how modern the windows and doors were. She was watching me, though, and I made certain that I went through the routine properly.

'You have gas and electricity?'

'Yes, though I don't use the gas.'

'Alright. May I see your electricity meter?'

We slowly made our way around the house, and my thoughts were soon elsewhere, principally on my lunch. I'd written Mrs Johanssen off as one of those very uninspired and uninspiring Christians who seem to think that anything above simple existence is somehow going to lessen their odds at being received into heaven. A bible in the dining room seemed to confirm this, but the main bedroom, hers (there didn't seem to be a Mr Johanssen, you can easily tell), made me doubt my prejudices. There was a small bookshelf which contained a number of modern thrillers and several books by Jane Austen and the Brontë sisters. It was rare to come across any books at all in the houses I surveyed, and I mentioned this to her as I opened and closed her still functioning metal windows.

'I like to read,' she said, again with that lilt, and I decided that her name sounded Scandinavian. She might certainly have looked Scandi-navian if her hair had not been black.

I meant to say how much I liked *Wuthering Heights*, but something made me remark on *The Tenant of Wildfell Hall* instead.

Her face remained as impassive as ever. 'My favourite book is *Jane Eyre*,' she said simply. And it was clear that was the limit of any literary conversation.

The bathroom was as clean and cold as the kitchen had been. The word 'scoured' came to mind. I was noting the very slight crack in the sink when I was suddenly surprised to see a man's razor on the shelf above it. Perhaps she had a husband after all? His presence was not to be seen or felt anywhere else in the house.

The second bedroom was different.

'My son's room,' she said, which explained the shaving gear in the bathroom. 'He lives with me. He has difficulty finding work.'

The room was not untidy, but it was quite a contrast to the rest of the house. There were framed prints of trains on the walls, and a stereo over which were shelves of records. A pile of magazines sat on the floor by a chair. It took me some time before I realised that it was also very tidy, although there was a colour and warmth that was missing elsewhere.

'His windows do not open,' she shook her head. 'The metal frames . . .'

'I know all about them,' I sympathised. 'We do have a replacement program, and we will be getting round to you soon, but resources are limited, and the elderly are getting priority at the moment.'

'I understand,' Mrs Johanssen said simply. 'I'm not asking for replacements.'

'The council will get around to you, but it might take some time.'

'That is not a problem.'

To be frank I was beginning get bored with the woman's quiet acceptance of everything, and I wondered if those tenants who moaned did not at least add some interest to the job. I walked back out into the hall and looked up for the loft hatch. Oddly it had been removed. The frame had been taken out and the hole very neatly sealed. The whole ceiling had been painted so that only a faint outline of its original position remained.

'Where's the loft hatch? Is it in your bedroom?'

'Why do you need to know?'

'I'd like to take a look up there. I need to check whether you have any insulation. We're trying to put a layer in all roofs. And I need to make sure that your water tank is lagged. It'll be a galvanised tank, I expect, but we're going to try and replace them all with plastic.'

'Oh, the roof is fine. My son insulated it all.'

'Excellent, but do you mind if I look?' I showed her that I had my own torch in my pocket. 'I have a ladder in the car if you haven't one easily to hand.'

She motioned towards her son's room and I walked inside and looked up. There was the hatch, quite newly and neatly put in by the look of it, but oddly it was locked with a heavy, old-fashioned padlock.

'My son has the key,' she apologised. 'But I can assure you that the loft is insulated, and so is the tank. I think he has put in a plastic tank already.'

'Really?'

'Yes, it is plastic, I am sure.'

'Good,' I smiled, and noted it down on my form. 'Very forward thinking. Of course, the rest of your plumbing *is* rather ancient.'

'It is all fine though. And you must write down that the tank was replaced quite recently.'

But something in her voice wasn't convincing, and it was such an odd matter to lie about. For some reason this annoyed me.

She was now beginning to look a little agitated. She had patiently followed me about the house before, but now stood out on the landing, as if prompting me to leave her son's room. She was fingering the top of her grey dress which, I noticed for the first time, was not entirely plain. There were small white flowers embroidered around the neck, and her fingers picked at them nervously.

'I have a few further questions, if I may?'

'Of course. Are you sure you would not like to have a cup of tea?'

'If you are making one for yourself,' I conceded, although I was not sure that it was a good idea. 'That would be nice,' and I stepped out of the room.

I had finished asking my last questions just before the tea was poured. Small talk was required, and I now regretted that I had accepted the drink. It was with some relief that I heard the front door open. She called through to the front of the house:

'David, I am in the kitchen.'

'Hullo, whose car's that parked outside then?' a young man asked just before he entered the room and saw me.

'This gentleman is from the council,' she introduced me. 'He is doing a survey of the house.'

'Oh,' he remarked, very defensively I thought. He was unprepossessing, tall like his mother, and with her features, but slightly overweight, and rather unkempt. 'What parts of the house?'

'All of it,' I remarked cheerily, and took a sip of my tea, knowing that her son was thinking about the loft. Now that I had met him I wondered just what it was he had up there that required it to be padlocked.

If I had left with my form filled in as it was nobody would have questioned what I had put down on it. In fact, there would be some relief that the insulation was already in place and the tank new. But my curiosity had been aroused, and there was usually so little of any real interest in the job.

'I was a little disturbed not to be able to get into the loft,' I said seriously. 'I am meant to have access to all parts of the house.'

'What did you want to see up there?' David Johanssen asked.

'The level of insulation, and the water tank.'

'Oh, it's well insulated, isn't it?' he asked his mother for confirmation. 'And the tank is quite new.'

'Metal or plastic?' I asked, thinking suddenly that I might be able to catch the pair out.

'Plastic,' said his mother.

'That's right,' he agreed.

'Why do you keep it padlocked?' I asked.

'No reason . . .' he looked to his mother for help, but she simply stared back at him with an expression that might have looked almost mischievous, if such a face could have registered emotion.

'I would get into awful trouble,' I lied, 'if they found out I hadn't seen inside the loft.'

'You just need to see the tank and the insulation?' he asked.

'Yes, that's all. And if there's daylight coming through the roof in too many places I'd have to note that down. . . .'

'Oh no, it's very well maintained,' he almost boasted. 'I see to that myself.'

I said nothing, but I put down my cup of tea and he nodded and asked me to follow him. His mother trailed after us, and we all climbed the stairs. There was only room for two of us to stand in the room as he placed a wooden chair under the hatch. From the landing his mother said nothing.

David Johanssen produced a small key and stood on the chair. Reaching up he unlocked the padlock and stepped back down again.

'The tank's right by the hatch,' he told me. 'And you can feel that it's lagged all around. I'm sorry I haven't got a ladder.'

I climbed onto the chair and pushed the hatch up a few inches.

'Feel around inside,' Johanssen suggested helpfully. 'It's all well insulated.'

He was right, I could feel the fibreglass prickling my hand. I pushed the hatch to one side and took my torch back out of my pocket. On tip-toes I could see from the little light available that it was lagged and my torch could pick out a shape that suggested it would be a modern, plastic one.

And then something glinted in the light and I suddenly saw that there was a ladder up there after all, on runners. Perhaps it was rash of me to pull it down, which necessitated jumping out of its way. The son moved the chair hastily and before he could do anything I was up the ladder and into the loft.

239

It was quiet down in the bedroom. Up there, under the roof, however, I could hear the muffled howl of the wind and rain outside. I swept the beam of my torch around and had a sudden fear that I was about to discover a heap of stolen antiques, a dead body, or some other good reason why I should have left with the mother's assurance that everything was in good order. Perhaps the very last thing I could have expected to see was a garden shed.

It was an ordinary wooden garden shed, standing three or four feet away from me, and it had a stable door and a little plastic window. It even had a green felt roof. To the side of the door stood a pair of boots.

'It all looks absolutely fine,' I called down, amused, and deciding that although it was rather strange it probably didn't conflict with the terms of their tenancy. I climbed back down, thinking that it was an odd way to make a roof space useable.

'I'll let you close it up,' I said to the son, who guiltily returned the ladder up on its runners through the hatch in the ceiling.

'Is everything alright,' David's mother asked anxiously as her son then stood on the chair and reached up to put the panel back.

'Yes, of course. It's just as you said; all well-maintained and properly insulated. I didn't doubt you, but I have my job to do.'

'Of course,' she replied, and followed me down the stairs and to the front door.

'Thanks for the tea.'

Mrs Johanssen did not point out that my cup in the kitchen was still almost full.

I had almost forgotten the whole incident when, over a month later, I received a message that Mrs Johanssen had telephoned and wanted me to go back to Coast Road. The reason given was that I had missed something in my survey that she wished to point out to me. She specified that I had to visit her in office hours, which caused some hilarity among my colleagues who all joked that she must want me to call while her husband was out at work. I was unwilling to deal with the matter myself, but as I had to be in Peacehaven that afternoon anyway I decided that it would be best to get it over and done with. I decided that I wouldn't raise the matter of the shed in the loft.

Coast Road was as uninviting as ever, although it was not actually raining, and a weak sun was doing its best to break through the clouds. I certainly didn't believe that Mrs Johanssen had any ulterior motive for inviting me back. My colleagues, especially the younger ones, often told stories of their adventures with bored housewives who let them in to survey their houses. None of it was true, of course. I'd never once been propositioned, although I had once taken advantage of a meal that was cooked for me. My work mates were all liars, though good-natured enough. One lad told the same story on every possible occasion of how he had surprised a rather good-looking woman who had been in the bath. Over time more and more detail emerged— certainly more detail than he'd have noticed in the couple of seconds he'd have been allowed to remain in the bathroom. I suppose I've fan-tasised about a couple of the women I met, but I never did anything about it. I think I can honestly say that I always behaved professionally.

On that afternoon I got out of my car and walked up to the door. The garden was as bare and uninviting as the house, but that may have been because of the time of year. I knocked and Mrs Johanssen opened the door immediately. You'd almost think that she had been standing there waiting. Perhaps she'd seen my car draw up? This time, she looked a bit flustered. She took me through to the living room and asked me to sit down.

'I am sorry to call you out on a pretence,' she apologised. 'But I didn't know what to do. My son has just found a job. I am alone in the house all day.'

My thoughts immediately went to the stories of bored housewives. Then she said:

'I am scared.'

'Scared of what?'

'Of what is in the roof. Tell me, what did you see in the roof when you went up there?'

241

'Nothing.'

'There can't be just nothing. Did you see someone?'

'No, nobody at all.'

'But my son goes up there for hours. I hear him making noises. Talking. And when he leaves the roof I hear nothing. But since he has started working I sometimes hear somebody up there.'

'I'm sure there must be some other explanation.' It was obvious that she wanted me to investigate.

'I'd offer to go up and have a look,' I said generously. 'But your son has the key.'

'He has, but I have made a copy. He left it in his trousers one day and I pressed it into some pastry. Then I took the impression to the locksmith and he said it was a standard key. Look, this is it.'

She passed me a small key. It sat in the palm of my hand.

'Will you please look up there for me?' she asked.

My eyes still on the key, I grudgingly agreed to investigate for her. The woman was plainly very scared, and to be completely honest I didn't feel much more at ease myself. I suppose I felt she was relying on me, and no gentleman should ever turn away from a woman in distress.

Once again I climbed the stairs, with Mrs Johanssen following me. In her son's bedroom I put the wooden chair under the hatch and opened the padlock. I looked around and saw the pole that I should have recognised before. I used it to push up the hatch door, and with the hook on its end I pulled down the ladder. I had to move the chair before I could transfer my weight onto the ladder, which then creaked in protest.

I climbed up, and, feeling for the light switch, flicked it on before raising my head carefully through the hatch. As I looked around, all seemed as before: the garden shed was unchanged; the boots were still beside the door. Now that I had the light on I could see that the loft space was large and that the shed was big too. It really was quite amazing how the son had actually managed to get it up there at all. I expect you know that sheds usually come in prefabricated panels, so he must have had to break those panels into smaller sections, and take them up the ladder and through the hatch a piece at a time.

For a moment I thought I might have heard a noise myself, but when I stopped to listen properly, all seemed quiet. Feeling a little more confident now, I climbed into the loft and then cautiously walked over the joists to the shed door. The woman in the bedroom below had said nothing, and was obviously waiting patiently. Slowly, my heart beating a little faster, I lifted the latch and opened the door in front of me.

I would have jumped violently, startled by almost anything that I saw inside. But the last thing that I expected to see was that Mrs Johanssen was already up there before me.

There were two red-shaded lights throwing a soft glow over heavy flock wallpaper, a deep-pile carpet, and a bed of rich silk sheets and velvet pillows. She lay on the bed, covered by one of the sheets, her skin no longer grey but warm and golden in the dusky light. She looked younger, and beautiful. Her limbs were long and perfect, her hair down around a soft and lovely face. She turned from her back on to her side and I could see the outline of her breasts through the thin sheet.

'Come here and love me,' she said in a soft voice. I wanted to, of course—how I wanted to! Her bright eyes might almost have been hooks, the way they seemed to drag me across the short distance towards her. I could see the sheet gradually sliding down her body. I could scarcely breath, and, as you can imagine, it was an horrific shock when a harsh voice came up from the bedroom below:

'What have you found?'

I had not realised that I was so far into the shed, by the bed, kneeling down and about to kiss those full, soft lips. In my confusion and horror I backed away from the bed and stumbled over a cushion. I grabbed at the door frame to steady myself, and the whole thing shook. I regained my balance and turned to look out of the shed towards the loft hatch. Suddenly I could hear her coming up the creaking steps.

'Nothing, nothing at all,' I nearly shouted as I took one great step over the rafters to the hatch. The grey-faced woman was there, looking up at me. 'No, nothing at all,' I said, backing down the steps and giving her no option but to climb down quickly.

As I descended I looked back once through the door of the shed and into its plush interior at the woman sitting on the bed, the sheet now covering only her lap. I flicked the light switch off and jumped down the last two steps. I pushed the ladder back up into the roof on its runners and, finding the pole, hooked the hatch and pulled it down. I moved the chair into position under it in the middle of the room and, in spite of my still-trembling fingers, re-padlocked the hatch.

Mrs Johanssen was sitting on the sofa in the living room when I had finished and walked, uncertainly, downstairs. I could see her through the door, but I let myself out without talking to her. I couldn't think of anything to say.

I often think about what I saw in that loft. I was mistaken, of course. Mrs Johanssen had been downstairs all the time. When I got home that night I found the key to that padlock in my trouser pocket. I still have it. It's a pretty ordinary, standard key, so I may find something else that it will unlock, one day.

Asphodel

Mr Gabo was an unlikely-looking author, but then most of their authors were unlikely-looking. Asphodel Books always attracted the improbable. As they were essentially a vanity publisher they were not in a position to turn down anybody who was willing to write a large enough cheque. Mr Gabo was perhaps seventy, and his face a mass of deep wrinkles, soft pouches and furry skin. His eyes peered out blearily from somewhere deep within his face. He looked like someone's great uncle, or great grandfather, with the life all but ebbed away from him. And he was very short indeed. He was standing in reception, wiping a finger over the dust on the books on display.

'I'm very sorry,' Marc apologized as he entered, 'But I'm afraid that both our managing director *and* our editor are out. Can I help?'

'That depends on who you are,' Mr Gabo said quite reasonably, and rather quietly.

'I'm the publicity manager. If we publish your book then I will be responsible for its promotion.'

'It will not be required,' the old man dismissed the young man's role. 'The book will sell itself.'

'Even the best books need to be presented to the public,' Marc justified himself.

'Not mine.'

'Well, that's a long way down the line.'

'The young are always biased against the old,' Mr Gabo stated, without any sign of rancour. 'You assume that because I'm so far removed from your own preoccupations and interests that I've lost touch, or am out of date. You forget that the elderly who shuffle around the streets of your city once knew the place just as well as you

245

do now. We fought wars and saw things that you could not start to imagine . . .'

'Fair point.' Marc put his hands up in defence. During the old man's softly spoken lecture he had advanced towards Marc slightly, perhaps trying to look threatening or menacing but not succeeding.

'Before I pay you a great deal of money to publish my book, I'd like to see around your operation here.'

'Of course,' Marc agreed, slightly disarmed by the man's matter-of-factness about the financial arrangements.

Marc Drake did not enjoy working for Asphodel Books. In fact, he had come to detest the job. That old feeling that he used to have as a youngster going to school, that heaviness in the stomach, was back with him as he made his way to work each morning. Even the night before that feeling would blight his evening. Sundays were the worst time: at least on Monday morning he was running around getting ready without a moment to think about it. He knew that it had all become too much for him when he would have that feeling for tomorrow before he had even left the office the previous day.

Which is what made those first few months at work seem so long ago. For those first few Sunday evenings he would actually look forward to going to work. He had things to be getting on with, people to phone; he knew that he would enjoy himself. Against all of the odds he had a job in publishing, a decent job (or so he thought), without any real experience. He had bluffed his way through his interview, had somehow given the right answers to questions he only half understood, and if the money wasn't that good, then at least there was a promise of more later on.

He knew so little about publishing that he failed to realise the implications of one of the questions asked at his second interview:

'Would you be confident that you could reassure an upset author that they hadn't wasted their money?'

'Wasted their money?'

'They are often expected to pay a contribution towards the costs of publishing their book. For some people it's quite a lot of money, and some expect great things. If they only sell a hundred copies they may not be very pleased.'

He replied:

'I'd try and impress upon them the positive things they'd received for their investment, talk about the possibilities for the future. Say how much I'd liked their book?'

It was the right answer and they moved on to 'If we offered you the job what sort of salary would you expect?'

He hadn't really thought about authors paying towards their book being published, although he later found out that it is quite common even among the most famous and well respected publishing houses. At Asphodel Books, however, authors didn't usually pay a *contribution* towards the publishing costs, they paid *all* of the costs, and left the company a contribution towards their profits. And for most people it *was* a lot of money. A hundred copies would have been a liberal average for sales. There were some successes, but there were also a few authors who would sell less than ten copies.

Quite how Mr Gabo would react to poor sales of his book Marc could not begin to guess. The old man had picked up his heavy-looking bag and was following him into the dark corridor.

'This is our managing director, Mr Jolly's office.' Marc opened the door but stood so as not to let Mr Gabo enter. 'As I say, he's not in, but I am sure he would love to meet you before going any further. He shut the door on the dusty and smelly room. It looked nice, with dark wood panelling and heavy old furniture, but there was an ineradicable smell of urine that did not often impress authors.

The company inhabited the top floor of an old Victorian building near the Gray's Inn Road. It was a warren of small rooms, and they came to the editor's next. Porter had recently had the heavy wood in his office painted a brilliant white and despite the heaps of manuscript, typescript and proofs, it had a fairly modern and industrious appearance.

'Our editor works out of this room.' This time he allowed Mr Gabo to enter. 'After the contract is signed most of your dealings will be with Mr Porter. Say, for the first six months.'

'Six months?' he was unimpressed. 'I did have a decent education, young man. I do know how to put together a coherent sentence. My book is ready to go to press without being mucked about with by an editor.'

'That's between you and Mr Porter.' Marc tried to inject a light-hearted tone into his voice.

Marc's room, the next kennel down the narrow corridor, was, frankly, a mess, and he passed by it quickly. It was a mess that he had inherited from his predecessor and despite various attempts to try and clear it up there were always more pressing demands on his time. Some people in the business thought it strange that a vanity publisher would have an editor and a publicity manager, for most of their competitors just took the money and ran. Marc, however, liked to think that Asphodel Books were slightly different. Of course, most people in the trade saw Marc mainly as window-dressing. And as far as Mr Jolly was concerned a good review was not a means of selling books, but of enticing other authors to sign up. Marc did try and do a decent job, if only to justify his existence, and he liked to think that he was quite good at it.

Marc and Mr Gabo reached Archie's office next. Archie smiled sweetly at Mr Gabo, asked after his health, and as soon as the old man's back was turned he stuck his finger up at him. Archie was the production assistant who should have found another job years ago, because he was never going to be promoted. He was paid badly, but was not expected to work very hard so he was content to remain in his lowly position. He had a fund of humorous stories, but soon after meeting him Marc noticed that the same jokes and quips were end-lessly repeated. Archie had been there longer than anybody else so he was the only one who knew the true genesis of the office in-jokes. It was painful to admit that everybody else became guilty of endlessly re-telling Archie's stories.

Marc explained to Mr Gabo that Archie's job was to design the dust jackets and occasionally lay out books that required photographs or illustrations. Other designers would create the artwork, but Archie would design the lettering, set the blurbs and add the author photo and bar code. Mr Gabo listened to Marc without any interest.

'And what have you written?' asked Archie brightly. It was a question that Marc always dreaded asking.

'Many years ago, young man,' Gabo said seriously. 'I committed a very great sin. My book is an atonement for that sin.'

'Really?' asked Archie, hoping his obvious show of interest would elicit details.

'Yes,' he replied simply but said no more.

Mr Gabo's explanation filled Marc with dread. If the author couldn't explain what their own book was about then Marc was not going to be able to do any better in his publicity campaign. There was an old saying in his native Norfolk that claimed 'You can't polish a turd,' but the saying was wrong. Asphodel Books often received these from illiterate and unimaginative authors and polished them until they achieved an unimagined brilliance. Despite the unkempt appearance of their offices, Asphodel's books looked good. Marc couldn't help it if they were unpalatable should any member of the public be stupid enough to read them.

Mr Gabo liked Archie and chose to deposit the manuscript on his desk.

'It does not need editing,' he told him. 'A plain and simple typeface, not too small, and decent paper. The cover is to be charcoal grey with gold lettering.'

'You wouldn't like to see a few examples of other designs we can offer?' Marc asked.

'No, I was told that it should look that way.'

'Well, if he's been told...' Archie chided Marc.

They exchanged glances, understanding that they should not ask from whom Mr Gabo had received his instructions.

'I assume that three months will be a reasonable time-scale?' Mr Gabo suggested.

'Until proofs?' asked Archie.

'Publication,' he said firmly.

'It is a little quicker than we can usually turn books around,' Marc started to warn him.

'Just send me an invoice. Whatever your usual price is, and if you can publish in three months I'll pay an extra ten per cent.'

'I'll have a word with Mr Jolly,' said Archie conspiratorially.

'Good.' He turned to Marc. 'And now you can show me out.'

As they walked back down the corridor towards reception he explained:

'Please don't think me rude, but the book really doesn't need publicity. It's all in more influential hands than yours or mine.'

'Good,' Marc said as he opened the door for the old man, and Mr Gabo walked out.

Archie had already worked out who the more influential hands belonged to.

'The end is nigh!' he wailed tragically as Marc walked back down to his office. 'The great prophet has entrusted us with the job of spreading the news. Well, as publicity manager he's entrusted it to you. His book is very philosophical, very deep.'

'No, it's out of my hands,' Marc grinned. He looked into the manuscript. It was handwritten in green biro, and consisted almost entirely of helpful suggestions for those preparing for the end of the world. 'Pay off your debts.' 'Be kind to everyone, including those you dislike.' 'Do not over-eat.'

Mr Gabo was obviously very serious, but his thoughts were broadcast about the office, and for some reason there was great hysteria when the author suggested that the end of the world was not a good time to consider obtaining a pet dog. What was of more interest, however, was his description of his own personal preparation. As a chosen prophet he had to make special arrangements; he was to give away all of his possessions, be cleansed, purged internally and externally, and then he would be transfigured.

Even Mr Jolly called Mr Gabo a 'fruitcake' on his return. Archie had moved the manuscript to Mr Jolly's desk, wondering what his opinion would be. Their boss was the main reason Marc hated his job. The man would not allow his staff to be critical of any of their authors, yet he was happy to complain about them himself. He would admit that a book was unreadable and then become angry when his staff were unable to sell copies. Over many years he had sought to offer the world a façade of respectability and success while he knew that the vast majority of his books were worthless. For some reason he kept up this façade even with those he worked with—those best placed to know the truth.

It would be wrong to suggest that all of their books were appalling. They published something like one hundred books a year and the odds were that they would publish a couple of reasonable titles among them, and they did, very occasionally, receive a good, high-profile review in a national newspaper. These, however, were exceptions.

And it would be wrong if anyone believed that their authors were actually ripped off. The worst vanity publishers tell prospective authors that their work is on a par with that of Tolstoy and that they will be rich in a very short time. Asphodel Books never stooped to these practices, and, in fact, authors were told not to consider publication as a money-making venture; they were told that there was a distinct possibility of not selling many books. There are degrees of duplicity, and strictly speaking Asphodel Books gave authors due warning. But too many people *are* vain and won't be told. If Mr Jolly had screamed at them 'Your book will not sell and nobody will review it, because it is a bad book' then many would still believe that they would be an international best-selling author. Sadly, few aspired to being the next Tolstoy.

By warning people Asphodel Books thus salved its conscience. Even in the instance of Mr Gabo, Jolly carefully put the warning into writing and satisfied his solicitors. But somehow their authors never realised that the warnings were meant for them. Marc warned Mr Gabo when he appeared in reception, unannounced, a few days before the publication of his book. The author arrived both excited and nervous.

'I'm worried,' he told Marc, 'that we haven't printed enough books. It was stupid of me not to insist on more. I need as many copies as possible.'

Marc looked at the stock report and told him that it so happened that there had been a small over-run at the printers and 512 copies had been delivered to the warehouse. He had taken a few copies for publicity purposes, he explained, and had kept back a couple of file copies.

'May I take them?' Mr Gabo almost pleaded.

'What, our copies?'

'Yes, if I can?'

'I would like to keep a few to send out for review.'

'No need,' he smiled for the first time. 'Those responsible will ensure that it is read by those who matter.'

'Well,' Marc replied, a little facetiously, 'I would like to do all that I can to help.'

Mr Gabo sighed and smiled a patronizing smile. He had apparently sent in his cheque for the publication of his book without any comment, prompting Mr Jolly to wish he had asked for more.

'I know that 500 copies will not be enough,' Gabo said.

'If the 500 copies sell, then we can always reprint it,' Marc pointed out.

'Of course,' he said, taking the books from the desk. Marc couldn't argue; after all, the man had paid for them.

'I'm glad to see that the cover is grey, and the lettering gold,' he nodded. 'I said it was to be a paperback, but I should have pointed out that ideally it would fit in a coat pocket.'

'It was produced to the specifications you gave us.'

'And on the day of publication you are to come around that evening and tell me how many we have sold.'

'Well,' Marc was horrified. 'That's far too early.'

'Nonsense,' he smiled.

'There will be some pre-orders from the library suppliers. But we really must allow for returns of unwanted books. Perhaps a statement after three months is the best...'

'No, that will be too late."

"What will have happened?"

'I will have been transfigured by then.'

'I'm sorry if I sound ignorant, or sceptical, but why?'

'When I was younger,' he said once again, 'I committed a great sin.'

Marc had been feeling sorry for Mr Gabo all this time, defending the man against some of the worst jokes of Archie and the editor (who had not been allowed to touch one word of the book), but suddenly he did seem rather a comic figure. Marc rounded up their file copies, a proof copy and a loose set of running sheets, and gave them to the grateful man.

He made the mistake of telling Archie of the conversation and the production assistant promised to remind Marc on the day of publication that he had to visit Mr Gabo in his south London flat.

Marc also told Jolly of the discussion.

'He's seriously disturbed,' Marc argued. 'Why are we taking his money when he probably needs psychiatric help?'

'He has serious religious convictions,' Jolly excused himself from behind his large desk. 'People have a right to their religious beliefs, don't they?'

'So the fact that his crackpot beliefs go under the guise of religion make them legitimate?'

'I'm not going to discriminate against anybody because of their religion.'

'Like you wouldn't discriminate against anybody with a mental health problem?'

'Exactly.' He seemed satisfied that he had won the argument.

As he said he would, Archie reminded Marc of his promise to visit Mr Gabo on the day of publication. He picked up the new stock report that Marc had not yet had a chance to look at.

'You'll need to explain to him why his book hasn't sold,' he said, looking through the titles. 'How many do you think've gone? Let's both make a guess and the one who's furthest away . . .'

'What's up?' Marc asked. He hadn't really been listening to Archie, but he did notice that he had trailed off.

'There's a stock figure of zero.'

'Ha, ha,' Marc mocked. 'What is it really?'

Archie passed him the stock report and Marc could see that he was right. A phone call to the distributors confirmed this.

'Where've they all gone?' he asked over the phone. He did wonder whether Mr Gabo had bought them all himself.

'The usual sources, library suppliers, wholesalers, individual shops and customer orders.'

'Are you sure it's not been mixed up with another book?'

'Very sure.'

'How the hell has it sold?' Marc asked.

'Quality will out,' Archie reassured him. 'Why are you looking so annoyed. At least you won't have to explain to him why none of them have sold.'

'No, but at least I'd know why they hadn't sold. What I can't explain is why they *have*.'

Marc could not bring himself to telephone Mr Gabo with the good news. He remembered that he had told the author that a reprint was possible if the book sold out, and Mr Jolly had impressed upon him that although this was in the contract, they were never to encourage the idea. Marc thought about writing to the author, but put this off too. Several days later an odd bloody-mindedness came over him, however, and without thinking he tried to call the man, but the number was unobtainable. That lunchtime, as usual, Mr Jolly had left early and would not be returning until late, and Marc decided that he would

254

visit Mr Gabo. He could probably do so in work time and if Mr Jolly returned first, well, after a liquid lunch he would probably not notice Marc's absence. He took a five pound note from petty-cash and left for the underground station two streets away.

It was a dismal day. London may not have smog anymore, but when it is damp and foggy the soot and grime seem to adhere to everything, and that included Marc's mood. His spirits had been further dampened, as the train clattered south of the Thames, by the thought that he had stupidly, very stupidly, given Mr Gabo every copy of his book that they had. He had also returned the manuscript and given the old man the proofs and running sheets. A reprint would cause trouble; their printers were competent enough, but they used disposable paper plates. Asphodel Books reprinted their titles so rarely that it was more economical to set up new plates than use metal ones. If Mr Gabo insisted on a reprint they might have to ask for his manuscript back, and that hardly looked professional. Perhaps the typesetter would still have a copy?

The journey went quickly. Out of the station he consulted his A-Z and crossed into Mr Gabo's road. It was a long, elegant street of white-painted terraced houses on three floors. As he passed them he noticed that most were flats and the author's was no exception. Marc walked up the brick path and climbed the three steps to the mock-Georgian front door. Something was not quite right.

The door had been forced open recently, and new locks had been fitted. The paintwork was mucky, and there was an acrid smell that he took a few seconds to identify. It was smoke. There had been a fire.

There were two doorbells. Mr Gabo's elicited no response, but when Marc rung the one over the name 'Smith' a bell rung from somewhere inside. Eventually he heard a door opening within the building, steps, and then the front door was opened.

'Yes?' asked a middle-aged, prematurely bald man.

'I'm sorry to trouble you, but I was looking for Mr Gabo?'

'Oh, are you a relative, or friend?'

'Neither. He was a client of ours. I tried phoning . . .'

'That wouldn't get you anywhere. There was a fire. We assume he's dead.'

'I'm very sorry.'

'Well, I didn't know him that well myself. I've only lived here three months, and he was pretty quiet. But I came home the other day to find the fire brigade had smashed open our front door and his flat, upstairs, was burnt out.'

'I'm very sorry,' Marc said again. 'Did it spread to your flat?'

'The fire? No. And there's not too much smoke damage, but the water! Sooty water through the ceiling and down the walls. It's horrible. And the insurance! Who knows whether *he* had any insurance. I did, but they want to claim from his insurers . . . My carpets . . .'

'But he died in the fire?' Marc asked with very mixed feelings.

'Yes, we assume so. It's all very odd. Do you want to come in?'

'No, thanks, really,' he backed down a step.

'They're doing tests.'

'On how the fire started?'

'That as well. The main test is to see whether he died up there.'

'You mean there's nothing left? It must have been an inferno?'

'Apparently not. The fire brigade say it wasn't too bad. A neighbour alerted them immediately. She saw a flash through the windows. It must have been an explosion of some sort. She saw it in bright daylight. Anyway, come and have a look.'

Marc really wanted to leave. He was sorry for Mr Gabo, but Marc felt that he could be forgiven for thinking that Gabo was one problem he no longer had to deal with. But Mr Smith was already inside and climbing the stairs. In no time he was out of sight and it would have been wrong for Marc to shout after him that he didn't want to go up there. It would also have been very bad form to simply walk away.

He entered the house and the first thing he noticed were all of the dirty footprints. There were horrible marks up the white walls of the stairs, from the firemen, he assumed. The door at the head of the stairs was wide open, but it was so dark within that he could see nothing.

The acrid smell caught at the back of his throat. He entered in trepidation, wondering that everything could be so black. The carpet was charred horribly, the paper had burnt on the walls but still adhered to it, and the ceiling was black and in places sagging. There were remains of curtains, and the discoloured hulks of formless and almost unidentifiable furniture. Although it had obviously been a terrible fire, it was odd that it was all so damp. He knew that this would have been from the fire brigade, but he had never been in a burnt out room before and it was somehow unlike what he had expected; not that he knew what he expected.

'There was a lot of muttering amongst the firemen afterwards,' the neighbour said knowingly.

'Why?'

'Well, they weren't sure if they'd found his body up here or not.'

'Really? Can't they tell?'

'They took some things away, all bagged-up, but nothing that looked the right size or shape.'

Marc was uncomfortable with the turn of the conversation. He was glad to be able to ask:

'What's that?'

The man had also heard it; from another room there was an irregular, angry flapping and the occasional sound of something hitting something solid.

'The floor's alright,' said Smith, walking over to a door, frowning. 'I had to pay an engineer to check that it wouldn't fall in on my flat below if people walked over it. The insurance people sent someone out, but he would only report back to the company.

The man pushed the door open with his foot and in the next room a bird was flapping uselessly around. It was even more frightened by their appearance and threw itself at the window. The panes were grey with soot and smeared where the bird had obviously hurled itself at the glass time and time again.

'Bloody hell,' the neighbour remarked. He gingerly made his way to the window and the bird cowered in the corner. The man tried to open the window and his hand was immediately filthy with soot. 'Bloody stuff,' he complained, looking for something to wipe his hand on, but there was nothing he could use. After some thought he decided that the soot was not worth worrying about. He pulled up the catch and gave the frame a shove.

With an instinct that birds do not always seem to display, the frightened thing made straight for the opening and was out in a flutter of dirty wings.

'I'd better be going,' Marc excused himself, backing towards the door.

'Oh, okay. So why was he your client?'

'We were publishing his book.'

'I didn't know he was a writer? Odd.'

'How would you know? Everything's burnt.'

'I've had a good look around and there's nothing here but a few old sticks of furniture. Absolutely no personal stuff, and certainly no books.'

Marc decided that if the neighbour had been rather too nosey, then he supposed that Mr Gabo was no longer around to care.

He returned to the office at four o'clock to find that he had not been missed. Nobody mentioned Mr Gabo after that, and a month or so later Marc resigned and took up selling second-hand nautical books — a hobby of his that finally turned into a full-time job. Within the general book trade he often advertised for Mr Gabo's book, but nobody seemed to be able to turn up a copy. Marc wondered if he had misjudged the man's writings, or misremembered them, but he wanted to read again the part which dealt with the author's end. All that Marc recalled for certain, because he had looked it up in the dictionary at the time, was the word 'transfigured'.

Where They Cannot Be Seen

'I think that love is best left to the young,' Donna said. 'I expect that one day it will be viewed by psychiatrists as a mental health problem rather than anything wonderful or spiritual.'

It was a pronouncement that nobody felt able to reply to immediately, and abhorring silence Donna continued: 'And as for sex, well, is it really necessary? I've always preferred a nice cup of tea myself.'

Donna found that she could not catch the eye of anyone else in the room. Her husband, Brendan, was staring at the crossword on his knee as though he had heard nothing. Terrance, on the two-seater sofa by the door with his wife Georgina was revolving the wine in his glass thoughtfully while she seemed to exchange a glance with Robert on the other sofa. Donna wasn't sure if Robert had actually returned Georgina's glance, for he was looking down at the magazine on his wife's lap which she, Wendy, was idly flicking through.

'So,' said Brendan, slowly, not looking up from his crossword, 'Do you not feel love for me anymore?'

'Of course I do, silly,' she replied. 'But, practically, it's really just another word for comfort or companionship.'

'So, I'm no different from some old, well-worn cardigan?' he asked, although without appearing to be hurt. He had long ago become resigned to his wife's lack of interest in sex. She liked romantic gestures, but only because it made her think that she wasn't being taken for granted. The previous year she had confided to Wendy that romance was rubbish but women insisted on it just to keep men on their toes.

'Surely there are good reasons . . .' Georgina asked, starting her question quite confidently but then losing heart; '. . . good biological reasons for love, and sex?' She realised that it was not a discussion that was worth continuing. Donna wasn't a woman who liked to explore ideas; she considered a good discussion to be when somebody of similar outlook made a statement that she could agree with, and perhaps elaborate upon. In turn the other person was expected to explore the implications of that elaboration, but at no time should there be any disagreement.

'Well,' Donna considered. 'Advances in medical science mean that men and women don't necessarily have to go anywhere near each other for a child to be produced.'

'Apparently some people enjoy making babies the old-fashioned way,' her husband said, still not looking up, and still without a hint of rancour.

'And look at all the trouble and heartache it causes,' Donna pointed out, and then yawned behind her hand. She saw the opportunity and everyone was happy for her to grasp it: 'Well, it's been a long and tiring journey to get up here today and I think I shall go up to bed. Goodnight everyone.'

Perhaps she could have been accused of trying to escape a discussion while she was ahead. Nobody would have done so, though; it would not have been worthwhile on the first day of their holiday, and anyway, it was customary for her to go to bed early. Everyone wished her a good night, and her husband assured her that he would follow once he had finished the crossword.

'There's no rush,' Donna told him, and she caught Robert grinning.

'That's enough of that,' she admonished him. 'You know me, I need my sleep.'

Once she had left the room her husband said: 'Well, she's right to a degree.'

'Really?' asked Terrance. 'How do you work that out?'

'Well, some people do spend too much time and energy thinking about sex. Once you've actually got married and had children it does become an unproductive effort, and only leads to frustration. I've never thought of having an affair myself; I can't believe that it would be worth all of the effort required? And the trouble it could cause?'

'Some people would argue,' Wendy said tentatively, 'that they couldn't help the attraction they felt for another person, and that it would actually be more trouble to try and repress their feelings.'

'You mean, after they were married? If they found somebody else?'

'Exactly.'

'Well, I'm old-fashioned enough to believe that such feelings should be kept under control.'

'Even if several people are made unhappy as a consequence?'

'I don't know,' he said, lifting his hands in tired exasperation. 'If you have children, and *we* all do, then those feeling should definitely be resisted.'

There was another silence, then Robert simply said 'James Thurber'. When questioned, he explained that Thurber's first book was called *Is Sex Necessary?* A further silence followed and then Georgina asked Wendy how her two children were, and the discussion wandered aimlessly over the academic achievements of their various offspring. When Brendan filled in the last answer of his crossword he smiled at them with quiet triumph, drained his glass, stood up and said goodnight as well. He and Donna were always the first to retire; she always said that the change of air and the different surroundings made her and Brendan especially tired.

All six of them, the three couples, met up for a week each year in a holiday cottage that Donna had booked, and they had been doing so for nearly a decade. The routine had been established; in February she would go through the brochures, make some enquiries and phone to make sure they were all happy with her proposed date and location. In their separate homes one hundred miles apart Terrance and Georgina, and Robert and Wendy would debate whether they really wanted to go on a shared holiday with the same people again, but would always somehow agree that they would.

'I don't think Brendan's followed her upstairs with too much optimism,' Terrance noted. 'Is she really as disinterested in sex as she says?'

'Apparently,' Wendy answered. 'When she was at school she wasn't really concerned about boys. When Brendan came along I think he offered her stability and reliability. He'd never cheat on her, no matter how frustrated he became.'

'I feel like they're another generation older than us,' Georgina said.

'That's only because they're like your parents,' Terrance replied. 'You can't ever imagine them having sex.'

'Well, like my mother and father, they have done so once, obviously,' she said. 'Otherwise, where did their daughter, Selina, come from?'

'Well, no matter what we think about their relationship,' Wendy said. 'They would do anything for Selina.'

'I'll be brutally honest,' announced Terrance. 'We come away to Donna's holiday cottage for a week each year so as to get away from our kids. . . .'

'Terrance!' Georgina punched him.

'. . . And to see you two,' he added. 'We haven't really got anything in common with Donna and Brendan, other than the fact that I went to school with him.'

'Well,' Robert admitted. 'I don't know about Wendy, because Donna was her school-friend, but I don't feel we've anything in common with them either. We like meeting up with you two. And you have to admit that Donna does choose some splendid holiday cottages. And yes, it's nice not to worry about the children.'

'Not that we need to worry about them anyway,' Wendy said. 'They're fourteen and fifteen now, and quite happy to stay with their grandparents.'

'The same with ours,' Georgina smiled conspiratorially. 'Jennifer and Adrian are thirteen and sixteen. At Terrance's parents they'll be staying up late, eating unhealthy food . . .'

And so the conversation continued. On the first night of their holidays they invariably caught up with the news, knowing that much of it would have to be repeated the following day for the benefit of Donna and Brendan. After another glass of wine Terrance admitted that he and Georgina had considered the possibility of going on holiday with just Robert and Wendy, but decided they couldn't; Donna in particular would be devastated if she found out.

'And besides,' said Robert, 'she does take on all the organising. All we have to do is keep the date free in our calendar and she tells us where and when we're all meeting up. And she does find some great holiday cottages, *and* she brings everything along for the first evening meal.'

'They always get the benefit of the master bedroom, though,' said Terrance. 'Which, as we all know, is wasted on them. Our room's got two single beds.'

'Well, we've got a double,' Wendy pointed out. 'But we don't have the en suite bathroom that you've got. We have to go down to the end of the hall.'

When they finally broke up and went to bed that evening Wendy took her turn in the bathroom first while Robert waited in their bedroom and read. After she had returned he went and washed and cleaned his teeth, and coming back met Georgina in the hallway, wearing a voluminous cotton nightie. She said she was going down to the kitchen for a glass of water and he said that he would follow her example; after all the wine they had drunk he agreed that it was a good idea.

'I'm taking this up with me,' she said after she had drunk a glass and refilled it from the tap in the kitchen.

'Well, goodnight,' he replied. Standing alongside her at the sink he kissed her on the cheek, but did not then move his head away. They both held the position; they had an understanding that neither of them would actually take their feelings for one another any further than this but, with his lips to her cheek he could not pull away. He breathed in a perfume that was a mixture of her own scent, moisturiser and cleanser.

She felt his stubble against her skin and his body touching hers, and she shivered. He smelt of soap.

Robert put his hand against her waist and felt her warmth through the material of her nightdress and she did not pull away. She trusted him to take it no further than this, but she let out an involuntary groan.

'Oh Georgina,' he said quietly and she drew slightly away, but with her free hand she held his hand to her waist.

'Have I got to sleep tonight with you just a few feet away again? With a wall between us?' she asked.

'I'll be sleeping right against the wall,' he said quietly.

'My bed's just the other side. We'll be so close to each other . . .' She raised her eyebrows and smiled.

'Goodnight,' she said and kissed him on the lips. There was nothing wrong with the kiss, nothing that a husband or wife observing them could have objected to, but a second later she leant forward once more and now kissed him again, deeply, lovingly. It was the first time in ten years of knowing him that she had allowed herself to do this. They kissed slowly and with tenderness, and then she pulled away and left him in the dark kitchen.

℘

That night, as he lay in bed, Robert could not sleep for the thought of Georgina in the room next to him, barely inches away through the wall. He considered how laughable it might appear to anybody else that in this modern day two people could be so in love and yet do nothing about it. Once, in the early days, when they had found themselves alone in the garden of some holiday cottage or other with their spouses elsewhere, she had said that their love was probably just a spiritual one. He had looked at her over the top of his sunglasses and told her that she could talk for herself; it was taking a great effort for him not to kiss her right then and there. And she had been forced to agree that she felt the same.

264

Robert could hear his Wendy breathing gently beside him and knew in his heart that he did not love his wife any less than when he had married her fifteen years previously. The last person he would ever want to hurt was her. And as for the children . . . He and Georgina had always asked what it would do to their children if they acted on their feelings for each other? But were these just excuses? Were they simply playing some game, creating a fantasy, building their love for each other up into something which they never expected to be consummated? He didn't think so, but after all these years of not acting on their feelings . . .

An hour ticked by, and then another, and he got carefully out of bed and stood up, deciding to go downstairs and read a book or watch a little television in an effort to make himself properly tired. As he stood he felt a little disorientated, and was then annoyed with himself that perhaps he had managed to fall asleep after all, for he couldn't quite remember where the bedroom door was. He felt about in the darkness and was surprised to find it to his left. He opened it quietly and went through, expecting the empty hall and was surprised to make out the form of Georgina standing before him in her white nightdress.

'I heard you get out of bed,' she whispered, and reached out for him.

He came close and held her, asking quietly, 'Are you sure we should be doing this?'

'After all of this time? I am sure, yes, but I also know we shouldn't be.' They held each other.

'You're as hopeless as me,' he said into her ear, and then pulled away slightly, feeling that something was wrong. His eyes had become accustomed to the light and he now realised that they were not standing in the long hallway as he had expected. He looked around. 'Where are we?'

'Outside our bedroom doors, silly.'

'No we're not.'

He let her go as she too looked around.

'There's a light switch here,' he said, his hand to the wall.

'Don't turn it on,' she said. And then, even more quietly, 'What if we've wandered into Brendan and Donna's bedroom!'

He stifled a nervous laugh: 'No, I came straight from my room. I'm not in yours am I?'

'Of course not,' she said slowly, and turning around she bumped into something. She felt down and discovered it to be a small table with a lamp.

'Perhaps I'll turn this light on,' she said, finding the switch under her fingers.

'Okay,' he agreed.

They were not in the hallway. In fact, they were not anywhere they had seen before. The room was long and thin and furnished simply with two nice old wooden chairs either side of an antique chest that sat before a shuttered window.

'I came through that door,' Robert pointed behind him.

'And I'm sure I came in this one,' she frowned at the second door. There was a third door opposite them.

'How did we miss a whole room before?'

'I don't know. It doesn't make sense . . .'

He turned back to her.

'Let's not question it?'

She smiled and moved close to him again.

'I don't know how much longer I can go on loving you, and not having you.'

He held her one again and then, looking down into her face he smiled and they kissed. When she pulled away it was to turn off the light.

'In case somebody comes in,' she said.

'But it'll look even more suspicious if we're found together in the dark! We'll hear anybody walking around at this time of night.'

But she did not turn the light back on. There was a soft carpet on the floor and in absolute silence they lay down together and kissed and talked quietly.

'Do you remember what Wendy said earlier,' asked Georgina. 'You know, about how some people couldn't help the attraction they felt for another person.'

'Yes. I don't think she was referring to us.'

'I just wondered if she'd guessed? She said it would be more trouble to try and repress feelings than act on them . . .'

They went no further than kissing, though their hands on one another excited them both to a degree that they found almost impossible to resist. Many years of restraint made them appreciate the closeness that they had managed to achieve, but they held their desire in check. They lay together, exploring each other, until the carpet no longer seemed as soft as before, and the cold started to creep over them. They parted reluctantly with no idea of how much time had passed. Each went back through their own door into their own bedrooms, to their own partners.

ℰᴑ

The following morning dawned dull and raining. Their cottage was in a clearing some distance from the road that cut through the Forest of Dean from Cinderford to Coleford and the trees seemed to press in and cast a sodden pall over the modern brick house. Donna normally found them period cottages to stay in, and the previous year they had rented an eccentrically furnished half-timbered house in Hereford with low ceilings and sloping floors. This house, though, was rather characterless, although furnished tastefully and offering three double bedrooms at a very reasonable rent considering that it was the high-season. It was hard to fault it for location, even if the trees seemed to cut out the light.

Inside the cottage, however, the mood that morning was bright. Georgina had already cleaned out the fire from the previous night, laid and lit a new one, and was teasing Donna about the summer clothes she had brought with her when the weather was so unseasonable. In the kitchen Robert was preparing an ambitious cooked breakfast on an

Aga that did not seem to be able to reach a temperature he would have liked. He was, nonetheless, very cheerful, and he and Georgina lifted the spirits of the others. Georgina wandered in and out of the kitchen teasing him about his cooking, which he took good-naturedly. Their happy industry infected the others who were trying to put up a rickety table tennis table in the large dining room. They had planned to walk through the woods to a local hotel for lunch and were debating whether or not breakfast would be ready before it was time to set off.

Like a carefully scripted farce it seemed impossible for Robert or Georgina to find themselves alone in any part of the house so as to be able to talk about the previous night. Even after they had eaten breakfast and the washing up had been done, while they were all preparing to leave to walk to the hotel, they were not able to talk. They had exchanged private glances on many occasions, and had been seen doing so by a bemused Donna at least twice. Her suspicions made them extra vigilant and during the walk to the hotel they made sure that they were not obviously seen together. At the bar they were unable to say anything, and although they ended up sitting next to each other for lunch they could discuss nothing of importance.

The six of them walked back to their holiday cottage in a leisurely fashion, in couples, enjoying the sunshine which had deigned to come through the clouds at last and offered some warmth for the first time. Georgina said that she would make the afternoon tea while the others started to play table tennis, and she contrived to find Robert alone outside when he went out to see if there were any spare bats in the shed at the end of the garden.

They met in the middle of the lawn as he returned. In full view of the dining room window, but knowing that they couldn't be heard, Georgina asked;

'Did I have a very lovely dream last night?'

She had her back to the house and he tried not to grin too widely.

'If it was the same one that I had,' he replied, noting that Brendan was at the window and looking towards them, 'then it certainly was astonishing. But there is one unanswered question.'

'I know. Where the hell were we?'

'I have no idea. There isn't another room upstairs. It simply doesn't exist.'

'I even tapped on the walls this morning, looking for secret passages!'

'So did I. But the rooms fit neatly into the outside shell of the house without any gaps. We must have gone downstairs.'

She laughed. 'You might have done, but I stayed upstairs, in a room adjoining my bedroom.'

'And did you find a second door in the bedroom when you looked for it this morning?'

'No, and nor did you, because I checked your room just as thoroughly as I checked mine.'

'But we were together last night, weren't we?'

'We were, and we shouldn't have been, but quite where we were is beyond me.'

'Can I suggest that we try and find that room again tonight?'

Robert had seen Brendan opening the window and at that moment he called out to Georgina that the kettle had boiled.

'Then put the water in the pot!' she called back over her shoulder and sighed. 'If I can find it again I'll be there,' she agreed. 'Where ever *there* may be.'

After several games of table tennis followed by a large meal they all watched a film together on the television and, as usual, Donna was the first to go up to bed. Brendan dutifully followed her a quarter of an hour later, and the remaining four quietly indulged in the usual character assassination of their friends. Terrance insisted that he was going to stay up and watch a concert on the television while the others decided to go to bed, and Robert and Georgina did not look at each other to express their frustration at this development. Upstairs Georgina said goodnight to Robert and Wendy on the landing and going into her room she closed the door behind her.

269

Robert lay awake for a while, listening to the distant, muffled sound of the television downstairs, waiting to hear Terrance come up to bed. His lack of sleep the previous night, however, the table tennis tournament of the afternoon and the large meal all conspired to make him fall asleep. He did not remember dreaming, but awoke at the sound of a door gently opening. He knew immediately who it was, although she said nothing, and satisfied that his wife was still breathing slowly and gently and must be asleep, he slipped out of bed.

He closed the door after him as quietly as he could and immediately yielded to Georgina's insistent kisses.

'Where have you been?' she asked after her initial frustration had been assuaged. 'I've been waiting here for ages, getting cold, wondering if you were coming at all.'

'I'm sorry. I must have nodded off.'

'Well, I had to wait for Terrance to come to bed and it was only after he was finally snoring that I came through here.'

'And where is here?'

'I don't know. While I was waiting I looked through the other door.'

'Where does it go? Into Donna and Brendan's room?'

'No,' she said slowly. Although it was very dark and he could only just make out her shape in front of him he knew she was smiling. 'Follow me,' she said, taking his hand.

They crossed the length of the room and she opened the third door. They entered a large room which was lit by two small lamps, one on either side of a large bed.

'Where's this?' he asked, incredulous.

'I don't know.'

'But what rooms are below us? I can't work it out in relation to the rest of the house.'

'It doesn't make any sense,' she admitted, letting go of his hand and sitting on the edge of the bed.

Robert walked to the window and tried the shutters, but they appeared to be fastened securely.

'It is rather worrying.'

'I know. The cottage is detached, isn't it? We haven't inadvertently gone into a house next door?'

'No,' he shook his head, frowning, not believing that when they arrived at the explanation that it could be anything obvious. Perhaps they would laugh at how, in the middle of the night, tired, when it was so dark, they had been so obtuse as not to realise where they were? Somehow he doubted it.

Georgina patted the heavy damask bedspread beside her and he padded over the carpet and sat down.

'Let's just make the most of this,' she said and they kissed. The room was not warm and so after some minutes it seemed natural for them to get into the bed. By the soft lamplight they continued where they had left off the previous night, but now they felt no inhibition and they made love properly, fully, for the first time. In the secret room they had discovered, in the large comfortable bed, it seemed quite natural and they did not feel any nervousness with one another. Neither felt any guilt, for both Terrance and Wendy seemed so far away at that moment.

Afterwards they snuggled against one another with the blankets tucked up around them and for a while thought and spoke of nothing but their love for one another.

'I will leave Wendy,' he said. 'Will you leave Terrance?'

'Yes,' she said, slowly, 'Tomorrow we'll work out how we're going to tell them.'

He agreed, and they smiled at each other and kissed, and after a while they closed their eyes. Robert awoke first and his heart leapt when he realised they had been sleeping. It was impossible to tell the time, so he woke Georgina gently and suggested they had to go back to their rooms.

'In a minute,' she replied sleepily. 'You go first.'

After a few moments got out of bed and looked around at the room once more. It was Victorian, he decided, not the same age as the rest of the house, and the dimensions were rather larger than elsewhere in the building. He looked over to where Georgina lay and felt an enormous tenderness for her. Why, he wondered, had they allowed themselves to take so long before they had come together like this? He noticed that she had fallen asleep again and he walked over and woke her once more. She sat up this time, tired, rubbing the sleep from her eyes. Then she shivered.

'You go now,' she said. 'I'll follow in a minute, just in case anyone sees us together.'

'Does it really matter if we're seen?'

'I don't want to discuss our relationship with anyone now, in the middle of the night,' she said. 'Go on, you go.'

He kissed her and went to the door, looking back at her as she sat up in the bed, happy and slightly dishevelled. As he walked back through the small room to his door he did not see her lie down at an angle onto the pillow where he had just been lying. He opened the door and found his way back onto the cold side of the bed next to his wife, and listened out for Georgina returning to her room. Perhaps he fell asleep sooner than he thought, or perhaps she left it a very prudent length of time before she returned, but he didn't hear any movement from her bedroom before he fell asleep.

The next morning Robert awoke and immediately his heart crashed in his chest and his stomach clenched. Now was the time to tell his wife that he was leaving her. He didn't know how he could do it, and hurt her, but he was certain that it had to happen. She kissed his forehead and said she would go down to the kitchen to put the kettle on.

He got up immediately and dressed. He would have to make sure that Georgina was in agreement that the time was right, and when he heard the door to the neighbouring room open he went out onto the landing. It was Terrance, who always looked a mess when he first got up on account of his thick growth of beard.

'Sleep well?' he asked.

'Thank you, yes,' Robert replied awkwardly, but Terrance did not seem to notice anything out of the ordinary. 'Wendy has gone down to put the kettle on.'

'Too late,' he said. 'I think Georgina's down there already.'

Robert walked down after him, wondering whether he and Georgina would have to exchange a nod of agreement before they gave their news. He had not felt quite as nervous as before. He alternated between wanting to forget the whole idea and needing to get the news out as quickly as possible. If Georgina suggested leaving it until later he was not sure he could stand the anticipation.

'I've put the kettle on,' Wendy said as the two men entered the kitchen.

'Where's Georgina?' Terrance asked.

'I don't know,' Wendy said. 'Is she up already?'

'I suppose so,' he said, sitting down, unconcerned.

Wendy walked to the door and found it was still locked. The keys were in the door. Robert wasn't really thinking it was odd that they didn't know where she was. He had suddenly been struck that they ought perhaps to tell their partners their news separately. He started to panic, hoping he could make the suggestion before Georgina said anything.

'She's not gone out.' Wendy said.

'Oh,' Terrance replied and got up, going first through to the lounge and then checking the dining room. He then wandered back upstairs.

Wendy was unconcerned, but turned to Robert and sensed he was troubled; 'You okay?' she asked, walking over and putting her hand to his forehead.

'I didn't sleep that well,' he excused himself.

'You were asleep when I got up, but I must have woken you. Why not go back to bed for an hour? I'll bring your tea up to you.'

He thanked her and went out to the hall. Terrance was coming down the stairs looking concerned.

'She isn't upstairs either,' he said.

'Who isn't?' asked Donna from the door to her bedroom.

'Georgina. She isn't in the house,' he explained. 'And the doors are locked.'

'She must have gone into the garden, or for a walk,' Donna suggested, and Terrance looked back towards the door. 'But her boots are still here, and her coat. And the keys are inside the locked back door.'

He turned and looked back up the stairs.

'Georgina!' he shouted. 'Where are you.'

There was no reply, but Brendan appeared at his bedroom door now and Wendy came into the hall from the kitchen.

'There's a rational explanation for it,' she said.

'Georgina!' he called again, loudly.

'You've checked your room, and the bathroom?' Donna asked.

'Of course I have,' replied Terrance, annoyed at her.

Robert pushed past him on the stairs and walked towards their room.

'I've told you, she's not there,' Terrance insisted.

In the bedroom it was obvious there was nowhere to hide, and he could see through the door to the en suite bathroom that she wasn't in there. Nevertheless he walked over and looked in, and it was then that he heard somebody stumble and fall behind him. He looked around and there was Georgina, on the floor in her nightie, looking distraught.

He ran to her and held her.

'I thought I'd never get out,' she said through a sob.

'You were in those rooms?' he whispered urgently, while putting his finger to his lips to encourage her to be quiet. He could hear talking down in the hall, discussion, and he hoped that he had to calm her down. He took her hands and her knuckles were grazed and sore.

'Come into the bathroom and we'll wash your hands,' he said. He could hear the others going out the front door and calling for her.

'I fell asleep. When I woke up I thought that I could hear you all and I tried to leave, but the door was gone. It wasn't there.'

'How did you get back?'

'I don't know. I was banging at the wall, pushing hard against it, crying, with my eyes closed, and suddenly I was back in here, on the floor.'

'They've been looking for you. You'd disappeared.'

'I know!' she said, raising her voice, and then calmed herself. 'I was stuck in those rooms.'

'I don't know what to tell the others.'

'Don't tell them anything,' she pleaded. 'Not yet. Not now. Maybe not ever. I don't want to go back there.'

He ran some warm water and she put her hands into the bowl. The raw red patches on her knuckles stung her.

'We need to explain where you'd disappeared to,' he said calmly.

There were now two or three distinct voices calling out to her from the garden. It sounded like the searchers were on the edge of the woods.

'I've got to tell them you're here, and okay,' he said, standing up and going to the window.

'And what are we going to say.'

'Perhaps we could say you'd fallen out of bed, you know, between the bed and the wall. You could say you'd somehow slept through everything.'

'We could try,' she agreed, uncertainly.

Robert opened the window and could see Donna out on the edge of the lawn in her dressing gown.

'It's okay!' he called. 'Tell Terrance I've found her.'

'We're not going to tell them about us today,' Georgina asked.

'No,' he agreed. 'We'll leave it for now. Let's discuss it later. Perhaps tonight?'

'Not in those rooms!'

'No. We'll find some other way to talk.'

The story they told was that Robert had checked down between the bed and the wall and had found Georgina lying there on the floor, sound asleep, muffled in her blankets. How she had hurt her hands she didn't know. Everyone said that it was incredible, and very strange that Terrance hadn't found her there, but it wasn't an unreasonable explanation. There were a number of jokes made at Georgina's expense by Donna, Brendan and Wendy about her strange sleeping habits, but more at Terrance's for losing his wife in their own bedroom. It took some time before either of them admitted that there was a funny side to the occurrence.

They spent the day in Usk as a group, principally because Brendan had a friend there who had promised to show them over the grounds of the Castle. They travelled in two cars and although Robert and Georgina contrived to sit together in the back of Terrance's, while he drove, they were unable to talk. They looked over the Castle and had lunch, and that afternoon walked along the river. Once again Robert and Georgina managed to walk together and Terrance walked ahead with Brendan and Donna, but Wendy held his arm the whole way. They had given up hope of talking alone when it was decided that evening to order a take-away from Coleford. Robert offered to drive and collect it and he asked who wanted to go with him and keep him company. Nobody offered, which allowed Georgina to say that she would.

Finally they had the opportunity to talk, but as they drove through the fine evening neither knew quite what to say. Finally, Robert asked bluntly:

'Are we going to tell them, then?'

She took her time before saying that she didn't know.

'After this morning . . .' she said, but trailed off.

Half a minute she said:

'I'm not going back into those rooms.'

He took a breath and then said that he understood.

'It is, though,' he pointed out, 'a place where we can meet.'

'But even if there was no danger of getting trapped in there, like I was trapped, where the hell is it?'

'I don't know.'

'I mean, is it real? Did we just dream it?'

'You're suggesting that we both had the same dream?'

'Is it any more unlikely as an explanation?'

'Okay, well, in my dream we were in a small, carpeted room at first with a couple of chairs and a chest by a window. And there was a small table with a lamp on it. The second time we were there we went through a third door to a larger room with a large bed. . .'

'I'm sure it was the same for both of us,' she said.

'So it couldn't have just been a dream. You weren't in the house this morning. Physically, you were in those rooms. You weren't just asleep, dreaming.'

'Maybe I had just fallen down the side of the bed.'

Annoyed, he pulled the car over to the side of the road and stopped. Another car behind them sounded its horn in displeasure as it passed them.

'Look, I made up that story to account for your disappearance.'

'Did you?'

'Are you denying that we met twice, at night, in those rooms? Are you saying that we never made love?'

She looked down at her hands in her lap and started to cry. When he put his hand on her shoulder she shrugged him off and leant down and gave in to her sobs.

He said, quietly:

'You don't have to go into those rooms again, not if you don't want to.'

'You don't understand,' she said, and then wiped her eyes with the back of her hands. Not looking at him but out of the side window she considered her reply. 'I would rather be in those rooms, forever, even trapped in them, but you have to be there with me.'

'Then let us go there again tonight. But I'll go in first. Open the door, but don't close it. Stand inside the open door until I come in.'

She nodded, then sniffed, then gave him a weak smile.

And so, that night, they both went into the rooms that could not possibly be there. Robert entered first and left his shoe in his doorway to stop it from closing. When Georgina came in he whispered for her to do the same, and stopped her from turning on the light. They fumbled their way over to the third door and into the far bedroom which was dark and felt cold. It smelt heavily of damp this time. Closing the door behind them he left her standing there while he made his way over to the side of the bed and felt for the lamp. It seemed to have been overturned so he righted it and flicked on the switch.

The room was in chaos. He didn't know how he had managed to navigate his way over from the door. The ceiling had partially collapsed on the far side of the room in front of the window, and the floor sagged dangerously in that part of the room and some floor-boards had actually rotted through. The bed listed dangerously to one side.

'What on earth's happened?' she asked.

'I don't know,' he replied, confused, walking carefully over to where she remained standing. The whole of the wall behind her was black with mould in the places where the plaster remained clinging to very rough, old brickwork.

At her side he looked back into the room and noticed that all of the material on the bed was rotten.

'I want to leave,' she said, scared.

'So do I,' he agreed. He tried to open the door, but it was stuck. By the dim light it looked as if it were jammed. The woodwork seemed to have warped.

'I'm scared,' she said, though quite evenly. Turning back to the room he looked at the holes in the floor and ceiling:

'I wonder if there's any way down there?'

'You're joking? This place is horrible enough without going any further into it.'

He turned his attention again to the door. He could see that although there was a gap between the door and frame at the bottom, they were tight against each other at the top. He tried the handle again, but this time put all of his effort into pulling. It moved a little with a disproportionately sickening shriek from the wood. He pulled again and with another screech it was open. They both hurried through the ante-room and could see a light through the door that lead back into Robert's bedroom. In Georgina's doorway there was movement and Terrance appeared.

'What's happening?' he demanded.

With a sudden inspiration Robert said 'We both went down for a drink of water and didn't realise the other was there. We frightened the hell out of each other.' And he bundled Georgina through her door before going back into his own. He faced Wendy who was sitting up in bed, looking worried.

'Was that Georgina screaming?' she asked, frightened. 'It sounded horrible.'

'I've just frightened the hell out of her, bumping into her in the dark,' he said, shaking all over. 'And frightened the hell out of myself. It's stupid.'

'Are you alright?' she asked, concerned.

He was becoming calmer now. The story came easy:

'I will be. Her scream scared me more than anything else,' he explained. 'I'll go through and check on her.'

Turning he could now see only one door. He went through it, and then knocked on Georgina and Terrance's door. In a moment Terrance opened it.

'What the hell happened?' he asked again.

'We bumped into each other in the dark,' he explained. 'In the kitchen. . .'

'She said it was on the stairs?'

'Well, I was coming out of the kitchen, and she was at the bottom of the stairs,' he lied as a compromise.

Terrance turned back to Georgina: 'Is this true?'

She was only able to nod.

'I don't think either of us knew the other was there until we bumped into each other. We terrified each other.'

Terrance turned and stepped back to where his wife was sitting on the bed, shaking. He sat next to her and hugged her.

'My poor darling. I think I understand,' he said. 'It's being in a different house. I was completely disorientated when I heard the scream. I wasn't even sure it was a scream. And it didn't seem to come from downstairs, or down the hallway. I don't know . . .'

'Is she alright,' Wendy enquired, making Robert jump. He hadn't realised she had followed him out of the room and was standing behind him. 'It woke me up and I couldn't work out where the noise came from. As we're all up and awake and jittery, why don't we all go downstairs, throw all the lights on, and have some hot milk before trying to get back to sleep again?'

Terrance was surprised that Brendan and Donna hadn't been woken by the noise, but Wendy pointed out that Donna, at least, used earplugs at night because of Brendan's snoring. When they heard the story the following morning she denied this, but both admitted that they hadn't been disturbed. Both Wendy and Terrance accepted the events that night at face value, but it was Donna who had her doubts. She was convinced that something else must have happened between Robert and Georgina, and when she remembered the odd glances that she had previously seen them exchange she became convinced that there was more to it. Apparently in corroboration of this, those glances had now ceased, and, in fact, Georgina seemed to go out of her way to avoid Robert's company and appeared to do her best not to meet his eyes when he looked at her. Certainly they did not speak to each other over the coming days, and Donna was faced with a dilemma.

She made her decision a few nights later after a long talk with Brendan. The next morning she took Wendy to one side and was told that she was talking rubbish and, frankly, it was none of her business. It caused Wendy some doubt, however, and she too began to scrutinise the two of them and voiced her concern to Robert on the day before they were all due to leave the cottage. Already frustrated by the turn of events, and some days after it had happened doubting his memory of them, he accused his wife of not trusting him and realised with annoyance that he was being hypocritical. He walked into the living room, thinking it was empty but found Terrance and Georgina there. He could never recall what Terrance had said to him or why he had taken offence, but the argument that followed was all the more unpleasant because it had not been about anything of importance.

The next morning, before they left, anyone who had spoken out of turn the previous day apologised to everyone else and good relations were re-established. When the three couples left in their separate cars only Donna was in tears, convinced that she had been misunderstood by everybody.

ॐ

That December Christmas cards were exchanged as usual, but the following year Donna felt unable to arrange the usual holiday for all six of them. Twelve months later Wendy booked a holiday cottage for four in the Peak District, and at the last moment Terrance and Georgina felt able to accept the invitation.

Afterword[1]

by Elizabeth Brown

In these stories Ray Russell presents us with situations in which apparently supernatural phenomena intrude, although rational or psychological explanations are also possible. No one explanation will account for everything that is meant to have transpired. Russell leaves the door open to the supernatural and his characters are forced to question what has happened to them, and in turn they start to doubt themselves. Their confidence is shaken, and it is in this respect that the drama of the stories is played out. They *are* tales of the supernatural and of the psychological, but they can also be considered tales of horror because the greatest horror is perhaps the realisation that you cannot rely on your own mind to interpret the empirical world around you. The stories are written to make the reader uneasy, and if it is of any comfort, then I am not certain that the author himself is sure of the answers to the questions he poses.

Ray tells me that he has an open mind when it comes to ghosts. He believes that it is highly unlikely that they are real, but he is not willing to discount the possibility entirely. He is cautious of anyone who dogmatically claims that they exist, but he is just as suspicious of anyone who insists that they do not. Science continues to make great inroads into territory where once only superstition supplied the answers, but he points out that there are still many areas left where science has failed to offer anything other than theories.

[1] From *Putting the Pieces in Place.*

AFTERWORD

He has suggested to me that it is quite probable that ghosts and other supernatural phenomena may one day be explained away entirely as the faulty operation of the human mind and senses. Being a bit of a Romantic, he acknowledges that this would be a shame, but our ability to be misled, and to mislead ourselves, is perhaps even more interesting to him than ghostly phenomena (which, in cases of 'true hauntings' appear preoccupied with the mundane and the trivial).

From time to time in our lives we all experience phenomena for which there appear to be no obvious explanations. If the supernatural offers a working hypothesis then our reaction to this will vary depending on our disposition; rationalists will simply refuse to believe what they have experienced, while the superstitious will offer it as proof of the supernatural. Many of us, I imagine, will simply assume that we were mistaken in what we thought we had encountered.

A magician's sleight of hand, misdirection and optical illusion can be just as entertaining when they are explained as they are remarkable when the methods remain a mystery. If we are predisposed to be responsive then our senses and minds are even easier to cheat, which is of course, how mediums often ply their trade. Nobody can doubt that apparently supernatural phenomena can be faked, and the reasons for fakery are themselves of interest. But Ray Russell is fascinated by the way that we can trick ourselves.

It is always astounding that two people who witness the same event can often have such different recollections of apparently objective facts. Perhaps it is down to the way that memory works: rewriting events every time we remember them and storing away the most recent version? If you are having problems recalling a detail from the past it would be reasonable to try to imagine various possibilities, discounting those that are the less likely. How we decide this will depend upon a number of conscious or unconscious factors, and can be susceptible to outside influence. Inevitably a particular possibility might make more of an impression than others, and when the question is considered later then it can happen that the memory you access is not of the event but the later reconstruction. And if you forget that you ever had doubts then it may be the only memory that you have available.

However, as I have already suggested, such explanations do not account for everything that happens in Ray Russell's stories. There is often something else at work, but how are we to know what it is? If we can't trust what our senses have told us and doubt the ability of our minds to make sense of any of it, then how are we to even ask for help?

Made in the USA
Monee, IL
11 April 2023

31703956R00173